SPHERE
OF
INFLUENCE

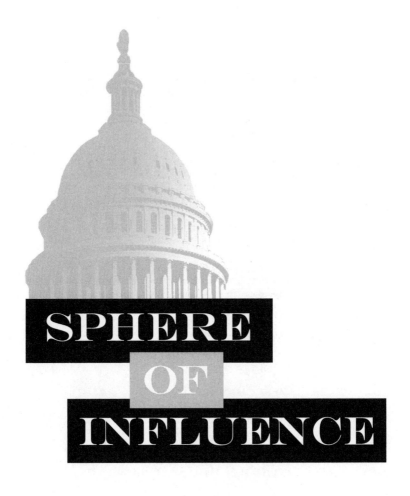

SPHERE OF INFLUENCE

KYLE MILLS

G. P. Putnam's Sons
New York

This book is a work of fiction. Names, characters, places, and incidents either are the product of the author's imagination or are used fictitiously, and any resemblance to actual persons, living or dead, business establishments, events, or locales is entirely coincidental.

G. P. Putnam's Sons
Publishers Since 1838
a member of
Penguin Putnam Inc.
375 Hudson Street
New York, NY 10014

Library of Congress Cataloging-in-Publication Data

Mills, Kyle, date.
Sphere of influence / Kyle Mills.
p.   cm.
ISBN 0-399-14934-1
1. Government investigators—Fiction. 2. Terrorism—Prevention—Fiction. 3. Undercover operations—Fiction. 4. Conspiracies—Fiction. I. Title.

PS3563.I42322 S64   2002
813'.54—dc21   2002024929

Printed in the United States of America

10 9 8 7 6 5 4 3 2 1

This book is printed on acid-free paper. ∞

Book design by Renato Stanisic

Let me assert my firm belief that the only thing we have to fear is fear itself.

FRANKLIN D. ROOSEVELT, MARCH 4, 1933

PROLOGUE

"HOW many people here consider the government to be highly efficient?"

Charles Russell adjusted himself behind his lectern and watched his opponent warily. Dr. Terry Gale, a popular professor of criminal justice at Harvard, was good-looking by any standard, with long brown hair tied back in a ponytail and the obligatory tweed jacket and faded jeans.

Gale had abandoned his own lectern and was moving back and forth across the stage, preaching energetically to the large auditorium. He was halfway through a highly successful ten-city tour for his latest book and had polished his delivery to a lustrous shine. *Crime Does Pay: The Inevitable Failure of America's War on Crime* had clawed its way to the bottom of *The New York Times* Best Seller List and was likely on its way to a top-five spot.

"Come on, don't be bashful. Let's see some hands. Who thinks the government is efficient?" He motioned toward Russell. "My opponent promises me that he hasn't installed any surveillance cameras in the auditorium, so vote your conscience here."

Russell started to frown but caught himself and laughed easily instead. As the director of homeland security and overseer of America's law enforcement agencies, he had been the target of Gale's acerbic wit on more than one occasion. Best to just let it roll off his back.

"Okay, I see a few hands," Gale said.

It wasn't many—maybe five, all bunched together at the front. Russell glanced down at them for a moment and then out over young faces crammed into the American University auditorium. With no television cameras—something he himself had insisted on when he'd agreed to this debate—the lighting was a little softer and more academic, allowing him to discern detail despite his aging eyes. What he saw was hostility: young, wealthy intellectuals who were there because they bought into Gale's fatalistic antigovernment ranting; children whose lives were still skirting the edges of the real world. Their parents were largely supporters of the conservative values he stood for, but their sons and daughters were still in a rebellious stage. At this age, with their fathers' credit cards still firmly in pocket, they had the luxury to be idealistic. In ten years, though, their loyalties would change. They would want to protect their money from excessive taxation, they would want their opulent homes and neighborhoods kept safe, they would want their children to attend a drug-free school that didn't teach down to the lowest common denominator, they would want to be safe from bomb-wielding fanatics. . . .

"Okay," Gale said, "it doesn't look like we're going to get a lot of hands. Big surprise. Let me ask another question: How many people think private industry is pretty efficient?"

Almost every hand went up.

"And I'll take that one step further. Obviously there are inefficiencies in private industry, but I'd argue that a lot of them are a direct result of government regulation. Compare the Post Office to Federal Express if you want proof."

"Is your suggestion to relieve private industry of excessive government meddling?" Russell cut in. "You're starting to sound like a Republican, Dr. Gale."

That got a titter from the crowd—something Russell knew he desperately needed.

"Of course not, sir. My point is simply that organized crime is, by definition, completely unregulated, making it almost infinitely efficient. And that, combined with the fact that the U.S. has no comprehensive policy on crime, makes the war on it a losing proposition."

Russell considered stepping out from behind his lectern, too, but then squelched the thought. He'd end up looking like Al Gore, trying to be hip. Better to just stick with . . . what did his son say? Old and crotchety.

"I'm not sure that's fair, Professor. Over the past few years we've increased the number of police on the streets, we've intercepted hundreds of millions of dollars' worth of narcotics coming into this country, we've had success in convincing narcotics producing countries to step up their output reduction efforts, we've put mandatory sentencing in place for a number of crimes, we've greatly expanded our antiterrorist efforts . . . I could go on. And we've seen results: a measurable drop in the use of various drugs as well as in some forms of violent crime—"

"But what was the *cause* of that reduction, sir? Additional arrests, convictions, and incarcerations? Statistics don't suggest that. The cost of drugs continues to go down as the quality improves, suggesting increased supply. Of course, some drugs go out of style and others come into style, but there's no net reduction in use. Typical of the government, we have initiatives and programs that are labeled successful simply by virtue of their implementation—it's all become just an expensive publicity stunt. We haven't had a repeat of the September 11 tragedy, but do I think that's a result of my no longer being able to take nail clippers on a flight? We see on TV that the American government has forced the Bolivians to reduce cocaine output, but no one talks about the fact that the Colombians immediately increased their exports to compensate."

Russell stiffened at the obvious personal attack. "Your suggestion, then, is that we concede? Throw our hands up and just let anyone do anything they want? Son, I'm guessing that you grew up in a nice neighborhood where everyone was rich and happy"—actually, he knew that for a fact—"but I grew up in a bad part of Detroit. I was scared every time I walked out my front door. . . ."

"My suggestion," Gale countered, "is that the policy makers decide what they want to accomplish and create policies to get there instead of creating showy policies with no real purpose. I mean, come on, Mr. Russell, your own economists estimate the international narcotics trade as being two percent of the world's gross domestic product. During its heyday the Cali cartel had estimated profits of about seven billion dollars a year. That's three times what General Motors was posting. When Pablo Escobar was fighting U.S. extradition, he offered to pay off Colombia's national debt if they refused to give him up."

"Pablo Escobar is dead," Russell said.

"So what? His death didn't even cause a ripple in the coke supply to the U.S. My contention, and the contention of my book, is that America is facilitating the growth of enormously sophisticated transnational crime syndicates. We're just repeating the same mistakes we've made in the past. Prohibition financed an unprecedented upsurge in the power of the Mob, and this is Prohibition times ten. There are people with net worths that rival Bill Gates's who we know nothing about. They control enormous political and financial power, they interfere in the operation of sovereign governments and manipulate wars, they buy raw opium from terrorist organizations that then use those funds to wage war on us. They pay no taxes and obey no laws. . . ."

"I found those chapters of your book to be very entertaining," Russell said, smiling sarcastically. "Who are these magnificent crime lords? I've never met one or even heard of one. It seems a little paranoid to assume that there's some 'man behind the curtain' controlling everything illegal that goes on in the world. I notice you gave no examples or suggested where we might find one of these people. You never even gave an indication of a pattern that would suggest central control. The criminals I've met and read about aren't all that bright or organized—and that includes people like Pablo Escobar."

"But that's the point, isn't it, Mr. Russell? These people don't want to be found. They move from country to country, they hold multiple passports, they provide money and arms to various regimes around the world to create safe havens for themselves, they use offshore accounts and corporations to move their money in a way that can't be traced. . . ."

Russell laughed into his microphone. "Let me try to understand your logic here, Professor. These people *must* exist because we can find no evidence of their existence. Does that about sum it up?"

1

HE'D been there for more than an hour, but the dirt loosened by his helicopter's downdraft continued to swirl around him in the aimless breeze.

Squinting against the dust and darkness, the man who called himself Christian Volkov moved gracefully through the jagged rocks, edging closer to the sheer cliff just ahead. The wind increased as he approached, getting caught in his jacket and overpowering the silence with the sound of whipping fabric. He lowered his head and continued forward, not stopping until the tips of his boots hung off what felt a little like the edge of the universe. Below him seemed to be nothing—like looking into the bottom of a well hundreds of miles across. The moon, in the proper phase for the night's events, provided just enough colorless illumination to make the snow-covered tops of distant peaks glow dully, but not enough to create contrast in the valley beneath him.

He averted his eyes slightly and searched his peripheral vision for the small settlement that he knew was there. After almost a minute of uninterrupted concentration, he thought he'd found it—an almost imperceptible glow with an unnatural steadiness that suggested a human origin.

He sat, letting his legs dangle over the edge of the cliff and reveling in the emptiness around him. He'd piloted the helicopter himself and told no one where he was going. No one except Pascal, of course. Pascal, who had debated, argued, and finally begged him not to go on this pointless errand—or at least to take a contingent of trusted men.

In the end, though, Volkov had refused. He had never shared Pascal's confidence in security. The only real security was anonymity—the ability to die and be reborn, to be many people and no one, to exist only as ink on paper and electronic blips in distant computers. What people could see they could fear and hate. And what they could fear and hate, they could destroy.

These brief moments of peace were so rare now. It had been months since he'd been truly alone—since he'd had a few seconds that he could free himself from the endless game of chess he'd doomed himself to play. A few seconds that he could enjoy the illusion of safety and calm.

When it finally started, it started as a flash of light, blinding despite the distance. Volkov gripped the edge of the cliff as he watched the column of fire rise and illuminate the encampment that had been so nearly invisible moments before. It took a few seconds for the sound to reach him—a dull rumbling that seemed impossible in this nearly uninhabited corner of the world.

For years this part of Afghanistan had been unusually quiet—subject to a "peace" that had been enforced by the Taliban and was now enforced by the regime America had inserted. Recently, though, the region had been plagued by brief, localized eruptions of violence. These attacks, carried out by the newly reorganized and energized al-Qaeda organization, were always the same—fast, brutal, and effective. As far as Volkov knew, not a single man, woman, or child had ever survived being overrun by these battle-hardened fanatics.

By Middle Eastern standards, the assaults were meticulously planned and precisely executed. Al-Qaeda's men were well armed with new, high-tech equipment, and their pre-op intelligence was always flawlessly accurate. The fact that Christian Volkov was responsible for this increased operational sophistication was known by almost no one.

The explosions ceased abruptly, leaving a long, rolling echo before being replaced by the staccato sound of gunfire. Volkov leaned forward, teetering on the edge of the precipice and concentrating on what little he could see of the scene below. The crescent of rifle flashes advancing steadily toward a group of burning buildings was easily visible at first but then faded into the unsteady light emanating from the fires.

While it was true that this part of the Hindu Kush mountain range had a certain stark beauty to it, the area had garnered much more attention throughout history than the desolate landscape seemed to deserve. Brutal tribal wars, the Macedonian Greeks under Alexander the Great, the Arab armies that brought Islam to the region in the seventh century, the Mongols, and then finally the Soviets and Americans. Volkov wondered what the farmers eking out an existence in the tiny oases of cultivatable land had thought when they first saw the magnificent cavalry of Genghis Khan.

A sad smile spread across Volkov's face as he recognized his own misguided romanticism. What those peasants had seen was the same thing the modern-day Afghans below saw in the dirty and fanatical men advancing on them now: slavery and death.

He couldn't help wondering what the people inside that burning compound were thinking in these last few moments. While they had no way of knowing who had ultimately condemned them to death, they certainly saw death approaching. Did they have doubts about their myths now? Were they afraid to give up the life they'd held so tightly in their hands for an afterlife that might not exist?

He supposed that he would learn soon enough. At forty-three, he was smarter than he had been at thirty-five. The experience he had gained more than offset the slight slowing of his mind and body. But that wouldn't be the case for much longer. He could already feel himself getting tired, losing his grasp of the minute details that kept him alive. The bouts of depression that he had suffered since he was a child could no longer be controlled by willpower alone and now responded only to a cocktail of prescription drugs. It wouldn't be long before he made a mistake. And when he did, he would finally get his chance to play the victim.

Volkov closed his eyes and lay back in the dirt. The sound of gunfire was slowing and he strained to hear the shouts and screams of the people below, although he knew the distance was too great. Soon the sound of the wind was all that was left.

MARK Beamon dodged clumsily, narrowly avoiding being clipped by the bus as he jogged across the busy street, only to be hit by a searing blast of exhaust as it passed by. By the time he made it to the sidewalk, sweat was stinging his eyes and his heart was pounding dangerously. He let his momentum carry him forward, skirting the densely packed office buildings in an effort to stay in the 105-degree shade.

His secretary had called his apartment at nine A.M. and woken him up. It was after eleven now and he was still half a mile from the office. As late and as hot as it was, it would have made sense to have parked beneath his building in the well-located space he now rated as the Special Agent in Charge of the FBI's Phoenix office. But in the end his normal hike across the sun-scorched urban landscape had seemed more attractive.

He told everyone who would listen that he parked a mile from the office to force himself to get a little exercise. That wasn't really the reason, though, only a desirable side effect. In truth it was nothing more than a twenty-minute delaying tactic—thirty if he stopped for an ice cream.

When Beamon finally made it to the edge of the stone courtyard in front of the FBI's new building, he took a deep breath and made a break for the fountain in front. There he hopped up and sat on its edge, letting the water mist protect him from the July sun. After a couple of minutes he was feeling cool enough to light a cigarette as his cell phone rang uselessly. He smiled when the caller gave up but felt the smile fade when the ringing began again almost immediately. He finally wrestled the phone from his pocket and flipped it open.

"Hello, D."

"If I walk over to the window, am I going to see you sitting on the fountain, smoking?" his secretary asked.

Beamon threw his cigarette down next to the fountain and ground it out with his toe. "I got hung up in traffic."

"ETA?"

"Three minutes."

"You realize it's almost lunchtime?"

"Good-bye, D."

Beamon kept his head down as he weaved through the densely packed cubicles that made up the FBI's Phoenix office, pretending not to see the agents scurrying to get out of his way. A few brave ones nodded and smiled, but most seemed content to just make a run for it. Beamon recognized the deterioration in his mood over the past year and knew he was in serious danger of becoming another of a million old, burned-out, pain-in-the-ass bureaucrats. But he didn't know how to stop what was starting to seem to be an inevitable slide.

"Skidding in at the last minute," D. said, appearing from behind a fake plant and following him into his fishbowl of an office. She looked at her watch. "Eleven twenty-five. You're supposed to meet with Bill at eleven thirty. . . . Wait a minute. Are you damp?"

Beamon fell into his leather chair and peeked out at her between the stacks of paper piled on his desk. "It's four hundred degrees out, D."

"So that's sweat and not fountain water?"

"As far as you know."

"Yeah, right. I'm having surveillance cameras installed on the front of the building tomorrow. You owe me lunch."

"Pick a restaurant."

"I told Bill you'd be in the conference room," she said, turning on her heel and disappearing through the door to his office.

It suddenly occurred to Beamon that almost everything lastingly bad in his life had begun in a conference room. While it was true that he'd been shot at, beaten up, dumped by countless women, and once even caught in an honest-to-God avalanche; the pain he'd suffered from those things had been relatively brief. By the same statistical logic that suggested you might live forever if you never entered a hospital, it seemed certain that a great deal of pain and misfortune could be avoided by simply never setting foot in another conference room.

He stared blankly at the table in front of him and the empty chairs surrounding it, remembering a similar setting when he first heard that he was going to be made an SAC. He'd left the meeting elated, acknowledging the promotion for what it was—a miracle on level with the parting of the Red Sea or the sheer perfection of a warm Krispy Kreme doughnut.

Thirteen months ago, his career—and by virtue of that, his life—had pretty much fallen apart. He'd managed to make an enemy of most of Congress with a political corruption investigation that had fallen in his lap despite every effort to dive out of the way. And after embarrassing the hell out of the Washington elite, he'd looked around and seen what little support he had from Bureau management quickly disappearing. Not long after, the FBI had decided to mend a few fences by offering him up as political sacrifice.

When it had looked almost certain that he would end up doing some jail time on a trumped-up charge, the political climate had suddenly changed. A new president was elected and his best friend ended up as the White House chief of staff. Suddenly he'd found himself transformed from scapegoat to golden boy. At the time it had seemed like his luck was finally turning around. Now he wasn't so sure.

"Mark?"

Beamon spun his chair around to face a man of about thirty-three with FBI-issue hair and suit. He had his head poked into the conference room but seemed reluctant enter. Probably a bad sign.

"Bill. Good to see you," Beamon lied. "Come on in."

He did, albeit a bit hesitantly. Beamon watched carefully as the younger man closed the door and slowly crossed the room, finally taking a seat and placing a thick folder in the center of the table.

"Got your black hood and scythe in there?" Beamon joked. At least, he hoped it was a joke.

No response. Another bad sign.

Every couple of years or so the FBI field offices had a team from headquarters descend on them and plow through every investigation, budget, report, and management decision, carefully second-guessing each one. Right now it was Phoenix's turn. Bill Laskin was the chief of the inspection staff that had been looking under the hood of Beamon's office for the last two weeks. And, for better or for worse, he was doing a hell of a thorough job.

"We're about winding down, Mark." Laskin said, pulling a thick document from the folder in front of him. "We've finished our draft report." His tone suggested that it wasn't entirely complimentary. "I thought we could go over a few of the points and then you could look at it and give it some . . . some thought."

Beamon grabbed the report unceremoniously, paging through as its author squirmed uncomfortably. With each page of neatly typed criticism he could feel what little strength he still had draining away.

"You know, Mark, last night I was sitting around my office and I started going through your report on the CDFA investigation."

Beamon didn't look up from the well-organized and meticulously documented report. Maybe he could find an appropriate quote for his tombstone when he finally had that well-deserved stroke.

"Why?"

"Because it was an incredible case. I mean, thousands of people died. The pressure must have been unbearable. I can't even imagine how you were able to hold it together and resolve it so quickly."

The case Laskin was referring to was the most infamous of Beamon's career. An ex-DEA agent had decided to try poisoning the U.S. narcotics supply to stem the use of illegal drugs. It had worked.

"Bound to happen, I suppose. Frustrating job, the DEA," Beamon said, his mouth feeling increasingly dry as he continued through the pages.

"The report's really clinical, though," Laskin continued.

Beamon flipped a few more pages. "Clinical?"

"What I mean is . . . well, I'm curious . . ."

"Spit it out."

Laskin cleared his throat. "How did *you* feel about the whole thing?"

That finally made Beamon look up. "What do you mean?"

"I mean, drug use was plummeting. People were dying, sure, but drug use was dropping like a stone. If you hadn't caught those guys, would people have just stopped using? In the end, would lives have been saved?"

Beamon stared past the man at the wall. It was tempting to talk about his old cases, his old triumphs. But those things were past. He wasn't the FBI's whiz-kid investigator anymore. He was a grown-up—a SAC.

"I was just following orders," Beamon said, affecting a thick German accent. The attempt at a joke sounded strained, even to him.

"No, seriously, Mark."

"I *am* serious," Beamon said quietly, sliding a finger beneath the back of the report and flipping it closed.

The young man took the hint and just nodded, eyes glued to the document lying on the table. He seemed to have lost his ability to blink.

Laskin was clearly a fan—something he'd proven over the last two weeks by being more knowledgeable about Beamon's past investigations than he himself was. The younger generation of agents liked to joke about people from Beamon's era, calling them "the gun toters" and de-crying their lack of sophistication while secretly worshiping them.

In many younger agents' minds Beamon was the last of the old-school investigators—the hard-drinking, chain-smoking, sometimes arrogant men who had created the larger-than-life myth of the FBI agent. The truth was less romantic. Beamon couldn't help feeling that this wasn't his FBI anymore. That he'd been left behind.

"Take some time looking that over, Mark. I'm interested in your comments. Obviously it's not set in stone. I think there are some areas where your ASACs could be giving you more support. . . ."

Beamon pulled out a cigarette and lit it despite the ironclad no-smoking policy in the building. "No."

"What?"

"Whatever's wrong with this office is my doing."

When Beamon glanced up from the inspection report in his lap, the office looked deserted. The sun was still streaming powerfully through the window behind him, reflecting off a clock that read six P.M. Taking off his reading glasses, he squinted through the glass wall that made up the front of his office. No one.

He shrugged and perched the glasses back on his nose. Normally the complete disappearance of his staff would be worth looking into, but the inspection report he'd spent the better part of the day reading had deadened pretty much everything in him, including his normally overactive sense of curiosity.

He reached over and picked up the untouched pastry D. had brought him, examining the almond-encrusted dough, damp with butter. These had once been his absolute favorite, but now the thought of eating it—or anything else for that matter—turned his stomach.

He tossed the pastry in the trash can and flipped to the next, and hopefully more positive, page in the report. After a quick scan it turned out to contain another sharp criticism of his number two that was, unfortunately, completely untrue. Beamon took a red pen from his desk and crossed through it. In the margin he wrote a brief note as to why the deficiency that had been uncovered by the inspection staff was, in fact, his own fault.

Sighing quietly, he flipped back through the report and scanned the similar commentaries scrawled on nearly every page. He couldn't help wondering if he was writing himself out of a job.

"Mark?"

Beamon looked up at the young woman hovering nervously in the doorway to his office.

"Sorry, Mark, I don't mean to bother you, but we thought you might have the inside track on this thing."

Beamon threw the inspection report on the desk. Enough for tonight—another ten pages and he was going to have to relocate to the ledge outside his window.

"Thing? What thing? And where the hell is everybody?"

She looked at him as though he were asking trick questions.

"We're all in the back, watching the news. Don't you know what's happened?"

Beamon shrugged and she nodded toward the television bolted to the wall. He pulled a remote from his drawer and flipped it on. When he looked back toward the doorway, he saw that the young woman had slunk away.

MSNBC's Forest Sawyer looked a little haggard as he leaned forward heavily on his desk. A logo across the bottom of the screen read "The Latest Threat."

"I think we have time to bring up the picture and audio one more time before we take you to the White House." Sawyer faded out, replaced by a still image that shimmered slightly on the screen. The exposure was a little dark, apparently lit only by a low sun filtering through dense overcast and distant mountains.

"The geological formation in the background has been preliminarily identified as the Wind River Range in Wyoming," Sawyer's disembodied voice said. "MSNBC, as well as a host of other news agencies, have received copies of this photograph and are having it reviewed by experts in the field. So far there is nothing to suggest that it is anything but genuine. . . ."

Beamon walked around his desk and jumped up on a chair to get a closer look at the photo on the screen.

The subject of the picture was something that looked like an overly simplistic artillery gun. It was nothing more than a large metal cylinder attached to a two-wheeled trailer. A man in traditional Arab garb, with his face obscured by swaths of white cloth flowing from his turban, stood between the gun and an open crate containing what looked like a ten-foot-tall rocket.

A scratchy hiss became audible through the television's speakers, followed by a heavily accented male voice. "Our targets are many: shopping malls, office buildings, schools. . . . We also have Stingers sold to us by your CIA to destroy airliners. . . ."

And that was it. Obviously a man of few words. The image switched back to Forest Sawyer.

"We're taking you to the White House press conference now," he announced as the screen flickered, finally stabilizing on an image of Charles Russell standing behind a lectern adorned with the presidential seal.

"We don't have a great deal of information yet, so this is going to be brief," Russell began.

Beamon ignored him and scanned the line of grave-looking people at the back of the podium, finally settling on a woman with blond hair pulled back into a severe ponytail and a conservative blue jacket and skirt. She was looking dutifully at the politician, but Beamon guessed she wasn't listening to a word he said. He knew from personal experience that she'd be calculating how long she was going to be stuck there, wasting time.

"We received a copy of the same photograph and audio as the media and it's being examined by the top people in the field. The FBI is taking the lead in this investigation and is already coordinating with the other U.S. and international law enforcement agencies to get on top of this as quickly as possible. As I said before, we don't have a great deal of information yet. We only received the photograph and the tape a few hours ago. Mainly what I want to say to the American people is to stay calm. All we've got here is a picture, nothing more. We need—"

Beamon pushed the MUTE button and jumped off the chair, backing slowly away as he watched Russell speak soundlessly on-screen. He kept his eyes glued to the television, but barely saw it as his mind focused itself on the problem of the photograph. Why just a picture? Why not use that rocket, kill a few godless Americans? Did it not work? Was it the only one? Were these Arab fruitcakes just real smart? If so, the rocket itself was the least of America's problems.

When Russell and his entourage finally filed off-screen, Beamon turned and began digging through the papers on his desk. It took a little effort, but he finally managed to find his Rolodex and dial a number from it.

"Laura Vilechi."

Now that he'd been kicked upstairs, Laura had taken over as the FBI's investigative savant. In fact, he was the one who had provided her with her first big break, tirelessly defending her against the still slightly chauvinistic organization they both worked for. She was an incredibly effective investigator, though her style was totally different than his. She was the master of detail and procedure—she missed nothing. Where Beamon tended to sneak up on criminals and spring out from the wood-work, Laura just wore them down.

"You look good on TV. Just the right mix of adoration and submis-siveness in Russell's presence."

"Mark?"

"None other. I haven't talked to you in a while. Anything new?"

"Very funny. Nothing I can talk about."

"Come on, Laura. Throw me a bone. Did they give it to you? Is this officially your case?"

"No one else wants it."

Beamon stifled a pang of jealousy. "So, what's the inside story? The picture's real, isn't it."

"We're still in preliminary—"

"Don't start. . . ."

She sighed into the phone. "Okay, Mark. Okay. Ninety percent certain."

"I knew it. Tell me more."

"I'm starting to feel like I'm having phone sex."

"I'm in management, Laura. I've got to get it where I can."

"I wish there was more I could tell you. The weapon's a modified multiple-rocket launcher. Normally it would be a bunch of tubes mounted together."

Beamon tried to picture that. What he didn't know about military hardware was a lot. "Like the ones the Japanese shot at Godzilla with?"

"A strange analogy, but yeah. Except this one has been torn apart and a single tube has been mounted to a trailer. Less destructive power but more mobile and easier to conceal."

"Who built it?"

"We don't know. The rocket has the characteristics of a number of different military models but doesn't really match any one of them. And like I said, the launcher's been heavily modified."

"Do you know what it can do?"

"We're guessing a range of about twelve miles, based on averages, and we're pretty sure it doesn't have any guidance system to speak of."

"What about the payload?"

"I don't know. Pretty destructive."

"Conventional, or could it be biological or nuclear?"

"Not nuclear in the sense of an atomic bomb, but there is the possibility that it could have radioactive material that would be spread around in a blast. We doubt biological: There are easier ways to deliver that kind of thing."

"Well, I guess it doesn't really matter."

"What do you mean?"

"Nothing."

"Come on, Mark. Give."

"They're not looking to use it. Think about it, Laura—when al-Qaeda knocked down the World Trade Center, we taught the world that the U.S. economy can be brought to a grinding halt by a few guys with box cutters. What did the audio that came with that tape say—that they were going after malls, office buildings, airlines . . . businesses. And by marking schools, they get parents to stay home from work with their kids. They'll keep making threats, keep the fear as high as they can. And when talk doesn't do it anymore and people start heading back to work, they'll blow something up. Then they'll start making threats again— milk the explosion for as long as they can until they're forced to blow something else up. How long until our economy implodes?"

"We came up with about the same idea. Kind of puts the government in a tough spot. Either whip up the panic, keep people at home, and cripple the economy, or downplay it and force a rocket attack."

"Any idea who these guys are?"

"The People's Front of Judea?"

Beamon laughed, a first for the day. That particular terrorist organization existed only in an old Monty Python movie. He'd always used it as a synonym for the multitude of crazies inhabiting the world. "What are you getting from the—"

"Oh, shit!"

"What's wrong, Laura?"

"Dave's coming. He'll kill me if he finds out I've been talking to you."

Dave was Dave Iverson, Laura's boss, and a man who hated Beamon with unbridled passion.

"Jesus, Laura, when is he going to let that go? I said I was sorry."

"Mark, you put a bra in his suitcase at a conference and his wife found it and left him. Sorry doesn't really cut it, does it?"

"I swear, people will never let me live that down. It was a joke; how was I supposed to know he was having an affair with a woman who wore that exact size?"

"Look, Mark, don't call me anymore. I'm serious, okay? I've got a lot on my plate here and I'm not looking for any extra trouble."

Beamon could hear the pain in her voice. They had been friends for years and it had obviously been a hard thing for her to say. Hard but smart. She'd watched him shoot himself in the foot over and over again and wasn't going to make the same mistake.

Beamon hung up the phone and flopped back into the papers on his desk.

Not your case.

He repeated that to himself precisely ten times to get it into his head. There was no way he was going to be able get involved. He was a SAC a thousand miles from headquarters. Terrorism was the worst kind of case, anyway. No matter how great a job you did, in no way would it deter the next wacko with an axe to grind.

Besides, why would he want to get involved in something like that when he could be curling up with an inspection report just bursting with colorful charts and graphs proving conclusively that he was an idiot?

3

MILES from L.A., in the more or less open desert, the temperature was probably ten degrees cooler than it was in the city. Despite that, Chet was sweating. A lot.

He focused on taking slow, even breaths that were shallow enough that the slightly artificial rise and fall of his chest wouldn't be noticeable beneath his soaked shirt. It was a bastardization of a breathing technique he'd seen on some cheesy early-morning yoga show led by an extremely attractive has-been actress in an extremely formfitting leotard. Who knew he'd ever put her principles to use?

Starting to feel a little calmer, Chet continued to slowly scan his surroundings. The only illumination was provided by a single set of headlights beaming from an idling car. He could see a distance of about twenty yards before the circle of light faded to gray, and then to a black expanse that went on for miles before being broken by the distant lights of L.A.

"You're Mohammed?" Carlo Gasta said, taking a few steps toward an Arab-looking man wearing dirty fatigues. Chet seized the opportunity to move left a few feet, into a position where the headlights were directly behind him. Hadn't it been John Wayne who suggested that you always keep the sun at your back? The Duke was rarely wrong in such things.

Although he was standing only ten feet away, Mohammed's age was impossible to determine. His deep-brown eyes had a youthful clarity to them, but what little of his face was visible behind his long black beard looked worn and tired.

"You're Mohammed?" Gasta said again, his tone hinting at the beginnings of anger. The New York accent and stylish suit that gleamed a little too brightly in the glaring light made him seem hopelessly out of place. By contrast, the man he was speaking to seemed a part of the desert that surrounded them.

"I am Mohammed." His accent was thick, and for some reason that made him even more imposing. Chet looked past him into the darkness. There was no way this guy was alone. The question wasn't *if* he had men out there but *how many*. How many just beyond the circle of light?

The man said nothing else, and Chet could see Gasta's head beginning to bob up and down in a mannerism he was unfortunately very familiar with. His boss was starting to get pissed off.

"What? Do you want to have tea? Where the fuck is it?"

Chet tried to will Gasta to stay calm. It had never worked before, but you never knew. If you wished hard enough . . .

"We don't have it," Mohammed said.

"Fuck!"

It was just like the movies. Time seemed to slow down as Gasta jerked back and went for his gun. Chet's breath caught in his chest and he went for his, too, trying to force back panic and thoughts of his new wife as he ripped his Beretta from its holster. He wasn't sure, but he guessed that it took less than a second for the meeting to go from civil conversation to the very edge of disaster.

Chet's hand continued to tighten on the grip of his pistol as he centered it on Mohammed's chest, causing sweat to wring from his palm and trickle down his arm. He was about to die—he knew it. That stupid wop was finally going to get him killed.

"You're fucking with the wrong person," Gasta screamed, retreating slowly with his gun stretched out in front of him. "I don't know who the fuck you think you are, but you're about to be dead!"

Chet tried again to will his boss to calm down, letting the words *Shut up, you stupid son of a bitch* echo in his mind. He knew what Gasta was thinking: that he had five heavily armed men parked less than a mile away. He seemed to believe that he was the only person clever enough to bring backup to this meeting. And it was apparently *completely* lost on him that, with the exception of Chet, the men he'd brought were fat, middle-aged wiseguys whose best weapon was the intimidation their rusty reputations could provide. The problem was, Mohammed didn't look intimidated. In fact, he looked a little bored.

Chet knew the man was from somewhere in Afghanistan, and that made it pretty much certain that he'd faced down a lot more intimidating people than a fortyish Mob boss and his freckled, redheaded lieutenant.

"Mr. Gasta, please," Mohammed said, spreading his empty hands wide. "You do not understand. We are very happy to have business with you. There has been a delay in our supply."

Chet couldn't figure out what was going on. Was this asshole telling the truth or just stalling until his men got in position? He shifted his gaze past Mohammed and stared intently into the darkness, trying to spot the pack of dusty Afghans he imagined were crawling toward them with knives in their teeth, then spun around, partially blinding himself, to make sure no one was sneaking up behind them.

"What the fuck do you mean, 'a delay'?" Gasta shouted. "We have a business arrangement here, you piece of shit!"

Chet winced. He had spent the last year working his ass off to move up in Gasta's organization, starting as a messenger boy, then being promoted to driver, then to soldier. And now, through a combination of luck, hard work, and brains, he'd gotten what he wanted: close to Gasta. Just in time for the son of a bitch to get him killed.

"I must apologize," Mohammed said calmly. "I just learned—"

"That one of your camels died?"

Gasta's confidence was being bolstered by the fact that both he and Chet were aiming guns at an unarmed man. He'd obviously decided he was in a position to push, but Mohammed remained serene.

"The reason does not matter. What is important is that we will have your shipment in one week."

"This might be the way you sand niggers do business at home, but now you're in a country where we live up to our goddamn agreements," Gasta shouted, stretching his pistol out in front of himself a little more.

Chet's finger tightened on the trigger as Mohammed removed the knapsack he was wearing and extracted a small package covered in duct tape.

"I have a sample. This is for you." He held it out and Gasta inched toward it. When he got within range, he slapped the package out of the man's hand and retreated a few feet. "I came here to buy a truckload of product and you insult me with this? Let me show you what I think of your fucking sample." Chet jumped when Gasta fired three rounds into it, sending a small cloud of heroin rising lazily into the still air.

Gasta glanced back at Chet before spewing a string of racial slurs that lasted a full ten seconds and then starting to slowly advance on Mohammed again. Chet knew the look and understood what Gasta wanted him to do. He was more than happy to oblige.

"Carlo, take it easy, man," Chet said, running up behind his boss and grabbing him from behind. "Take it easy, it's not worth it."

"You come into *my* country and insult me? We should have just killed every fucking one of you after what you did to the World Trade Center," Gasta screamed, making a show of struggling against Chet's grip, giving every appearance that he wanted to break free and tear Mohammed apart with his bare hands. It was all for show, though. In the end, Carlo Gasta was a coward.

4

"Bonjour, *Christian. Ça va?*"

Through the trio of five-meter-tall windows behind his desk, Volkov could see a deep glow building on the horizon. In a few more minutes the darkness laid out before him would begin to gather color and shape until it became the ocean and jungle-topped cliffs that bordered his home. He wondered if he would ever tire of the metamorphosis.

"Christian?"

Volkov answered in French. Although he was a brilliant administrator, Pascal had no gift for languages. "I'm fine. And you?" He remained transfixed by the evolution of the dawn as he spoke.

"I am very glad to have you back from Afghanistan safely."

"You worry too much, Pascal."

"You do a great deal to fuel my fears."

Volkov smiled sadly. "I know I do, and I'm sorry. So what news, my friend?"

He heard the bank of televisions set into the far wall come to life and glanced at their reflections in the window in front of him. He could follow all the commentaries at once without difficulty—one of a number of unusual mental gifts he'd developed over the years.

Euronews, Fox, and CNN were continuing their minute to minute coverage of the rocket launcher photograph in America, with the BBC taking a moment to run a brief story on a recent coup in Laos. Volkov focused on the BBC report for a moment, concentrating on the reflection of an Asian man in military garb speaking energetically into a bouquet of microphones.

"As you can see, Christian, there is a great deal of news."

Volkov continued to gaze at the empty Cuban landscape that spread out behind his isolated home. The red limestone of the cliff that bordered the western boundary of his property began to glow as though it had its own power source. It was a spectacular sight that lasted for only a few moments. "Has there been an official announcement from the Americans as to the authenticity of the photograph?"

"No, no official word. However, the independent experts hired by the news agencies have completed their examinations and unanimously declared them unaltered. The American government will eventually do the same."

Volkov took a deep breath and let it out slowly but didn't speak.

"Perhaps the Americans shouldn't have celebrated Osama bin Laden's demise so energetically, eh, Christian?"

Volkov nodded silently. Before bin Laden had been transformed from a fundamentally flawed human being into an omnipresent martyr for radical Muslims to rally around, he had chosen the formerly obscure Mustafa Yasin as his successor.

Yasin, a former economist, had shrunk the ranks of al-Qaeda, restructuring it using principles developed by Special Forces and organized crime. The remaining operatives, numbering less than a thousand, were well educated, well trained, and highly motivated. It was now more likely to find an al-Qaeda operative studying engineering in a foreign university than bombs in a dusty training camp in Somalia. At least that would have been true a year ago. Now more and more of these elite troops were being drafted to carry out Yasin's takeover of the Middle Eastern heroin trade.

"Have they identified the weapon yet, Pascal?"

"No. Apparently it doesn't fit any known model. There was some early speculation that it might be a fake, but I believe most experts are now saying that it is likely real. They correctly speculate that it is an unsophisticated system being built by criminal concerns inside the former

Soviet Union. The possibility that it could contain radioactive or biological material is also being put forth by the media."

"And what is America's reaction?"

"The military is being mobilized and the navy is going to sea, though I don't think anyone knows to what end. The FBI is—"

"What's *America's* reaction?"

Pascal nodded his understanding. "Fear. Air traffic has nearly ceased, though it seems likely that if the terrorist actually had Stingers in the country, they would have shown them in the picture. Schools are running at half capacity, businesses are closed . . ."

Volkov leaned back in his chair and laced his hands on top of his head. "Al-Qaeda has always believed that they were responsible for the collapse of the Soviet Union, and now they believe that they can do the same to the United States." He let out a short laugh. "With Mustafa Yasin leading them, they may be right."

"But this is hardly of the same magnitude as the destruction of the Trade Centers. . . ."

"No, it's much worse. Why is America the world's only superpower, Pascal? It's certainly not their military. Missiles cannot be used against friends, or countries with the ability to respond in kind, or against weak countries with strong patrons, or even against countries that have something they need. And while the Americans certainly can bomb the small number of countries not included on that list, they cannot gain control over them because of their unwillingness to send their sons to die on foreign soil. So, in the end, the practical use of their armies is extremely limited. America's power is in its economy—its ability to dominate other countries financially. Yasin understands that if he can destroy that wealth, he effectively pulls America's teeth."

Volkov closed his eyes for a moment and tried to concentrate. His situation had been hopelessly complex two days ago. Now it was impossible. He attempted to conjure a reasonable hypothesis as to what this would mean to him going forward but quickly gave up. The permutations seemed endless.

"The investigation will be led by the FBI," Pascal said. "With whatever assistance they need from the other American and international law enforcement organizations. Officially, David Iverson, the assistant director in charge of the counterterrorism section, will be the lead man. Our sources suggest that the driving force behind the investigation, though, will actually be Laura Vilechi—apparently a woman of uncommon intelligence and tenacity."

"And what has she learned so far?"

"According to our sources, very little. With nothing concrete to grasp, they can do very little but round up Arab immigrants and illegals, hoping to find something. . . ."

"Are they making any progress identifying the origin of the weapon?"

"No. They're trying to enlist the help of the Russians, but without actually obtaining the unit and tracing the individual parts to the former Soviet states, the Russians will be unwilling to take responsibility and cooperate in any meaningful way, even without our interference."

"And we won't interfere," Volkov said. "We are completely silent on this, do you understand?"

"Of course."

Volkov tried to ignore the sensation of his carefully constructed anonymity slipping irretrievably away. "And the CIA?"

"We understand that Ms. Vilechi has contacted them. For obvious reasons, it seems fairly certain that the FBI will receive very little useful information from the Agency."

Volkov nodded. "What about our contacts? What have we been able to discover?"

"Nothing beyond what the media has been able to put together. In order to find more, I would have to make direct inquiries. Do you want me to do that?"

"No. . . . We need to focus on drawing as little attention to ourselves as possible. At some point, that will become impossible, but for now, let's try to stay far in the background."

Volkov spun his chair around and for the first time that morning faced Pascal. "Is there anything else?"

His assistant just stood there, staring down at the floor.

"Pascal? Are you all right?"

Finally he looked up again. "What does it mean, Christian?"

Volkov glanced over at the bank of televisions, watching the images playing across them for a moment. "To us? I don't know. But there's nothing we can do now except to try to protect ourselves from any immediate danger." He paused for a moment. "We leave for the house in Chile as soon as possible. We've been here too long. Don't make any preparations or inform anyone we're moving until the last possible moment. And then only inform people who absolutely need to know."

"May I suggest the house in Seychelles instead? We have good people already there, and it will cause less disruption when we arrive."

"Fine. When can we leave?"

"Elizabeth and Joseph are taking care of it. Can you be ready to board a plane in two hours?"

Volkov nodded and his assistant started for the door.

"Pascal?"

The man stopped and looked back over his shoulder.

"Thank you."

"Of course."

5

"ARE you going to eat that or just play with it?"

Beamon stabbed a tortellini and popped it in his mouth. It took almost more energy than he had to chew and swallow.

"Come on, Mark. Quit being so tight-lipped."

"I'm just an honest, hardworking SAC, Carrie. Nobody tells me anything anymore."

A disbelieving frown spread across Carrie Johnstone's face—a really spectacular one. She was wearing her shoulder-length auburn hair down tonight, and the loose curls framed her face perfectly, though he knew from experience she hadn't given much thought to it.

Like him, she was wearing glasses nearly full time now. The difference was that his were nothing more than a badge of advancing years, while hers—little round lenses with almost imperceptible wire rims that somehow seemed just a bit subversive—seemed to enhance her features.

"There are terrorists running around America with a rocket launcher, and you're telling me you don't know anything about it," she said.

Beamon looked around the nearly empty restaurant, trying to spot their nervous waitress. "I guess I haven't been paying that much attention."

Another beautiful frown. "I saw Laura on TV, but she pretty much said the same thing you guys always say: 'We have numerous leads and are following up on them rigorously.'"

"Laura said *rigorously*?"

"She might not have used that exact word, but it was something similar. Have you talked to her?"

Not since she'd told him to piss off.

"Nope."

Carrie sliced thoughtfully into the bland-looking vegetarian dish she'd ordered and looked around the cavernous room. "Couldn't we have just eaten at your place? This is creepy."

"What is?"

"What do you mean, 'What is?'? The fact that any minute now, some fanatic could just blow us to pieces."

"I doubt anyone would waste a rocket on a mid-priced Italian restaurant in Phoenix."

"But you don't know that. You don't know for sure."

Beamon shrugged. There was just no goddamn way he was going to let some Middle Eastern fruitcake with a piece-of-shit surplus rocket launcher keep him from doing exactly what he wanted to. "Thousands of people die getting run over by drunk drivers every year, and all anyone ever worries about is terrorists and plane crashes. You have a better statistical chance of being killed by a shark in your hot tub."

"I know it's irrational, but it's hard to help, Mark. The fact that something could come out of nowhere . . . One minute you're just working or talking about nothing with a friend, and the next you're dead. I guess it's like snakes. Most are harmless but . . ." She shuddered.

The image of the World Trade Center flashed briefly across his mind. He blinked hard and watched Carrie as she popped something that might have been eggplant into her mouth. What if she had been in it when it had collapsed?

After twenty-odd years in the FBI, it was easy—critical to what was left of his sanity, really—that he view crime as clinically and dispassionately as possible. But what if she had died that day in September? What if she had been taken from him just because a bunch of semiliterate Muslims decided God was angry.

"You still there, Mark? What are you thinking about?"

"Nothing."

He ran a finger absently along the edge of his plate as she continued to eat. They'd been together for what seemed like a long time now—easily the longest relationship of his adult life, if he optimistically assumed that they still had a relationship.

The year before, when he'd become the target of the FBI and Congress, he'd made the monumental mistake of dumping her. He'd done it with the best intentions: He loved her and he didn't want to drag her and her young daughter down with him. She hadn't seen it that way, though. What she'd seen was a lack of trust—a lack of commitment. And maybe there was some truth to that. Or maybe he'd just wanted to cut loose of everything. With the benefit of hindsight, though, that break-up had positioned itself firmly at number one on the rather long list of dumb things he'd done in his life.

So now, despite a fairly obscene amount of groveling on his part, they'd "slowed things down." That's what women said when they were on the fence as to whether or not you were a compete loser: "I think we should slow things down."

There was still hope, though. The necklace he'd given her as a peace offering was dangling from her neck. It shone in the candlelight like . . . well, not like forgiveness, but maybe like the distant possibility of forgiveness.

"What's happening with the inspection?" Carrie said, dabbing at her mouth with her napkin. "You haven't said a word about it all night. Is it over?"

An interesting choice of words.

"Just about."

"And?"

Beamon quoted a line from the report that pretty much summed it up. "'While the office has been effective, this has been despite the management and administration, not because of it.'"

"That seems unfair."

Beamon blew air from his nose in an audible rush. Not quite a laugh.

"I guess it is, in a way. It should have been worse. The kid running the inspection seems to think I'm a cross between Sherlock Holmes and Jesus Christ. He softened the blow."

Finally spotting their waitress standing by a window, searching for terrorists, Beamon drained his beer and motioned for a refill. "Kind of a strange position to be in. Every time I turn around these days, politics are working for me instead of against me. It's hard to get used to for some reason."

Carrie nodded thoughtfully. "Why do you think that is?"

"Am I going to get a bill for this?"

Carrie was the director of psychiatry at a hospital in Flagstaff, a qualification that many people felt made her uniquely qualified to take on the task of being his significant other.

"Pick up dinner and we'll call it even."

"I don't know. Seems like it's about time the system worked for me instead of against me."

"I don't think anyone could say you haven't paid your dues, Mark. You finally got the promotion you'd deserved."

Beamon didn't respond. Maybe it was what he'd deserved—a punishment, though, not a reward. He'd had more than a few chances to ride into the sunset as the FBI's top investigator—some people might have even said the best they'd ever had. He was starting to think he should have just lived up to everyone's expectation and just self-destructed. But he'd convinced himself that it had been time to grow up.

"I guess so," he said, reaching for the pocket of his jacket before remembering that he couldn't smoke in the restaurant. Probably for the best: Maybe he'd manage to come in under two packs today. Instead he just drummed his fingers on the table and waited for his beer to arrive. Carrie wouldn't say anything about that. Giving up his beloved bourbon for light beer was actually one of his successes. What she didn't know, though, was that lately he'd caught himself slowing down when he drove by liquor stores.

"You know, Mark, I have this friend. She was a salesperson. Made lots of money, really good at her job. So good, in fact, that they gave her a big promotion and moved her upstairs into management. She absolutely hated it. Three months later she'd gone back to sales."

"I can't go back, Carrie. And I'm a little young to retire."

She examined his face carefully. "Mark, I've worked with some of the top surgeons in the country; I know college professors, researchers—you name it. And you're still the smartest guy I ever met. You *can* do this job if you buckle down. This is an issue of discipline, not ability."

He pushed his plate away and dug a toothpick from his pocket. Not as satisfying as a cigarette, but it took the edge off. Carrie just stared at him.

"What?"

"I'm worried about you, Mark."

"You've been worried about me since the day we met."

"No, I used to worry that you'd get yourself shot, or fired, or arrested. Now I'm worried about *you*." She motioned toward his still-full plate. "You don't eat anymore."

"The doctor said I had to lose weight."

"Yeah, I know your doctor and don't think he suggested substituting cigarettes and stress for two of the four food groups."

He shrugged. Whatever the reason, he'd lost the weight—almost fifty pounds. That, along with the beard that he'd grown to even out his thinning hair and the glasses he now wore, made it hard to recognize himself in the mirror every morning.

"I called you last Thursday at home at one P.M. and woke you up," she said.

"I guess I'm still adjusting to my new life as a successful FBI executive."

"Are you? I'm not sure. This new job—and the loss of your old job—is . . . I'm afraid it's beating you."

"I think you're being a little melodramatic, Carrie. I've been almost killed more times than I care to remember, and I just narrowly avoided being thrown in jail for God knows how long. I don't think sitting behind my desk and getting a bad report card from some kid is going to kill me."

"Isn't it?"

"Quit answering me with questions."

She nodded and fell silent for a few seconds. "You know one of the things I like best about you, Mark?"

"I didn't know there was anything anymore."

She kicked him under the table. "I've told you this before. What I like best about you is that, without fail, you always do what you think is right. A lot of times you're kind of misguided, but you're one of the only people I've ever met who really tries."

He actually remembered the first time she'd told him that. It had been about three minutes before he'd dumped her. Hopefully she'd forgotten.

"In fact, I think I told you that right before you dumped me."

Great.

"In the past it was always you against the establishment," she continued. "That's not the case here. What you're telling me is that you think they're right and you're wrong. That must be hard for you."

He didn't answer.

"Maybe you need some help—someone to talk to. Someone impartial."

"I'm not crazy, Carrie."

That elicited a little smile from her. "Don't fool yourself, Mark. You're as crazy as anyone I've ever met."

For once, he welcomed the sudden ringing of his cell phone. His dinner conversation with Carrie hadn't started out particularly flattering, and it looked like it was only going to get worse. He dug the phone from his pocket and pressed it to his ear. "This is Beamon."

"Evening, Mark."

"Laura? What happened to 'I never want to hear from you again'?"

"Don't beat me up over that, Mark."

"Does your boss know you're talking to me?"

"He suggested it."

Beamon felt his eyebrows rise involuntarily. "Dave Iverson suggested you call me? I find that hard to believe."

"Strange but true."

"I'm intrigued. What . . . ?" He let his voice trail off. Time to get his goddamn priorities straight for once in his life. "But I can't talk now."

"It's about the launcher," she said, baiting him with something that he would normally find absolutely irresistible.

"I don't care what it's about."

"What do you mean?" she said, obviously confused. "I don't understand."

"I'm having dinner with Carrie."

"Really? Good job, Mark. Give her the phone, I want to say hi."

He held it out. "It's Laura."

Carrie flashed a wide smile and snatched the phone, "Laura! How've you been?"

Beamon concentrated on his beer, trying to ignore the conversation that soon degenerated into smirks, ironic laughter, and brief phrases designed to be indecipherable to him. It went on like that for five minutes before Carrie finally handed the phone back.

"Go, Mark!" Laura said. "It sounds like you're softening her up. Call me when you get home, okay?"

"I don't know. Might not be able to get back to you till tomorrow."

Her laugh crackled through the earpiece. "I don't think you've softened her up that much."

6

Mark Beamon stepped into the cold air of his apartment and slammed the door before the July heat could slip in behind him. He looked around at the immaculate living room and sighed quietly. He'd cleaned it up that morning—or at least hidden everything dirty—in case things went better than expected with Carrie. Of course they hadn't and she'd escaped back to Flagstaff and her daughter. Who could blame her? He'd been less than a sunny companion lately. That was something that needed to change.

He dropped onto the sofa and picked up the inspection report he'd left there the night before. After staring at the blank cover for a few seconds, he dropped it in his lap and flipped to a dog-eared page about a third of the way in. This page, he told himself, would be the turning point. Things were going to start looking up from here on.

After a quick scan, it turned out to be yet another inaccurate criticism of one of his assistant SACs. Instead of crossing it out and writing a note as to why it was his fault, he just tossed the report on the floor and flipped on the television, surfing the channels at high speed, looking for something uplifting. There wasn't much to choose from—mostly doom, gloom, and wild speculation about pending biological and nuclear attacks. He finally settled on Charles Russell speaking passionately to a television camera. His message seemed uncharacteristically confused: half prediction of impending death and destruction, and half plea for people to climb out from under their beds and support the economy. As he always did when something bad happened, Russell eventually segued into a fire-and-brimstone speech on why the government needed more power to "root out these evildoers." Even as a senator he'd had the disturbing philosophy that if the U.S. would just incarcerate three quarters of its citizens and severely restricted the freedoms of the other quarter, America would be transformed into some kind of utopia. The guy was so goddamn law-and-order, even cops thought he was a pain in the ass.

Russell pointed right at him. "We have to give law enforcement the tools to—"

"Careful, America . . ." Beamon cautioned, starting to flip through the channels again. Yet another brutal civil war in Southeast Asia, casualty reports from a recent school shooting, rocket launchers, rocket launchers, and more rocket launchers. He finally settled on the Cartoon Channel. Carrie's daughter had turned him on to it. Some of the most intelligent programming on cable.

Settling a little deeper into the sofa, he tried to lose himself in the old episode of Scooby-Doo. It was the one with Mama Cass as a guest star. A classic.

After a few minutes he caught himself drumming his fingers relentlessly on the cushions. He laced his hands tightly across his stomach but couldn't keep the phone next to the sofa from looming larger and larger in his peripheral vision. He lit a cigarette, despite his ironclad rule of not smoking in his apartment, and focused on the elegant plot unfolding on the television.

The truth was, he was more than a little put out at Laura's smug prediction that he'd strike out with Carrie—not to mention her certainty that he'd call her back after she'd snubbed him last time they'd spoken.

What did she want? Why would Iverson suggest she call? It would have to be important. . . .

"Goddamnit," he said in disgust at his own lack of willpower. He glanced at his watch. It would be one-thirty in the morning in D.C. Hopefully he'd wake her up from a good dream.

She picked up on the first ring, sounding wide-awake.

"It's Mark."

"Home so ear—"

"Don't say it," he warned. "Just don't even say it."

"I guess I've caught you in one of your moods."

"My relationship with Carrie seems to be in a permanent stall and she thinks I'm crazy." He jabbed his cigarette out in an ashtray cleverly disguised as a candy dish. "I don't think she's seeing anyone else, but at this point I honestly don't know. Shit, if she isn't, she probably should be."

"She isn't seeing anyone else, Mark."

"I wish I could be so sure."

"Look, she's put her hand on the Mark Beamon stove, what, three times now? She was bound to learn eventually. She loves you, Mark. But you make things so damn hard. . . ."

"I have professionals pointing out my failings, Laura. I don't need you to."

"You want me to talk to her?"

"No. . . . Thanks, though. I'll work it out."

"You can, you know."

"Yeah. Now, what do you want?"

"Have you been watching the news?"

"Not really. I assume that they don't know anything and are just trying to whip up a little panic. It took me a goddamn half an hour to find a restaurant that was open." He let his head loll to the right. Scooby and Shaggy were being chased by a monster. He wouldn't have predicted that plot twist.

"Mark? Are you still there?"

"Yes."

"Where's the commentary? Normally, I can't shut you up."

"It's not my case, Laura. I mean, I feel bad that there's a rocket launcher floating around out there somewhere, but the Director, Dave, and all the other powers that be aren't going to want me involved in this thing. They're more than happy to just let me hang myself here in Phoenix."

"I'm sorry about the 'Don't call me anymore' comment, Mark. I didn't mean—"

"I know you didn't."

"So? What do you think?"

Beamon laughed. "About what? I don't know anything. I hear you're leaking that al-Qaeda is behind it. Is that just bullshit to feed the media?"

"At least for now Mustafa Yasin looks good to us."

"I don't know, Laura. I don't envy you. Now that we've shown we can be hurt, we're never going to get rid of these assholes. The war against terrorism has the potential to end up like the war on drugs."

"Not my problem, Mark. I'm just trying to find a rocket launcher."

"Have you checked with customs?"

"They're making sure their asses are covered. We figure Yasin's people would have sent the launcher in pieces. It'd probably just look like construction material or equipment. The rocket would be tougher to disguise, but smaller."

"I'm guessing they don't have many of those," Beamon said.

"Why?"

"Like you said, harder to smuggle in. Besides, if they had a warehouse full of them, they'd have started this thing out with a bang. No, I figure they've got one or two and they're going to milk them for all they're worth while they try to get more across the border."

"We came to the same conclusion. In fact, we figure they only brought the rocket and launcher together briefly for the purpose of taking that photo. We're working under the assumption that one terrorist cell has the launcher and that there are one or more with the rockets. Yasin learned from the Trade Center investigation: He's a fanatic for keeping his cells completely separate. In the Trade Center case we found letters and wills and even tattoos of Osama bin Laden. This time I wouldn't be surprised if the different cells don't even speak the same language."

"It pays not to put all your eggs in one basket. What about the audio?"

Laura groaned. "Don't remind me. We have a hotline set up for anyone who might recognize the voice. We're getting literally thousands of calls. People are phoning in about anyone with a beard and an accent."

"So you pretty much have nothing."

"Well, we have our informants, who are pointing to Yasin as the mastermind here."

"Are you sure they aren't just telling you what you want to hear? Yasin's taken bin Laden's place as the poster child for everything that's wrong with the world."

"We've been hearing about something big for a while now. I'm actually fairly confident that he was involved on some level."

Beamon nodded into the phone. Laura never made statements like that unless she was pretty much dead certain.

"Well, I guess it's all pretty academic. I seriously doubt we'll ever see him in an American jail."

"Not my problem either. I just want the weapon."

Beamon lit another cigarette. "I have to wonder why you're telling me all this, Laura."

"Dave and I . . ." she began hesitantly. "Well, we met with the CIA about this yesterday."

"And?"

"And we both agreed that they're holding out on us."

"What's that mean to me?" Beamon asked, although he already knew the answer.

"I'm just going to come out and say it, Mark. We need your influence at the White House to get them to open up. We need to apply a little pressure."

Beamon blew a smoke ring at the ceiling but didn't speak.

"Look, Mark, you know damn well that if it was my call, you'd be on this case. Hell, at this point I'd love to just give it to you and walk away. But it's not my call."

"What's in it for me?"

"What do you want?"

Good question. A glowing inspection report that he didn't deserve? Involvement in a case that wasn't his to help him forget about the job that *was* his? Hell, did he even want to be an FBI agent anymore?

"Dinner. Next time I see you, you have to cook me dinner."

"I don't cook, Mark—"

"And it has to be really good. And it can't be out of a box. It has to be from scratch. And I want a pie for dessert. Apple. No. Rhubarb."

"Rhubarb? Do you even know what a rhubarb looks like?"

"You heard me."

"Fine."

"Honestly, Laura, I don't even know where Tom is. Didn't I hear that you guys have some evidence that the White House has been targeted and the President's been sent to Kansas to hide?"

"Nebraska, actually. But the White House being targeted was just something the press secretary made up so the President wouldn't look like he was cowering. Tom's still in D.C."

"Okay, I'll make some calls."

Silence.

"Is this where we say good-bye, Laura?"

"There's one more thing."

"What?"

"I think it would be best if you were at our meeting with the Agency. It's just one day. I know you're busy, but it's common knowledge that the White House chief of staff is your best friend and that you can just pick up the phone and call him anytime. It might keep them honest."

"Dave went for that?"

"I had to throw a tantrum, but yeah, he went for it."

"Must have been some tantrum."

"You have no idea. So it's agreed? You'll come?"

"There are no flights."

"I'll send the jet for you."

"All right. Fine. Let me know when."

"I owe you one. I'll talk to you soon: I've got to go and force myself to get some sleep."

"Doesn't sound like you've got anything better to do."

"Thanks a lot, Mark. I appreciate you reminding me."

7

THE plane's sudden loss of altitude created yet another unpleasant sensation in Jonathan Drake's already nauseated stomach. He leaned over in the uncomfortable canvas seat and brought his face close to the window. Despite the fact that his watch, still set to Washington, D.C., time, told him that it was only late afternoon, he could see nothing but deep, unbroken darkness.

After thirteen hours on a luxurious private jet and two more in this small, unstable prop plane, he could only make semieducated guesses as to where he was. The plane's most likely destination was somewhere deep inside the former Soviet Union—well out of his sphere of influence and perhaps even outside the tracking capability of his people. Once again he found himself isolated, alone.

He leaned into the window again as the small plane continued its descent, but still, the only light visible was the dim glow coming from the cockpit. The sudden lurch as the landing gear made contact with the runway sent a jolt of adrenaline through him and he strained to see something—anything—outside as they rolled to a stop. But there was nothing.

The pilot, a tall black woman, appeared from the cockpit and opened a small door in the side of the aircraft. Drake felt the cold air wash over him but didn't immediately move. While it was clear that she wanted him to get out, he wasn't anxious to be left standing alone in the pitch black.

In the end, though, there was little choice. He unbuckled his seat belt and walked to the front of the plane, jumping down onto the dirt runway and hearing the hatch immediately close behind him. He took a few unsteady steps forward as the whine of the motor began to rise in pitch, then turned to watch his only source of light and transportation take to the air again.

The cloud cover must have been low and dense—no moon or stars were visible and he lost sight of the plane almost immediately. It was a weather pattern that he had expected; the heavy overcast would make it even more difficult for his people to track him.

He folded his thick arms around himself, already feeling the cold, thin air penetrating his shirt. It had been over ninety in D.C., making the idea of bringing a jacket seemed absurd. He took a step forward and nearly lost his balance in the blinding darkness. What if no one came? What if they had just left him here? When the sun finally came up, would he find himself in the middle of an endless, empty wilderness—stranded in an uncharted part of Siberia or Uzbekistan? What time was it? Would it get colder? Was it possible that he had been left here to freeze?

It was almost a half an hour before the sound of an engine began to emerge from the silence. Drake turned toward it and concentrated on the low hum. His eyes were well adjusted to the darkness, and it wasn't long before he was able to discern a weak glow in the distance. Soon there was enough light to see the outline of the densely packed trees that he had known surrounded the airstrip from the heavy scent of pine. When the gray Chevy Suburban glided to a stop in front of him, its headlights illuminated the faded Cyrillic writing on a dilapidated hangar, confirming Drake's suspicions as to his general location. He climbed into the backseat unbidden and found himself separated from the front by a panel of opaque glass, leaving the driver silent and invisible.

It was another hour of nothing but poorly maintained dirt roads lined by impenetrable forest before the car veered off onto what looked more like a wide trail than anything else. The vehicle continued forward at not much more than a walking pace for another fifteen minutes before it jerked to a stop in front of an old log cabin. Drake took a deep breath and stepped out, examining the isolated building in the vehicle's head-lights. It looked abandoned. Part of the roof was missing and the walls appeared to be on the verge of collapse. The only sign of life was the smoke billowing from a crumbling chimney and the flickering light coming from inside.

He straightened, rising to his full six foot three, trying to look more confident than he felt as he marched forward and pushed through what was left of the cabin's door.

Fueled with fresh evergreen branches, the fire inside was raging. He averted his eyes slightly, making a quick sweep of the cabin's single room. There wasn't much to see: a broken table, the rusting frame of a bed, two chairs.

"You wanted to see me, Jonathan?"

Christian Volkov was sitting in one of the chairs, leaning back enough to bring the front legs off the floor, seemingly at ease. Drake approached slowly, examining the man carefully.

Although they'd met four times during their association, Drake was always surprised by Christian Volkov's unremarkable appearance. He was of medium height, maybe five foot nine, and thin in a vaguely athletic way. His eyes and hair were a deep enough brown to give him a slightly ethnic look, but his fair skin and the gray at his temples softened the impression. There was no aura of power or charisma, no piercing intelligence or ruthlessness visible in his moderately handsome face. Overall a rather forgettable man of around forty.

Despite the uncertainty of his situation, Drake's confidence began to return to him, as it always did when he saw the diminutive Volkov. He strode across the room and took a seat in the empty chair, his height and bulk creating a substantial presence.

"You asked for this meeting," Volkov said, motioning around him through the firelight with a dead expression on his face. "What is it you'd like to talk about?"

His accent was upper-class British, though Drake knew that English wasn't his native language.

"I thought it was important for us to meet, Christian. I thought I should tell you face-to-face that everything's moving forward as planned."

"I see," was Volkov's only response.

Drake tried to read him—the real purpose for this inconvenient and dangerous meeting—but the combination of Volkov's slack expression and the erratic shadows from the fire made it impossible. "Obviously there are additional complications and we're going to have to take care of those—tie up some unanticipated loose ends. I want you to understand that and to be prepared for it. There's no need for you to be concerned."

"What kind of loose ends?"

Jonathan shrugged in an attempt to make the question seem trivial. "We're going to begin blocking any paths that could lead to us . . . or to you. That's going to mean removing some of the people who aren't necessary to the operation going forward. As I said, it's not something you need to concern yourself with. What you need to focus on is that we still expect you to deliver on your agreement."

Volkov folded his hands in front of his face, gazing past them at the crackling fire. For a few moments he looked just like the literature professor that Drake's intelligence suggested he had once aspired to be.

"What happened, Jonathan?"

"That really isn't your concern, either. It's enough for you to know that everything is moving forward as before."

Volkov slammed his hand down on the table and Jonathan scooted back involuntarily, despite his superior size and physical strength. He had never seen Volkov express anger—or any other emotion, for that matter—and it suddenly reminded him of where he was: thousands of miles from home, sitting in front of one the most powerful organized-crime figures in the world.

"You've made it my concern, haven't you, Jonathan? Your stupidity and ambition have involved me in the potential deaths of hundreds of people—of women and children. American women and children. You used my contacts to arm al-Qaeda with a powerful portable weapon and you allowed them to outsmart you and smuggle it into the United States—despite my repeated warnings. Why should I trust you to fix a situation that only a fool would create?"

Drake tensed at the personal insult. Volkov's arrogance had infuriated him from the beginning. The man was nothing but a drug dealer—a petty criminal who had grown fat on easy business opportunities. He hoped he could be there when Volkov died. He wanted to see that icy veneer stripped away. He wanted to see Volkov beg.

"I have my people working on it," Drake replied in a calm, practiced voice. "We expect to resolve the situation within a week. If there are problems, of course we'll contact you. But we don't anticipate any."

"I wonder if your FBI will have something to say about that. They're under a great deal of pressure to find these terrorists and their weapon. They tend not to give up easily."

"You understand that I can't give you details, Christian, but you can believe me when I say we have this under control. The FBI will learn only what we want them to learn."

"And what will that be?"

Drake didn't answer; instead he just stared back at Volkov, who seemed to shrink and fade into the wall behind him.

"I will do what I said I would," Volkov said finally.

Drake simply nodded.

"But you, Jonathan . . . you make sure you do the same."

"It's cold, Christian."

Volkov threw a log that had once been part of the structure around him into the dying flames. He could feel the heat on his face almost immediately.

"Come closer to the fire," Volkov said in French.

The man did as Volkov instructed, bending at the waist and holding his hands out to warm them.

Jonathan Drake had gone more than hour ago and would soon be boarding one of Volkov's planes for his return to America. The question was, what would he do when he arrived there?

"The car is waiting," Pascal prompted for the third time, but Volkov ignored him. His friend was unaccustomed to being outside the well-protected and luxurious compounds that they had scattered across the globe. Volkov, on the other hand, never missed an opportunity to enjoy a brief parole from those opulent prisons. For the second time in a week, he found himself with an opportunity to enjoy a few moments of silence and distance. A rare treat.

He watched as Pascal leaned in closer to the fire, finally sitting down in the dirt and folding his tall, thin body into the space between the hearth an the table.

Volkov allowed very few people to get close to him—a sometimes depressing philosophy that had nonetheless kept him alive longer than he'd had a right to expect. Of those people, Pascal had been with him the longest—almost fifteen years now. And while the Frenchman lacked anything that could be described as imagination or humor or passion, he more than compensated with his loyalty and genius for the maze of off-shore accounts, corporations, houses, and passports that had become so indispensable. Pascal was responsible for a great deal of Volkov's success, prosperity, and . . . and what? Happiness?

"Do you believe him, Christian?"

"I honestly don't know."

"It seems impossible that he would try to end his support of al-Qaeda now. It would almost certainly have a devastating effect."

Volkov smiled absently. Pascal's mind worked only in logic; he had little understanding of human nature. "The Americans can always be counted on to do what is in their own best interest, with little regard to anyone else. The problem is that they often don't know what their interests are." He closed his eyes and listened to the sound of the fire. It had always been certain that getting involved with Jonathan Drake would be a mistake. But what choice had he been left with?

"Then, what do we do, Christian?"

Volkov shrugged. "We move forward. Commitments have been made."

Pascal nodded silently.

"Is there any news from Laos?" Volkov asked, moving to a different and equally difficult subject.

"We're still trying to set up a meeting. General Yung is agreeable in principle but vague with details."

Yung had just orchestrated a brutal and apparently effective coup in Laos that had taken even Volkov by surprise. While it was unlikely that the changeover in governments would weaken his position on the Pacific Rim in the long term, the temporary disruption of his power base there couldn't have come at a worse time.

"Do we have any reliable reports as to the general's strength at this point?"

"He is still in the process of consolidating his power. Support for the former president still exists, though it is scattered and appears weak. Yung seems to be quite intelligent and understands that this is his opportunity to deal a crushing blow to the opposition before they are able to reorganize. He'll move decisively."

Volkov sighed quietly. "Another psychotic general . . ."

"In the end, though, a positive change, don't you think, Christian? The prior regime was certainly friendly to us but rather communistic and bureaucratic."

"Better in the long run, perhaps. But exhausting. Sometimes I think I prefer the communists." He looked down at Pascal. "Unless your meeting with Yung looks completely safe, I don't want you to go. Do you understand?"

"He has Luang Prabang locked down. I don't anticipate any problems."

"All I'm asking is that you err on the side of caution."

8

ACCORDING to the clock on the wall, this particular tirade had been going on for and hour and twenty minutes. To be entirely accurate, though, Carlo Gasta had been spewing an almost constant stream of empty threats and epithets for two days—ever since they'd returned from their aborted heroin buy. Chet ran a hand through his curly red hair, careful not to sigh audibly, and took another delicate sip of the vodka in his glass.

"Cocksucker!" Gasta screamed, continuing to pace violently back and forth across the living room for the benefit of his captive audience.

"This is fucking America! If those sand niggers want to come to this country and do business, they better learn to run their fucking organizations! If not, they're gonna find themselves dead."

There was yet another murmured assent that Chet made sure he joined in on.

"Cocksucker!"

Chet let himself sink a little further into the oversized leather sofa and continued to watch his boss march from wall to wall. The scene was almost laughably stereotypical. The decorator, no doubt specializing in Mob clients, had missed no opportunity to load the house with glass, chrome, and animal prints—except when a Roman bust or pillar got in the way. When Gasta suddenly stopped and spun to face Chet, the jewelry around his neck swayed hypnotically. His overstyled hair, though, didn't budge.

"You shouldn't have held me back," he said for what must have been the hundredth time. And for the hundredth time, Chet answered, "Shit, Carlo, if I'd let you beat him to death, we'd have ended up in a war with those assholes. We'd have spent the next five years shooting Afghans. And that'd attract a hell of a lot of attention. Particularly now, with this fucking rocket launcher thing."

The statement didn't necessarily make a hell of a lot of sense, but it seemed to please his boss, who started to pace again.

Chet was just glad to be alive. Their meeting with Mohammed could have easily gone the other way. It had been the first time he'd ever pulled his gun for real, and he'd be perfectly happy if it was the last time.

Gasta stopped again, this time in front of an elaborate stereo, and turned up the volume, filling the room with retro dance music. "The question is, what are we gonna do about these towelheads?" he shouted.

Chet didn't say anything, but he was pretty sure towelheads were Indians.

When no one in the room dared answer, Gasta made a frustrated gesture with his free hand and stumbled to the bar to make another drink. He looked like he was having a hard time lining the ice cubes up with the glass.

Chet wondered how long he'd have to work for Gasta before he finally figured the man out. Carlo was the only son of the highly respected and now dead Carlo Gasta senior, an extremely powerful organized-crime figure from New York. As nearly as Chet could tell, though, the younger Gasta had little in common with his father. While Carlo senior had shunned the spotlight, his son had never met a camera he didn't like. He seemed to think he was a movie star and could often be found having drinks with semifamous actors and actresses at the most exclusive restaurants in town. The public had always been fascinated with the Mob, and Carlo junior was about as Mob as you could get.

So far, the best the L.A. cops had been able to do was to pick him up for a few bar fights and for kicking a dent in the car door of a woman who had cut him off in traffic. Nothing had stuck, though. As soon as the witnesses and victims found out who he was, they tended to become very forgetful. So he continued to operate right beneath the noses of federal and local law enforcement, taking great pleasure in driving both absolutely nuts.

Chet couldn't bring himself to be too critical of people who were drawn to Carlo's persona, though. It was partly that persona that had attracted him to the man. That and the rumor that Gasta was trying to make a splash in the heroin trade. At first the idea of hitching his wagon to Gasta had seemed like a hell of a good one. Now he wasn't so sure.

The more time he spent around the mobster, the more evident it became that Gasta was nothing more than an insecure little boy. Even worse, he was stupid—a real card-carrying moron. He didn't do what he did for money or even for power, really. He did what he did to get attention. And that was a dangerous addiction for a career criminal.

"Chet! What the fuck are you doing sitting there, staring at your feet! Are you even listening?"

Chet straightened up abruptly and lied. "Yeah, I'm listening, Carlo. But I'm thinking there isn't a whole lot we can do right now. Mohammed said he'd have the stuff in a week. I figure we give him a week. If he doesn't deliver, then we start making a plan."

"Bullshit! If we just sit here and take this kind of shit, we look weak. We end up with those dune coons laughing at us."

If nothing else, Gasta was an encyclopedia of ethnic slurs.

"The people I'm dealing with expect things to get done—you understand that, Chet? I don't like having to explain delays. When I have to start explaining delays, I start fucking killing people."

And there, in a nutshell, was what made Carlo so intriguing. Who were these people he was "dealing with"? As near as Chet could tell, most of Gasta's schemes were no more profitable or successful than last night's drug deal, but there always seemed to be money lying around. Everybody got paid; there were cars, houses, women. And when a few million was needed to buy a vanload of heroin, well, that just suddenly appeared too.

Where it all came from continued to be a mystery to Chet, despite having been recently promoted to a position that allowed him to keep a watchful eye on the organization's accounts. Despite his press, Gasta was really just another small-time dumb-ass wise guy, but the people supplying him with his cash might not be. And those were the kinds of people that Chet was very anxious to meet.

9

THE corridor had no windows or inhabitants and was starting to look as if it had no end. Beamon stayed alongside Laura Vilechi as she closely followed the young woman ushering them through the CIA's Langley headquarters.

"The place looks different than last time I was here . . ." Beamon said, in yet another attempt to strike up a conversation with their guide. He had tried the weather, local attractions, current events, and now decor—all to no avail. Other than the stern look he'd received when he'd started to hum, she didn't seem to want to acknowledge that they were there.

The woman's momentum began to falter and she finally stopped, pointing to the only door in a dead-end hallway to their right. "If you could have a seat in there, someone will be with you as soon as possible."

"Is there a Coke machine or something around here?" Beamon asked.

"No."

"Thank you," Laura said, pushing him forward. "We'll be fine."

The door closed behind them and they found themselves alone in a little box of a room furnished only with a long table and ten chairs. Another damned conference room. Beamon resisted the urge to test the doorknob to see if they were trapped.

"So where's Dave?" Beamon said, referring to Laura's boss.

"He has a lot going on."

Beamon fell into a chair and put his feet up on the one next to it. "Still can't stand to be in the same room with me?"

"It was part of the deal," she admitted. "If you came, he didn't. He's still pretty angry with you, Mark. But he appreciates you helping us."

Beamon nodded silently. His friend at the White House had called the CIA director at home and parroted Laura's concern that his organization was withholding information that might be useful in the FBI's investigation. Not surprisingly, this meeting got scheduled in a hurry.

"So how are things going?" Beamon said through a yawn. The simple act of sleeping through the night was getting harder and harder for him.

"Well, I wouldn't want to bore you any more than you already are," she snapped.

Beamon stared at her for a moment. The stress was already starting to show. He knew it was impossible, but it seemed that new lines were etching themselves into her face almost hourly.

"The captain's chair isn't that comfortable, is it?"

Her expression softened a little and she actually seemed to blush. "Things aren't going that well. We know exactly where the photograph was taken and we've been able to pinpoint the time based on the weather. There's not a town within fifty miles and no one we can find saw anything—no Middle Eastern–looking men, no trucks, no usable tire tracks or footprints. We're watching all the roads out of there and looking into the sale and rentals of trucks big enough to carry that thing, but I'm not hopeful. We're covering all the bases on possible radical groups, right down to the animal-rights people. In the end, though, it's going to be al-Qaeda. I'm ninety percent certain. . . ."

"Getting anywhere on the audio?"

"We've got a decent voice print off it and we're running it against the tips we're getting and any possible suspects. Nothing."

He really didn't envy her this one. The media was doing a hell of a job convincing America that missiles were going to start falling from the sky like rain and that many of them would have nuclear and biological payloads. If al-Qaeda managed to get a shot off, it didn't take a whole lot of imagination to figure out who was going to take the blame for letting it happen.

"How's Brian doing with all this?"

Laura's three-year marriage to a Georgetown University geology professor—and generally good guy—was starting to falter.

That blush again. "This isn't what we needed right now. It's the hours: We never see each other anymore. He said we might as well not even be married. He actually said that." She averted her eyes toward the ceiling. "And he's right. I'd actually started doing a little better—being more careful with my time, but now this . . ."

The door opened and she fell silent. Beamon didn't recognize the man who entered and dropped his laptop and files a little too hard on the table. He was actually kind of an impressive figure. Well over six feet tall with the thick chest and arms of a serious weightlifter and not just someone who popped into the gym every once in a while to alleviate guilt. His skin was well tanned, and his slicked-back black hair was a little longer than would normally be expected. The blue slacks and white shirt he wore were obviously tailor-made and created a well-thought-out backdrop for an expensive-looking tie. If he were to smile, which seemed unlikely, it was almost certain that his teeth would be ruler-straight and designer-white.

Laura rose from her chair and stuck her hand out. "You must be Jonathan Drake. I'm Laura Vilechi."

Beamon smiled. At times there was definitely something to be said for having the White House chief of staff as your best friend. Until now Laura had been confined to working with Drake's underlings, never laying eyes on the man himself.

Drake gave her hand a cursory shake and sat. He turned toward Beamon for a moment but didn't offer any kind of a greeting. It didn't matter. This was Laura's show.

"Ms. Vilechi—" he started.

"Call me Laura."

"Fine. Laura, then. Apparently you had Tom Sherman call the DCI, who then called my boss, Alan Holsten, who has in turn called me with some vague notion that my people are not fully cooperating with you and your investigation."

Laura opened her mouth to speak but he silenced her with an impatient and rather rude gesture. Beamon smiled. He and Laura were pretty good friends—it could even be argued that he was at least partially responsible for her meteoric rise through the FBI's ranks—and he still wouldn't have the guts to in any way suggest that she shut up. Maybe this meeting would turn out more entertaining than he'd thought.

Drake continued in an irritated toned deadened by fatigue. Beamon had initially been dazzled by the man's impeccable grooming but now saw that behind it, he looked as if he hadn't slept in a couple of days.

"Your belief that al-Qaeda is involved in this may be correct or it may not, Laura. Either way, we've shared everything we've got on them with you. What do you want from us? We can't do your job for you. . . ."

Beamon had to stifle a laugh. Five more minutes of this kind of attitude and Drake was going to find himself at the hospital, having his laptop surgically removed from his ass.

". . . And since all you've provided us with on the weapon is a bunch of poorly supported theories that you seem to gave gotten from the media, we've got no leverage with the Russians. Until you have something that's at least got some basis, they're going to deny that this is anything but a model built from materials purchased at Home Depot."

Laura didn't answer immediately, instead nodding thoughtfully at his lecture.

"You're right, Jonathan, the FBI has been slow in turning up concrete evidence. That's my fault and I'd like to apologize. We're hoping to get you more soon."

Beamon had been wondering if Laura's suspicions about the CIA had been just an impression or if she had something more solid. The affected sweetness of her voice answered that question.

"What I'm looking for," she continued politely, "is some information on the recent skirmishes that have taken place in Afghanistan, Turkmenistan, and Pakistan. Maybe even a few in Iran and Turkey: I'm not certain of my intelligence, there. I understand that it's possible the al-Qaeda organization is involved."

Beamon had guessed from Laura's tone that she was about to lower the boom and had been watching Drake's face intently as she spoke. He was good—there was no denying it—a natural-born liar. Whether it was his obvious fatigue or just surprise at the little blond woman's attack, Beamon spotted a split-second glitch in Drake's expression as he shifted gears.

"We have been picking up some activity—"

"I see," Laura said. "So when you said you'd shared everything you have, that wasn't entirely accurate."

Drake had himself completely back under control when he spoke again. "Come on, Laura, this kind of thing isn't unusual and you know it. We've stabilized that region as much as it can be stabilized, but it's still wall-to-wall with warlords, Muslim fanatics, terrorists, and people who don't know how to do anything but fight. And as far as al-Qaeda being involved, who the hell knows? These guys aren't as easy to identify as they used to be—and as you know, they were never easy to identify."

"But there's been an increase in the frequency and scale of the attacks over the last six months, isn't that right? And they cover a pretty wide geographic area, don't they? Too wide to be an individual warlord fighting over some piece of ground."

The silence that ensued probably lasted no more than two seconds, but it spoke volumes. Drake was trying to calculate how much she knew and the absolute minimum he could reveal without seeming evasive.

"You're assuming that the individual battles are connected in some way, and I don't think there's any evidence of that," he said finally. "This kind of violence ebbs and flows. We may just be seeing a reaction to the American-supported regime in Afghanistan, possibly with the involvement of displaced Taliban or al-Qaeda. Or it could be more perception than reality. We're just looking harder than we used to. In any event, I don't see how that would be relevant to your investigation. In fact, you could argue that if Mustafa Yasin is tying up his limited manpower in petty skirmishes on the other side of the world, he might not be involved with this rocket launcher at all."

Mistake, Beamon thought.

"So you don't think information relating to Yasin's possible innocence and someone else's guilt would be relevant to our investigation?"

It was Drake's turn to flush.

"Could al-Qaeda be trying to take control of Afghanistan again, Jonathan? Could Yasin be trying to initiate radical Islamic revolutions in the surrounding countries?"

"I hardly think that the activity we're seeing is of that kind of magnitude. And again, we don't know that al-Qaeda is involved."

"So someone over there is just feeling a little pissy," Laura said. "Sort of Muslim PMS."

Beamon had to bite his lip to keep from laughing.

"*What I'm trying to tell you,*" Drake said angrily, "is that the people in that region like nothing better than to kill each other and anyone else they happen across. I mean, look at their stance on the United States. We pour billions into their economies and helped the Afghans drive the Soviets out of their country, and now they call us infidels and run planes into our cities."

Beamon was a little slow in stifling his laugh this time, and Drake spun toward him. "Did you have something to add?"

Beamon had an Ivy League degree in history—something he rarely admitted to—and the CIA's revisionism always struck him as funny in kind of an absurd way.

"I'm sorry. No, nothing."

"Please, Mr. Beamon. If you have something to say I'm sure we'd all like to hear it."

The guy sounded like his second-grade teacher.

"Well, I'll tell you, Jonathan: As I remember it, the CIA armed the Afghan people to the teeth in order to fight the Soviets and adopted a kind of 'We'll fight to the last Afghan' policy. Then, when the Soviets were driven out, we just flipped them the bird and walked out of there. In return for helping us bring down the Soviet Union and end the Cold War, we left them with half their male population dead or maimed and their country in ruins. And as far as pouring money into the economies over there, I think it's less goodwill than the fact we like to drive big cars. . . ."

"I'm sick of people telling me that because we helped the Afghans fight off an occupying force, we somehow owe them. They had every opportunity to create a viable government after the Soviets pulled out, but they didn't, because they're a corrupt, violent, uneducated people. It wasn't our job to save them from themselves."

"What we owed them or didn't owe them is neither here nor there, Jonathan. That fact is that al-Qaeda's mostly a bunch of non-Afghan Muslim fanatics that the CIA encouraged to go to Afghanistan and help the mujahideen. As I recall, you guys paid Osama bin Laden to build training camps so that we'd be dead sure that every nutcase in the Middle East could shoot a Stinger with either hand. Wouldn't it have made a little bit of sense to have stuck around and tried to create something productive for these guys to do? To have given them a little guidance?"

"I don't have time to sit here and debate history with you, Mr. Beamon. It has no bearing on our discussion."

"I'm curious as to what criteria you use to decide what is and isn't relevant," Laura said.

The air rushed out of him in an exasperated gush and he threw his hands up.

"Is there any pattern to the skirmishes we're seeing over there?" Laura asked.

"No."

"Are they using weapons similar to the one in the photograph?"

"I don't know."

"Do you know anything about who exactly has been attacked?"

"Not really."

"Have there been offensives against cities of any size or importance?"

"Not that we know of."

Beamon tilted his head back and stared up at the ceiling. That was it: This guy had his back up and Laura wasn't going to get anything more out of him.

"Look, Jonathan," Beamon said, keeping his eyes trained on the ceiling. Laura would undoubtedly be glaring at him for interfering. "We don't want to take up any more of your time than we have to. Just give us the four *W*'s and we're out here."

"I'm sorry?" Jonathan said.

"Don't be sorry. Just tell us who, when, where, and why."

"I think it's a little more complicated than that."

"And maybe we're too dumb to understand it," Beamon said, leaning forward in his chair and looking directly at Drake. "Should we fly to Nebraska and finish this meeting with the President? He's a pretty smart guy—maybe he could help us understand the complications you're talking about. One thing I know for sure is that he's real interested in finding that launcher. From what I hear, it's about all he thinks about these days."

Drake stared back fiercely but it didn't mean much. He would have checked into just how well connected Beamon was and would know that he could make good on his threat.

Drake grabbed a thick cable protruding from the top of the table and connected it to his laptop. When he turned the computer on, the images on its screen were transmitted to a large monitor built into one of the walls. He tapped a few keys and a map of the Middle East appeared.

"Where," he said simply.

Beamon and Laura both leaned forward and watched as the screen zoomed in on the map and red dots appeared representing recent guerrilla activity. They seemed to be concentrated in, but not limited to, the Helmand province of Afghanistan and its borders with Pakistan and Turkmenistan.

"All attacks were on insignificant encampments of no military or strategic value that we can discern," Drake said, tapping a few more commands into the computer. A moment later the "when" part of Beamon's question appeared next to the dots in the form of dates.

"Who? We're not sure. Warlords, former Taliban, al-Qaeda, various tribes, all of the above. We just don't know. As far as why goes, your guess is as good as ours: ethnic hatred, religion, territory, money. Take your pick."

Beamon glanced over at Laura but she seemed content to let him stay in the lead.

"Okay, Jonathan, now we're getting somewhere. I can get my mind around this. What I'd like is for you to give us everything you've got on this subject, including inquiries you've made that came to nothing. Why don't you have it couriered over to Dave Iverson in two hours. And copy Tom Sherman at the White House. I'll let him know when to expect it."

Beamon stood, not bothering to wait for Drake's response. "I guess that's about it." He nodded toward Laura. "Unless you have something else."

"No, I think that'll do it." She moved around the table and shook hands with an unhappy Jonathan Drake. "It's been a pleasure," she lied. "I appreciate all your hard work."

As they walked out into the hall and joined their less than bubbly escort again, Laura looked over at him and carefully mouthed the words *thank you.*

"I told you to be careful!" Alan Holsten shouted, slamming the door to the conference room behind him. "They came in here with vague suspicions and left certain that we're hiding something. You read the files on Vilechi and Beamon and you still underestimated them."

Holsten, the CIA's deputy director of operations, had been listening to the entire meeting through a microphone hidden beneath the table.

"What did you want me to do, Alan? Tell them the truth—that we're involved in supplying Mustafa Yasin with weapons and that one of those weapons made its way to the United States? Or did you want me to tell them absolutely nothing, even when it was obvious that they knew we had something?"

"*You* are involved in supplying Yasin," Holsten said forcefully. "Not we—*you*. This is your operation and it has been since the beginning. You made guarantees, Jonathan. And now . . ." His voice trailed off, leaving a silent threat hanging in the air.

Drake was careful not to let the anger and suspicion he felt read on his face. While it was true that this particular off-the-books operation had been his concept, it was just as true that Alan Holsten had enthusiastically approved it. But that didn't matter now. Holsten was getting scared, and a man in his position could be very dangerous when cornered.

"Our exposure on this is insignificant," Drake said calmly.

"Insignificant? Are you kidding me? I just listened to you stutter through an interrogation by the FBI's two top investigators. How are you planning on withholding the information they asked for now?"

"I'm not. I have to give it to them. I have no choice."

Mark Beamon's insistence that he send everything they had—even avenues that had come to nothing—was designed to keep the CIA from omitting information. If there was an obvious thread that hadn't been pulled or a line of inquiry that hadn't been pursued, it would be glaring.

"You're just going to hand over our files on al-Qaeda's operations?" Holsten said through clenched teeth.

"Like you said, Alan, I read the file on Beamon. It seems that it was accurate: He's not as dumb as he looks. But he's still five steps behind us. I anticipated his request and had a clean set of files prepared that will lead them exactly where we want them to go."

Holsten didn't sit, choosing to remain standing by the door. "Very clever, Jonathan. But you're still giving them something to sink their teeth into. And the truth is, we don't know where that's going to lead them."

"It won't lead them to us."

Despite Drake's effort, his boss continued to look skeptical.

"What will Mark Beamon's involvement be going forward?"

"Limited. He's having problems at home with his inspection, something that we can amplify and use to distract him. Also, he and Dave Iverson can't even be in the same room together. That's why Iverson wasn't here today."

"We don't want him involved in this, Jonathan. He's smart, experienced, and lucky. That's a very bad combination."

Drake shrugged. "This is Laura Vilechi's investigation. Beyond her using his contacts at the White House, Beamon has nothing to do with it. The only reason he was here today was a clumsy attempt to intimidate me."

"What do we know about her?"

"She's tailor-made for us. Certainly an exceptional investigator, but unlike Beamon, she's chained to procedure. That makes her predictable. Also, we can count on her to file regular detailed reports that we'll have access to. We'll always know exactly where she is and where she's going."

Holsten nodded slowly. Drake was relieved to see that his boss was calming down a bit. "You say the files you're sending won't lead to us. Will they lead to Volkov?"

"Not in any obvious way. The FBI isn't even aware he exists right now. It's strange, but J. Edgar Hoover's early refusal to admit that organized crime existed seems to have held on in their culture: They don't seem ready to admit to the existence of people like Christian Volkov. Eventually, though, they'll come to him. That's the way we set it up. All roads eventually lead to Volkov."

"But we counted on him being a corpse at that point."

"He will be."

"And Carlo Gasta?"

"I'm taking care of it. Don't worry, Alan. All the FBI has is the photograph and the audio that came with it. *We* know everything. Within a few weeks we'll have destroyed the weapon and the people involved. Then there will be nothing for the FBI to get a hold of—nothing at all left to link us to any of this."

Holsten turned and grabbed the doorknob but stopped before opening the door. He didn't look back when he spoke. "You've created a very dangerous situation here, Jonathan. There's no more room for errors."

Drake let out a long breath when he was alone again. "You've created . . ." he repeated quietly. You've created . . .

Drake had been the head of the highly secretive Organized Crime Division since its inception five years ago. It was his job to deal with the growing number of international criminal organizations that were beginning to influence world politics and economies. Despite the fact that some had annual incomes greater than the gross national products of many second-tier nations, the State Department did not solicit or recognize these organizations. And despite the fact that they controlled the markets in such things as narcotics and illegal arms, they were ignored by U.S. law enforcement because of the impenetrable jurisdictional mazes they operated in.

It had taken a great deal of time and effort, but Drake had finally been able to contact and form a relationship with Christian Volkov, the head of what he estimated was the most powerful criminal organization in the world.

Initially the relationship had been somewhat guarded and tentative. Volkov had been suspicious and Drake hadn't been sure what his mission was exactly. Slowly, though, the potential of his small unit had become obvious. Instead of just intelligence gathering and relationship building, why not go operational? If these enormously powerful and efficient criminal organizations could be used—manipulated—there was almost no limit to what could be accomplished. Unaffected by law, politics, or morality, they could be an incredibly deadly weapon if wielded correctly.

After the destruction of the World Trade Center and the demise of Osama bin Laden, it had become obvious to the intelligence community that by winning individual battles, America was dooming itself to losing the war on terrorism. Bin Laden had been replaced with the infinitely more dangerous Mustafa Yasin, and the victory in Afghanistan had left no terrorist target on which to unleash America's impressive military— only a loosely connected, highly trained group of fanatics scattered across the globe. It was this situation that had created an opportunity for Drake to use Christian Volkov to America's advantage.

Mustafa Yasin saw the world through an odd filter of Allah and economics, making him the obvious choice to carry out Osama bin Laden's economic fatwa against the United States. What had been less obvious, though, was Yasin's obsession with funding. He'd cut al-Qaeda's ranks by at least ninety percent so that he could focus what was left of his resources on the elite ten percent remaining. But those resources turned out to be hopelessly inadequate. Just as Yasin understood that money was the key to America's power, he knew that he would have to repair al-Qaeda's shattered financial network in order to effectively wage his jihad.

It had been a little over a year ago that Drake's division had begun to hear whisperings of al-Qaeda operatives methodically reclaiming and expanding their presence in the Middle Eastern heroin trade. Yasin had apparently decided to defer an immediate attack against America in favor

KYLE MILLS

of rebuilding his infrastructure. And if he succeeded, al-Qaeda would have billions of dollars to fund its religious war.

Would it be possible to play on Yasin's obsession with funding? Volkov had a great deal of credibility in the narcotics trade. If he were to supply al-Qaeda with the necessary intelligence and weaponry to step up their campaign to take over the heroin production and distribution lines in the Middle East, Yasin would have to concentrate his forces in one area, and would create a brief but inevitable disruption in narcotics exports from that region during the worst of the fighting.

Of course, Drake wasn't naïve enough to think that he could actually bring about a long-term reduction in the availability of narcotics in the U.S.; in fact, he was counting on not being able to. If a sufficient disruption in the flow of Middle Eastern heroin could be created, the market would react to fill the void. With the help of the CIA, Volkov's contacts in Thailand, Myanmar, and Laos—the Golden Triangle—could move in and replace the Middle East as America's heroin dealer of choice.

The potential of the plan had been almost limitless. The Asian crime lords would cut off al-Qaeda's primary source of funding, but more importantly they would cut off one of the Middle East's most important exports. It wouldn't take long for the region's smugglers, warlords, and governments to turn on the men Yasin had sent to the Middle East and, with the help of the CIA, destroy them.

Of course as limitless as the benefits of the plan were, the risks were just as limitless. And now the worst had happened.

Drake looked up at the map still glowing from the screen on the wall. It was all over now. He had been so close, but this operation died the moment al-Qaeda had managed to smuggle a rocket launcher across the border. All that mattered now was that none of this be traced back the CIA. All that was important was that he and Holsten were not implicated.

10

THE house itself was almost identical to the one in Cuba: large windows overlooking a rugged tropical landscape that finally gave way to the endlessness of the sea. Except for the slightly different shade of the water and the smooth gray of granite replacing red limestone, it was as if he hadn't moved at all.

"Is it on?" Pascal said in French as he strode into the office. Volkov just pointed to a television bolted to the wall.

"With everything that is happening, Charles Russell is making the announcements himself?" Pascal remarked. "Interesting."

Russell had just come on-screen and was shuffling papers across a broad lectern. The American news agencies' round-the-clock coverage of the rocket launcher issue had relegated this particular news conference to C-SPAN, and it probably wouldn't have rated even that had Russell not made a personal appearance. America's ridiculous narcotics certification program had become one of his pet programs and he obviously felt obligated to support it no matter how trivial it now seemed.

Russell cleared his throat and Volkov used a remote to increase the volume.

"Before I talk about this year's decision, I'd like to give everyone a bit of background on the process. Under U.S. law, the President certifies the antinarcotics efforts of the major drug-producing and drug-transporting countries. If a government is not certified, it is ineligible for most forms of U.S. assistance. The law also provides for waivers for those countries which, because of their strategic importance to the U.S., should be exempted from sanctions. While some governments resent this process and some members of Congress would like to see it repealed, I believe it is an extremely effective way to keep this important issue at the forefront and to create cooperation between the U.S. and countries with heavy narcotics-producing capability. In the past few months we've seen significant initiatives in the target countries and no less than five extraditions of major drug traffickers. The timing is obviously not a coincidence—these countries know that their action or inaction will play in the President's decision."

A hand must have gone up somewhere in the crowd, because Russell waved his own dismissively. "I'll take a few questions at the end—relating to this topic only—but first let me go through this year's list. . . ."

Volkov pressed the mute and turned to Pascal. "Haiti and Cambodia will remain decertified but get national interest waivers. Myanmar will remain decertified with no waiver." He paused dramatically. "Mexico will be decertified with a national interest waiver."

Pascal shook his head. "This is going to be the year you're finally wrong, Christian. Myanmar has done almost nothing to curb heroin trafficking, but it's more than Nigeria is doing. The Americans certainly wouldn't be swayed by Nigeria extraditing two insignificant drug traffickers last month. And they wouldn't dare decertify Mexico, no matter how corrupt the new government is."

Volkov put his finger to his lips and turned the television's sound back on.

"The President has certified twenty of the twenty-four countries," Russell continued. "Myanmar has been denied certification as it was last year. Haiti and Cambodia were not granted certification but have been granted national interest waivers." He paused just as Volkov had. "Also, this year, in light of the poor record of its new administration, Mexico has been denied certification but has been provided a national interest waiver." Russell held up a hand, again fending off questions. "Following President Fox's assassination—"

Volkov turned off the television and smiled. "My flawless record remains intact."

Every year since the certification program's inception, he and Pascal weighed in with their predictions. And every year he was right and Pascal was wrong.

"I'm told that Carlo Gasta's experience with Afghans isn't the only evidence of disruption in the heroin supply line this week," Pascal said, changing the subject. He obviously didn't want to dwell on the fact that he'd lost their little competition again.

"Really?" Volkov said, deciding to wait until dinner to gloat.

"We have reports of five separate instances that promised heroin shipments could not be delivered."

"And the Mexicans?"

"They're angry. Obviously they have their own production capability, but it certainly isn't sufficient to meet demand."

Volkov nodded silently. Most of the heroin that flowed into America every day originated in the Middle East, was transported into Mexico, and then was smuggled across the border by a confusing confederation of Mexican organized crime, police, and military. Problems, until now unheard of, could create dire consequences for the extensive but delicate Mexican distribution system.

"We aren't seeing any open fighting between the Mexican smuggling cartels," Pascal said. "But if the unreliability in supply should continue—and particularly if it should worsen—I don't think fighting is far away."

One of their informants had told them of the Afghans' failure to deliver product to Carlo Gasta in L.A., and Volkov found that failure telling. It had been a direct transaction, quietly circumventing the Mexicans. These deals would be prioritized, as the quick cash they provided was critical to al-Qaeda's operations.

"Exactly what you predicted is beginning to happen, Christian. Mustafa Yasin's ambitions are becoming known throughout the region. Refiners and transporters are expecting the attacks, making al-Qaeda's victories more costly. More importantly, though, they are resigning themselves to their eventual defeat. They are strategizing to inflict as many casualties on al-Qaeda as possible and then completely destroying their own infrastructure and warehoused product so that Yasin comes away with very little."

Volkov took a sip of water from a heavy crystal glass on his desk and listened to the rain begin. In a few minutes they would have to raise their voices to be heard over what would undoubtedly be a magnificent storm. "Are the Mexicans aware that Yasin is going around them and sending people to the U.S. directly?"

"No. Those types of transactions are fairly limited at this point—just enough to keep his cash flow positive while he tries to solidify his position. Should I make the Mexicans aware of it?"

Volkov shook his head. "Not yet."

"When?"

"I don't know," he answered honestly. "This has always been a difficult situation, but now, with the CIA's involvement uncertain, it's almost impossible."

"At some point, though, al-Qaeda will complete its task and consolidate its power. Then they'll have the opportunity to create a relationship with the Mexicans. We have to act before that happens."

Volkov leaned forward, resting his elbows on his desk and trying unsuccessfully to put order to the events of the past week. What he did know, though, was that his own best interests and those of the CIA might well have irretrievably diverged. His survival depended on him guessing when al-Qaeda was at its weakest and being ready to move at that moment.

"Where does our relationship with Charles Russell stand?"

"It's excellent. We've provided the Republican party with a great deal of money over the years and we were a strong supporter of his during his senatorial campaigns. Obviously this was all done through our legitimate U.S. corporations. He has no idea you even exist."

Volkov leaned back in his chair again. As he'd predicted, the wind was beginning to vibrate the windows behind him and the rain was creating a dull roar as it pounded the roof. "I think it may be time he learns of my existence."

Pascal didn't bother to hide his surprise. "I'm not sure I understand."

"I believe it's time that Mr. Russell and I meet."

"Christian, are you sure that's wise? I could have a CEO from one of your stateside companies meet with him on your behalf. Or perhaps we could set up a teleconference. . . ."

Volkov shook his head. "No. What I have to say to him will have to be done personally."

Pascal was silent for a moment, knowing better than to ask for details not offered.

"Of course, Christian. When?"

"As soon as possible."

"I'll set it up before I leave for Laos."

"You've been able get the general to agree to a meeting?"

"I spoke with him directly. I leave tomorrow."

Volkov spun his chair to face the windows. This situation was becoming unbearably dangerous. It seemed likely that both he and Pascal would be gone at the same time, with neither of their returns guaranteed. But what choice was there? Time was quickly running out.

"You understand as well as I do that our power base in Laos is almost nonexistent now," Volkov said. "If things look too unstable, turn around and come back immediately. I'd be very disappointed if you let yourself get killed."

The storm was already subsiding and he could hear Pascal start for the door. "I'll be fine, Christian."

The door closed and Volkov was alone again. He closed his eyes and laid his head against the back of the chair. He was only forty-three years old and it was already starting to become hazy how he had come to be to be where he was. The same thing had always driven him, he supposed: necessity. Not a particularly noble or powerful motivator, really, just a by-product of the hopeless poverty he'd been born to.

His first memories were of living on the streets in Bucharest, being cared for by a ragged and pale little girl that he now guessed had been no older than thirteen. She had told him that she was his sister but he had no reason to believe they had any real biological connection. But she had protected him and fed him and taught him to steal, so the title seemed legitimate.

By the time he was old enough to contribute, to repay her for what she had for some reason done, she'd fallen ill. Possibly an early victim of AIDS contracted from years on the streets as a prostitute. He would never know for sure. All he knew was that for all the power he now had, he'd been unable then to do anything to help her or to even ease her suffering. She'd finally died lying under a torn plastic bag he'd found to try to keep the rain from soaking her.

Volkov stood and walked out onto the stone terrace, splashing through the water pooled there and looking down on the dark ocean.

He'd taken the knowledge she'd given him and added to it, eking out an existence the only way available to him—as a small-time criminal. But even as he achieved a few minor victories and managed to rise from the constant fear of starvation to mere poverty, he began to understand the trap he'd walked into. Every deal seemed to lead to another larger and more dangerous one. His childhood hadn't really allowed for anything so grandiose as ambition, and he'd had no real thirst for power or excessive wealth, but he knew that if he didn't involve himself in that next transaction, someone else would. And if they could use the money and goods they obtained to buy allies, or guns, or knives, then they would become a threat to him. In the dangerous and highly competitive business of crime under Ceauşescu's reign in Romania, one moved forward or died.

And now, after years of unavoidable transactions, he found himself at the head of an empire. He honestly didn't know how large, though Pascal had once told him he was one of the world's wealthiest men. A meaningless distinction as far as he could tell. He had no hope of ever retiring and enjoying the things his wealth could buy. His future was the same as his past—one necessary transaction after another until the day he finally made a fatal mistake.

11

THE FBI's Phoenix office was almost completely silent as Beamon weaved through the empty cubicles toward his office. At the threshold he reached for the light switch, but then thought better of it and just made his way to his desk in the semidarkness.

The FBI's jet had dropped him off at ten-thirty and he'd decided to come here to the office instead of going home. The truth was that his meeting with the CIA earlier that day had actually cheered him up a little. While the case still wasn't his, he'd actually accomplished something positive for a friend. Instead of wasting his rare good mood, he figured he'd expend some of it on Bill Laskin's inspection report. By his estimate, the warm fuzzies he'd garnered from helping Laura stick it to the CIA, combined with the six-pack he'd purchased on the way in, would be just enough to get him through the final pages without hanging himself.

After a half and hour of what felt like hard work, he'd managed to get through two beers but only three pages. He tried harder, blocking out everything but the report on his lap, to no effect. He just couldn't seem to absorb any of it tonight. Grabbing the television remote from a drawer, he pressed the POWER button and watched an old video of Osama bin Laden standing at the mouth of a cave, speaking into a microphone. The translator's voice was heavily accented.

"—of Allah's greatness. America will pay for—"

He hit the MUTE button. If there was one thing he truly hated, it was revolutionary jargon. The world had finally gotten rid of the communists and their "imperialism" this, "capitalist dog" that, and now you had to listen to these idiots. Hardly an improvement.

The video was strangely riveting and he watched until the screen faded into current scenes from America's cities. Restaurants and stores closed, offices empty, silent street interviews with haggard-looking people who for some reason had been forced from their homes and into the dangerous and malignant world.

Beamon looked down at the report in his lap for another few seconds but then just tossed it on his desk. The fact that he had to spend his time worrying about whether his debits equaled his credits while some nut was running around the country with a rocket launcher was really cruel.

Not your case.

He was still repeating that to himself when he pulled a sheet of paper from the breast pocket of his shirt. On it was a rough drawing he'd made of the map Jonathan Drake had projected on the wall in Langley. Normally, Beamon wasn't really a detail person, but when it came to interesting crimes, his mind could grab and hold things with almost photographic detail.

He ran his hand across the paper, smoothing out Iran, Pakistan, Afghanistan, and all the other -stans, focusing on the little dots representing recent fighting. They meant something—he was sure of that. But what?

He reached for another beer but immediately dropped it and sent it rolling across the floor.

"Jesus Christ!" he said, grabbing his chest. "You scared the shit out of me. What are you doing here this late?"

Neither of his two ASACs replied; they just stood there in the doorway to his office like extras from *Night of the Living Dead*. "What?" Beamon said, spinning his chair to face them.

His number two, Rick Sterling, finally took a step forward. "We've heard some things."

"What things?" Beamon motioned to the chairs in front of his desk. "You guys want to sit?"

His other ASAC answered by moving through the door and leaning silently against the wall.

"We . . . we hear that the inspection report doesn't look good," Sterling said. He'd apparently drawn the short straw and was stuck with the job of spokesman. "We hear that you and Bill Laskin are going to hang us out to dry."

Beamon nodded silently. He supposed he should have expected something like this. Inspection results were perhaps the worst-kept secret in the FBI.

"Is that true, Mark?"

"Some of it," he said, grabbing another beer from the bag on the floor. Warm foam spewed from the top as he opened it. "The report definitely could be better."

"And?" Sterling said.

Beamon flipped the report open to a section criticizing the support he was getting from his management team and turned it around on his cluttered desk so that Sterling could read it beneath the desk lamp that was the only light on in the office. Nearly the entire page was crossed out, and in the margin Beamon had written why the noted deficiency was his responsibility. After reading it, some of the grave certainty was gone from Sterling's face.

"I'm not sure I understand."

Beamon slammed the report shut. "Look . . . Bill Laskin's a good kid who's heard too many bullshit stories about me. He's got nothing against either of you but he's having a hard time criticizing me."

Sterling stared down at the closed report, looking a little unsure. "Where does that leave us?"

"I've got my faults, Rick, but making excuses isn't one of them. You'll get a copy of the report, with my comments, when I'm finished. Then we'll get together and talk about it before it goes back to the inspection staff. Fair?"

Sterling looked back at his colleague. He hadn't seen Beamon's notes but seemed content to follow Sterling's lead.

"Yeah, that's fair, Mark."

Beamon watched them go and, when they were completely out of sight, let out the breath he was holding.

"Jesus," he muttered, leaning forward and beginning to bang his forehead gently on the hand-drawn map he'd left on his desk.

There was no way out of this. He was completely screwed.

Despite the weight of that realization, he couldn't concentrate on it for more than a minute before he sat up and started examining the map again. The dots on it had kind of a hypnotic quality, filling his mind and driving out thoughts of his career's imminent demise.

Mark Beamon rang the doorbell for a second time, resisting the urge to bang on the door in deference to the nearby houses that made up the quiet suburban neighborhood. A light came on somewhere inside and Beamon dried the sweat from his forehead with a handkerchief, then rang the bell one more time for good measure. It was after three in the morning but still felt like it was over a hundred degrees.

"Who is it?" came a muffled voice on the other side of the door.

"It's Mark."

"Mark who?"

"Mark Beamon, you asshole. Let me in, I'm melting out here."

Jaime Mastretta opened the door cautiously, wearing only a pair of sweatpants. A 9mm hung from his right hand.

"Mark? What's going on?"

"I have a question."

"It couldn't wait until tomorrow? Do you know what time it is?"

Mastretta was the head of the local DEA office and an encyclopedia of normally useless information about the narcotics trade.

"It's just a quick one."

Mastretta didn't look excited about it but finally stepped aside. "Okay. Come on in. But take your shoes off and be quiet—Lisa's asleep."

Beamon followed him through the house and into the kitchen, where Mastretta carefully closed the door.

"I hope this is important, Mark. I've got to go to work in a few hours and I'm never going to get back to sleep."

Beamon pulled out the now sweat-dampened map and laid it on the table. "What do you know about Afghanistan?"

"They supply almost three quarters of the world's heroin. I know everything about Afghanistan."

"Okay," Beamon said. "This is a map I drew of it."

Mastretta squinted at the poor rendering. "It is?"

"Use your imagination, asshole."

"What are the dots?"

"Those represent small encampments that have been recently attacked."

"By whom?"

"This is just between us?"

Mastretta nodded.

"Maybe by al-Qaeda."

That got the DEA man's attention. "Does this have something to do with the rocket launcher?"

Beamon shrugged and tapped the map again. "Like I said, the places that have been attacked are more encampments than towns or cities—small, you know?"

Mastretta fished a pair of reading glasses from a drawer and peered down at the map, nodding thoughtfully.

"Any ideas, Jaime?"

"I'm guessing you have one already."

"I have a suspicion. But you're the expert."

"The dots on your map correspond to areas we know are active in the heroin trade—agricultural and distribution centers in the Helmand province of Afghanistan, refining and transportation points along the borders, especially the borders with Pakistan and Turkmenistan."

"You feel pretty confident about that?" Beamon said.

"It's interesting that you bring this up . . ."

"Why?"

"We've been seeing some weird things lately. . . . It seems like the heroin supply isn't as reliable as it's been in the past—nothing major, just a few missed shipments and things like that. If there's fighting going on, it may explain that."

A slow smile spread across Beamon's face. "I thought the new Afghan regime was putting an end to poppy cultivation."

Mastretta laughed. "That's the party line. The truth, though, is that they give seminars on how to grow them more efficiently. They took that page out of the Taliban's book."

"And the government officials take a cut."

Mastretta nodded. "We're actually not talking about a whole lot of money, though. The real money is made by the people who refine it, cut it, transport it, and sell it. Back when the Taliban was more or less taxing heroin imports, they were seeing only about twenty mil a year out of what's really a multibillion-dollar industry."

"So this stuff mostly comes to the States?"

"Most of it, though they're major suppliers to Europe too. Like I said, probably about seventy-five percent of the world's heroin is coming out of Afghanistan right now."

"What about Burma—Myanmar? I thought they were major suppliers."

"They're actually the second largest producer now, the leader of the Golden Triangle, which also includes Laos and Thailand. They've been getting squeezed by the Afghans over the past few years, though, and they're pretty pissed about it. . . . I figured you for an expert on drugs, Mark."

Beamon shrugged. He had a talent for quickly forgetting things that didn't matter—it cut down on mental clutter. As far as he was concerned, the drug war had been lost a long time ago.

"How does all this heroin get here?"

"Lots of ways. For the most part, though, it's smuggled in through Mexico."

Beamon folded up his map and shoved it in his pocket, lost in thought for a moment.

"What's going on behind those beady little eyes, Mark?"

"I'm not sure," he said honestly.

"Oh, come on. You're thinking that al-Qaeda's trying to get into refining, transport, and sales—the money end of the heroin business. And if that's the case, you figure they used their new money and contacts to get ahold of that rocket launcher and smuggle it into the States."

"What if I do think that? Would it be a reasonable theory?"

Mastretta took his reading glasses off and flopped into a kitchen chair. "It might be. We've been doing a pretty good job cutting al-Qaeda off from its money. First we run most of them out of Afghanistan, then we start putting heavy pressure on financial institutions and Arab charities—not to mention coercing those asshole Saudis and Egyptians to stop stabbing us in the back. . . ."

"Thanks, Jaime," Beamon said, heading for the kitchen door. He stopped with his hand on the knob. "And I was never here, right?"

"Well, if you need any more help with what we didn't talk about just now, give me a call."

"Laura!"

"Mark?"

Beamon leaned forward over the wheel, surveying the desolate street before running the stop sign in front of him. "Didn't wake you up, did I?"

"It's four in the morning."

He laughed. "I didn't. I didn't wake you up."

He heard her sigh over the cell phone. "I don't sleep much these days."

"Did that ass Drake send you the stuff we asked for?"

"Yeah, we got it—by the truckload. We're just starting to dig through it. You called at this hour to ask me that?"

"Not just that."

"What, then?"

"I've got something you should follow up on."

"I'm listening."

"I had a thought that the fighting Drake told us about is over heroin production and transportation facilities—that it relates to Mustafa Yasin expanding his presence in the narcotics business. Think about it. What could be more perfect for him? He sells heroin to the U.S., addicting our kids, and then uses the money to buy sophisticated self-contained weapons. And as a bonus, he gets access to the smuggling lines into the U.S. to get those weapons here. From a radical Muslim perspective, it's got kind of an elegant symmetry to it, don't you think?"

"Where are you getting this?"

"Just a thought I had. I ran it by Jaime Mastretta and he seems to feel pretty good about it. You should talk to him."

There was silence over the phone for a moment. "What about the CIA? Wouldn't they have figured this out?"

"I guess it's possible that they missed the connection, but I doubt it. I mean, they were the catalysts for the Afghan drug trade. The caravans that the CIA used to get weapons to the mujahideen were coming back empty. It didn't take long for somebody to start loading them up with opium."

"Why wouldn't they tell us?" she asked, but her tone suggested she already knew the answer.

"My guess would be that they've got interests in the heroin trade over there and are using the money to finance some of their off-the-books stuff. Wouldn't be the first time: Remember Nicaragua and Laos?"

"It's an interesting theory, Mark, but it seems pretty academic to me right now. The question I need to answer is: Where is the launcher?" Her tone turned thoughtful. "How can I use this to find the launcher . . . ?"

"Think drugs, Laura. Middle Eastern heroin is smuggled through Mexico by a fairly organized and efficient group of people. If the launcher came in that way, it could be that somebody will remember something. Maybe somebody noticed a few Middle Eastern heroin dealers acting suspiciously—more suspiciously than Middle Eastern heroin dealers usually act, I mean. I saw that the Mexicans were just decertified. If it comes out that they were somehow involved in this, life's going to get even worse for them. Maybe you can use that to get a little cooperation."

"Maybe. . . . Let me think about this, Mark."

"Does it sound like something worth following up on?"

"As much as I hate to admit it, it's probably the best lead I've got right now."

12

"CARLO? What's up?" Chet said groggily. He stepped back from the door and let Gasta walk by him. "What time is it?"

"Get dressed."

"Why? What's going on?"

"Just get your clothes on. You've got three minutes."

Chet blinked hard, trying to clear away the remnants of the deep sleep he'd been awakened from. "Sure, Carlo. Sure."

He hurried into his bedroom and pulled on a pair of slacks, trying to run through the last few days in his head. Had he said or done anything that could have pissed anyone off? Had he confused any of the constant stream of lies that kept him alive? Getting woken up in the middle of the night and ordered to get dressed in three minutes was not a good sign in his business. The Mob didn't give warnings.

"Get a fucking move on!"

Chet looked away from the window he'd been thinking about crawling out of and saw Gasta standing in the bedroom door. His arms were crossed in front of his chest and his stare was clear and intense.

He seemed like an almost completely different person. First, he was completely sober. Second, he looked vaguely nervous. Gasta didn't get vaguely nervous; he had only two demeanors: overconfident arrogance and scared shitless arrogance. And finally, he was wearing a suit. Not the normal retro-gangster fashion he favored, but a normal, conservative suit. Like one a . . . Chet tried to stifle the thought but couldn't: like one an undertaker would wear.

"What's going on, Carlo?" Chet said again as he slid a tie through his collar and hoped his hands weren't shaking too much to tie the knot. "Where are we going?"

Gasta just stood there.

When he was finished dressing, Chet reached for the .45 on his nightstand.

"You won't need that," Gasta said. "Let's go."

Chet had expected to be driving, with Gasta watching him and giving him directions to a secluded corner of the empty desert surrounding L.A. Instead he was in the passenger seat, looking out the window as Gasta maneuvered his Corvette through the nearly silent streets of Century City. Chet still had no idea where they were going or why, but if Gasta was going to put a bullet in his head, it seemed like he would find a more practical place to do it. Or would he? Chet kept his hand close to the door handle, just in case it became necessary to bail out and make a run for it.

"What's this?" Chet said as Gasta turned into the parking garage of glass high-rise. Again, no answer.

They stopped in a dark corner of the nearly empty garage and Gasta got out. Chet didn't immediately follow, quietly swearing to himself in the deep leather seat. The building above would be empty this time of night. Maybe Gasta just didn't feel like driving all the way out in the desert. He'd do it here and have Tony pick up the body for disposal.

Chet jerked away from the sudden banging on the window. A moment later Gasta yanked the door open. "Jesus Christ, Chet, what's your problem? Get the fuck out of the car."

Chet did so slowly, looking around him for an escape route. He was unarmed but a hell of a lot faster than Gasta. There was a chance, albeit a small one, that he could make it to an exit before Gasta—well known for his poor marksmanship—could put a bullet in him. Or he could just use his college wrestling skills to try to get the gun away from the older man. That was probably a better bet.

He moved to within a foot of Gasta, crowding him enough to make it difficult for the man to pull his gun. "I've worked my ass off for you, Carlo. I've been nothing but loyal. You taking me for a ride, here?"

Gasta's brow furrowed for a moment and then a smile began to spread across his face. "You know what you're gonna die of, Chet? A fucking ulcer—that's what you're going to die of. Now, quit being such a dumb-ass and let's go. We're gonna be late."

When he started walking again, Chet didn't follow. The speech had seemed sincere, but was it?

Gasta stepped into an open elevator and turned around. "Jesus Christ! Would you get in the goddamn elevator?"

Chet finally convinced his legs to move and he walked slowly forward, taking a deep breath before stepping through the elevator doors. Gasta stuck a key into a slot above the buttons and they started up.

When the doors opened, it was onto a generic but well-maintained hall. They walked past a number of large doors with business names stenciled on them, finally stopping at one belonging to the First Federal Development Bank. Gasta pulled another key out and they went inside.

The outer office was dark and empty, but there was a dim light coming from an open door at the back of it. Gasta straightened his jacket and squared his shoulders, then started forward.

Chet followed his boss into the inner office, trying to take everything in so that he could remember important details later. Overall there wasn't much to look at: a desk, a few chairs, and some pictures that you could buy already framed at Kmart. The only illumination was provided by a single desk lamp that had been turned slightly toward the door, creating an uncomfortable glare.

Gasta sat in a chair in front of the desk and Chet took a position behind him. It would look properly subservient, but he actually figured it as the best spot to see around the glare and get a look at the man sitting behind the desk. He seemed tall, with dark hair kind of slicked back. His shoulders were extremely broad and heavy-looking through the deliberately formless jacket he was wearing. Probably muscle and not fat, but it was impossible to be certain. His face had no features prominent enough to be obvious in the bad light and was partially obscured by large tinted glasses.

"Who the hell is this, Carlo?" The man's voice was cold, but the anger beneath it was obvious.

"This is Chet. I told you about him."

"Why is he here?" This time the words were spoken through clenched teeth.

"He's my new right hand—handling a lot of the business end for me now. All he does is worry, but he's smart as shit. I thought you two should meet."

Chet ignored the compliment, still trying to identify the man behind the desk. He wasn't a player in any of the New York families—of that, Chet was certain. A drug lord he wasn't aware of, maybe? A greedy investment banker that Carlo had met through one of his celebrity playmates?

"You thought we should meet," the man growled.

"Relax, John. He's okay. I'd trust him with my life, all right?"

Chet was only half listening at this point, focusing on concocting a plan to get close to the man sitting in front of him. Was this the mysterious source of Carlo Gasta's money?

"You trust your life to anyone you want, Carlo, but I make my own decisions about who I deal with. Do you understand me?"

Gasta nodded and stared at his feet.

"Now, get him the hell out of here."

Gasta twisted around and waved toward the door. "You heard him. Get the fuck out."

"Goddamnit!" Gasta shouted. It was the first sound he'd uttered since climbing into the Corvette and pulling out of the parking garage.

Chet's ears actually rang a bit from the sudden volume of it as he watched Gasta pound on the dashboard. Obviously the meeting hadn't gone as planned.

"You okay, Carlo?"

"Shut up! Just shut the fuck up!"

Chet leaned his head against the window and looked out at a police barricade set up in front of a sprawling hospital. He'd heard the new threat by the asshole with the rocket launcher on the radio earlier that day. It seemed he was considering blowing up a hospital now. According to the news, seriously ill people all over the country were fleeing their sickbeds as if they were on fire. Between them and the people who got sick or hurt and just stayed home, predictions were for a significant death toll.

"Fucking towelheads! Trying to make me look like an asshole in front of—" He cut himself off and jabbed Chet hard in the chest. "No one in the organization hears about this until I tell them. You got that?"

"Hears about what?"

"Fuck . . ." Gasta muttered.

"Hears about what, Carlo?"

"John said that those sand niggers have the product; they're just stalling, trying to see if they can find someone who'll pay more. He says they're showing it around—that they'll do this one deal with me, but afterward they're going to cut me out." He banged on the wheel again, making the car careen across the centerline of the empty street.

"Sons of bitches come in here like they own this country. No loyalty, just bullshit."

"What are you going to do?" Chet said.

"I'm going to teach them some respect."

"What does that mean?"

"These people understand war, Chet. They understand a handshake deal. But they think Americans are soft. And they think Catholics are shit under their heel. They would never treat one of their own this way."

Chet turned and watched the city lights play across Gasta's face. Those weren't his words. Gasta couldn't find the Middle East on a map if you put a gun to his head. He'd heard that little speech from whoever this John was.

The guy was good—Chet had to admit that. Telling Gasta that the Afghans were looking for bigger and better things played well to the feelings of inferiority beat into him by the years of being compared to his father. And the religion thing—that was a nice touch. Gasta liked to wear his meaningless Catholicism on his sleeve, just like the old-time gangsters he worshiped.

"That doesn't answer my question, Carlo."

"You want me to answer your question? Okay, I'll answer your question. I'm going to put a bullet in the head of every last one of those fucks and piss in the hole. Then I'm going to take their heroin to pay for my trouble. I'm going to teach them that in this country we live up to our agreements. They either deal with me or they deal with nobody."

That's exactly what Chet had been afraid of.

"Hold on, now, Carlo. Let's think about this for a second. What did you just tell me? These people understand war. They don't care if they die, man. They go into the military when they're six years old, for Christ's sake."

"Fucking kicked their asses in Afghanistan."

"No we didn't. We dropped bombs from the stratosphere and let the Northern Alliance kick their asses. Jesus, Carlo. What're we gonna do? Ask the Air Force to cover us at our next meet? Drive there in a tank? We're going in there with the same guns they got. We don't have an edge."

"What, are you scared of these assholes? Maybe I need to find somebody with balls to work for me."

"You saw that Mohammed guy, Carlo. He's badass and he isn't alone. At that last exchange I'll bet they had ten guys out there with rifles aimed at our heads. That's the way they work, man. It's like going up against a bunch of psycho Marines."

Chet could see from Gasta's face that at least some of what he was saying was getting through.

"Who is that guy, Carlo? You trust him?"

Gasta's hand shot out and he grabbed Chet hard by the back of this neck. "You just forget all about him. You understand me?"

"Sure, Carlo. Sure. I understand."

Gasta released him and went back to his erratic driving. "We can't walk away from this, Chet. There's too much money on the table."

And that was the problem, Chet knew. The financial rewards that came with the heroin trade were sky-high—enough to make Carlo the big man he'd always wanted to be. And while it was true that Carlo Gasta's fear was stronger than his anger, his vanity lorded over all.

"What are we talking about here, Carlo? I mean, how would we do it?"

"They said they'd have the stuff this week—after they've fucking shopped it around to everybody on the West Coast," he said, starting to sound a little hesitant. "So we go to the buy and blow their god-damn heads off—send a message about what I do to people who try to fuck me."

"Jesus, Carlo, they got, like, those machine guns that sit on tripods and shit. They're desert fighters, man—they're born to it. If we just go in there shooting, we better hope we get killed quick, 'cause if not, they're going to take us back to wherever they came from and spend a few days cutting us apart."

Gasta just stared through the windshield.

"I mean, do you know where we could find them, maybe? Then we could hit them when they're not expecting it."

Gasta shook his head and Chet blew out a long breath. The silence that descended on the car lasted almost fifteen minutes.

"What about your old boss?" Gasta said finally.

During the long lull in the conversation Chet had actually said a prayer that this wouldn't come up, breaking his steadfast policy of never bothering God with business problems.

"I don't think he'd be interested," Chet replied tentatively.

"What, he doesn't want to do business with me? I'm not good enough for him?"

"That's not what I meant, Carlo. I just don't think this is his kind of thing."

"You don't think," Gasta repeated angrily. "I don't want you to think. I want you to call him and ask."

Chet knew he was pretty much backed into a corner now. Playing up his relationship with the notorious criminal known only as "Nicolai" had been how he'd managed to finagle his way into Gasta's organization. It could become a major problem if he didn't now produce. In fact, it could get dangerous.

"Honestly, Carlo. That was a long time ago. I'm not even sure how to contact him anymore."

"You're a smart kid. You'll figure it out."

Chet knew the tone, the low voice, the short answers. Gasta wasn't going to let this go. It had taken a long time and a hell of a lot of work to gain Gasta's confidence—he didn't need to blow it now. Besides, if he could help make things work out, maybe he'd impress this John guy and get some recognition from him—get a chance to move up.

"I'll see what I can do. You know he takes a hundred grand just for a meeting, right?"

Gasta nodded. "Not a problem. The cash out on this deal will be fucking huge."

13

PASCAL braced himself on the seat in front of him as the heavily armored vehicle skidded to a stop in what seemed more like an extraordinarily long mud puddle than a road. The driver rolled down his window and began speaking Lao to the leader of a group of men who had suddenly appeared from the dense jungle and surrounded them. Pascal ignored the damp breeze blowing through the open window and the scent of sweat and explosives that it carried, instead staring through the front windshield at a man aiming a handheld rocket directly at him.

The undecipherable conversation became heated, drowning out the erratic bursts of gunfire coming from somewhere nearby. The driver seemed strangely adamant for a man who had a missile aimed at him, but his steadfast resolve prevailed and the men surrounding them reluctantly melted back into the jungle. The vehicle's engine roared again and they jerked forward, continuing toward the city of Luang Prabang.

General Yung could scarcely have picked a worse time to rise up and overthrow the Laotian government. Christian had enjoyed a long and very profitable relationship with the former president, who had been intimately involved in the cultivation and export of heroin from his country. Now, though, nothing was certain. Poppy fields and refining facilities had almost certainly been destroyed in the coup, supply lines would be made unsafe by inevitable rebel activity, and there was no guarantee that General Yung would honor his predecessor's agreements where his country's number-one export was concerned.

None of this could be tolerated. When the time came for Volkov to turn against al-Qaeda, the transition from Middle Eastern to Asian suppliers would have to be seamless to the point of being almost transparent. Yasin, while hampered by his own unwavering religious fanaticism, was in no way a stupid man. There could be no warning that might afford him time to protect his position and no cracks remaining for him to slither through after the transition was complete.

The palace at the center of the city seemed to be untouched by the violence that had gripped Laos over the past weeks. Pascal stepped from the vehicle into a hot, drenching rain and walked toward a man wearing an impeccable military uniform. He was flanked by myriad well-armed guards and civilian assistants, one of whom seemed to have the sole purpose of holding the general's umbrella.

"General Yung, I am Pascal."

The Asian man smiled pleasantly and offered his hand. "I am so sorry that Mr. Volkov could not come personally," he said in accented but perfectly acceptable French.

"You understand he's extremely busy right now," Pascal replied.

Something flickered in Yung's eyes but Pascal didn't know what it was. He had always wished he had Christian's insight into human nature, but knew he never would. His talents revolved around numbers, precision, and efficiency—a different but equally valuable gift.

"Please follow me," Yung said, turning in a military fashion and striding through the broad door centered in the building. "I'm looking forward to our discussion."

His office was a bit haphazard—a cheap desk in the middle of what looked like an ancient library—an effective combination of austerity, tradition, and learning.

"Can I offer you a drink, my friend? I think you'll enjoy it. I make it myself."

"No, thank you, General."

He didn't want to be here any longer than was absolutely necessary. Once again this brutal, half-educated little man's timing had been the height of inconvenience. At this moment Christian was on a plane for America to attend his mysterious meeting with Charles Russell, leaving the entire organization in the hands of loyal but inexperienced children.

"Can I offer you something else?"

"Nothing."

"Then please have a seat," he said, pointing to a folding chair. "What is it you came all this way to discuss?"

Pascal sat stiffly. "Our future."

"Indeed?"

"We're concerned about the stability of Laos following your takeover. There still seems to be a significant amount of fighting, and we have reports of groups loyal to the former president organizing in the jungle."

The general nodded gravely.

"Our concern is that the flow of heroin from your country will become unreliable."

The general's eyes widened at the word *heroin*, as though he were unaware that it was the basis of Laos's economy.

"My concern," Yung began, "was to throw off the yolk of communism, to bring my country into the twenty-first century. I will provide freedom to my people and create opportunities for education and economic development. . . ."

Pascal frowned. He simply didn't have time to indulge the general's delusions of grandeur.

"And does that plan for economic development include the continuation of your country's relationship with Mr. Volkov?"

Yung's smile was polite but a bit strained. "Of course, I have nothing but respect and admiration for your employer. And I would be honored to discuss a relationship that would be mutually beneficial."

"Then may I suggest—"

"But you have concerns," the Yung interrupted. "And I want you to feel . . . confident." He motioned toward the open doorway to the office, and Pascal craned his neck to watch one of Yung's guards approach.

"You understand that I am quite busy right now," the general continued. "And I am afraid that I have some things to attend to. Please accompany my assistant. He will take you on a tour of the city and the outlying areas. I believe that you will be satisfied with the stability of my country. And tonight I would be honored if you would be my guest for dinner, where we can talk more."

Yung pulled a stack of papers from his desk and began shuffling through them before Pascal could protest. He had been dismissed by this arrogant little man whose entire country wasn't worth half the assets Volkov controlled. And now he would be forced waste his time dining in this godforsaken country instead of being on a plane back to the Seychelles.

He nodded respectfully toward Yung, knowing there was nothing else he could do.

Pascal sat impatiently in the passenger seat of the armored car as his driver took him to every island of calm in the area, pointing out the uncommon serenity of their country in broken French, ignoring the sound of gunfire and distant columns of smoke with almost comic diligence.

"Yes, that's fine. Very informative," Pascal said for the tenth time. "Could you please take me back now?"

Yung's assistant ignored him, swinging the vehicle onto a narrow mud road leading into the jungle. Pascal twisted around, looked past the smiling men crammed into the back of the truck, and watched all evidence of civilization disappear. Soon, even the seemingly omnipresent sound of killing was swallowed by the thick, wet plant life that had closed in behind them.

"You've done and excellent job showing me the area," Pascal said, deciding to take another approach. "And I intend to tell General Yung how helpful you were. But I believe he is expecting me back and will be concerned if I don't return soon."

The man didn't respond, concentrating on maintaining the truck's momentum in the thick mud. Pascal clenched his teeth and tapped his foot impatiently on the rusted floorboard of the vehicle. He let thirty excruciating minutes pass before he spoke again.

"This is ridiculous! We are in the middle of nowhere. Take me back to the city immediately!"

For a moment he thought his outburst had worked. The driver stepped on the brake and the truck came to an abrupt halt. But then he turned off the engine.

Pascal leaned forward, peering through the humidity-fogged windshield. The clouds had parted and he had to squint against the glare of the sun to see the grass hut standing on three-foot stilts in the middle of a small clearing.

"Come," the driver said, throwing his door open and stepping out.

Pascal heard splashes as the men in back jumped to the ground.

"Why? Where are we?"

"Come." His voice was more insistent this time.

Pascal didn't move, trying to grasp what was happening. Why would he have been brought to such a place?

The passenger door was suddenly yanked open and he was dragged out into the mud. Confused, he didn't bother to struggle as he was pulled roughly to his feet and marched toward the hut. When he twisted around to look behind him, he saw that no less than five rifles were trained on him.

"I want to speak to General Yung! I want to speak to him now!"

He was shoved up the makeshift stairs and into the even more oppressive heat of the hut, where he was forced into a chair constructed of bamboo. A few moments later his hands and feet were secured tightly to it.

The men who had bound him retreated outside, and Pascal looked around, his eyes beginning to adjust to the gloom. A recognizable shape began to form in a pile of debris next to the wall, and he leaned forward to see better. It was a man, lying as though discarded, with a profound stillness that could only signify death. His face was swollen and broken, making it unrecognizable, but his clothes revealed his identity: It was the broken body of his pilot.

The sound of an engine suddenly flared in the silence, followed by the splashing of tires as the truck that had brought him started back down the road.

"Wait!" Pascal shouted, starting to feel his own heart beating powerfully in his chest. "Wait! Is anyone there? Hello?"

He pulled hard on the leather straps securing him to the chair, but it was hopeless. The bonds were tight enough that his hands and feet were already starting to go numb.

"Hello?" he shouted again.

No answer. Just the buzz of insects and call of birds. He felt another surge of adrenaline at the sound of a snapping stick outside the hut, and he swung his head desperately toward the open door. What had made it? An animal? Was it watching, trying to decide whether he was safe prey?

"Go away," he shouted, trying again to free his hands but succeeding only in opening a cut in the top of his wrist.

"Is there anyone out there? Hello?"

14

CHET watched the crowd part respectfully, letting Mikey through the bar untouched. The stocky fifty-year-old made his way straight to their table, five beers dangling from his thick fingers. He forced himself into the booth next to his four companions, overcrowding it to the point that Chet could barely free his arm enough to get his beer to his mouth.

"Goddamn weeknight and you can't hardly move in this place," Mikey complained. "You used to be able to come in here at nine o'clock on Saturday and the place was empty."

Despite the cheesy and threadbare atmosphere, this former Mob-only hangout was becoming increasingly hip with the local yuppie crowd. While it was true that the pasta was cheap and above average, the well-dressed twenty-somethings who poured in every night were less interested in the cuisine than they were in mixing with the "criminal element."

Chet hated the place. He felt on display. But the aging and amply fed men surrounding him loved it. Their chances of slinking off to a cheap hotel with some slender young thing just out of college increased from zero to five or ten percent here—still far from a sure thing, but more than they had a right to hope for. The notorious Carlo Gasta, who made an appearance at least twice a week, generally batted a thousand.

"Well, we're all here," Mikey said, twisting around as best he could and looking directly at Chet.

"Yeah, I can see that."

"So, you gonna tell us what's going on?"

Chet shrugged and took a sip of his second beer of the evening. Mikey had put a third down in front of him and he was wondering what he was going to do about that. Two was his absolute limit tonight, even with the huge plate of carbonara he'd just put away.

"What are you talking about?"

"What the fuck do you mean, what am I talking about? I'm talking about the sand niggers."

The wall of flesh surrounding him leaned forward in unison and murmured quietly. Chet couldn't make out distinct words over the horrible eighties' music blaring from overhead speakers, but he got the gist.

"I don't know, man. I don't know what's going on with those guys."

"On the level? You're not bullshitting us?"

Chet nodded. He'd always liked Mikey, and he hated to pile on yet another lie, but Gasta had been clear that he was to keep his mouth shut on this particular subject.

"Damnit," Mikey said, taking another hit off his beer. "I don't mind telling you that I have a real bad feeling about this whole thing. I think that son of a bitch is finally going to get our asses shot off."

Chet looked around him at the thick faces of his colleagues. The dissent in the ranks had obviously been discussed and was unanimous.

The five men crowded into the booth made up the group closest to Gasta—his main management and muscle. At thirty-four, Chet was the youngest by probably fifteen years and the only one who was looking to make a name for himself. The others had already paid their dues with Gasta's father in their younger years and weren't looking to drag their bad backs and clogged arteries into another shooting war. If Chet told them that Gasta was planning on executing and ripping off the formidable Mohammed and his partners, half of them would probably have heart attacks right there in the bar.

"Look, guys, don't worry about it," Chet said, pushing against the enormous man next to him.

"Where you going?" Mikey said. "You ain't gonna finish your beer?"

"Nah, I got some thinking to do and I need a clear head."

"Thinking? What kind of thinking?"

"I'm gonna think about how to keep you from getting your fat ass shot off."

That seemed to be the right answer because Mikey let him out. Chet was halfway across the bar when he heard someone yell his name. He spun and looked back at the table he'd just left.

"You think hard on that," Mikey shouted. "Okay?"

Chet ate the last of an entire roll of Life Savers but he knew he wasn't going to fool anyone. He was sitting in his car, parked a quarter of a mile down a dirt road that branched off a rural highway outside of L.A. It was an ideal spot. He'd been able to see miles behind him for most of the drive there. There were always risks, of course, but he felt confident that no one could have followed him.

He was a little early, and probably five minutes passed before a set of headlights appeared over a rise, easily visible in the darkness despite the distance. He watched as they continued along the highway and then turned toward him.

Chet stepped out into the still air and walked forward as the approaching headlights went out and car glided to a stop in front of him. It was too dark to see the faces of the two people who emerged until they were only a few feet way.

"Chet?"

He nodded and the blond woman offered her hand.

"I'm Laura Vilechi. I don't think we've ever met."

Her handshake was firm but not so strong that it was like she was trying to prove something. Based on her reputation, he supposed she already had.

"Nice to meet you. You're a friend of Mark's, aren't you?"

"Mark Beamon? Yeah, I am."

"I used to work for him in Flagstaff," Chet said, "before I got transferred to L.A." When she released his hand, the man standing next to her took it.

"How are things, Chet? Everything all right?"

"Yeah, I'm good, Scott. Things are still going good."

Scott Reynolds was the special agent in charge of the FBI's L.A. criminal division. The fact that he and Laura Vilechi were here in person meant that the Bureau had taken the report Chet had filed a lot more seriously than he'd thought they would. This was a whole lot of high-level management to be standing around in the desert with a guy who'd only been an agent for five years.

"You okay to talk, Chet?" Laura said. She obviously smelled the beer on his breath.

"I just had a couple. Didn't have much of a choice, you know?"

She shrugged casually in an unsuccessful attempt to put him a little more at ease. "That's undercover work."

"You're running the rocket launcher investigation, aren't you?" Chet said. He couldn't believe she'd flown all the way to L.A. to meet with him. What if he'd wasted her time?

"I'm sorry to say that I am."

"Uh, so . . . what are you doing here?"

"Scott sent me your last report. I thought it made for interesting reading."

"Really?"

The report she was referring to was his description of Gasta's meeting with Mohammed. Chet had toyed with the idea that there might be a connection between him and the terrorist in the photograph, but hadn't really given it all that much thought. There were a lot of Afghans and Arabs in the world. Ninety-nine point nine percent of them weren't psychos. Some of them were just plain old drug dealers.

"Look, Chet, there's a chance that the people with the rocket launcher might be tied to the Afghan heroin trade. Actually, it's an angle that Mark Beamon came up with. Far-fetched but . . . well, you know Mark: When it comes to things like this, he's right more than he's wrong."

Chet grinned. "Mark's pretty much nuts but I think he may be a genius."

"Yeah, that about sums up how I feel about him, too. Now, is there anything else you can tell me about this Mohammed?"

"Not much," Chet said apologetically. "I mean, the word is he's Afghan—or, more accurately, that he's from Afghanistan. But then, I heard that from Carlo Gasta, and he isn't exactly a geographer, you know? Jeez, Ms. Vilechi, when I wrote that report, I didn't think you'd come out here personally. The whole thing is probably nothing."

"Probably," Laura said. "On the other hand, we think al-Qaeda may be trying to expand its presence in the heroin business. There could be a connection."

Chet tried to remember any detail of the meeting with Mohammed that he might have left out of his report. There was nothing, though. They'd talked, Gasta had thrown a tantrum, and then they'd left.

"Your write-up said that Mohammed postponed the transaction. Do you know when your next meeting will be?"

Chet shook his head. "I'm not sure what's going on right now. I haven't had time to put this on paper yet, but Gasta took me to meet someone last night." He looked over at Reynolds. "I think it's the guy we've been looking for."

"The money man?"

Chet nodded. "We met him in an office in the Sun America Center in Century City: it has *First Federal Development Bank* on the door."

Reynolds wrote the name on a small pad.

"The guy was pissed that Gasta brought me and didn't let me stay for the meeting. But when Gasta came out he had the idea that the Afghans were shopping for another contact. Now he's planning on killing them at our next meeting and grabbing the drugs. I don't think it's his idea, though—I think it's coming from this other guy."

"Can you describe him?"

"Not very well. Big guy, stocky. He looked tall, but he was sitting, so I can't be sure. His hair's almost black, short, and kind of slicked back. I'm honestly not sure I'd know him if I saw him again."

"Name?"

"Just John. He's nobody I've ever seen. Not connected to the families as far as I know."

Reynolds finished writing in his pad and stuck it back in his pocket. "Maybe there's a security camera tape. We'll get on it."

"There's more."

"What?"

"Gasta seems pretty set on hitting the Afghans, but he's worried about it. I managed to convince him that they weren't going to just roll over and play dead. . . ."

"Yeah?" Reynolds prompted.

"He wants me to bring in Nicolai to help."

Reynolds took a deep breath and blew it out. "Great."

"Who's Nicolai?" Laura said.

"I'll explain on our ride out," Reynolds answered. "What do you want to do, Chet?"

"I'm not sure . . . I take it that getting ahold of this Mohammed guy is kind of a priority now."

"Top priority," Laura said. "I admit it's a long shot, but under the circumstances it has to supersede your organized-crime investigation. We've got a rocket launcher floating somewhere out there. . . ."

Chet stared off in the dark for a few moments, considering his position. "I'll tell you, Scott, my read is that I need to produce on this. If I can't set up a meeting between Gasta and Nicolai, my credibility is going to be shot to hell. And if that happens, I could find myself out of the loop on the next meeting with the Afghans."

Reynolds nodded. "All right, Chet. Call me tomorrow and we'll try to have something put together."

15

PASCAL thrashed back and forth violently but he couldn't dislodge it. The insect, a large cockroach, continued its slow march up his leg, perhaps drawn to the odor of urine that now permeated his trousers.

His fear that the jungle's predators would instinctively sense his helplessness and slowly creep up on him had not materialized. The truth was so much more terrifying. The insects that had scurried away in terror at his thrashing six hours ago were becoming bolder. Would they devour him a millimeter at a time?

He threw his body right again, nearly upsetting his chair but managing to dislodge the roach and send it toppling to the floor. It righted itself and began to wander away. But it would be back.

By following the shadow of the doorway as it moved steadily across the floor, Pascal determined that he had been there for somewhere around fifteen hours. Another long night wasn't far away.

He tilted his back and opened his mouth, catching a few precious drops of water and letting them trickle down his raw throat. Thankfully, it had rained intermittently since he'd been trapped there, soaking through the thatched roof and providing him with enough liquid to at least partially quench his growing thirst.

He wondered again whether Volkov was concerned about his absence yet, but he knew the answer was no. Even if Christian hadn't been caught in a similar trap in America, he would undoubtedly assume that Pascal was peacefully negotiating a business relationship with General Yung. He probably wouldn't become concerned until midday tomorrow. And what then? Pascal trusted him—something rare in the business they'd chosen—but he didn't hold much hope. Volkov's power base in Laos had disintegrated after Yung's coup. It was why he had been sent here.

A second droplet of water missed his mouth and splattered across his forehead. It didn't matter: He wouldn't survive for long on what could filter through the roof. Truthfully, he wasn't sure he wanted to. While dehydration wasn't reputed to be the most pleasant way to die, there were certainly worse alternatives.

"Not thirsty? I would have thought a cool drink of water was exactly what you needed."

Pascal jerked his head in the direction of the door and saw the broad form of a man backlit in the entrance.

"Who are you?" Pascal said in English. His throat would barely allow the words out.

The figure moved through the door and walked around the perimeter of the small hut, pausing for a moment to look down at the body of the pilot and cover his nose with his hand against the rotting stench that was quickly gaining strength.

"You," Pascal said quietly.

Jonathan Drake's smile was perceptible even in the dim light. "You'll have to accept my apologies for making you wait so long. I assure you that I was on a plane as soon as I heard you were . . . available."

Except for Volkov, Pascal was the only person in the organization who was aware of the CIA's involvement in supplying Mustafa Yasin with weapons and intelligence. Obviously this was enough of a concern to Drake to use the CIA's influence in Laos to have him brought here.

"I have a few questions for you, Pascal. Let's start with the most interesting first. Does Christian believe that the CIA is going to continue with this operation, or does he think we're going to back out?"

Pascal considered his position as carefully as his exhausted mind would allow. He would be dead soon, of that there was little doubt. By nature he wasn't a fearful man, but he was realistic. He would not be able to remain silent in light of what Drake was willing to do to him. And he didn't think that Christian would expect him to.

"Don't make me repeat myself, Pascal."

"He doesn't know what to believe."

"But he doesn't trust me."

"Christian trusts few people."

"What is he doing to protect himself?"

"He is doing nothing at this point. He sent me here to negotiate with General Yung. This should tell you that he is preparing to honor his agreement to help you replace the Middle Eastern heroin producers with his Asian contacts."

Drake looked down again and watched the insects writhing over the corpse at his feet. "Okay, Pascal. Here's another interesting one. Where is he?"

In the end, that was the piece of information Drake really needed. Of course, he would want whatever general information he could pry out of Pascal, but finding and killing Volkov would go a long way toward ensuring that he and his organization were never linked to the weapon that al-Qaeda had managed to smuggle into America.

"This has gone too far," Pascal said, trying to give himself time to think. "Christian warned you of the risks of your plan. He never wanted to be involved in any of this, but you forced his hand. To not see it through now makes no sense. It is true that people—that Americans—may fall victim to this rocket, but there will be many more to follow if you allow al-Qaeda to solidify its position in the Middle Eastern heroin trade."

The only effect his argument had was to make the CIA man's anger come to the surface.

"I asked you where he is," Drake growled. "I suggest you focus on that question."

"Christian has made commitments," Pascal said. "He has no choice but to see what you have started through to the end. Talk to him. Ask for his help in protecting your anonymity. He can be trusted. It is convenient for him to have ties to the CIA."

Drake stared down at him. "It's *convenient,* is it?"

Pascal didn't see the blow coming, but it wouldn't have mattered if he had. Drake's fist came across his face with startling force.

"You are nothing!" Pascal heard through ringing ears. "You are a fucking arrogant little drug dealer. You and Volkov live or die at *my* convenience. Do you understand that?" Drake grabbed Pascal's hair and pulled his head back, staring into his eyes. "The fact that I even have to deal with people like you makes me sick."

Pascal laughed, spraying spit and blood onto Drake's shirt. "It's funny: Christian feels the same way about you."

The second blow was even harder—delivered with much of Drake's considerable weight behind it. Pascal was certain that his jaw was broken, but the pain wasn't as bad as he would have expected. The end wasn't far away.

"Where is he?"

Pascal's disdain for the man standing in front of him continued to grow. Drake cared nothing for the people who would fall victim to a better-funded, more powerful al-Qaeda. He cared nothing for the people whose lives depended on America's FBI finding the launcher. He was only concerned about protecting himself.

"Cuba," Pascal lied. As his anger rose, so did his courage. Time was his and Christian's enemy now. The longer he could keep from revealing Christian's location, the better the chance that he would survive to kill this bastard.

"Cuba," Drake repeated quietly. "Okay. That's a start. But I think we need to make sure."

16

AFTER an hour of concentrating on them, the endless columns of numbers in front of Beamon had completely lost their meaning. He squinted and tried to focus, but it was pointless: They had become nothing more than indecipherable symbols.

He tossed the budget report on his desk and leaned back in his chair, trying to block out the buzz of activity outside his office door and let his mind go blank. As usual, it didn't work. After about twenty seconds he found his thoughts wandering back to his dinner with Carrie.

She had been right, of course. While it was doubtful that he had the tolerance for boredom necessary to be the greatest SAC in the history of the bureau, he could certainly do this job at a competent level. The bottom line was, he just didn't want to. In fact, he was starting to wonder if he wanted any of it anymore.

He'd put everything into the Bureau—never marrying, working fourteen-hour days, often seven days a week, no kids, hardly any friends outside the organization. No real life at all.

Not that it had been what he would call a terribly painful sacrifice. He'd loved it. How much luckier could you get than to have somebody pay you to chase bad guys all day. Honestly, he'd have done it for free.

Things were different now, though, and it wasn't just the SAC job. During his last investigation, the FBI—his family—had turned on him. And as if that weren't bad enough, they'd done it just to make life a little easier for a bunch of low-life politicians. He imagined that this was what it felt like to have a spouse cheat on you. You still loved her, but something was gone. Something that would never come back.

Of course, there were the people he'd helped—there would always be that. And he'd made a few true, lifelong friends over the years. But the rest was just starting to look like smoke. He sometimes found himself half wishing that he'd just gone out in a blaze of glory—gunned down, fired, or slammed his credentials down on the director's desk. God knew there had been multiple opportunities for all three.

For the first time in his life he was thinking seriously about resigning, but at this point he had to admit to himself that he wouldn't be storming out, he'd be crawling out. That plan also made it kind of critical that he figure out what he was going to do with the rest of his life. A complicated issue.

There was another option, of course: He could always request a demotion. Hell, if he just waited a few more weeks for that inspection report to come out, asking probably wouldn't even be necessary.

"Mark? Mark!"

Beamon blinked his eyes hard and sat up abruptly.

"Laura. Are you early?"

"Actually, I'm late," she said, dropping into a chair in front of his desk. "Are you all right?"

"Fine," he lied. "I'm fine." It occurred to him that he wasn't sure how long he'd been sitting there, lost in thought. Looking at his watch was out of the question, though. Laura would almost certainly pick up on it.

"Are you sure?"

"Yeah. What about you? You look tired."

"A little jet lagged is all," she said. "I just came in from Los Angeles."

Beamon decided not to bring up the fact that an hour's time difference rarely resulted in jet lag. "What were you doing in L.A.? Seems like a long way from Washington."

"I was there talking to a guy who's undercover in Carlo Gasta's organization."

"Carlo Gasta? That asshole Mob guy?"

She nodded.

"Spreading yourself a little thin, aren't you? The rocket launcher thing isn't enough to hold your attention?"

Laura rubbed her eyes with the palms of her hands. "Last week he and Gasta met with a heroin dealer from Afghanistan."

"Really," Beamon said. "So you think there might be something to my idea about al-Qaeda staking itself to a piece of the drug trade?"

"Probably not. Having said that, though . . ."

"You're desperate."

"That pretty much sums it up. The stock market's dropping like a stone, the airlines are looking for another bailout, retail sales are through the floor . . . People are afraid to leave their houses: They're just sitting around with the TV on, listening to all the horrible things that could potentially happen to them. The economy is on the verge of crumbling, thousands of lives are at risk, and I'm just standing around with my mouth hanging open."

Beamon had never seen her like this. The cool façade that she showed the world, the one she'd been wearing ever since he'd known her, was coming apart right there in his office. And behind it there was something that looked like . . . panic.

"I don't think there's anybody who could do more, Laura. You're as good at this game as anyone I've ever met."

"But am I as good as you? Could you do more?"

Beamon tried to smile, but it seemed uncomfortable under the force of her stare. She was actually expecting a straight answer.

"Too technical for me, Laura. All those suspects and foreign governments and politicians and weapons systems . . . no, this one's tailor-made for you. I have a feeling the answer will be in the details."

"You're so full of shit. You *do* think you could do better. I know you do."

"I'm an obsessive-compulsive egomaniac, Laura. Of course I think I could do better." He grinned. "Do you have time for a drink? Maybe more than one?"

She shook her head. "The jet's waiting to take me back to D.C."

The silence that ensued looked to be in danger of getting overly long.

"I'm guessing you didn't come here just to say hello. What do you want? More access to the White House?"

She shook her head.

"Then, what?"

"I have a problem . . ." she began.

"Somehow I guessed that."

"I want to pursue this angle of investigation . . ."

"You mean the Afghan drug dealers?"

She gave him a short nod. "And I want you to be involved. But Dave and P.C. aren't going to go for it."

Beamon nodded knowingly. P.C. were not only FBI Director Peter Caroll's initials but an acronym for his political leanings. A former liberal judge with no investigative background, he was a man who actually called short people "vertically challenged."

"I think you're pissing into the wind here, Laura. I mean, Dave gritted his teeth and agreed to use me for my contacts, but he and P.C. aren't going to let me take an active role in this investigation. No way."

"You know Scott Reynolds in L.A., don't you?"

Beamon nodded.

"He agrees that this is something worth looking into. He's willing to prioritize getting the Afghans over getting Carlo Gasta."

"Reynolds is a good man. You can trust him."

"I agree. He also said that he's willing to keep this angle of investigation quiet from management."

"I don't understand, Laura. Why would you want to do that?"

She ignored the question. "We hear that Gasta has orders to kill these Afghans at their next meeting and steal their heroin."

"Orders from whom?"

"We don't know exactly.

"I still don't see what this has to do with me," Beamon said, careful not to let himself succumb to the hypnotic effect that drug dealers, mafiosi, and rocket launchers always seemed to have on him.

"We were able to get an undercover FBI agent close to Gasta two ways. First, we have an informant inside Gasta's organization and he vouched for our guy. Second, our guy told Gasta that he used to work for Nicolai."

Beamon searched his brain for the name but came up empty. "Who?"

"Nicolai is a criminal transaction specialist—assassination, drugs, arms deals, theft. If it's big and complicated, he's interested. But he's strictly a free agent, not affiliated with any particular organization."

"Never heard of him."

"That's probably because he doesn't really exist."

"Excuse me?"

"The FBI conjured him out of thin air. Well, not exactly thin air— more like out of unsolved crimes and classified FBI operations. We created him for just this kind of a thing."

Beamon kicked his feet up onto his desk and thought about that for a few moments. "A creative and interesting idea," he said sincerely. "Did you come up with it?"

"Not me. Actually, I don't know who did."

"You still haven't answered my question. What does this have to do with me?"

"Like I said, Gasta has orders to hit these Afghans. The problem is, he's a little scared of them."

"Who would have thought he was that smart?" Beamon said.

"He wants our guy to call Nicolai and get him involved."

Beamon couldn't help laughing. "Let me guess: Nicolai is about my age and build."

"He sure could be."

"You're too much, Laura."

"Look, Mark. We've got to move on this, and the 'Nicolai' file is pretty thick. You've got a hell of a memory for crime when you try. There aren't too many people in the Bureau who could get on top of the material in the time we've got. Plus, it's your angle—your idea. And . . ."

"And?"

"You're going to make me say this, aren't you?"

"Say what?"

"Look, I don't think this is going to come to anything, but I want you involved. I'd feel better if you were involved. Okay?"

"I'm not sure what to say," Beamon responded honestly.

"From what I'm hearing, you should turn me down—stay here and buckle down."

"News travels fast," he said.

"So what do you think?"

It had been years since he'd gone undercover, and he didn't remember particularly liking it. On the other hand, Laura looked like she was on her last leg; turning her down wasn't going to be easy.

"What I'm talking about is basically one meeting, Mark. You go in, you play our guy up in front of Gasta, and then you tell him you've got other commitments."

"I don't know, Laura. I've done some fairly high-profile stuff in the last few years. What if somebody recognizes me?"

"Is that a joke?"

She was right, of course. With all the weight he'd lost, the beard, and the continued graying and thinning of his hair, he barely recognized himself. Combined with the glasses that only his optometrist knew were bifocals, he was starting to look more like a college professor than an FBI agent.

"I don't know, Laura . . ."

"It's up to you."

The truth was that there was nothing for him to do in Phoenix right now. He was waiting for his ASACs to finish going through his comments on the inspection report, and the stress would most likely kill him before the weekend. Maybe this would be good for his mental outlook—help out a friend and get a little break from his life.

"What about this informant that helped our guy get inside?"

"What about him?"

"You said you don't know who ordered Gasta to hit the Afghans. Does your informant have any information?"

"We don't know. Probably not. We're trying to initiate contact with him, but it takes time. We'll catch him before you go in . . . *if* you go in."

"When?"

"Soon. Tomorrow or the day after at the latest."

"Your undercover guy. Is he any good? Reliable?"

"You ought to know: You pretty much trained him. It's Chet Michaels."

Beamon's eyes widened, remembering the glow-in-the-dark red hair and freckles that spread from Chet's nose across his pale cheeks. "You sent Howdy Doody undercover?"

Laura shrugged. "That's the other reason you're perfect for this job. He really did work for you for a couple of years."

One of the primary rules of undercover work: Keep it as real as possible. The more lies you told, the more chance you'd trip yourself up.

"Chet Michaels," Beamon said quietly, shaking his head. "Okay, you've sold me. Send me the files."

A tired smile spread across Laura's face. "Your secretary's copying them as we speak."

17

BEAMON had a hot pan of Kraft macaroni and cheese burning one hand and a beer freezing the other when the phone rang. He ran across the living room and searched for a safe place to put the pan, finally just dropping it on the coffee table next to the three burned crescents already there.

"Yeah, hello?" he said, grabbing the phone and digging a magazine from beneath the sofa to use as a pot holder.

"Mark! It's been a while. How are you?"

The voice was still clear and youthful, though some of the uncontrolled enthusiasm seemed to have dimmed a bit. The ravages of maturity.

"Chet. Yeah, it has been a while. I'm good. I hear some idiot put you undercover with the Mob."

"Can you believe it? And they love me. I guess as much as I don't look like a crook, I look like an FBI agent even less. Who would ever suspect?"

"You make a good point," Beamon said, finally tracking down the manual to his phone and flipping quickly through it.

"Hold on, Chet. I'm going to see if I can conference Laura in."

"Hey, Mark?"

"Yeah," Beamon said, skimming the instructions.

"I appreciate you doing this. I mean, being a big-shot SAC and all, I know you have better things to do."

"You'd be surprised," he said, cutting Chet off and dialing Laura to connect her. Miraculously, it worked.

"Okay, Chet. You first. Do you have anything new since the last time you talked to Laura?"

"Not really. Gasta's getting himself worked up to hit these Afghans, but as far as I know he hasn't been contacted by them to set up another meeting yet. He hasn't even mentioned that John guy since the day we met him, but I'm still convinced that he's the money man we've been looking for."

"And you still think he's the one putting Gasta up to this thing with the Afghans."

"Absolutely."

"Okay. Laura, how about you? What have you got?"

"As far as the mysterious 'John' goes, not much. The security tapes for the night Gasta met with him seem to have miraculously disappeared. There were no useful prints we could find in the office, and we got nothing from the other tenants on that floor. The company itself, First Federal Development Bank, is a shell corporation chartered in Niue, which is basically a medium-sized rock sticking out of the Pacific. Where the Afghans are concerned, we're not doing any better. We've run through pretty much every informant the DEA has and we've got nothing on a group of Afghans shopping around a big load of heroin—or any heroin at all, for that matter. It's looking like we're going to have to count on Chet to find them for us."

"And that's where Nicolai comes in," Beamon said.

"Right," Chet agreed. "I played up my relationship with Nicolai to get Gasta to take me on. I have a feeling that if I don't produce, I'm going to lose a lot of credibility in his eyes. If that happens, I could get frozen out of the deal and then I won't be able to do anything to help you get your hands on these Afghans.

"But if Nicolai makes an appearance, you're okay, right? Even if Nicolai says no to Gasta's proposal?"

"The important thing is to make it look like we've got a good relationship and that you respect me. Call it a scheduling conflict and that you'd be interested in doing something with him in the future. Gasta's really susceptible to flattery."

"If Nicolai's got all this built-in credibility, could he help you get close to the money man you're after?"

"It's a good idea, Mark, but I don't think it will work. Unless I miss my guess, Gasta will keep Nicolai's involvement quiet. He wants to impress this John guy—particularly after pissing him off by bringing me to that meeting. He'll want to take all the credit for pulling this thing off."

"So all he's looking to do here is hire Nicolai to help him kill these Afghans and steal their product. Then he'll just pay Nicolai's fee and no one will ever know Gasta didn't plan and execute the whole thing."

"Exactly."

"And you're sure it's not going to hurt you when Nicolai says no."

"I'm not dead sure but I don't think so. I said I worked for the guy—not that I had any influence over him."

"Okay," Beamon said, pulling the phone to the full length of its cord and shoving a spoonful of mac and cheese in his mouth. "Set up a meeting."

"I'll get in touch with you when I get a time and place."

"Mark," Laura cut in. "I opened an account for you in the Caymans and an e-mail account with a server set up in the Czech Republic. I faxed all the information to one of the techs at your office. He's setting up a laptop with all this stuff. Nicolai takes a hundred thousand just for showing up to a meeting."

"Sounds good. What about the informant you told me about—the one who introduced Chet to Gasta? Have you been able to get in touch with him yet?"

"We're still trying to set up a meeting," Laura said. "What about you, Chet? Can you get to him?"

"I don't think so, Laura. I've moved way beyond him and never really see him anymore. I think my trying to contact him now would look weird and wouldn't be worth the risk. I mean, I know it pays to be thorough, but this guy is too low on the totem pole to know anything that could help us."

"Okay, then," Laura said. "Is that it?"

"Seems like," Beamon said.

"I'll keep after that informant, Mark, and I'll let you know what I find out. Oh, and, Chet, if I don't talk to you, good luck and thanks for the assist." There was a click on the phone as she hung up.

"You still there, Chet?"

"Yeah, I'm here. It's gonna be fun working with you again, Mark. I've missed the sort of surreal quality of it."

"Uh-huh. What's the girl with the nose ring think about all this?"

"My *wife* is fine with it. But I told her this was the last time."

"That's a promise you should keep," Beamon said seriously, "but the Bureau won't make it easy. From what I hear, you've done a good job, and that means they'll want you to go under again. Don't let them get to you. Your relationship with your wife's all that's important."

There was a fairly long silence before Chet spoke again. "I don't get it. Are you being sarcastic?"

"No, I'm not being sarcastic. I'm giving you the benefit of my age and wisdom. Do as I say, not as I've done."

"Sure, Mark. I will. Hey, how's Carrie?"

"Good. She's good."

At least as far as he knew; he still hadn't called her. He wanted to have some kind of coherent plan for the rest of his life first.

18

WOLFGANG had been motionless since before dawn, half buried in a mound of dead foliage near two granite boulders. The small muscular knot that had begun to tie itself in his lower back three hours ago was now bad enough to impair fast movement should it become necessary. He needed to stretch, to relieve some of the pressure, but that was out of the question. It seemed that every year he felt the discomfort of his job a little more acutely—the cramping muscles, the wet, rotting jungle soaking through his fatigues, the sharp rocks beneath him. At twenty-nine, it was already time to think about the day that he would no longer be capable of this kind of work.

Another interminably long hour passed before he heard it: a sound too quiet to be a coconut falling through the trees, but too loud to be one of the small reptiles scurrying around him in the dead leaves. He held his breath and flexed his hand around his rifle. It was possible that it was some kind of animal—something he hadn't seen yet, but he doubted it. The noise had an unnatural hesitancy to it that usually meant a human source.

It took another five minutes before the first one became visible, striped by the sunlight filtering through the canopy. Wolfgang watched him and the others as they appeared, moving only his eyes. They closed efficiently on the boulders near him, training their weapons on an obvious indentation between them, which is why he had avoided that more strategic position.

It was a pleasure to watch them work. The grace, the near total silence, the almost telepathic integration of the unit. Obviously a group of men who had honed considerable natural talent with years of sacrifice and training. Men to be respected and, if one was wise, feared.

He continued to watch as they moved past, taking in every detail. He calculated their speed and adjusted for the terrain he knew was ahead, letting them go what he estimated was a quarter mile before daring to move his fingers to his throat mike.

"This is Wolfgang," he said in English. "Five men have passed my position and are now approximately four hundred meters north of me, moving toward the house. Estimated arrival in a half an hour. Stand by."

When all of his men had acknowledged the transmission, Wolfgang moved his green-painted hand silently to his pocket and punched a button on the satellite phone secured there. It was picked up immediately. The voice on the other end was surprisingly clear through his earpiece.

"Yes?"

He'd never laid eyes on his employer and this was only the second time he'd spoken to the man directly. In the end, though, it didn't matter. The wire transfers he received for his services were very real and substantial enough to ensure a comfortable retirement for him and his family.

He switched to German, which he was more comfortable with, knowing that his employer had no real preference as to language. "We've made contact. They're moving toward the house."

The house he was referring to was one of the only things on the small island in the Seychelle chain—a structure perched on the edge of a smooth granite cliff. His orders had been to rig it with explosives and to make it look as though it were still occupied. He and his men had set enough Plastique to more or less disintegrate it.

"Any idea who they are, Wolfgang?"

"Definitely not Laotian and probably not American," he said quietly, continuing to scan the jungle for movement. "Based on their equipment and appearance, I would guess mercenaries of various nationalities."

"How easily could they be captured?"

"It would be extremely difficult, even with surprise on our side. I've seen five but there are probably more: There are other obvious insertion points and lines of attack. As I told your people years ago, this house is impossible to properly secure."

"It has a wonderful view, though."

Wolfgang wasn't sure how to respond to that comment, so he ignored it. "If you are intent on capturing some of them, sir, the best way would be to wait for them to get close to the house and then blow it. Their point men will be killed and we can use the confusion to try to take the men at the rear. What would you like us to do?"

Christian Volkov pressed the phone to his ear a little harder, trying to block out the hum of the small jet as it descended through the clouds and revealed a landscape of endless snowcapped mountains.

There was no real point in trying to capture one of these men, he knew. It was unlikely that they would know the identity of their employer, and the potential loss of Wolfgang or the members of his team would be a devastating. Especially now.

"Destroy the house."

"Now? They are probably still more than two kilometers out."

There was also no point to killing them. Violence was best used sparingly and only when absolutely necessary. Had they been Laotian or American, perhaps acquiring one alive would have been helpful in ascertaining whether General Yung or Jonathan Drake was involved. But mercenaries . . .

"Destroy it now and get your men out of there safely. Payment will be in your account by tomorrow."

"I understand."

Volkov shut off the phone and pressed his forehead against the cold window next to him. When he'd lost contact with Pascal, he'd immediately abandoned the Seychelles house and sent Wolfgang to look after it. Now, only a few hours later, there were already men closing in. Whoever had masterminded the attack moved quickly.

The obvious answer, of course, was General Yung. He certainly had known the time of Pascal's arrival and could have had a group of mercenaries on standby while he retrieved the information on Volkov's whereabouts. That was far from certain, though. It could have been any one of a hundred enemies whom he had collected over the years. The disintegration of his power base in Laos would not go unnoticed, and it was not unreasonable to expect someone to take advantage of his temporary weakness there and attempt to move in on his business interests.

If the situation were reversed, it was exactly how he would have done it: pay off the men driving Pascal and get rid of the plane. Then, if the attack was unsuccessful, the general would be the obvious suspect. And either way, Yung would be suspicious of Pascal's sudden disappearance and would assume that he had just been there as a spy.

Of course, there was also Jonathan Drake and the CIA, an organization with a significant presence in Laos. Despite his protests to the contrary, was Drake trying to end their relationship?

The truth was, there was no way to know. It wasn't the first time he'd been attacked like this, and it probably wouldn't be the last. The problem in this case was that his business with General Yung, one way or another, had been left unfinished. Despite the uncertainty of his situation, he would have to reach out to Yung again. Soon.

"Christian? Are you all right?"

Volkov looked up at the man sitting in a deep leather chair across from him. He was thirty-three but looked younger, with dark, smooth skin and closely cropped, curly black hair. While certainly not ready to take Pascal's place in the organization, he was nevertheless a very talented young man.

"I'm fine, Joseph. A bit tired from my visit with Charles Russell. It was a long flight." Volkov pointed to the laptop in the younger man's lap. "Where do we stand?"

"The procedures were very clear and detailed. It's all going smoothly."

Everything was temporarily in flux. They were flying toward a house that no one, not even Pascal, had known about. New corporations were being formed, bank accounts were being closed and new ones opened, houses were being burned and new ones purchased. Volkov estimated that the loss of Pascal would cost over fifty million U.S. dollars. Legal fees alone would rise into the millions.

Volkov leaned his head back on the seat, feeling the darkness that he was so familiar with trying to descend on him, to leave him helpless and broken as it had so many times before. He couldn't allow it, though. Not now.

"Pascal has a sister in France," he said quietly. "You'll need to tell her that he is . . . he is dead. Tell her it was an auto crash or some other accident. He had a five-million-dollar life-insurance policy through one of our European corporations. See that there are no delays in her receiving the money." He paused for a moment, finding it suddenly difficult to speak. "And tell her that . . . tell her that he was a good friend to me."

19

DESPITE the seriousness of his situation, Beamon had to struggle not to smile.

He was in the backseat of a black Cadillac with way too many gold accents, sandwiched between two enormous mounds of Italian-American flesh. The mound to his right, inevitably named Tony, had a nose that looked like it had been broken at least a hundred times and dark, beady eyes that were beginning to disappear into his fleshy face. Mikey, an equally stereotypical specimen, had a slightly straighter nose but made up for it with a seventies-looking clip-on tie.

"So tell me, Mikey," Beamon said, prying himself free and leaning forward a bit to stretch his back. "How many track suits do you own?"

The man just stared straight forward with a military intensity. Obviously he didn't have much of a sense of humor and thought that Beamon—Nicolai—was trying to pry important information out of him.

"I don't know. Why?"

"Never mind," Beamon said, looking over the front seat at the winding road in front of them. He'd thought the meeting was to be held at Carlo Gasta's downtown office, but when he'd arrived, he'd been ushered into this car. He wasn't crazy about this type of thing not going as expected, but so far there seemed to be nothing to get worked up about.

"Where are we going?

Silence.

Every attempt he'd made to pry something useful out of these overweight bookends had gone nowhere, so Beamon decided to use the time to review the countless facts he'd shoehorned into his mind over the past forty-eight hours. The files that combined to create the fictional persona Nicolai encompassed fifteen years of complex crimes and scams. He thought he had a grasp on most of it but sincerely hoped there wouldn't be a quiz.

Finally exhausting his limited capacity for concentrating on detail, Beamon focused on the bigger picture. What did the individual acts contained in those files say about Nicolai? What kind of a man was he?

Beamon had always thought that undercover work and acting were the same thing. In this case you read the file—basically a script—then you created a person in your head who would do those sorts of things. It was a form of applied schizophrenia—something he should be pretty good at, according to Carrie.

They turned off the road and into the driveway of a smallish house built into the side of a hill and Beamon followed Tony—or was it Mikey?—out of the car and took in the rolling quilt of city lights spread out below.

"This way."

He was marched to the porch and one of his new friends knocked gingerly on the front door. It took probably a minute before Beamon heard footsteps approaching from inside.

"So this is the famous Nicolai," Carlo Gasta said, pulling the door open and stepping out of the way as his men ushered Beamon inside. "I thought you'd be taller."

Beamon was going to offer his hand but it felt strangely unnatural. Nicolai, as it turned out, wasn't a handshaker. And neither was Gasta, apparently. He turned and led them through the gaudily decorated entry, trailing the distinct scent of alcohol and aftershave.

When they entered the living room, Chet rose from a sofa to greet him. Beamon decided that Nicolai would make an exception and shake hands with his old assistant.

"It's good to see you again," Chet said respectfully. "We appreciate you meeting with us."

Beamon just nodded and sat down on the sofa uninvited.

Gasta was standing with his back to them at a bar, mixing himself a drink. Beamon saw that he was swaying a little from the ones he'd had already and that worried him a little, though he wasn't exactly sure why.

"What do you drink, Nicolai?"

"Nothing."

"I don't trust a man who won't drink with me."

Beamon surveyed the room casually. The men who had brought him there were standing against the wall with their eyes locked on him.

"I don't care."

Gasta looked a little angry when he turned around. It was likely that he was accustomed to being firmly in command—particularly in his own home.

"You know what made me think of you on this deal," Gasta said, pulling a pack of cigarettes from his pocket and smacking them against the palm of his hand. "It was that job you did in Detroit."

Beamon called up the details of a multimillion-dollar diamond heist he'd read about in one of the files Laura had given him. Gasta's glassy eyes suddenly became just a little bit probing.

"I understand you have something that might interest me," Beamon said, ignoring the inference.

"That was a hell of an operation," Gasta said, obviously not willing to let the subject go. "The one in Detroit, I mean."

Was it possible that he could be any more obvious? He undoubtedly has some kind of information on that job that would suggest Nicolai wasn't involved.

"The FBI and Interpol blame me when it rains, Carlo. I had nothing to do with that. As I recall, two security guards were killed—but not before they'd managed to get a few shots off." He shook his head in disgust. "I don't make a practice out of getting into gunfights with eight-dollar-an-hour rent-a-cops."

Gasta looked disappointed. "Well, then you haven't really done much in the U.S., have you?"

"I haven't. You have better class of law enforcement here. I prefer to avoid the FBI."

That got a laugh out of Gasta. "Bunch of fucking idiots." He spread his arms wide, a drink in one hand and a cigarette in the other. "They've been busting their asses for years and they can't touch me."

It was odd but true. Beamon had never been able to figure out how someone like Carlo Gasta had stayed out of prison for so long. Perhaps it had something to do with the mysterious banker Chet had met.

"Hats off to you. You've done well for yourself."

Gasta took a seat in a chair across from Beamon, and his people took that as the signal that they, too, could sit. A moment later Beamon found himself between his sweaty new friends Tony and Mikey again. Chet, wisely, took the chair next to Gasta.

"So, do you know why you're here?" Gasta said.

"Chet tells me you want to steal a shipment of heroin. Is that correct?"

Gasta nodded.

"Then I have to ask the obvious question. Why?"

Gasta looked at the two men flanking Beamon and laughed. They took the hint and laughed along.

"For the money. Why the fuck else?"

Beamon acted as though he was considering Gasta's statement for a good thirty seconds. He saw Nicolai as a thinker, a man who didn't speak without carefully considering his words. "I'll tell you, Carlo, my involvement in the drug trade has been fairly limited, so I'm no expert, but isn't the markup on this stuff enormous—ten, twenty times? It seems that with those kinds of numbers, the initial cost of the product is almost irrelevant."

"I don't consider two million dollars irrelevant," Gasta said.

Beamon nodded thoughtfully. "I came here because Chet's proved himself to be smart and reliable, and I respect him. But honestly, if I was going to get involved with this, I'd be more inclined to just invest the money." He knew that Chet just wanted him to suck up to Gasta and say he had a scheduling conflict, but it seemed out of character. Why would someone like Nicolai show up to a meeting like this if he already knew he was unavailable?

"Hey, you want to give me a couple of million dollars? Fine. Give me a couple of million dollars."

Tony and Mikey laughed on cue but they were sounding increasingly nervous. Chet remained silent.

Beamon opened his mouth to explain why he wasn't going to be writing Gasta a check anytime soon but was interrupted by the ringing of his phone. He'd just bought it and Laura was the only person who had the number. "Excuse me a moment," he said, pulling it from his pocket and flipping it open. "Yes?"

"Can I talk?" she said.

"Go ahead."

"We found the informant, Mark. He's dead."

Beamon nodded serenely as she spoke, but his mind was racing, trying to recalculate his position.

"We have to assume that they know about Chet."

"I agree," he replied simply.

"Are you in Gasta's office?"

"No."

"Can you tell me where you are?"

"No."

"Can you get out of there?"

He thought about that for a moment. "It doesn't look good."

"Talk to me, Mark. What can I do?"

"As near as I can tell, nothing. Just sit tight. I'll get back to you."

He cleared his suddenly very dry throat and stuffed the phone back in his pocket. "I'm sorry about that. Now, where were we?"

"We were finding out that the great Nicolai is afraid of a bunch of sand niggers," Gasta replied with a flash of his infamous temper.

Beamon remembered the reports Chet had written on Gasta. He drank a lot, but he drank even more when he was scared. At first Beamon had assumed the man was just nervous about his first meeting with Nicolai. But it was more than that—an incongruous combination of fear and arrogance. Beamon thought about lighting a cigarette to calm himself down but he couldn't bring himself to do it. Unfortunately, it seemed that Nicolai didn't smoke.

The men sitting next to him had relieved him of his .357 before he'd gotten in the car with them. He hadn't thought much about it at the time—standard procedure. Now, though, he wasn't so sure.

"I *am* afraid of them," Beamon replied calmly. "Your average Middle Eastern heroin dealer isn't a forgiving man, Carlo. They're violent, unpredictable, and they hold a grudge. Anyone who would cross them for an insignificant amount of money has either very poor judgment or an ulterior motive."

This time Gasta laughed hard enough to get himself coughing. "Which do you think it is, *Nicolai*? Bad judgment?" He looked over at Chet. "You think *I* have bad judgment?"

That was it. Gasta's syntax and body language clinched it. Somehow Chet's cover had been blown. Now the only question was what Beamon was going to do about it. He didn't immediately respond, giving himself time to run various scenarios in his head—trying to come up with one that didn't end up with him and Chet dead.

"That would be my guess, Carlo. You probably don't even know that Chet is a federal agent. I'd call that bad judgment, wouldn't you?"

Beamon had to struggle not to look over at Chet in the silence that ensued. *Come on, kid. Protest already.*

"What the fuck are you talking about?" Chet said finally, rising from his chair and pointing at Beamon. "This is bullshit, Carlo. He's trying to fuck us. He probably wants the heroin himself."

"Oh, please," Beamon said, waving a hand lazily in the air and ignoring the fact that the two men who had been on the sofa with him were now standing behind Gasta with guns drawn. He could tell from the orchestration of their movement that they'd known the entire time. The whole thing had been a setup.

"In fact I did know," Gasta said, trying to sound forceful but not quite succeeding. Beamon beating him to the punch had deflated him a bit.

"What I want to know," Gasta said, jabbing a finger toward him, "is who the fuck *you* are!"

Beamon looked over at Chet for a moment. The poor kid looked like he was on the verge of panic, but Beamon knew he could be counted on to hold it together.

"You already know who I am, Carlo. Chet and I have a mutually beneficial arrangement. He provides me with useful information and points out opportunities like this one. And for that, he won't have to live on his government pension in his old age. Works well on both sides, don't you think?"

The story wasn't exactly airtight but Gasta's uncertainty was definitely growing. If Beamon could fan it a little more, he and Chet might just walk out of there.

"You're full of shit!" Gasta shouted.

Beamon reached into his pocket, ignoring the added attention he got from the men pointing guns at him, and pulled out a cigarette. Time for Nicolai to start smoking.

"Come on, Carlo," he said, taking a lighter off the table in front of him. "Why would I lie? Why would I even bring it up if it weren't true?"

"*Fuck!*" Gasta screamed suddenly, jumping from his chair and throwing his drink in Chet's face. A few moments later Gasta was pacing back and forth across the room, running his hand through his hair compulsively.

"What are you so upset about, Carlo? I'm guessing that Chet was going to hit you with this sooner or later. He's a greedy little bastard but he can be damn useful. I'm guessing there's all kinds of evidence that he can make disappear."

Gasta stayed in motion, an expression of panicked concentration etched deeply into his face. Beamon literally would have given a number of fingers off his right hand to know what the man was thinking.

"Carlo . . ." Beamon began.

Gasta came to an abrupt stop and spun to face him. "*Shut up!* Just shut the fuck up!" His words were punctuated by Mikey pulling the hammer back on his revolver. Or was it Tony?

Beamon watched Gasta take a cell phone from his pocket and start dialing, then stop, then start again. He finally put it up to his ear.

"We have confirmation." There was a long pause as whoever was on the other side of the line spoke.

"There's something else. . . . Yes. . . . We've got information that he's on the take." Pause. "No, I think it's good information. No . . . I don't know. I think it's worth looking into."

The next pause seemed to go on forever. Who was he talking to? The only answer Beamon could come up with was the man Chet had met a few days earlier. John the Banker.

"But it's a— Yes. I understand, but—"

The more desperate Gasta's tone became, the tighter the knot in Beamon's stomach got. He sucked hard on his cigarette but it wasn't helping anymore. He'd figured he had a fair chance of controlling this Mob moron, but he hadn't counted on the man on the other end of that phone. All he could do was sit there on the gaudy animal-print sofa and watch this thing spiral out of control.

"All I'm saying is that maybe we should check it out. He might . . . yes. I said yes. Okay." Now the desperation had turned to resignation. Beamon dared a quick look over at Chet. He'd heard the change in tone too. Gasta was being convinced to do something he didn't want to do. And that something was almost certainly killing an FBI agent and an unaffiliated criminal named Nicolai.

"I understand," Gasta said, and turned off the phone. He went straight to the bar to replace the drink he'd doused Chet with.

"Carlo . . ." Beamon tried again.

"I told you to shut up," he said without turning around. He downed a third of a glass of vodka and looked at Beamon's reflection in the mirror on the wall. "Do you know how much trouble you've caused me? I brought Chet into my organization because of his relationship with you. Now I'm fucked—I'm going to have to go underground."

The drink, the speech . . . He was clearly working himself up to something.

"Goddamnit! He was into all my finances, met the people I work with, knows everything I'm into!" Gasta was shouting now, the spit flying from his mouth visible in the powerful track lights. He walked around his men and grabbed Beamon by the front of his shirt. "Do you know what you've done?"

Beamon grabbed one of Gasta's fingers and bent it backward. The man winced in pain as Tony walked up and pressed the barrel of his pistol to Beamon's temple. Or was it Mikey?

"Don't push it, Carlo," Beamon said, ignoring the gun. "I didn't just come here without telling anyone." He released Gasta's finger and the mobster stumbled backward, fury clearly visible in his face.

"Carlo, take it easy," Chet said, speaking slowly and calmly. "I can make a whole lot of the stuff the FBI's got on you pretty much worthless. You need me. Let's work something out."

Gasta's expression went dead as he looked down into Chet's hopeful face. "It's already been worked out."

20

THE moment the helicopter's skids hit the ground, Christian Volkov threw open the heavy door and jumped out. He ran forward, crouched low against the sand tearing at his clothes and skin as the Russian gunship's engine went from a roar to a scream. By the time he'd made it twenty meters, the helicopter was already in the air and accelerating toward distant mountains.

Volkov had no reason to expect trouble, but he also no reason to be careless. A Russian attack helicopter in the vicinity would be a subtle but effective threat to people who understood the capabilities of such a machine.

He wiped the dirt from his eyes and looked around him as the dust slowly settled. The dead brown land undulated gently, occasionally broken by artificially geometric bursts of green, creating a bizarre patchwork that spread out in every direction before getting lost in the heat distortion.

When the air had completely cleared, he spotted a small group of men moving toward him on foot. There were five of them in all, some dressed in baggy white shirts and pants called *shalwar kameez*, others in more military dress. All were armed.

"*As-salaam alaikum,*" Volkov said when they got close enough to hear. Arabic wasn't his strongest language, but he could get by.

The man in front just nodded. Volkov had met him before: Wakil. His brown skin was deeply creviced from the sun and wind, making him seem older than he probably was. The long black beard covering the lower half of his face was devoid of gray, and his teeth were white and strong.

"Your journey was a pleasant one?" Wakil said, looking him in the eye and then gazing past him at the retreating helicopter.

"It was, thank you."

"Please follow."

Volkov was immediately surrounded by Wakil's four companions and marched toward a long, straight column of smoke about a kilometer away. Its source soon became discernible, as did the distinct odor of burning oil and flesh. Volkov's breath became instinctively shallower as they approached the shattered remains of a wood and stone structure.

"Congratulations on your great victory," he said as they passed a body hanging from the barrel of a burned-out tank. The men surrounding him smiled blankly.

Volkov wondered idly if he would end up in a similar condition before all this was over. He was still unable to tell with any certainty if Jonathan Drake was continuing his support of Mustafa Yasin's capitalist ambitions. It seemed more likely that the CIA had pulled back and that Drake and his boss, Alan Holsten, were now focused solely on protecting themselves.

Unfortunately, Volkov didn't have the same luxury. He had made commitments to his Asian associates, and based on his word, they had made significant investments of time and money. Despite his own considerable power, he was not inclined to disappoint them. The Asians expected their business partners to live up to their agreements and exacted extremely high penalties when they didn't.

To compensate for the possibility that the CIA was abandoning this operation, Volkov had no choice now but to step in and personally supply al-Qaeda with the instruments to continue their war. Everything had to be made to look seamless: Any disruption in the flow of weapons or intelligence would arouse Yasin's suspicion and possibly prompt him to cease his expansion and focus his resources on holding the ground he'd already gained.

"As you can see," Wakil said proudly, "we have complete control over this refinery. With Allah's help we were less than an hour taking it."

Volkov nodded respectfully as they passed through what was left of the facility's walls, wondering if Allah really got personally involved in the butchering of children to secure a heroin production factory. When the day came, who would God be more angry with: men like him who acted with no regard to His will, or men like these who used Him to justify their own brutality and ambition?

Volkov stopped near the center of the compound and looked around him at the shattered buildings and the silent, blackened corpses inhabiting them. Only half of what Wakil had said was true. While certainly they did control this particular piece of ground, it could no longer be called a refinery. Yasin, in his zeal, had managed to turn one of the region's most productive heroin processing plants into a useless shell. For Volkov, this was an extremely positive development. For al-Qaeda, it would likely prove to be a disaster.

The men surrounding him turned in unison and shuttled him out of the compound again, leaving the dead to lie in the powerful sun and the choking stench to float slowly to heaven.

The large tent had been hastily constructed just upwind of what was left of the refinery. Volkov stepped inside, followed closely by Wakil, who closed the flap behind them.

"Christian. It brings me great joy to see you."

The man sitting ramrod straight in the middle of the tent slowly became visible as Volkov's eyes adjusted to the semidarkness. He had always considered Mustafa Yasin to be one of the most impressive and regal-looking men he had ever met: his thin, dark face, the long, straight nose that flared like an ancient arrow head at its base, the eyes brimming with intelligence and religious fervor. He exuded single-minded determination even more powerfully than Osama bin Laden had.

Yasin motioned to one of the pillows strewn across the ground and Volkov sat, aware that Wakil had taken up a position behind him.

"What you have accomplished here is most impressive," Volkov said in Arabic. Yasin spoke a number of Western languages but considered them vulgar. "But I understand that it is only the last in a long string of great victories."

"Allah has been kind."

"And your recent activity in America . . ."

Yasin just nodded a serene acknowledgment.

Volkov chose his next words carefully. The man sitting across from him was by no means stupid and would expect some protest.

"While I admire your courage and see that you've made the Americans' blood run cold, your threat of an attack on them makes our business . . . more difficult. It was my understanding that you were going to complete your business here before continuing your war on the United States."

"The Americans are weak—even weaker than the Soviets. And, Allah willing, they'll be even easier to destroy."

Volkov sometimes wondered if Yasin really knew where he ended and God started. While it was this quality that was responsible for his inexhaustible charisma, it made him something of a precarious and unpredictable business partner. To Yasin, Volkov was just a convenience—a disposable device of little value beyond the ability to serve al-Qaeda's perverse version of Islam.

"I acknowledge America's considerable crimes against your people and against Islam," Volkov said. "But until we are able to solidify your position, I would ask you to pull back and consider the future."

"I will consider it."

Of course, he wouldn't. The people in this part of the world never considered anything but the present. Ironically, if Volkov set aside the likelihood of an irrational reaction from Jonathan Drake and the CIA for a moment, this was a perfect scenario for him. Terrorists made the Mexican narcotics distribution machine even more nervous than it already was.

"The Americans hated you before," Volkov said. "Now they fear you."

Another nodded acknowledgment from the cleric. This time accompanied by a thin smile. Of course, what Yasin had taken as a compliment was really an acknowledgment of his irrationality. Volkov hadn't completed his thought aloud.

And what the Americans fear, they destroy.

The heavy thud of a helicopter became audible in the distance and Volkov stood, motioning to Yasin. "Please. If you would join me."

The Arab considered the invitation for a moment and then rose gracefully. Wakil held the tent flap open and Volkov stood aside to let Yasin precede him.

The approaching helicopter was easily visible against the uniform blue of the sky. It was much larger than the one Volkov had arrived in— a massive cargo carrier. By the time it landed, Yasin's men were already running toward it, shouting excitedly and waving their rifles like the warrior tribesmen they were at heart.

When Volkov and Yasin arrived, the helicopter's massive side doors were wide open and crates were being passed quickly to the ground, where they were immediately pried open.

"The disruption in the flow of heroin caused by your operations here is beginning to make the Mexicans uncomfortable," Volkov said as Yasin examined the weapons lining the interior of the crates. "And their discomfort will become worse if the Americans discover that you smuggled the rocket launcher through Mexico."

The Arab was running a hand along the stock of a Russian machine gun, only half listening.

"We need to move faster," Volkov continued. "We need to consolidate your position here and stabilize the distribution system."

This, of course, was all true. But it was also a strategy that would, for a brief time, exacerbate the problems and fears of the narco-trafficking community. Any increased intensity in the fighting locally would help to further disrupt the flow of product through Mexico.

Two men excitedly worked the lid off another crate, and Yasin peered inside at the land mines it contained. "Are there rockets?"

Volkov stared at him, now absolutely certain that the man hadn't heard a word he'd said. His self-appointed role as God's sword hand was all-encompassing.

"There will be no more rockets. The dealer who sold the system to you is concerned that the Americans will use their resources to trace them back to him," Volkov said. That was actually an understatement. When Volkov had talked to the man who had supplied the weapon now plastered across every television screen in the world, he was already dismantling his entire operation and planning a permanent move to South America.

Yasin's disappointment was visible but understandably mild. His men still had a launcher in America, and according to Volkov's information, three rockets as well.

21

MARK Beamon managed to twist his body at the last second and he hit the dirt shoulder first, face second, instead of the other way around. He struggled to his knees, a thick film of dust caked to his sweat-soaked body. Despite the late hour, it was still over ninety degrees.

A kick from behind surprised him and he went down again, but this time he was unable to rise. A hard boot pressed down on the rope binding his hands behind his back, keeping him facedown in the dirt. He craned his neck and watched as a similarly bound Chet Michaels was dragged from the car and thrown to the desert floor a few feet in front of him.

The man hovering over Chet reared a leg back to kick him in the head but then seemed to changed his mind. His face was illuminated in a combination of starlight and the distant glow of L.A., but it wasn't enough to read his expression.

"What the hell are you doing?" Beamon finally managed to get out after spitting the dirt from his mouth. "Are you crazy?"

The boot planted against his bonds twisted skillfully and for a moment he thought his wrists were going to break.

"Shut the fuck up!"

"Mikey," Chet said, "he's right. This is nuts. I can help you. I'm inside the FBI. All I want is a little taste of the action. You can't blame me for that, can you?"

"Jesus, Chet, just shut your mouth," the man hovering over him whined. "Why the hell did you have to be a Fed?"

"It doesn't matter," Chet said. "We can work together. I can do a lot for you guys. Shit, ask Nicolai all the stuff I did for him. And I've moved up in the Bureau since then."

Mikey didn't answer, instead turning around and walking about twenty feet into the desert. He stood there, staring out into the darkness for almost a minute. Then he took a deep breath audible even to Beamon, yanked out his gun, and stalked back toward Chet.

Beamon looked into the young agent's face, searching for the accusation and suspicion that he knew would be there, but didn't find it. Having not heard the call from Laura, Chet would have no idea why Beamon had blown his cover and landed him out in the desert with an armed killer standing over him. Beamon searched harder and found something that cut him even deeper: a hint of trust. Chet believed in him. Believed that he had a plan. Believed that he would get them out of this.

"Mikey—stop!" Beamon said. The man already had his gun aimed at the back of Chet's head. "Killing an FBI agent is never profitable. Never! Right now, they let that dumb-ass you work for parade around like a rock star, but you kill one of theirs and the gloves are gonna come off. And when they show up at your door, Gasta isn't going to be there telling them he's the one who gave the order—he's just going to point his finger at you. There's no reason to do this."

When Mikey turned the gun on him, Beamon felt an inexplicable sense of relief.

"I thought Tony told you to shut the fuck up!"

"Mikey, calm down," Beamon said. "Get Carlo on the phone— I want to talk to him before this gets out of control."

The man stared at him and for what seemed like a long time, and Beamon thought he might have gotten through. But then he aimed his pistol at the back of Chet's head again. The young agent couldn't see the gun but obviously sensed what was happening and squeezed his eyes shut.

"Fuck!" Mikey screamed suddenly, stepping back a few feet. "I can't do it. This prick's been like a little brother to me." He looked up at Tony, who was busy keeping Beamon pinned to the ground. "You do it."

"Fuck that. I like him as much as you do."

Chet had opened his eyes and was staring directly at Beamon while the men argued. He didn't seem to hear when Mikey moved forward again. Beamon squirmed violently enough that Tony had to drop a knee into the small of his back to keep him on the ground.

This time Mikey found the resolve he needed. There was the crack of the gun, Chet's face being jerked down into the dirt, the warm spatter of blood and bone that Beamon felt shower his face. And then the silence after.

Beamon started coughing uncontrollably, struggling to keep from vomiting. A small stream of Chet's blood was cutting its way through the dust toward him, and he tried to pull away from it, but Tony's weight kept him immobile. Finally he just closed his eyes, blocking out the piece of dead flesh that had, a moment before, been a thirty-four-year-old kid.

"This is your fault, you fuck!" Mikey screamed. Beamon opened his eyes and looked straight into the barrel of the man's gun, willing him to pull the trigger, wanting to see that last flash and then nothing. Mikey was right. It was his fault.

"You fuck!" Mikey shouted again as he walked to the car and pulled a shovel from the truck. He came back alongside Beamon and raised it in the air. "Look what you made me do!"

The blow from the flat edge of the shovel wasn't as bad as he imagined it would be—less painful than the boot to the ribs that immediately followed. Strangely, he could hear the two men battering him, but after a few seconds he couldn't really feel it. He remembered Chet's wedding: Carrie had gotten pretty drunk that night, shirking her responsibility as designated driver and forcing them to take a cab home. He remembered meeting Chet's parents. They were a lot older than he'd expected and they worried about their son getting himself involved in such a dangerous profession. Beamon had assured them that being an FBI agent was far less dangerous than working in a liquor store, and they'd left feeling better.

The sound of the blows became less frequent as the two men began breathing harder and harder. Beamon hoped he wouldn't lose consciousness. For some reason he wanted to see death coming.

It was still dark when Beamon opened his eyes, and it took him a few moments to come to the obvious conclusion that he was still alive—that they hadn't killed him. Tony, Mikey, and their car were gone. There was no sound other than the ringing in his ears.

"No," he said quietly, and then slipped back into unconsciousness.

When his eyes opened again, he found himself staring up at the stars shimmering through the heat and smog.

Still not dead.

Except for his head and face, there didn't seem to be a square inch of his body that wasn't injured. It occurred to him that his hands had been freed, and he managed to push himself to his knees but couldn't muster the balance or strength to stand. He crawled twenty feet to a small tree and used it as a crutch, managing to pull himself to his feet with a badly bruised arm. He couldn't put much weight on his left foot, but he forced himself to hobble forward anyway. A coughing fit doubled him over, and his contracting muscles amplified the pain that seemed to come from almost everywhere. Oddly, though, the spit running from his mouth looked clear, suggesting no internal injuries and no cuts in or around his mouth.

He kept going, but he wasn't sure where. Tears came up in his eyes, making it even more difficult to see and forcing him to stop. He tried to recall the last time he had cried.

He hadn't been prepared for this. When Gasta's men had started beating him, he assumed the end result would be death—an infinitely uncomplicated state. But he wasn't dead, and despite a considerable amount of pain, he didn't think he was dying. He wanted to drop to his knees and search for Chet—for the grave Gasta's men had dug with the shovel they'd beat him with. But what would be the point? He'd seen it all. They'd killed him. He'd watched the life suddenly ripped from those clear, trusting eyes, and he hadn't done anything to stop it.

The anger started slowly but grew brighter and hotter as his mind cleared. He started down the barely visible dirt road toward the highway that he knew was only a few miles away, ignoring the excruciating pain every time he weighted his left foot. They'd regret leaving him alive. He'd make them regret it.

22

"A GODDAMN FBI agent! Jesus Christ! Do you have any idea how fucking dangerous this is?" Alan Holsten shouted. The shades to the conference room were down, covering the soundproof glass that looked out onto an empty corridor. It was Saturday and the CIA's Langley headquarters was nearly empty, but Holsten obviously wanted to make sure that he wasn't seen with Jonathan Drake.

"How could you let it go this far?"

Drake remained passive, sitting motionless at the table. His boss's tirade was just a release of fear and frustration: There had been no choice but to get rid of Chet Michaels, and Holsten had approved the sanction personally. However, it had been a barely audible verbal authorization given in the small office he kept in his home. There would be no paper trail to follow if it should ever come to that.

"I gave Gasta strict orders that no one was to know of my existence, Alan. I told him that if anyone ever found out, I would pull my support from him. There was no way to know he was going to ignore that order."

"I told you we shouldn't get involved with that son of a bitch—that we'd end up getting fucked."

That wasn't even vaguely true, of course, but it was undoubtedly how Holsten remembered it.

"We've talked about this before, Alan. Gasta is arrogant, has an inferiority complex, and is stupid. The first two made him easy to manipulate, but the last always had the potential to make him unpredictable. But we needed him. We needed someone who could take on a fair amount of Afghan heroin—to keep the money flowing to us and to al-Qaeda. It's not like we could just ask Congress for the financing—"

"You said you could control Gasta."

"I said that he was the most controllable person who met our criteria. Going with someone bigger, smarter, or more powerful would have been too dangerous. They wouldn't have needed our support as desperately and they would have asked questions."

Holsten laughed bitterly. "Jesus Christ, Jonathan. This whole thing is crumbling around you and you're giving me a dissertation on why you've made all the right decisions. Well, you haven't made the right decisions. And you failed to control an uneducated street punk from Brooklyn."

Drake ignored the insult. Alan Holsten seemed to think that the world moved along an even, predictable path—that all things could be modeled and statistically analyzed, just as his Harvard professors had taught him. But this was the real world.

The fact that Chet Michaels had seen him was, at first, a more or less minor issue. When a background check on the man revealed him to actually be an FBI agent, though, there had been little choice as to what action to take.

"I want to know what you're doing to make this all disappear, Jonathan. And I want to know now!"

Drake forced himself to remain calm. Holsten was the CIA's deputy director of operations and the only other man in the Agency who knew the full details of this operation. He had the potential to become extremely dangerous if he lost confidence.

"Alan, you have to understand that we didn't kill Michaels, Gasta's men did. Anyone investigating his disappearance would simply assume that his cover was somehow blown and that Gasta did away with him. The fact that Gasta is still on the street is a major embarrassment to the FBI, and they'll be happy to have something to pin on him."

"But is Gasta under control, Jonathan? He's scared now and that could make him even more unpredictable."

"I don't think so. He brought an undercover agent to meet me and he gave the order to have him killed. He recognizes that he's in a dangerous position and he's going to look to me for help and advice. From here on he'll do everything I say, exactly."

"You're sure about that," Holsten said, gripping the back of the chair he was standing in front of tightly enough to turn his knuckles white.

Drake nodded. "He has no real choice. I pulled the money we originally wired him for this drug buy and I've made it clear that there will be no more coming."

"What about the FBI? They're going to come after Gasta when they find out that their man's disappeared."

"But that works perfectly for us, Alan. Gasta's already gone into hiding. He won't be able to draw money from his normal operations, and we've cut him off. With no other source of cash, he has no choice but to go after the heroin. "

"And you're confident that the FBI won't be able to find him?"

"Absolutely. I have people in Washington who are keeping me up-to-date on the L.A. office's investigation into Gasta as well as Laura Vilechi's investigation into the rocket launcher. I'll always be one step ahead of them. But as far as Gasta is concerned, it doesn't really matter: He'll be dead before the FBI even realizes their man is gone, and that will be the end of it. Gasta will be posthumously blamed and there will be no reason to look any further."

Holsten didn't speak for a long time, and Drake could feel the perspiration starting at his hairline.

"You're very smooth, Jonathan. Very convincing. But I sometimes wonder what's really going on in your head."

"If you don't think I've told you the truth, I suggest you check it out yourself."

"Oh, I think it's the truth. But I think it's been attractively packaged. You've allowed al-Qaeda to smuggle a sizable weapon into the U.S. and hold the American people hostage. We know from our intelligence that they have three operable rockets, but you have no idea where they are. And now the FBI agent. . . . You're very good at telling me how this all works for us, but I'm not convinced. Chet Michaels met with a drug supplier from Afghanistan, and Laura Vilechi knows from us that the Afghans are fighting in the Golden Crescent. The drug connection isn't going to be something they miss forever."

"Like I said, Alan, I've got ears high up in the FBI, and I'm hearing nothing about Gasta in relation to the terrorism investigation. He's being handled out of the L.A. office as nothing more than another organized criminal."

"When is Gasta meeting with the Afghans again?"

"A week."

"And you guarantee that no one will walk away from that meeting?"

Guarantees were dangerous, but there was little choice at this point. "No one will. Gasta will attack them based on my orders, and anyone who survives that firefight will be taken care of by our people. It will just look like a drug buy gone wrong."

"Gasta is top priority," Holsten said, stating the obvious, as he often did when he was frightened. "If we can't get the Afghans, so be it. Let them drive away. Recovering the launcher, whatever al-Qaeda is or is not accomplishing in the drug trade—that's all second priority now. We have to focus on the CIA's exposure."

"It's all being taken care of, Alan. We're in the process of cutting off contact with al-Qaeda and destroying all evidence of our involvement. But we have to do it carefully. We don't want to tip Volkov off that we're shutting this operation down. The illusion of continued business with him is critical to our being able to get close enough to kill him."

Holsten's expression darkened. "It hasn't done much good so far, though, has it, Jonathan? Does he know we were behind the attack on his house in the Seychelles?"

"We would certainly be one entry on a very long list. All of his enemies would know that he would have to send someone to reassert his power over Laos. In any event, with Pascal dead, he's weakened."

Jonathan knew that this was true but wondered now if killing Pascal would have the devastating effect he had hoped for. The few bank accounts they knew about were already gone, and large fires had sprung up in areas where the CIA suspected Volkov had houses. The speed and efficiency with which he had cut himself off from everything he had built was startling, though this was something better left unsaid at this point.

"You're keeping in touch with Volkov," Holsten said. "Keeping him reassured?"

"Of course."

"We have to get to him, Jonathan. Everything the FBI uncovers has to lead to a dead end. Nothing can go through to us."

"I understand. But Gasta and his people have to be our first priority. Volkov will be difficult for the FBI to reach, even if they discover his existence. Based on my information, the investigation into the launcher is pretty much stalled now. They have no physical evidence to work with and aren't getting much international cooperation."

Holsten nodded slowly, and for a moment Jonathan thought the discussion was over.

"What about Mark Beamon?"

"I had the information regarding his inspection report leaked. It was perfect for us: heavily critical of his ASACs, blaming them for his own failings as a manager. The implication is that he was going to let his ASACs go down in his place. He's got his hands full with them right now. That, combined with the fact that he and Laura Vilechi's boss can't even be in the same room together, should keep him out."

23

MARK Beamon opened his eyes to a woman dressed in white, holding his wrist and looking at her watch. He tried to pull away, but she was stronger and more determined than she looked.

"Stop being such a baby," she said. "You're going to be fine. You have quite a few cuts and bruises, and a sprained ankle, but no broken bones. Do you understand? You're going to be fine."

Apparently satisfied with his pulse rate, she dropped his arm unceremoniously and held up something that looked like a business card. "The police officer that brought you here told me to give you this. When you're feeling up to it, he'd like to talk to you." She placed the card on the table next to his bed and disappeared through a door without another word.

His head was beginning to clear and he managed to push himself into a sitting position and look around him at the private hospital room. Satisfied that he was alone, he fell back onto the mattress. His memory of the night before was hazy at first, but once the images started to come, he couldn't make them stop: his meeting with Gasta, Chet's death out in the desert, Mikey and Tony beating the shit out of him, finally finding the highway and being picked up by a disinterested cop.

Chet.

Beamon felt the tears starting again, but he forced them back with thoughts of a drunk, swaggering Carlo Gasta. What had happened? How had Chet's cover been blown? The answer was obvious. The mysterious man behind Gasta had taken the time to do a little digging after his accidental meeting with Chet and had somehow come up with his real identity. It was him who Gasta had called last night. And it was him who had given the order.

Beamon threw the covers off and slid carefully from the bed. The pain when his left foot touched the ground was excruciating, but he stood anyway, putting his full weight on it in a pointless act of defiance. Gritting his teeth and refusing to favor his injury, he walked stiffly to the bathroom and looked in the mirror.

An examination, made easier by the less-than-modest hospital gown, suggested that the nurse was right. Most of the skin on his arms, legs, and torso was an uneven yellow/brown, broken by the occasional laceration. Only a few of the cuts had been bad enough to warrant stitches.

His face was another story entirely. Other than a few little scratches he'd gotten when Tony had thrown him to the ground, there wasn't a mark on it. He ran a hand along his dirt- and sweat-matted beard, looking for hidden swelling or abrasions. Nothing.

A brief search of the room turned up his glasses but not his clothes or what was left of the cell phone he'd had in his pocket. Ignoring a crutch propped against the wall, he pushed through the door and started down the hall, watching everyone he passed carefully with semicontrolled paranoia. In the end, though, no one seemed to be particularly interested in a middle-aged man hobbling by with his ass hanging out.

He finally found a pay phone near the elevator and dialed Laura Vilechi's cell number.

"Yeah, hello."

"It's Mark."

"Mark! Jesus, we've been going nuts trying to find you. Are you all right? What happened? Where's Chet? Was his cover blown?"

Beamon looked around him and confirmed that there was no one within earshot. "Look, I've only got a second, okay. Listen carefully. I'm at the San Bernardino County Hospital. Call Claude Heiss—I think he's still working out of the L.A. office. He grew up in Quebec. Tell him to come here and meet me. He's Nicolai's bodyguard and doesn't speak much English, mostly French. You got that?"

"Mark, what's going on?"

A couple of people stopped a few feet away to wait for the elevator.

"We'll talk later. Tell him I need him now. And, Laura, no one else comes within ten miles of this hospital—do you understand?"

"I'll take care of it."

"And . . . and could you call Carrie and tell her I'm okay but that I won't be able to talk to her for a little while?"

"Sure, Mark. But what—"

He hung up the phone and made his way back to his room, closing the door firmly behind him and pulling the drapes shut against the possibility of a sniper firing from the building next door. It was hard not to dwell on the fact that he was weak, injured, and completely unarmed. Glancing at the clock, he wondered how long it would take Claude to get there. Carlo Gasta was probably just getting over his hangover and would be wondering if leaving Nicolai alive had been such a good idea.

The next hour and a half turned out to be one of the longest he'd ever lived through. He'd tried watching television, but every channel was still harping on the recent terrorist threat against hospitals—not exactly what he needed at this point. He'd turned it off, but without anything else to occupy his time, he'd started second-guessing himself and creating elaborate scenarios that could have saved Chet. He tried to focus on his hatred for Carlo Gasta and the mysterious man behind him, but it didn't work. All he could think about was how young Chet had been— the years that had been taken away from him.

When the door to his room was suddenly thrown open, Beamon jumped off the bed, ready to make whatever pathetic effort at defending himself he could manage. He'd been ready to die last night, but now he was ready to live. He was going to find the son of a bitch who had ordered Chet's death. And, if possible, he was going to put a bullet in him.

"Nicolai," the man said through a thick French accent, closing the door behind him.

Beamon fell back onto the bed, the adrenaline-provided illusion of strength dissipating quickly. "Claude. Jesus Christ."

Beamon hadn't seen Heiss in years, but he was still perfect for the role. Six feet tall, broad shouldered, and weathered from a lifelong obsession with sailing.

Beamon motioned him over and leaned into his ear. "Laura gave you some background?"

"A little," Heiss whispered back.

"Okay. You're high-class muscle. You don't speak much English. Are you armed?" He nodded again. "Good. It's possible that Carlo Gasta is going to come after me, but I don't know. We just need to play it cool."

"Do you think someone is listening?" Claude whispered.

"Not really, but paranoia's working for me so far."

Claude nodded and retreated to a corner by the door, his hand inside his suit jacket.

He looked the part as much as anyone could, and he was a solid agent. The drawback was that, as far as Beamon knew, he'd never pulled his gun in the line of duty. Hopefully the image would be enough.

24

THE television bolted to the wall across from his bed glowed with a recap of the week's events as they related to the "The New Threat." Beamon recognized the strategically timed and somewhat vague releases from the FBI as an indication that Laura's investigation was either crawling or completely stalled. To the experienced eye, the official reports were being shampooed—given more body and volume than they actually had.

Not that the media seemed to notice. They were more than able to fill their dance cards with endless interviews of terrified victims, demonstrations of the destructive power of various rocket systems, endless replays of called-in terrorist threats, details on possible biological and chemical payloads, far-fetched speculation as to when and where death would come streaking across the sky.

Interestingly, the government wasn't doing much yet to rein in the panic. Support for struggling businesses and laid-off workers was in the offing, but pleas for America to go about its business were few and far between. He assumed that was Laura's doing. It seemed likely that as long as the panic was running high, the terrorists wouldn't waste their precious ammunition.

He wondered how she was holding up. The recriminations hadn't started yet, but his infallible instinct for such things suggested that they would start within the week. The television audience would soon become numb to the endless hours of guesses, and when they started to tune out, the media would have to find a new angle to bring them back.

How would Laura handle her sudden transformation from brilliant, hardworking civil servant to the woman who was going to allow al-Qaeda to start blowing up suburban kindergartens?

"Shit," Beamon said under his breath.

Claude looked over at him and Beamon just waved a hand dismissively, sinking deeper into the pillows behind him. The constant nausea that he'd been learning to live with over the last year was getting worse. It seemed to be spreading to his mind, keeping him trapped in this bed and interfering with his ability for logical thought.

Leaving him alive and killing Chet was just another in a long list of cruel tricks the gods had played on him. If one of those fat fucks had put a bullet in him instead, who would have really cared? His ASACs would certainly be happy to be rid of him. Carrie would get a chance to find herself a nice, stable man to be with. Chet, though . . . There were so many people who loved him. There was so much he'd planned to do.

Beamon was staring at the wall, lost in himself, when Claude suddenly jumped to his feet and went for his gun. Beamon knew he should be scared, or at least startled, but for some reason he felt neither of those things. He actually had difficulty even generating enough curiosity to roll his head toward the door. When he finally did, he found himself looking at Carlo Gasta, flanked by the two men who had killed Chet and beat the hell out of him. Tony and Mikey stayed by the door, trying not to shrink under Claude's withering stare, as their boss centered himself at the foot of Beamon's bed.

The hate and rage that suddenly gripped Beamon quickly eclipsed the despair and self-pity he been sinking into. It felt good.

"Nicolai," Gasta said simply.

He didn't look much better than Beamon did. There were dark circles beneath his eyes, and his skin actually looked gray under the strong lights. The familiar stink of a near-terminal hangover was quickly filling the room.

Beamon remained silent; his throat felt so constricted, he wasn't sure he could speak even if he wanted to. He tried to force Chet from his mind but failed miserably. His second method worked better. He replaced himself with Nicolai. He'd let Mark Beamon have his wish and be dead for a while.

Gasta motioned toward Claude. "That's not your doctor."

"I told you I wasn't traveling alone," Beamon said, surprised by the coldness of his—Nicolai's—voice. Applied schizophrenia.

Gasta glanced around the small room, looking increasingly nervous. He was undoubtedly wondering how many of Nicolai's other "associates" were lurking just out of sight.

"Can we talk?"

Beamon thought about it for a moment. *"Claude. Cinq minutes, s'il vous plaît."*

He'd practiced that and a few other simple phrases until they rolled from his tongue effortlessly. Nicolai, he'd decided, was multilingual.

Heiss strode across the floor with impressive confidence that Beamon knew he didn't feel and paused to allow Gasta's men to precede him into the hall.

"What kind of work does Claude do?" Gasta said after the door clicked shut.

"He does the kind of work you'd think he would."

Gasta nodded, and for some reason the meekness of the motion enraged Beamon. The fact that this small-time, badly dressed little pissant could cause the death of someone like Chet . . .

He forced his anger back again by remembering who he was. Nicolai didn't care about Chet Michaels. "What do you want, Carlo?"

"I told you. I want to talk. To make peace."

Chet's assessment had been right, Beamon realized. Gasta had brought Nicolai in on his own. His boss, whoever that was, didn't know and wouldn't be there to protect him from Nicolai's wrath. Gasta was scared. And why not? Nicolai was a fabrication to be feared.

"You can start by telling me that the hundred thousand you owe me is in my account."

When he didn't answer, Beamon shook his head. "Carlo . . . what am I going to do with you?"

Gasta just stood there, frozen.

"You ordered the death of an FBI informant who I spent a great deal of money cultivating," Beamon said. "And then, to make it worse, you had your men beat the hell out of me. Those were fairly grave errors on your part."

"I told Mikey and Tony not to touch you," Gasta said hesitantly. "They liked Chet. . . . They didn't listen to me. . . ."

Beamon hadn't thought it possible, but his hatred for his worthless piece of shit notched a little higher. Gasta had gotten drunk and lost control, giving an order that he shouldn't have. And now he was blaming his own bad judgment on two men who had been with his family since before he was born. For all he knew, he had just condemned them to death.

"They could have killed you, but they didn't," he said hopefully.

"And that's the only reason you're still alive, Carlo. If I'd been two more hours finding a phone, Claude and his men would have been paying you a visit."

Gasta finally managed to muster the courage to make a pathetic effort to look defiant, but didn't speak.

"I'll tell you, Carlo. I can't decide whether it's worth the trouble to kill you or not."

"I had orders," Gasta said, once again trying to deflect blame from himself. "I didn't want to kill Chet—you heard me on the phone. It wasn't my decision. You have to understand that Chet left me exposed and exposed people I worked with. They don't tolerate things like that."

"Then maybe I should be talking to them?"

"Don't think that's possible."

Beamon stared at him for a long time, trying to decide what Nicolai would do in this situation. How much energy and time would he expend on this little man? How much of this would he take personally?

"I had over a million dollars invested in Chet, and now that investment's gone," Beamon said finally. "And then, of course, there's my pain and suffering, which I expect to be compensated for. Tell your boss I expect two million dollars in my account by noon tomorrow, New York time."

Gasta stared at the floor and then gave the answer that Beamon had counted on. "He isn't going to do that."

"Then I guess you owe me the money."

"I don't have it."

Beamon nodded slowly. "I don't want you to take this personally, Carlo, but I have a reputation that I have to protect to maintain my credibility. People don't cross me and survive. I'm sorry."

Beamon surprised himself again by how easy it had been to tell the man in front of him that he was as good as dead. He wondered if he should be worried about how well Nicolai's persona was beginning to fit him.

Gasta took a step backward but didn't otherwise seem to know how to react to the offhand statement. He finally managed to process what it meant, and the stench of his hangover intensified noticeably as he started to sweat.

"It's because of Chet—and you—that I don't have the money. I don't know what he told the Feds—I've had to go underground. I'm completely cut off from my businesses and most of my people."

Beamon didn't answer. Gasta's problems seemed irrelevant to the situation at hand. While politics and law enforcement could be insufferably complex, crime was refreshingly simple: money or death.

"I can get it," Gasta blurted. "But not by tomorrow."

"I'm not really in the mood to negotiate, Carlo."

"The drug shipment Chet told you about—it's real and it's happening in a few days. When I get it, I'll sell the drugs and you'll have your money."

Beamon nodded slowly but didn't speak. He had suspected that this was the way things would go. Gasta's men hadn't done any lasting damage to him—except for the ankle, which was probably an accident. And even more telling was the fact that they hadn't so much as touched his face, leaving no marks that might draw attention.

The fact was, Gasta still needed him. He needed cash and needed to redeem himself in the eyes of his boss. That meant this heroin heist had to go off without any problems.

"When?" Beamon said.

"Soon. This week," he said hopefully.

"Fine. I'll extend your deadline. But if I don't have my money within a few weeks, I'm sending Claude back for you."

Altough Beamon's tone was obviously a dismissal, Gasta just stood there, staring at the floor.

"I need your help," he admitted finally.

"Let me get this straight: You want me to get my own money?" Beamon said, laughing. "I didn't want to be involved last night, and believe me, my opinion of you hasn't changed." He paused and affected a thoughtful expression. "But then, you probably can't pull it off alone, can you?"

Gasta wouldn't meet his gaze.

Beamon remained silent for a long time, as though he were considering the situation, which actually was progressing exactly as he had hoped.

"Okay, Carlo. My fee would be one million plus the two million you owe me."

Beamon assumed that the number would be satisfactory to Gasta, since his alternative was death.

"And then we'd be even?"

"And then we'd be even."

Of course that wasn't true. He would use Gasta to find the man who had ordered Chet's death and then he'd crucify them both.

"Okay," Gasta said finally.

"Okay, what?"

"We have a deal. Three million. When can we talk? There isn't much time."

25

DESPITE four inches of rock-hard snow beneath his feet, it was almost unbearably hot. Over the past three hours Christian Volkov had stripped off layer after layer of clothing until he was left in only a pair of work boots, jeans, and a T-shirt.

He hefted an armload of firewood onto the neat stack that he had been constructing for the better part of the morning. There was something about physical labor outdoors that always helped him step back and think.

"Christian?"

Volkov turned and leaned against the woodpile. Joseph was hopelessly out of place here: His dark, worried face and slight build seemed to get swallowed up by the endless landscape of Kazakhstan that spread out around them.

"The young FBI agent is dead."

"We have confirmation of that?"

"Yes. We're certain."

The first of many deaths, Volkov guessed. Jonathan Drake was beginning the process of severing connections between al-Qaeda and the CIA. It was to be expected, of course, and Drake had been careful to warn him that these kinds of actions would be forthcoming. But an FBI agent . . .

"And what have we discovered about this man Nicolai?" Volkov said.

"Our man inside Gasta's organization says he's still alive and in hospital. It was apparently Nicolai's contention that he was aware Chet Michaels was an FBI agent and that Michaels was on his payroll."

A hundred meters behind Joseph, Volkov saw another figure leave his new house and begin running gracefully toward them through the snow.

"Do we have any indication that Drake is behind Nicolai's involvement?"

"No. The contrary seems to be true. Every indication is that he came to Gasta through Chet Michaels. It's possible that the CIA isn't even aware of Nicolai's existence. I've put everything we've been able to find so far on him in your computer. It isn't much."

As the figure grew nearer, its youthful, feminine figure and long, dark hair became visible. When Elizabeth stopped next to Joseph, she was breathing hard. Despite that, she managed to silently mouth "General Yung" and hold out a satellite phone.

Volkov looked at it but didn't immediately reach for it. The fact that the general hadn't returned any of his calls since the disappearance of Pascal wasn't as telling as he wished it was. The Asians disliked confrontation and the delivery of bad news. They'd rather just kill you.

He finally took the phone and pressed it to his ear.

"*Bonjour, Général. Comment allez-vous?*"

Volkov heard a voice on the line translate his words into Lao, although he knew Yung to speak excellent French. The general was obviously nervous and thought he might need the extra time to consider his words more carefully.

Volkov heard him reply and the translator spoke moment later. "I am well and hope that you are the same, Mr. Volkov. Please accept my apologies for not calling sooner, but I had no information to impart about your man, Pascal. You understand that he insisted on going out into the countryside against my recommendation. While it is largely under my control, there is rebel activity in the area. We regret that we still cannot locate him but are making every effort to do so."

Volkov nodded into the phone. Pascal was dead, of that he had little doubt. Whether or not General Yung was involved in his murder was another matter. At least for the moment it was an unanswerable question and therefore irrelevant. What was relevant, though, was that without Yung's cooperation, Volkov's entire plan was in jeopardy. He had no choice but to continue to try to create an alliance between the new Laotian regime and his organization.

"I assure you," the translator continued, "I am most anxious to continue the promising dialog begun with your man regarding the future of our business relationship."

Volkov tossed another piece of wood on the pile. "As am I, General. As am I."

26

THEY were late.

It was something Beamon hadn't counted on when he'd agreed to the meeting place. He tried to roll the window up tighter, but the mechanism just hummed uselessly. The dusty scent of the California desert was seeping into the cracks of the car, overpowering the filtered air blasting from the air conditioner, trying to make him remember Chet. He lit another cigarette with a shaking hand and felt himself calming down a little as the smoke filled the car.

Twisting around in his seat, he squinted against the powerful afternoon sun and surveyed the empty desert behind him. Heiss had trailed him at a distance of about a mile to make sure he wasn't followed—his last duty on this fucked-up operation. The memory of Claude would be enough to keep Gasta in line.

The quiet purr of an engine began to separate itself from the light desert breeze, and Beamon stepped from the car with the assistance of a cane he'd purchased after checking himself out of the hospital. The approaching vehicle appeared over a rise, and Beamon raised a hand to block the glint off its windshield as it rolled to a stop in front of him. He quickly jumped into the backseat.

"Mark! What the hell's going on?" Concern and exhaustion were equally visible in Laura's face as she turned around in the passenger seat to face him. Scott Reynolds, Chet's boss—former boss—just watched him in the rearview mirror.

"What's with the cane, Mark? Are you all right? Where's Chet?"

"Chet's dead."

"What?" Reynolds said. "What did you say?"

"He's dead. Gasta had him killed."

The silence that descended on the small car lasted a long time. The wind was starting to pick up, and all Beamon could hear above the persistent ringing in his ears was the dust being driven against the window.

"What happened, Mark?" Laura said, not bothering to protest when he lit another cigarette.

"The informant you found dead must have given him up," Beamon said, concentrating on keeping his voice steady. "They . . . they took us out into the desert, shot him, and then kicked the shit out of me."

Scott Reynolds sagged forward as Beamon spoke, resting his forehead against the steering wheel.

For a moment Laura didn't seem to know what to do or say—an unusual position for her. "Mark, I want you to tell us exactly what happened."

Beamon took a deep drag on the cigarette and let the smoke roll from his mouth as he spoke. "Gasta was drunk when I got there . . . arrogant, belligerent. The way he was acting seemed kind of off, but I couldn't put my finger on what was wrong. The more we talked, the more I thought he knew something that I didn't—that he was building up to something. Then you called and it all made sense. . . ."

Reynolds's head came up from the wheel for a moment. "What happened? What did you do?"

"I tried to maintain my credibility. I said Chet was an FBI agent before Gasta could come out with it. I told him that Chet was on my payroll." Beamon had to stop talking for a moment when his throat constricted, but tried to play it off with another drag on his cigarette. "I thought I could convinced Gasta that Chet was dirty and he could just cough up a little money and make all his problems go away."

"But it didn't work . . ." Laura prompted.

"It was going fine until Gasta made a phone call. He was scared and was looking for an excuse not to kill a Federal agent. Whoever he talked to changed his mind."

"Shit," Reynolds said quietly.

Laura pulled her feet up on the seat and leaned back against the dash. No one seemed to know what else to say. A young FBI agent was dead, and despite more than sixty years of law enforcement experience among them, no one was sure what to do.

"Do you . . . do you have any idea who he called, Mark?"

Beamon shrugged, sending a shooting pain through his neck. "I figure the obvious answer is the right one. We know that Gasta took Chet to meet that guy John and that he wasn't very happy about the meeting. It seems to follow that the guy would check Chet out. Somehow—probably through your dead informant—his cover got blown. It seems pretty likely that this same guy was on the other end of the phone, ordering him dead."

Reynolds didn't lift his head from the wheel when he spoke this time. "We know that Gasta has heavy support from somewhere—somebody big backing him financially and helping him force his way into the heroin trade. But we've never been able to figure out who it is. Gasta's just a dumb-ass wise guy who wants to be a movie star. I'd bet just about anything that he wouldn't have the balls to kill an FBI agent on his own."

Another long silence.

"Mark," Reynolds said, looking back at him for the first time. "Where . . . where is he?"

"Out in the desert. They buried him."

"Jesus. . . . We can't just leave him out there."

Something in those words sent a surge of adrenaline through Beamon. For a moment it was as if he were outside his body, watching himself lose his carefully constructed illusion of control and powerless to do anything about it. He reached out and grabbed Reynolds by the shirt, pulling him partway over the seat.

"You think I want to leave him out there rotting in the fucking desert?" Beamon screamed. "Is that what you think?"

Laura came to life and jammed her arms between them, pulling them apart with surprising force. "Mark! Calm down! That isn't what Scott meant and you know it."

"Hey, fuck you," Reynolds said, making a grab for Beamon that Laura managed to block. "Chet worked for me, not you. I liked the kid too. And I'm the sorry son of a bitch who's going to have to go to his house and look his wife in the face and tell her he's dead, you sanctimonious prick!"

"Shut up, both of you!" Laura shouted. "Look . . . Chet's dead. There's nothing we can do about that. Let's try to concentrate on things we can do something about."

"Like what?" Reynolds said.

"Like getting the people responsible. Like getting the rocket launcher. Chet's dead, but the people al-Qaeda could kill with that thing aren't yet. We can still save them."

"So what are we talking about?" Beamon said, managing to get at least partial control over himself.

"As I see it, we've got enough to put Carlo Gasta on death row. The question is, do we want to? If we take down Gasta now, the chance of us getting the man behind him goes to about zero: He'll run far and fast. And so will the Afghans. I mean, the connection here is thin, but . . ." She seemed to weaken as she spoke. "But it's as good as anything I've got."

Beamon leaned back in the seat and looked out the window, trying to remove himself from the conversation. He already knew what he was going to do.

"What you're saying," Reynolds said, "is that you want to just leave Gasta on the street."

"Look, Scott, I know how you both felt about Chet. I'm just thinking out loud, okay?" She looked at Beamon through the smoke hanging in the air. "Mark, where do you stand? If we were to leave you in, is there any chance you could get to the guy behind Gasta? Or better yet, the Afghans?"

"Gasta's painted himself into a corner," Beamon said. "He thinks that Nicolai is seriously considering putting a bullet in the back of his head."

"Do you think you can convince him to trust you?"

"I already did."

"What do you mean?"

"He came to visit me in my hospital room."

"Your hospital room!" Reynolds cut in. "What are you talking about?"

"Haven't you wondered why he didn't kill me too? He still has to pull off this heroin heist. He's got to regain face with his boss and he is desperate for the money. The problem is, he isn't sure he can do it alone."

"He still needs Nicolai . . ." Laura said.

Beamon nodded. "I told him he owes me three million dollars and I'd have him killed if he didn't pay up. The heroin heist is the only way he can get the money, and I agreed to consult on the job to make sure he gets it."

Laura was nodding silently, calculating their position, but Reynolds was looking increasingly worried.

"This is nuts," he said. "First of all, we're on pretty thin ice legally: We have an FBI agent threatening someone with their life if they don't break the law. Second, we seem to be coming up against a well-informed and totally unidentifiable crime lord with a lot of money and apparently no problem with killing federal agents."

"Life's full of risks," Beamon said.

"Look, all I'm saying is that we need to talk to the Director."

"I agree," Laura said. "But when we do, what are we going to recommend?"

They all just looked at one another for a moment. Beamon spoke first. "I intend to get the son of a bitch who ordered Chet dead. I'd prefer to do it with the FBI, but I'll do it alone if I have to. And if I can find some terrorists and a rocket launcher in the process, more's the better."

"Mark . . . this isn't your fault—you understand that, right? Chet's cover got blown and you did everything you could to try to save him. Under those conditions there aren't many people who could have thought coherently enough to come up with the story that Chet was on the take. I don't think I would have. . . ."

"Me neither," Reynolds admitted, not willing to meet Beamon's eye. "It was a smart play. But smart plays aren't always enough."

"What I want to know is," Laura continued, "if we go forward with this, can you stay objective?"

Beamon thought about that for a moment. "I don't know."

A long breath escaped her and she leaned back on the dash again. "Okay. I think we're clear on Mark's position. And I agree with him, but not for the same reasons. Getting hold of the man behind Chet's death isn't going to bring him back. But if we have a chance, no matter how remote, of getting a lead that will take us to that launcher, we have to take it."

"This just gets worse and worse," Reynolds said. "Mark just admitted that he doesn't know if he can stay objective—"

"What's your vote?" Laura said.

"Shit. . . . If we do this, I'm going to have to call Chet's wife and lie to her—tell her that he's okay. Shit. . . ."

"What's your vote, Scott?"

"Okay. . . . Yes. I'm with you."

27

THE house was a serious dump, a tiny cube covered in peeling paint and topped with a bowed roof. It looked appropriately anonymous in this low-income neighborhood on the outskirts of L.A. but probably didn't fit into the lifestyle Carlo Gasta had grown accustomed to.

Beamon finally had to admit to himself that renting the conspicuous gray Lexus had been a mistake and considered just driving by. There just wasn't time, though: Trust had to be quickly conjured from thin air, and one thing that promoted trust was punctuality. He slowed the car to avoid a child on a rusted bicycle pedaling across the street and then turned into the dirt driveway.

Taking long, slow breaths of the cool air inside the car, he shut out the memory of Chet, the rocket launcher—everything. He was Nicolai, and Nicolai cared about only one thing: money.

Aware that someone was probably watching, he stepped out of the car and hobbled toward the front door, which opened before he could knock. The man on the other side, standing so he couldn't be seen from the street, looked nervous. Actually, he looked scared.

Beamon crossed the threshold and reached into his coat pocket, causing Mikey to freeze. He looked relieved when Beamon's hand reappeared with only a set of keys. "Get someone to move my car. It'll attract attention."

Mikey nodded and Beamon continued through a narrow hallway, feeling the sweat starting to roll down his back in the stifling heat. The room he came to was a little cooler and a lot darker, the windows having been covered with old towels held in place with nails. The inevitable odor of garlic filled the air.

"Nicolai. Right on time."

As near as he could tell from Gasta's steady voice and smooth stride, he was stone sober.

"Carlo."

"Can I get you something cold to drink? We've got iced tea." He pronounced each word a little too carefully. Fear.

"Sure."

Gasta motioned to Tony, who was sitting at the vinyl-topped kitchen table, but the gesture turned out to be a dismissal and not an order. Gasta poured the tea himself as Tony disappeared into the hall.

"You doing all right? Anything you need that I can get you? Anything at all?"

Beamon shook his head and sat down at the table, ignoring the map spread across it.

"Thank you for coming," Gasta said, setting the glass in front of Beamon. "I think you'll be glad you did."

"I wonder."

"You're still going to help me out, right? Sure you are: You wouldn't be here otherwise. . . ."

"The police are interested in me," Beamon said. "I told them I got mugged, but it was a tough sell with a wallet full of money."

Gasta scrunched up his face. "You'll never hear from them again— trust me. If you don't make a stink, they'll be just as happy to go back to the doughnut shop and forget all about it."

He was almost certainly right. The questions the cop who had brought him to the hospital asked led Beamon to believe this kind of thing wasn't all that uncommon. As far as local law enforcement was concerned, he was just another guy from out of town who had messed with the wrong hooker or gotten a little too obnoxious in a strip club.

"We were talking about ripping off some Afghan heroin dealers . . ." Beamon prompted. Nicolai wasn't one for small talk.

"Yeah."

"I seem to remember not being able to figure out why you would want to do something so stupid."

"After the thing with Chet, I'm going to have to disappear for a while. That's going to cost money and I'm cut off from my businesses. . . ."

"Oh, I understand why you're going to do it now. But why were you going to do it last week?"

Gasta didn't answer immediately. He was obviously being a little more careful in choosing his words than he normally was. "I have information that they're shopping for other buyers—that after this deal they're going to cut me out. I want to teach them some respect."

"By killing them and taking their product?"

"It makes a point."

Beamon took a sip of the cold tea, staring over the glass at Gasta. He couldn't remember ever wanting someone dead so badly. "What point is that, Carlo?"

"If they try to fuck me, they end up dead. If they deal straight with me, they make a lot of money. That's the kind of thing these people understand. They understand strength. You have to make them respect you."

Beamon shrugged. "I guess it doesn't matter. As long as I get my money."

"You'll get it. I promise."

Beamon tapped the map on the table. "I take it you have a plan?"

Gasta nodded and pointed to a barren section of desert outside L.A. "This is where we're meeting—where they want to make the exchange. It's a place with big rock walls on three sides—"

"A natural amphitheater."

"Yeah—a natural amphitheater. Anyway, you turn off the highway here and drive along a shitty dirt road that's not on the map to get to it."

"Uh-huh."

"So we get there early and then, when they show up, we take 'em out."

Beamon stared at him, waiting for the rest. After about thirty seconds Gasta became uncomfortable and started talking again.

"So then we, uh, drive their van out and take it to our warehouse."

Beamon remained silent.

"Then, you know, we break it up and cut it, and then we can distribute it."

The widely held opinion that this man was a complete idiot was starting to look overly charitable.

"That's it?"

Gasta shrugged. "What do you mean? Yeah, that's it. What do you think?"

Beamon laughed and drained the rest of his tea. He considered it a personal insult that the FBI had never been able to nail this asshole.

"What about the cops? I mean, you start shooting a mile from the highway and somebody with a cell phone might just make a call."

"It's kind of a rural highway—not all that busy. And it'll be late at ni—"

"What if the Afghans have a chase vehicle—a bunch of guys with machine guns hanging back, just in case?"

"Well, I—"

"What if they have guys set up in the rocks with rifles? What if one of those fat-asses you have working for you gets in front of a bullet? Then you've got a dead body to deal with that's going to leave blood at the scene that can be traced back to the bleeder."

"It was just an idea," Gasta said angrily. "That's why I asked you here. I thought you could help me tweak it. You know, polish it. So, you gonna help me or not?"

"Well, if I don't, I'm sure as hell never going to get my money. Though I won't have to worry about killing you. The Afghans will do it for me."

Beamon shook his head and pulled the map off the table, holding it closer to his face. Like most FBI agents, he'd always been fascinated at the thought of being on the other side. There were people who thought he was one of best investigators in the modern era of law enforcement. Did that mean he'd also make one of the best criminals?

His eyes slowly scanned the map, examining the blank areas that represented empty desert and the narrow lines that represented the myriad roads, ramps, and bridges that connected the millions of people settled around L.A. "Tell you what, Carlo. Let's see if we can come up with something a little more elegant.

28

"WHERE'S Laura?" Beamon said, wadding up the cigarette pack in his hand and throwing it on the ground in disgust. He was up to three and a half packs a day, and despite the vivid warning labels, he wasn't dying. Goddamn false advertising.

"She didn't come," Scott Reynolds said. "She went back to D.C."

Beamon nodded and watched the wind take his discarded pack and send it rolling across the dark, barren landscape. He suddenly wanted to be home, to be back at his crappy job, to sit on his own sofa, to see Carrie again, to forget Chet Michaels. Mostly he wanted to escape Nicolai before he lost Mark Beamon.

"Can't we meet in a bar like normal people? I hate this fucking desert."

Reynolds ignored the question.

"I don't know how to say this, Mark, so I'm just going to say it. We talked to the Director and he said no."

"No? What do you mean he said no?"

"I mean, we told him what happened and he went through the ceiling. It wasn't too hard to predict—bringing you in on this without approval, following a line of investigation no one knew about. Honestly, if it wouldn't cause a huge PR problem, Laura would probably be finishing out her career in the Anchorage office."

Beamon opened his mouth to speak, but Reynolds held up a hand and silenced him. "A young agent's dead and you heard Gasta give the order, Mark. The Director isn't interested in speculation about someone on the other end of a phone line. He isn't willing to take the chance on losing Gasta."

"Son of a bitch—"

"Look, Mark. He's worried. The FBI's gotten a lot of black eyes lately, and now he's sitting on a terrorism investigation that isn't going anywhere. You can bet he's going to play this one right down the middle."

Beamon couldn't think of anything to do but laugh. "Gasta's a nobody—a thug. We both know that—"

"The other thing we know is that Gasta's been an embarrassment to law enforcement for years. Getting him is going to be a major coup and it's going to divert some of the attention away from everything else that's going on."

"Goddamnit!" Beamon shouted to the empty desert. "We bring down Gasta and my cover's blown. His boss is going to disappear into thin air. And what about the Afghans? Instead of diverting attention from the fact we can't find the rocket launcher, why not actually get out there and find it? You can't possibly agree with this."

Reynolds hesitated. "I understand that this is how it's going to be."

"What about Laura?"

"Laura understands that too."

"Fuck!" Beamon turned and walked aimlessly for a few moments, finally stopping at the edge of a dry ditch and looking out into the dark. "We can't just let this go, Scott."

"It's over, Mark. A swing and a miss."

"No. No way. Look, this drug deal is going down in a few days— I don't know exactly when, yet, but soon. We grab Gasta there along with Laura's Afghans."

"We already suggested that. The Director thinks we've got an entrapment problem that's going to muddle our case against Gasta."

Beamon spun around to face Reynolds. "Does nobody give a shit about the fact that we've got a rocket launcher floating around the country?"

"Face it, Mark, we've got nothing on this Mohammad guy that could connect him to the launcher other than the fact that he appears to be from roughly the right part of the world. With the millions of Middle Eastern people in the country, what are the chances that he's linked to any of this?"

"Okay let's forget the fucking rocket. Everyone agrees that these Afghans are driving around with a truckload of heroin, right? That's still illegal isn't it? We take them all out at the buy—it's the only logical decision."

"The buy when? A 'few days' from now? A lot can happen in that time, Mark, and you know it. We still don't know how Chet's cover was blown. Yours could be next. Then Gasta just makes himself disappear and we look like a bunch of idiots."

"Get the Director on the phone. I want to talk to him."

"No way. He specifically said that the discussion was ended. That this was a direct order."

Beamon threw his half-finished cigarette down and stomped on it violently, instantly regretting the act. It had been his last one. "Bullshit! You want me to blow an opportunity like this so you can bust a guy who wears silk tracksuits and spends his time shaking down strip clubs?"

"Gasta was directly involved in Chet's death, Mark."

"I know that," Beamon said. "But who was *behind* it?"

"Don't get cute here, Mark. I know you've gone up against management and won in the past, and I know you're friends with Tom Sherman. But you can't win this one. You'd be protecting the guy who had Chet killed—that's how the Director would spin it. Right or wrong, the rest is too complicated to make good TV. It'll be your job and your reputation . . . what's left of it."

"Hey, fuck you."

"You're a hell of an investigator, Mark. Maybe the best ever, who knows? But I'm speaking nothing but the truth here and you know it."

Beamon considered bending down and trying to salvage the smashed cigarette, but decided he hadn't sunk quite that low. Soon, probably, but not yet. Instead he just turned and started walking toward his car.

"Mark? What are you going to do?"

He honestly wasn't sure. Did he really care about his job and his reputation anymore? Could he just stick his head in the sand while the FBI prostituted itself for a little good press?

"Mark!"

Beamon stopped. "When does the Director want Gasta?"

"Now. Tonight. Tomorrow at the latest. They want a full breach. SWAT, press, the works. It's got to be big or we won't be able to get it on TV." Reynolds paused for a moment. "When we get him, we'll put the screws to him over the Afghans. You have my word."

Beamon shook his head slowly. "Don't you think I've already done that, Scott? Gasta wants my help to rip them off; I guarantee you he's told me more than he's going to tell you, and it's nothing. He doesn't know who they are, who they work for, where they are, or who they associate with. Nothing. We take Gasta out before the buy and they're gone."

"Then they're gone. Look, Mark, as far as I'm concerned, you're in the right here. But it doesn't matter."

Beamon knew that he was finished at the FBI one way or another. Even if his inspection report were to disappear into thin air, there was the fact that someone would have to be blamed for what happened to Chet. And if he'd learned anything during his long career at the FBI, it was that there always had to be someone to blame.

29

DESPITE pretty much cleaning the hotel room's bar out of liquor, Beamon couldn't sleep. Those puny little bottles didn't do shit. He closed his eyes, trading the blank white of the ceiling for empty darkness, trying again to clear his mind.

And once again he failed. There were too many things swirling around in his head: Chet, the Director, Laura, Gasta, the Afghans, the rocket launcher, Carrie, his future. What the hell was he going to do? How far was he willing to go? And if he decided to throw away what was left of his career, what was his motivation? He hoped it was something more than revenge and self-pity.

He was still wide-awake at three A.M. when the phone rang.

"Yeah?"

"What the hell are you doing, Mark?"

"Hello, Laura."

"Scott called me. He said he delivered the Director's orders and you said 'I'll think about it'? Did you really say that?"

"I don't know if I used those exact words, but that was the gist."

"Jesus, Mark. This isn't a game. The Director's made a decision—and he didn't make it alone. I don't like it any better than you, but there's nothing we can do about it." She didn't sound completely convinced.

"Have you heard what he wants to do, Laura? He wants to grab Gasta and immediately plaster it all over the TV. You can kiss your Afghans good-bye."

"I know, Mark, I was in the meeting. He isn't going to budge on this—I already tried. I did everything but choke the son of a bitch with his tie."

"Maybe you should have."

"It wouldn't have done any good. I can't make the Director believe in the connection between the launcher and Gasta's heroin dealers."

Beamon sighed quietly. "I guess the silver lining here is that we're holding some pretty good cards where Gasta's concerned. He'll have no choice but to spill everything he knows about his boss."

There was a long silence over the phone.

"Laura? Are you still there."

"I . . . I wouldn't count on that, Mark. I don't think tracking down the man behind Gasta is going to be a priority."

"What are you talking about?"

"They're going to go for the people under him, Mark. They want—they need—him to look like the top man. Trying to get him to roll over on some shadowy figure pulling his strings makes getting Gasta look like a failure, not a success. And I'll tell you right now, they're going to want the death penalty. That's a bargaining chip they aren't going to let us use."

Beamon sat up on the bed. "What are you talking about?"

"I'm sorry, Mark. This is my fault. If I was getting somewhere on finding this launcher . . . But I'm not, and the press is starting to come after us. The fact is, the FBI needs some good publicity."

"Jesus Christ, Laura, Gasta's a nobody!" Beamon realized he was starting to sound like a broken record.

"You and I know that, but the public doesn't. To the man on the street he's the personification of organized crime—the mastermind behind the Mob. This is going to be a big coup and it's going to take some of the heat off us."

Beamon rummaged through the tiny bottles on the floor, looking for one he hadn't completely drained. "Until a rocket goes off. After that, no one's even going to remember Carlo Gasta's name. Then Chet's death is going to be nothing more than a failed publicity stunt."

"Then, call Tom at the White House—get him to intervene."

"No, he was willing to help us squeeze the CIA, but he isn't going to countermand a decision by FBI management. The White House's whole schtick is getting the politics out of the agencies and letting the experts do their jobs. Besides, Tom doesn't do anything without knowing every angle. We don't have the time."

"So, what are you going to do, Mark?"

That was a good question. One he needed some time to think about.

"I don't know where Gasta is," Beamon lied. "But I can probably find him. Tell the Director I need a day to track him down and set him up. If we have to do this, I'd like to do it in a way that doesn't get any of our SWAT guys shot. We'll make it look smooth and professional for the cameras."

There was a confused silence over the line for a moment. "That's it?"

"I'm sorry to disappoint you, Laura. But I'm getting too old to tilt at windmills."

He hung up the phone and closed his eyes again, though he knew he wouldn't sleep.

30

THE random mix of tiny liquor bottles the night before, while creating no particular effect at the time, had left Beamon with a surprisingly durable hangover. That, in combination with the fact that he once again found himself in the empty desert—this time in the full heat of a cloudless afternoon—was putting him in danger of throwing up at any moment. Not really the image he was looking to project.

He scooted his lawn chair back a few inches to escape the blazing sun that was beginning to sneak around the beach umbrella overhead and reached into the cooler next to him for a beer. "Come on, guys, we don't have all goddamn day!"

Three overweight middle-aged Italian men simultaneously stopped what they were doing and glared as threateningly as they could under the circumstances.

"You heard the man! Get your fat asses in gear!" Carlo Gasta was sitting next to Beamon on an uncomfortable-looking rock. He seemed afraid to encroach on the shade the umbrella provided and was already starting to redden in the sun.

Beamon popped the top off his beer and let some of the icy liquid slide down his throat. Pressing the cold bottle against his sweating forehead, he once again examined the dead, rolling landscape. Except for the poorly defined dirt road fifteen feet in front of him, there was no sign of civilization at all. Of course, that was an illusion. If taken west for about a mile, the sandy path dead-ended into a moderately traveled highway bordering the sprawl that surrounded L.A. And if taken east an equal distance, it dead-ended into the natural amphitheater where Carlo Gasta was to meet his Afghan suppliers three days from now.

Beamon closed his eyes for a moment and constructed a map of the area in his mind: the confusing jumble of interconnecting highways, secondary roads, and off ramps that made a previously impassible desert into just another gateway to suburbia.

"How hot you figure it is, Carlo?" he said, opening his eyes again and watching Gasta's men attacking the sandy road with shovels.

"It's gotta be over a hundred."

One of the men suddenly jerked upright and began rubbing his arm. Sensing a heart attack in process, Beamon leaned forward and watched with ghoulish anticipation.

"Mikey! Get back to work!" Gasta shouted.

"I think I pulled something in my arm, Carlo."

Beamon fell back into his lawn chair. False alarm.

"I don't give a shit about your arm. Get it in gear!"

Beamon took another sip of his beer and watched the man start digging again, favoring his injured limb. They were almost finished, and with the exception of sunburns that would undoubtedly blister before tomorrow, none looked much worse for the wear. It must have been the goddamn breeze.

Beamon pushed the bag of ice off his ankle and stood, limping slightly as he hobbled up to the deep ditch that bordered the south side of the road, and jumped painfully over it. Fortunately, the landing was soft.

"Hey! We just did that part," Tony whined. "You're packing it down!"

Beamon ignored him, admiring the work that had been completed. Gasta's men had dug down a good foot and a half in the road, carefully sifting the dirt and then gently replacing it, creating a thirty-foot-long sand bog.

This particular spot was perfect. On one side of the road was the ditch Beamon had just crossed, and on the other was a low but steep berm. The Afghans' van, heavy with men and product, would make its way up the road toward the amphitheater and become hopelessly stuck in this unavoidable trap.

Beamon rolled his beer across his forehead again, wondering for the hundredth time what the hell he was doing. He'd told Laura, and she'd told the Director, that he was going to find Gasta and set him up for the FBI today. Instead he was standing in the desert, supervising the groundwork for the plan he'd come up with to get Gasta his heroin.

His new cell phone was turned off so he wouldn't receive the desperate calls that were undoubtedly being placed to it. He honestly wouldn't know what to say.

"All right. I think that's enough," Beamon said.

The three men stopped working and leaned on their shovels for support.

"Now we're going to run through this. Is everybody clear on what they're supposed to be doing?"

Gasta jumped over the ditch and joined his men, who were nodding with what little energy they had left.

"Okay, put your masks on."

They all looked at one another and then at their boss, who was staring at his feet.

"We've been talking about this," Gasta started hesitantly. "We don't see the reason for the masks. These guys are going to know who we are."

It was a perceptive observation. The reason for the masks was simply to intensify the heat and to see if he could make one of these sons of bitches die of heatstroke. It had taken no small effort for Beamon to find four wool ski masks—in the appropriate sun-absorbing black—during the dead of the L.A. summer.

"Look, Carlo, we've already talked about this. If you want to go it alone . . ."

Gasta shook his head and pulled a mask from his back pocket. His men reluctantly followed his lead.

"Okay, are we ready?" Beamon said when their heads and faces were properly covered.

More nodding.

"And no shooting, right?"

"You know . . . that's another thing we wanted to talk to you about," Gasta said, his voice sounding a little muffled through the small hole in the wool. "Why don't we just kill these guys? It doesn't make sense to leave them alive."

Beamon let out a bored sigh. "We're a mile from the highway. We don't need anyone hearing gunfire and calling the cops—or worse, some soccer mom catching a stray through her window. Besides, you said you wanted to send a message. Well, this is a clear message that you're not even afraid of these guys enough to bother to kill them. It also leaves you with some options. You can pay them after you've sold the stuff if you want—teach them that a deal is a deal and that you won't be fucked with."

Beamon had devised that speech over two hours the night before. The logic was a little strained, but Gasta was as dumb as a box of rocks. And, more importantly, he was afraid of Nicolai.

"Okay, okay," the gangster said. "Fine. We'll do it your way."

Beamon stared directly into the man's eyes. "You understand that I expect people to live up to their agreements. No screwing around."

"I said okay. What the fuck do you want from me?"

Beamon didn't answer, instead strolling down the road toward a panel van parked fifty yards away. He'd rented it earlier that afternoon and had one of Gasta's men fill it with debris from a construction site to weigh it down. He slid behind the wheel and started it, turning the AC up to full. When he looked up through the windshield again, Gasta and his men had already scurried to their designated hiding places.

"I hope you know what you're doing," he said quietly to himself as he released the emergency brake.

He figured that the plan he'd hatched had about a thirty percent chance of working—assuming he actually had the guts to go through with it. Gasta would steal the van full of heroin and Beamon could have the local FBI pick up the Afghans while they were walking home. Then, when he made contact with Gasta again, the Director could have his testosterone-drenched SWAT maneuvers under the television lights. Everybody won.

Or not.

Beamon gunned the engine, accelerating to a slightly unsafe speed on the rough road. When the van hit the sand bog, it stopped a little more violently than he'd expected, throwing him hard against his seat belt. He managed to turn his face away from the side window just before it was smashed in by a hammer and a gun was pushed through the hole.

"Get the fuck out of the car!" The masked man screamed as the van's other windows were similarly shattered.

Beamon unlatched his seat belt and stepped out, feeling an uneasy sense of déjà vu as he was forced facedown to the ground and a boot was pressed into his back. From his prone position he watched a beefy-looking four-wheel drive come rumbling up the road. A rope was connected to the rear of the van and it was quickly towed back onto solid ground. The pressure of the boot on his back disappeared and Beamon pushed himself to his feet, glancing at his watch.

"Three minutes," he said, brushing the dust from his cotton slacks. "Not bad, but we can do better."

The men groaned.

"What about what you said before?" Gasta asked as his men unhooked the van and the four-wheel drive retreated out of sight again.

"What do you mean?"

"What if they have a chase vehicle? Or if we run into cops on the way out of here?"

Beamon climbed back into the van and leaned out through the broken window. "You let me worry about that, okay?"

31

CHRISTIAN Volkov squinted at the open book in his lap and read the page for the fourth time, but it still meant nothing to him. He adjusted the lamp on his desk to better illuminate the page. Now it was indecipherable and well lit.

He had never been able to abide organized religion, seeing too much of the hand of man in it. But he still had a strange compulsion to glimpse the mind of God. As with all his previous attempts, though, this path seemed to lead nowhere.

Volkov leaned back in his uncomfortable new chair and admonished himself again for not rescuing his old one. The office around him appeared overly large and nearly empty, although it was fully furnished. Volkov had an obsessive distaste for paper and other tangible records of his business, making things like filing cabinets and bookshelves useless. His life—his entire history—was contained in billions of encrypted electronic impulses that were nearly impossible to intercept, simple to relocate, and could be destroyed almost instantly. An interesting by-product of this philosophy was that when he died, he would leave almost no trace. If *Fortune* magazine was aware of his existence and recognized men in his profession, he would be listed as one of the wealthiest men in the world. His innovations in the businesses he was involved in and his success at integrating the undisciplined capitalist elements in former Soviet Union might have been taught at universities.

Not that he really cared. He had no ambition for notoriety. In fact, there was something strangely appealing about living at the very edge of civilization. It wasn't without cost, though. His freedom from the arbitrary rules and dictates of society was more than paid for with uncertainty and loneliness.

"Christian?"

Volkov smiled as the young man approached his desk hesitantly. "Joseph! What wonderful timing." He held up the book he had been reading and the young man leaned over the desk to see the title.

"It tells the story of a mathematician who solved one of the last great math problems," Volkov explained. "Are you familiar with it?" Joseph had a master's degree in mathematics.

"Fermat's Last Theorem? Sure. But I haven't read that particular book."

"Well, I have," Volkov said, tossing it on his desk. "Twice. And as hard as I've tried, I can't comprehend it. I just read a rather long passage on imaginary numbers. What good is a number if it's imaginary? Isn't that like an anthropologist studying the anatomy of a dragon?"

Joseph laughed. "Imaginary numbers are multiples of the square root of negative one. They are one of the axes of the complex plane."

Volkov stared at him blankly.

"I think it might take some time to explain."

"I suppose so. Maybe we could discuss it over dinner. François is doing his duck tonight."

"Thank you, Christian. I'd love to."

"Now, what do you have for me?"

Joseph spread out a map of the Los Angeles area on Volkov's desk. "We've managed to pinpoint the place and time of Carlo Gasta's meeting with Yasin's people." He tapped an empty spot on the map well outside the overpopulated confines of L.A. "Our informant says they will be here at midnight American Pacific time on Saturday."

Volkov nodded slowly. He'd almost hoped that Joseph would fail in obtaining this information. It forced a difficult decision.

"Our informant also tells us that Nicolai is involved."

"Really?" Volkov said, genuinely surprised. The preliminary information Joseph had provided on Nicolai had been intriguing. Now, though, Volkov's interest was quickly turning to suspicion. Why would an extraordinarily well shrouded and apparently extremely effective private operator like Nicolai get involved with someone as unpredictable and well known as Carlo Gasta?

There seemed to be only one explanation: that Jonathan Drake was involved in the sudden appearance of this mercenary after all. It seemed likely that Drake was going to use this drug transaction to do away with both Gasta and the Afghans, thus severing two critical connections between al-Qaeda and the CIA. Could Nicolai be part of that plan—Drake's inside man?

"When am I going to get the remainder of the information on Nicolai?" Volkov asked.

"You already have it. The file's in your computer." Joseph whisked the map from Volkov's desk and began running it through a shredder by the wall.

"Why didn't you tell me?"

"I'm sorry. You seemed to be concentrating."

"He's working for Drake at the CIA," Volkov said matter-of-factly.

To his surprise Joseph shook his head. "Every indication is that he's not. You should look at the file. I think you'll find it interesting reading."

Volkov rose from his chair and turned on a portable stereo that was substituting for the elaborate sound system he'd left in the Seychelles. Louis Armstrong's rich voice—one of America's greatest contributions to the world—filled the room.

Volkov knew that he no longer had the luxury of not taking a position. It was time to decide whether he thought the CIA was going to renege on their agreement with him or if, as Drake insisted, they were continuing forward. Nothing that had yet occurred was proof of either hypothesis. Gasta and the Afghans were pawns that would logically be sacrificed in light of the FBI's investigation into the rocket launcher photograph.

Despite that, he strongly suspected that Drake was no longer committed to his ill-conceived plan to destroy al-Qaeda. And if that was true, he would do whatever was in the Central Intelligence Agency's considerable power to see Volkov dead. But were his suspicions enough to start a war with America's CIA?

Volkov made his way back to his chair amid the strains of "Mack the Knife." He knew the answer—he just didn't want to face what would probably be the end of him and his organization. He wasn't ready for that yet.

"What do you want me to do, Christian?"

"I think we have no choice but to try to divert Jonathan Drake's attention a bit."

"And Nicolai?"

"Let me look at the information you've gathered and I'll make a decision by tomorrow. Thank you, Joseph."

The young man turned and started for the door but stopped when Volkov spoke again.

"And, Joseph—don't forget my mathematics lesson tonight. By dessert I want to completely understand the world of modular functions."

Joseph gave him a short nod and then disappeared through the door. He would undoubtedly spend the rest of the afternoon desperately trying to come up with a way to explain advanced number theory over the course of an hour and a half. He was a very bright, very conscientious, and very likable young man. But Volkov was still far from certain that he would ever be able to replace Pascal.

32

"COUNT OFF."

"One, in position."

"Two, in position."

"Three, in position."

"Four, in position."

"Leader, in position."

Jonathan Drake leaned against the cliff wall behind him, feeling the jagged rock press painfully into his back. He concentrated on the discomfort for a few moments, sharpening his senses and focusing his mind. It wouldn't be long now.

The tiny space he'd concealed himself in was almost too small for his frame. The stone behind him bowed precariously, sweeping over his head at a height of no more than four feet. In front and to the sides of him were large boulders that had detached themselves from the cliff and now provided perfect cover.

Drake crawled forward, dropping to his stomach as he squeezed through a tight gap, stopping when he had an unobstructed view of the small natural amphitheater that he was at the edge of. The floor of it, some twenty feet below, was basically round and just over two hundred yards across at its widest point. The edges were defined by loose, steep slopes topped with sheer ten-foot cliffs and broken rock. The only entrance was to the west—a barely visible dirt road leading through a narrow gap of dirt and stone.

The topography gave him and his team excellent cover, an elevated position that afforded unobstructed visibility and numerous options for escape.

Drake scooted forward a few more inches and scanned the cliff band bordering the far side of the clearing, but could see nothing that would suggest that he had snipers strategically positioned at regular intervals along it. Nothing would survive that he didn't want to survive.

Drake looked down at the softly glowing hands of his watch. Nine fifteen. Less than three hours before Carlo Gasta and the Afghans were scheduled to arrive.

"Wait until the last possible moment," he said into his walkie-talkie. "After Gasta's men attack, let them fight among themselves for as long as you can."

The invisible men surrounding him in the rocks counted off again, acknowledging his orders, although they already understood their role. They were to perform a cleanup function—to make sure Gasta and his men didn't survive and, if possible, to capture one or more of the Afghans alive.

Despite the quickly dropping temperature, Drake found himself sweating more profusely as the time drew closer. He told himself again that he had considered every eventuality and that nothing could go wrong, but he knew that something always went wrong. What would it be?

Would Gasta ignore the orders he'd been given?

Inconceivable. Drake had spoken to him again that morning and again expressed his anger at Gasta for exposing him to Chet Michaels. Besides, Gasta had no money to purchase the heroin and needed cash badly.

Would someone hear the shooting and call the police? Irrelevant. He had set up a man with a machine gun a couple of miles away. Any activity on the police scanner and he'd start shooting, leading the police away.

The most likely problem would be that the Arabs' van would be too badly damaged in the gunfight to drive away. A minor inconvenience. He had a tow truck parked a few miles down the highway.

The worst-case scenario was that the Arabs wouldn't show up. But since they were as desperate for money as Gasta, it was unlikely. If they should fail to appear, Drake's men would simply kill Gasta and his people themselves. And when the gangsters' rotting bodies were found, the FBI would be happy to call it a Mob hit and blame Gasta solely for the death of their undercover man.

It left the problem of the launcher being found by the FBI, of course. If he was able to capture or kill the men making up al-Qaeda's L.A. cell, it would put the CIA even further ahead of Laura Vilechi and her investigation.

Drake retreated to the cliff wall again and managed to find a marginally comfortable position as the deep glow in the west faded and surrounded him with darkness. He closed his eyes and continued to compulsively run through possible scenarios for tonight and the weeks that followed. It was going to be all right, he told himself.

The sound was so distant and so low that it almost seemed imaginary at first. When the hum persisted and became more defined, though, Drake crawled forward again, trying to identify it. It took only a few moments for it to become obvious that the source was getting closer and for the rhythm of the sound to become apparent. Drake peered around the large boulder in front of him and craned his neck, searching the night sky. Three separate lights had just become visible on the horizon, still distant but quickly approaching.

Helicopters.

It didn't matter: There was still more than two hours before Gasta was scheduled to appear. Even if they flew directly overhead, they would be gone in ten minutes. He struggled to stay calm as the sound of the blades churning the air deepened and increased in volume until it became a pounding in his chest. He watched the helicopters' forward momentum evaporate, leaving them hovering directly over the amphitheater.

Drake suddenly found himself engulfed in the dust and tiny rocks dislodged by the powerful downdraft. He partially covered his eyes as the helicopters began to descend. There was just enough light to pierce the haze around them and make it possible to read the lettering on the fuselage: L.A.P.D.

Drake pushed himself back desperately, ducking behind a large boulder and pressing his back into it. He clawed the walkie-talkie off his belt and shouted into it. "Hold your position. I repeat. Hold your position!"

He had to think. What the fuck were the police doing here? Who had tipped them off? He whipped his head around the corner and saw that the skids of the first helicopter were almost to the ground. It didn't matter: He had to—

Powerful hands suddenly grabbed him from behind and dragged him back, prompting a wave of panic to wash over him. He struggled, but despite his considerable strength and bulk, he was unable to break free. Something brushed against his ear and he heard a familiar voice. "We're getting out of here!"

Drake felt the arms holding him slip away and he spun around to face the leader of the team he'd brought there. "No! We . . . we have to complete this operation."

There was just enough light penetrating the rocks for him to see the man shake his head and bring a walkie-talkie to his mouth. Drake lunged but wasn't quick enough. A moment later he found himself pinned against a rock wall with a knife against pressed against his throat. There was nothing he could do but watch helplessly as the man began speaking into the radio.

"Retreat using primary escape paths! Rendezvous at area A! Repeat: Retreat using primary escape paths. Rendezvous will be at location Alpha!"

The man shoved the radio back in his pocket and grabbed Drake by the hair, dragging him into a narrow split in the cliff. He wanted to break away, but the sharp blade against his throat kept him from fighting back.

After about twenty yards the gap narrowed and lowered, forcing Drake to his stomach.

"Crawl," the man ordered. He did, moving quickly as the sound of the helicopters grew loud again. "They're going," he said when they came out the other side of the gap and saw the helicopters rising into the sky. "Look, they're going!"

The man shoved him into a shallow ditch and jumped in behind. "They're not gone, you stupid son of a bitch. They were inserting a SWAT team."

"You work for me! If this operation isn't carried out, it will be a disaster for this country. Do you understand? A disaster!"

"I expect that America will still be standing in the morning either way," the man said, sheathing his knife.

"You have no idea what's at stake here! You agreed to carry out this operation and you've been paid."

"I agreed to be involved in the deaths of a bunch of drug dealers— not to execute L.A. cops."

"Look," Drake said, concentrating on regaining his calm. "Just listen to me for a second . . . please. When Gasta and the Afghans get there and find out it's a bust, they'll start shooting. Right?"

The man didn't respond.

"Right," Drake said, answering his own question. "All you need to do is help it along—help escalate it. Make sure that Gasta, his men, and the Afghans all die. You don't have to kill any cops. Hell, you'd be helping them."

"SWAT's already taken up our positions," the man said. "I guarantee you that. And do you think those copters are gone? They're not: They've just moved to a safe distance. They're not going to just let us walk away after we start shooting."

For obvious reasons Drake had been unable to use a CIA team for this operation, and that left his authority completely financial. "I'll double your fee. Triple it. You name your price."

"Shut the fuck up." The knife reappeared and Drake stumbled backward.

"Understand this," the man said. "Me and my guys are getting the hell out of here. You can come with me or I can leave your body here."

"I need my phone," Drake said. He had to call Gasta. Warn him off. He couldn't let him fall into the hands of the police.

The man grabbed him by the arm, spinning him around and pushing him forward.

"For God's sake! If you won't do your job, you have to let me at least use the phone!"

"Shut up and move."

33

WITH every minute that went by, the butterflies in Beamon's stomach felt more like a flock of birds from the Hitchcock movie.

"One more time," he said into the microphone suspended in front of his mouth. "Come in from a different angle and let's gain some altitude."

The pilot veered the helicopter right and increased power, further agitating Beamon's gastric aviary.

They'd gone over the area twice already and this was the last pass Beamon could risk. He didn't know any Middle Eastern drug wholesalers personally, but he was guessing that they didn't like helicopters buzzing around when they were about to do a deal.

This time the pilot flew south, keeping in line with the moderately traveled highway beneath them. Beamon peered through a powerful pair of binoculars, finding it almost impossible to hold a steady image in the bucking helicopter.

Fortunately, there wasn't much to see, other than the light late-night traffic moving along the road below. No one seemed to be in any particular hurry—no erratic driving, no cops. The most unusual thing he found was a tow truck parked behind an abandoned car about two miles from the dirt road that was the subject of that night's festivities.

"Keep going?" the pilot said.

"Yeah. Just a quick peek."

A little more than a minute later Beamon spotted the almost invisible entrance to the dirt road in the headlights of a passing semi. He scanned it as they passed but couldn't make much out in the darkness. Another minute and he saw a black midsized sedan parked in the median. He brought the binoculars to his face again, steadying his elbows on his knees. The car looked empty for a moment but then was briefly lit by a reddish glow as a big-haired woman inside dragged on a cigarette. Not exactly a highly trained operative, but she and her friends had been cheap and seemed well qualified for the jobs he'd given them.

Beamon laid the binoculars down and rolled his head around on his neck, trying to untie the knot that was tightening between his shoulder blades. He knew that he was playing a game he couldn't possibly win. He was under direct orders to find Carlo Gasta and sic the local FBI on him. Obviously he was interpreting those orders fairly loosely. At this point, if everything went right, he'd probably still get fired. But at least he'd go out with Laura a few steps closer to her terrorists and a really stylish "fuck you."

The pilot whacked him on the shoulder and then pointed to the road below. "Is that what you're looking for?"

Beamon followed his finger and saw a decent-sized panel van moving south along the highway below. Judging by the other cars on the road passing it, the van was probably going exactly the speed limit. Beamon picked up the phone sitting in his lap and shouted into it. There was no need to dial. He'd opened the line to Gasta a half an hour ago.

"Carlo? Can you hear me?"

"Barely! Go ahead."

Beamon twisted around in his seat and the pilot adjusted their trajectory to give him a better view of the vehicle below. "We've got a possible. Stand by."

The van began to slow even more and Beamon saw its headlights jump as it hit the edge of the dirt road. "This is it, Carlo! They just turned off the highway. ETA approximately four minutes. Stay cool. And remember: no goddamn shooting!"

"We're ready!"

Beamon motioned to the pilot and he put the helicopter into a lazy arc that carried them over a small plateau and would eventually take them over Gasta's ambush.

By the three-and-a-half-minute mark, they were closing from the east, and through his binoculars Beamon could see the tiny swath of desert illuminated by the van's headlights. He began counting slowly to himself and had made it to forty-three when the lights suddenly stopped making forward progress. He signaled the pilot to slow and steadied the binoculars again.

Everything looked textbook. Three men piled out of the van and looked down at the wheels of the stuck vehicle. Unfortunately, the driver appeared to have stayed put, but it was the scenario he'd trained Gasta's men for, so he didn't expect it to present a problem. Beamon watched as the three men put their shoulders to the back of the van and started to push. When they were completely focused on the task at hand, Gasta and his men suddenly appeared out of the darkness.

"Beautiful, Carlo," Beamon whispered to himself. "Just stay cool and hold it together." He motioned the pilot forward, keeping his binoculars trained on the scene unfolding below. Probably less than fifteen seconds passed from the time Gasta and his men first appeared to the moment they had the driver out of the van and all four Afghans lying facedown in the dirt.

"Very nice," Beamon mumbled. It was starting to look like his inordinately stupid plan was actually going to work. In a few minutes Gasta would be calmly pulling the van and the heroin out onto the highway and Beamon would be calling the local FBI office to tell them that there were four Afghan gentlemen in need of a ride home. Then tomorrow he'd turn Gasta over and the Director would get his news footage with the added benefit of a backdrop that included a couple of million dollars' worth of heroin. Everybody wins.

Thirty seconds.

Beamon adjusted the focused on the binoculars.

Forty-five seconds.

"What are you doing, Carlo?"

Gasta and his men weren't towing the van out. In fact, they weren't doing anything other than standing motionless over the Afghans with their guns drawn.

One minute.

Beamon felt the birds in his stomach suddenly start to peck and scratch. He grabbed his cell phone again. "Carlo! Don't even think about it! If you fuck this up, I'll track you down like an animal and put a bullet in the back of your head! Do you understand me!" Beamon made it through his entire tirade before he realized the connection was dead.

The flashes were surprisingly bright, considering the distance. Beamon watched in horror as Gasta and his men emptied their guns into their captives.

"Jesus Christ!" Beamon heard the pilot shout. "Fuck this!"

The helicopter banked hard and the noise of the engine increased as they sped back toward L.A. Beamon leaned his head against the vibrating glass and squeezed his eyes shut. It was suddenly hard to breathe. Maybe he was finally having that well-deserved heart attack.

Probably a minute passed before he was forced to face the fact that he wasn't having a cardiac incident and that he had just helped carry out the execution of four human beings. His stylish "fuck you" had just turned into a moronic "fuck me."

"Jesus Christ! Son of a bitch! Goddamnit!"

Beamon looked over at the pilot, who was emitting a constant stream of obscenities as he tried to coax a little more speed out of the helicopter. Gasta had set Beamon up with the man, but it appeared that he hadn't been quite prepared for the night's events.

"Gasta's gonna kill me. I know too much. Shit!"

Beamon bit down on his lip hard, using the pain to clear his head but quickly regretting it. What did he have to think about? The fact that he had just completely and irretrievably screwed himself? That when the FBI got hold of Gasta, he'd be more than happy to tell them all about Nicolai's role in this? That he had gone from FBI agent to murderer in a matter of minutes?

"Damn," he said quietly to himself. He'd been so angry. About Chet, about the FBI settling for Gasta and not wanting to go after the man behind him, about the Director playing politics with people's lives. He'd just closed his eyes. This had always been inevitable.

The phone, still in his lap, suddenly started to ring. Beamon hesitated but finally answered it. Gasta's panicked voice came through the earpiece almost immediately.

"Nicolai! Nicolai, can you hear me?"

Beamon stared out into the darkness, not answering.

"Nicolai! We got cops coming up on us! You hear me? Cops!"

"I told you not to shoot, you dumb son of a bitch," Beamon yelled into the phone. "Someone heard you."

"Fuck you! It's not one cop. They're coming out of the woodwork! You set me up, you piece of shit!"

Beamon twisted around and looked behind him. In the distance he could see the flashing blue and red lights moving along the highway toward the dirt road that Gasta was just about to come out of. Where the hell had they come from?

"Turn around," Beamon said to the pilot.

"Fuck you."

Beamon sat there for a moment, considering his position. It didn't take long to confirm that he was utterly and completely fucked. Laura would get some dead Afghans, which was better than nothing; Gasta would get caught by the cops and would, for a change, be prosecuted for something he was actually guilty of; and no one would ever look for the man really responsible for Chet's death.

Beamon looked behind him again. The police cars were still visible but only barely. What did he have to lose now?

He pulled another cell phone from his pocket and hit a speed-dial number. When a woman picked up, he said simply "Now" and then dialed another and said the same thing. Next, he pulled his .357 from his pocket and stuck the barrel against the pilot's head. "Turn around."

"Fuck you. You're not going to kill me. We'll crash."

"Very clever. You're right. I can't kill you now. But you've got to land sometime."

The pilot considered that for a moment and then the chopper made a sharp turn and started speeding back toward the highway.

"Carlo!" Beamon yelled into the phone. "Are you still there? What's your situation?"

"Why should I tell you, you fuck?"

He'd be heading south on the highway by now—that much Beamon knew. "Carlo, look behind you."

The chopper crossed over the highway and Beamon could see a southbound traffic jam starting about a mile before the dirt road Gasta had come out of. A number of police cruisers were trying to get around it, but their low-slung cars weren't fairing well off road.

"What the fuck? How'd you do that?" Gasta said.

"Don't worry about that now," Beamon said, unfolding a map on his lap. "Tell me where you are exactly."

"About a mile from where we got on the highway, heading south at about eighty-five. That's as fast as this piece of shit will go. Where the fuck did all these cops come from?"

"I have no idea. Are any of them on your tail?"

"There's one coming up fast. He's a ways back still, but not for long."

"What about northbound? Anybody that could jump the median and come after you?"

"It's weird, but there's no cars over there at all. It's totally empty."

Beamon motioned for the pilot to gain altitude. After a few hundred feet he could make out a similar traffic jam a few miles ahead of Gasta's position in the northbound lanes.

"Carlo. You've got an on-ramp to the freeway coming in about a mile. Take it east. Do you hear me?"

"East. I got it."

Beamon grabbed the cell phone in his lap and hit a speed-dial number that he had written down on the map.

"Hello?" came the woman's voice.

"Get ready. You're looking for a blue panel van coming up on your position at about eighty-five miles an hour."

A good minute went by before she spoke again.

"It's coming up the ramp."

"When it passes, go!"

He was just hanging up that phone when Gasta started shouting over the other. "Nicolai! Nicolai! We got a police chopper right above us! Fuck!"

"Don't worry about it, Carlo—that copter can't do anything. Just stay cool and take the route we talked about to the mall."

"You're sure?"

"Trust me."

Beamon motioned the scared pilot forward. They had to give the LAPD chopper a wide berth but managed to find a position that afforded them a reasonable view of what was going on. When the van took a ramp leading to an even busier section of highway, Beamon pressed another speed-dial number. "Go."

The van and the police chopper were soon out of sight, but there were no police cruisers following. Beamon looked down at the traffic backing up on the off ramp and the flashing lights hopelessly stuck in the middle of the mess.

As they flew overhead Beamon focused his binoculars on the cause of the traffic snarl. One of the strippers he'd hired, standing in the headlights of her car, was already down to her bra and panties.

His other nine little helpers would similarly disrobe on critical junctions along Gasta's route to the underground parking lot of an enormous shopping mall. The police chopper would see him go in, but by the time any cruisers could get there, the drugs would have been switched to another vehicle and it, as well as twenty decoy cars, would be slinking off into the Los Angeles night.

34

ANOTHER wave of nausea gripped Mark Beamon and he crawled quickly across the stained vinyl floor of the bathroom. Coughing violently, he hovered over the toilet, managing to keep from vomiting by sheer force of will. When the spasms subsided, he leaned against the tub and lit a cigarette with a shaking hand.

He'd left the hotel room's television on and was now regretting it. Reports of his little drug heist had actually preempted the 24/7 coverage of the rocket launcher threat, and the newscaster was starting to sound downright giddy at the new subject matter. High-speed chases, guns, and strippers. What more could you possibly want in a story?

It seemed that all the girls he hired to snarl traffic had been arrested—but then, they'd expected that and built it into their fees. Reports were just starting to come in regarding rumors that "a number" of bodies had been found in the desert and that they appeared to be of Middle Eastern descent. Wild speculation regarding a connection to the launcher was starting to fly, based solely on the color of the dead men's skin and their obvious religious leanings.

Beamon pinched the filter off his cigarette and drew in the heavy smoke. What the fuck had he just done?

It was a question that was depressingly easy to answer, as it turned out. He'd just planned and helped execute a drug heist that had left four men dead. He pulled his knees up to his chest and laughed. "What do you think, Chet? How am I doing so far?"

The stress and guilt wreaking havoc on his stomach started to subside a bit and he pulled out the two cell phones he was carrying. The one that Laura had the number to had been turned off for days now—ever since he'd decided to ignore the Director's orders. He'd bought the other a few days ago: It was Nicolai's phone. Gasta had that number.

He flipped Laura's on and dialed her number from memory. She picked up on the first ring.

"How'd you like the show?"

"Mark! Jesus Christ. I've been trying to get in touch with you for days. . . ." She didn't seem to know what else to say.

"You watching the news? Your Afghans are all dead, I'm afraid. It sounds like the LAPD has them."

"They do. Scott's already got fingerprints, pictures—the works. We'll have a thousand people working to identify them within the hour."

"Good. That's good. I hope it gets you somewhere. I think it will."

"What the hell happened, Mark?"

"A lot."

"I want to talk to you."

"You are talking to me."

"Face-to-face. I'm on the Bureau's jet. I'll be in L.A. in an hour."

He thought about that for a moment. If the FBI wasn't throwing everything they had at finding him now, they would be soon. In a couple of weeks his picture just might make the wall of the post office. Hopefully, they wouldn't use one that made him look fat.

"I don't think I want to do that, Laura."

"Just you and me, Mark. You have my word."

He still wasn't sure he wanted to talk. The truth was, he didn't know what he was going to say. But he didn't have any real reason to refuse. Laura's word was good.

He gave her directions to the run-down hotel he'd holed up in and turned the phone off again. After a shower he felt marginally better. All except for the part about being completely, irretrievably doomed. He put on the same clothes he'd been wearing earlier and looked down at the unopened liter of bourbon lying on the bed. The answers he wanted probably weren't in there, but that was no reason not to look.

The knock was quiet, timid. Just what one would expect from a brilliant, anal retentive, team-playing FBI agent who was edging way too far out on a very narrow limb. Beamon opened the door and Laura jumped through, pushing it immediately closed and looking around to make sure all the curtains were shut.

"Mark. You look terrible. Are you all right?"

"I'm okay," he said, walking a little unsteadily to the bed and propping himself up on a stack of pillows. At his feet the TV was speculating on the mysterious man behind the traffic-stopping strippers and using that as an excuse to send their cameramen to some of the more colorful local clubs. He pushed the MUTE button.

"The cops knew where the buy was happening, Laura. They were all over the place. Did you have anything to do with that?"

She sat down in a pumpkin-orange vinyl chair. "If I'd have known where they were meeting, I would have sent our own team. Besides, you told me you were going to play ball."

"How, then?"

"The word is that they got an anonymous tip with a location and time. They thought it was all going to go down in a little valley about a mile from where it really happened."

Beamon frowned deeply. "Why do I find it improbable that they would put that kind of manpower behind an anonymous tip?"

"There's anonymous and there's anonymous, you know?"

"Uh-huh."

"Are you going to tell me what happened?"

He didn't answer.

"I guess the popular theory right now is that the van was driven by the Afghans and got stuck in some sand on its way to the meeting place.

All four of them were shot and killed, then the van was towed out—we assume by Gasta and his men. When the van hit the highway, I guess the cops thought they had Gasta dead to rights."

Beamon watched a particularly nubile stripper gyrating against a chrome bar bisecting the television screen. How had he missed her?

"You planned it, didn't you, Mark? Gasta might have figured out the sand bog, but not the women."

"No one was supposed to get killed," Beamon said. "I told them guns would make too much noise."

"But the guy behind Gasta was clear on that point, wasn't he? He wanted those Afghans dead," Laura said. "Chet told us as much."

"I thought I'd convinced Gasta that leaving them alive would send an even louder message. I bet everything on the fact that Gasta wouldn't renege on an agreement with Nicolai—that he'd be too afraid."

Beamon reached for the bottle of bourbon on the nightstand and took a swig. It burned going down, but that seemed to be the only effect. "I guess he's more afraid of the guy he works for."

"Scott asked you if you could trust your judgment, being so close to this. . . ."

Beamon shook his head slowly. "I should have just given Gasta up and walked away. Now people are dead and I . . . Shit, even *I* think I belong in jail. . . ."

Laura rocked back in the rickety chair and pushed her blond hair from her eyes. She was wearing jeans, a blouse, and a pair of running shoes—not her normal corporate look. Beamon wondered if it was a disguise or if she was too exhausted to put on anything else.

"You're right about one thing: You're in uncharted territory now. But the other stuff is pretty much crap."

He squinted at her, not sure he'd heard right.

"We've got the Afghans, Mark. I can pretty much guarantee you they wouldn't have talked if we'd gotten them alive, so they're just as good to us dead. Maybe better, who knows? Dead men don't hire lawyers." She shrugged. "As I see it, we got them without putting any cops or FBI agents in harm's way. And we can still have Gasta. Nicolai can. Sounds like a textbook operation to me."

"What textbook are you reading?"

"Look, Mark. We've got a lot of politics flying around here. We've got powerful people who've wanted Gasta for years—and they see Chet's death as their big chance. But we've also got a rocket launcher floating around somewhere, and that has to be the priority. The way I see it, you had the guts to rise above all the noise and go after what was important."

"You paint a lovely picture, Laura, but I'm not sure it's accurate. I think maybe I sunk below the noise more than rising above it."

She shrugged again. "Whatever. It was a huge gamble. But the jury's still out on whether or not you lost."

"What are they saying about this at the Bureau? They must want to string me up."

"Why? You had nothing to do with any of this."

"Excuse me?"

"I'm just guessing here, but I'd say you had no idea when or how this heist was going down. Gasta strung you along and then at the last minute froze you out. He had people watching you, so you couldn't call us and you weren't able to find him. What a shame."

Beamon flipped his feet off the bed and sat up. "Laura—"

"And Gasta . . ." she said, cutting him off. "That guy is up to his neck in prostitution and strip clubs. Who but him could have put that diversion together?"

"No way, Laura. You're not going down with me on this."

"There's no evidence out there linking you to anything. I'm just making logical conclusions."

"No, you're moving toward that uncharted territory too."

"Don't be such a prima donna, Mark. You aren't the only one willing to hang it out there on this. I don't want to be the one who held back when one of those missiles hits a school or something."

Beamon wasn't sure where she was going with all this. What he did know, though, was that Laura didn't do anything without an elaborate plan. It took two hours of prep time for her to grill a couple of burgers. If nothing else, it should be interesting to hear what this new, outlaw Laura wanted to do.

"We've got a license number on the van from the police and we're already tracing it. Between that and the bodies of the Afghans, we might just turn something up. And if it leads us to the launcher . . ." She made the sign of the cross in the air. "All your sins may be forgiven."

It was still before dawn and there wasn't much activity on the street. Beamon lit a cigarette and limped slowly down the sidewalk, not having any real idea where he was going. Laura had gone a half an hour ago—back to her hotel, her job, and the real world. He'd tried to sleep but he had too much going on in his head. The movement and fresh air seemed to be helping, though. The night had turned cool, and for the first time in a month he could feel a slight chill beneath his light shirt.

Laura had seemed strangely desperate. Not so much about the launcher, but to convince herself that he hadn't just thrown away what was left of his life. She seemed to want to believe that the elaborate story she'd concocted was something more than the very brief reprieve it realistically was. She *had* bought him some time, though. The question now was what he was going to do with it.

The bottom line was that he wanted the man who'd ordered Chet's death. Of course, he knew it wouldn't change anything—Chet would still be dead and he would still be alive. But sometimes revenge was all there was left.

He knew now that his plan to deliver Gasta and the Afghans had been a carefully contrived fantasy. Even if everything had worked the way it was supposed to, he'd never really planned on leading the FBI to Gasta. In the end he would have used the success of the heist to stay close to Gasta and get his hands on the man's boss.

Now, though, his investigation—if anyone in their right mind would call it that—was dead in the water. Gasta had disobeyed him and owed him money, making it kind of unlikely that the mobster would be anxious to ever get within rifle range of Nicolai again.

Beamon lit a cigarette and just kept walking. There didn't seem to be much else for him to do, and despite a little residual pain from his injuries, it felt good.

He'd made it almost a mile when his cell phone rang, confusing him for a moment. Hadn't he turned it off? A jolt of adrenaline ran through him when he discovered that it wasn't the phone Laura had the number to that was ringing.

"Yeah."

"You live up to your reputation."

Beamon didn't answer immediately, taking a moment to calm down and slip back into Nicolai.

"Do I?"

"Shit yeah!" Carlo Gasta laughed drunkenly. "Strippers! You are the man. *The man!* We made those cops look like a bunch of assholes!"

"What the hell happened, Carlo? Why'd you shoot?"

"Look, Nicolai . . . I'm sorry about that. Really, I am. My boss wanted those guys dead, you know? What could I do? And we used twenty-twos with silencers. The cops didn't hear us. That's not what brought those fuckers down on us."

"Then you have a leak in your organization," Beamon said. "My sources tell me that the police knew exactly where you were supposed to be. If you'd gone all the way to that amphitheater, you'd have found a SWAT team waiting for you."

"Bullshit! This ain't coming from my guys. I'd trust them with my life."

"Then you should be more careful who you trust," Beamon said, letting a little anger creep into Nicolai's voice. "Because if it wasn't for my intervention you'd be calling me from prison."

"Hey, take it easy, man. No question that you saved my ass and I owe you for that. Look, I know it wasn't the prettiest deal you ever did, but everything worked out. Can we put it behind us?"

"Where's my goddamn money?"

"We're cutting the product up now. You'll get it soon. Relax. You earned it." Gasta laughed loud enough to make Beamon pull the phone away from his ear. "Goddamn strippers! You are the shit, man. Look I gotta go. Gotta go work on getting you your cash."

"Give me a number where I can reach you, Carlo. I've got people in the LAPD If they turn up anything interesting, I'll let you know."

"555-3847 is my cell. Talk to you. . . ." The line clicked as he hung up.

"Great," Beamon said to the empty street. Somehow Gasta contacting him didn't make him feel better, and the reason was obvious. He really *had* earned that three million dollars. It suddenly occurred to Beamon that not only was he an organized criminal, he was a really good one.

He'd more or less lost track of where he was when he came upon a pay phone that looked like it had escaped the wrath of the local vandals. After sticking in a few coins, he dialed Carrie's number. She was out of town until tomorrow but for some reason he wanted to hear her voice.

"Hi, you've reached the home of Dr. Carrie Johnstone. You can leave a message or, if it's an emergency, you can beep me at 555-9394. Sorry I missed your call."

He hung up, feeling like a middle-aged adolescent. That didn't stop him from digging in his pocket for more change, though. Something about her voice provided a brief illusion that none of this had happened.

"Nicolai?"

Beamon dropped the phone and spun around, reaching behind him for his gun.

The weathered, broad-shouldered man standing at the curb didn't react at all, other than to smile politely. He was probably in his early thirties and spoke with what might have been a German accent.

Despite the fact that Beamon already had his hand wrapped around the butt of his .357 and the young man standing in front of him had his hanging at his sides, Beamon knew he was outmatched. If he pulled his gun, this kid would kill him. Or worse, take it away from him. Frankly, he just didn't need that kind of humiliation right now.

"And who are you?" Beamon said, surprising himself with his calm tone. No doubt Nicolai's influence.

"My name is Wolfgang. My employer wanted me to ask if you would be available to meet with him."

Beamon released his gun. "Who's your employer?"

"That is probably something you should talk to him about."

Beamon looked up the road and saw a gray Mercedes gliding toward them. How had this guy tracked him down? The FBI obviously couldn't.

"When were you thinking?"

"Now, if it's convenient."

Of course it didn't really matter if it was or not, but at least the kid was polite.

"Sure. Why the hell not?"

35

"**W**HAT the fuck happened, Jonathan?" The temperature in the conference room seemed to drop as Alan Holsten walked through the door. "There were police everywhere. Where the hell did they come from? And where the hell were you?"

Drake shifted uncomfortably in his chair. He wanted to stand and use his superior height and bulk to assert himself, but knew it would be pointless.

"It was an anonymous tip, Alan. Someone phoned in an anonymous tip. It wasn't possible for my people to complete the mission."

"An anonymous tip," Holsten repeated. "From whom?"

"I don't know yet. It could have been anyone—one of Gasta's enemies, someone being paid off inside his organization . . ."

"Or it could have been Volkov."

Of course that was a possibility. If Volkov had ears inside Gasta's organization, he might have guessed that the CIA would use the heroin transaction as an ambush. If he was working under the assumption that the CIA was abandoning its plot against al-Qaeda, he could be interfering. By protecting Gasta, Volkov knew he would create a distraction that might temporarily deflect attention from him. Drake would be forced to concentrate his resources on hunting Gasta down before the police did.

"It's possible, Alan, but unlikely, I think. A much more probable—"

"Then, tell me how Gasta got away. How did a man that you

described as stupid and completely under your control orchestrate what we're seeing on television?"

Drake had spent most of the day trying to come up with an answer to that question. Only an hour ago he'd gotten his first shred of useful information on the subject.

"He didn't orchestrate it, sir. Someone else did. According to my sources, Gasta hired a man named Nicolai to help him plan the operation."

Holsten nodded coldly. "Nicolai. Why didn't we know about this?"

Drake knew he had to tread lightly here. "Because Gasta wanted to please me. He solicited Nicolai to help him complete the mission I sent him on because he was afraid to fail. But when he succeeded, he wanted to take the credit."

"Your operation has completely fallen apart, Jonathan. The FBI has the bodies of the Afghans and they're going to use them to trace the launcher. Gasta is still alive, and if the police find him before you do, they'll have a direct path to us."

"They won't find him."

"Prove it to me. Prove to me that you aren't just blowing sunshine up my ass like you have for the past two weeks—that you actually have a fucking single clue what you're doing."

Drake stiffened but remained silent.

"Are you in touch with Gasta? Do you know where he is?"

The truth was, he didn't. Gasta had hidden out with the spoils of his victory against the Afghans and wasn't answering his cell phone. Thinking that he'd successfully completed the task Drake had charged him with, he would see no need for immediate communication.

"Not yet," Drake said. "But he'll call me in the next day or—"

"That's not good enough!" Holsten screamed. "What else is there, Jonathan? What else have you done to fuck this thing up?"

Drake laced his hands calmly in his lap but didn't immediately respond. He had information that Volkov was personally supplying al-Qaeda with weapons and intelligence so that they could continue their destabilization of the heroin supply flowing into the U.S. through

Mexico. But he couldn't tell Holsten that. The time for honesty was gone; his position was becoming more and more precarious. All that mattered now was protecting himself.

"There's nothing, Alan. I'll find Gasta and get rid of him. He'll be dead in the next two days. I guarantee it."

"And what about this Nicolai?"

"I assume he's holed up with Gasta, though I can't be sure. We're working on identifying and locating him now."

Holsten pulled a file from under his arm and threw it at Drake. "Let me save you the trouble. Nicolai is Mark Beamon."

"What?" Drake clawed the file open and began sifting through its contents.

"Laura Vilechi sent him undercover when Michaels reported meeting an Afghan heroin dealer. She thought there might be a connection."

Drake pushed aside an old article on Beamon from *The Washington Post* and uncovered Michaels's report.

"So far," Holsten continued, "the FBI is keeping the fact that they had men inside Gasta's organization quiet. They haven't been able to contact Beamon, but they're working on the assumption that Gasta froze him out of the deal. I'm guessing it won't be long before they find out he ignored his orders to arrest Gasta and was directly involved in the deaths of those Afghans."

Drake looked up at Holsten. "That doesn't make sense. Why would he get involved in something like that? Why wouldn't he just hand Gasta over?"

"Because, you stupid son of a bitch, he was there when Gasta called you. He was there when you told Gasta to kill Michaels. And now he's after your ass."

"But . . ." Drake fell silent. He wasn't sure what else to say.

"You know what's at stake here, Jonathan. You've supplied one of America's most dangerous enemies with weapons. You've allied yourself with a major international organized-crime figure. You've ordered the death of an undercover FBI agent." Holsten slammed his hand down on the table. "You *will* bring this operation under control *immediately*, do you understand me? I'm giving you one more chance before I get involved personally."

Holsten turned and walked from the room without further explaining his vague threat. Drake felt the perspiration start to leak from his forehead as the deputy director of operations slammed the door behind him. His life was now in danger. If he was dead, Holsten could paint him as a rogue agent and deflect blame. There could be no more mistakes. But if there were, he had to make sure he had a way out.

36

WITH great difficulty Beamon had refused repeated offers of top-shelf booze, instead opting for coffee and Cokes in an effort to sober up. He'd been less coy when the scent of garlic and herbs filled the cabin and had already packed away more than he'd eaten in any given twenty-four hours over the last year. Why? He wasn't sure. The fact that it was some of the best food he'd ever tasted might have had something to do with it. But there was something else. The condition of his stomach, after reaching an all-time low about ten hours before, seemed to be improving. Maybe there was a silver lining to being completely doomed. With absolutely no upside, there wasn't all that much to left to worry about. It was a badly tarnished silver lining, to be sure, but a silver lining nonetheless.

He sliced into a shrimp ravioli dabbed with a complex green sauce and popped it in his mouth. Fantastic. Wolfgang, his young chaperon, was sitting in a deep leather chair on the other side of the plane, reading a book. He seemed wholly unconcerned that Nicolai was still armed and now also holding a sharp knife—confidence that was undoubtedly well founded.

Beamon finally pushed the plate away, fearing that if he shoveled in another bite, he might actually injure himself. A moment later a woman who'd thought was the stewardess but now suspected was the pilot appeared and cleared the plate.

"Did you enjoy your meal, sir?"

Beamon looked up at her. "It was wonderful, thank you."

She was a striking woman, over six feet tall, with smooth, dark skin, dramatic bone structure, and the pleasant accent of a native African. When she smiled, she revealed a truly magnificent set of teeth. "In that case, can I interest you in dessert? We have—"

"Thank you, but no. As much as I'd like to, I better not risk it." He motioned to the complete darkness outside the window next to him. "Where are we?"

"Not far from our destination," she said vaguely.

"Oh, right. I went on vacation there last year. How much longer?"

Another stunning smile. "Not long. If you're tired, there's a bedroom in the back. Please feel free to use it."

"I'm fine. But thanks for the offer."

Beamon watched her move back toward the cockpit and looked around the plane again. He knew almost nothing about private jets, but he'd been on enough to know that this one was big—much larger than the FBI's. And a hell of a lot nicer too. All leather, exotic woods, and heavy brass. He'd obviously managed to get someone's attention.

Another two hours passed before an obvious loss of altitude saved him from the onset of a nasty food coma. He glanced at his watch, which read eight P.M., and then out the window. The sun was bright and low on the horizon. Dawn. He tried to calculate in his mind where in the world it would be early morning if it was early evening in L.A., but that kind of math just wasn't his forte. It didn't really matter anyway.

As they descended, he watched the endless carpet of tightly packed pine trees get closer and closer. There wasn't much else to see—no towns, no roads. For a moment he thought they might be crashing and wasn't quite sure how he felt about the possibility. It would go a long way to solving his personal problems.

As they continued to descend, though, what had looked like a long gouge in the trees became a well-maintained runway. Beamon kept his face pressed to the glass as the plane touched down but still couldn't see anything of interest. By the time the plane rolled to a stop, Wolfgang was already busy opening the door. He didn't get out but invited Beamon to.

The weather was cool, almost fall-like, as he stepped down onto the tarmac. A pleasant change from L.A. and Phoenix. He put his sunglasses on and watched a tan Ford Expedition speeding toward him. It came to a hurried stop a few feet away and the driver jumped out. He was black, too, but with a smaller frame and lighter skin than the pilot. Beamon guessed that he was in his early thirties.

"Nicolai. I'm Joseph, Christian Volkov's executive assistant." The Australian accent nailed it. Aborigine blood. Quite an international crew.

"Christian Volkov?" Beamon, said, shaking the man's outstretched hand.

"I'll take you to him now."

Beamon climbed into the vehicle and they were immediately on their way. The pavement was replaced with a rutted dirt road after less than a mile, slowing their progress significantly.

"It's a beautiful spot," Beamon said as Joseph carefully maneuvered around a deep pothole. "Where are we?"

"Not far from Christian's home."

Beamon nodded as though that was a credible answer. He might as well give up trying to place himself on a map.

The house was impressive but not spectacular. Probably seven or eight thousand square feet, constructed primarily of gray stone and glass. The setting was the most remarkable thing about it: fantastic views of some mountain range or other, and nothing but pristine wilderness in every direction. With the exception of the airstrip, Beamon wondered if there was anything more than an old mine or hunting cabin within five hundred miles.

As he stepped out of the vehicle, it suddenly occurred to him how alone he was. His status as an FBI agent, tenuous as it was, generally could be counted on to carry some weight. Here, though, it was completely meaningless. Right now, for all intents and purposes, Mark Beamon didn't exist. There was only Nicolai.

The house was haphazardly furnished and Beamon found himself skirting the occasional box or crate as he was led through it. His years of investigative experience weren't necessary to deduce that whoever Christian Volkov was, he'd just moved in.

The room he was finally ushered into was quite large, with a back wall made almost entirely of glass and an enormous fireplace complete with stone gargoyles to the right. Heavy beams that looked as if they had been hewn from the local trees supported an arched ceiling. Again, most of the furniture seemed to be missing, but for some reason the sparse decor looked more studied here: A large desk with a bright red iMac on it and a few chairs was about all there was. The man behind the desk was staring at the computer screen, slowly maneuvering his mouse.

Joseph had already disappeared and Beamon moved forward, examining his apparent host carefully. He was seated, but it was still clear that he wasn't particularly tall—perhaps five foot nine or ten. His hair was medium length and he had a slight but solid build. Age? Early forties, based on the lines around his eyes and the chiseled angularity of his slightly sunburned face. His eyes glowed a little as they picked up the light from the computer screen, but didn't seem particularly piercing. There was something, though . . . something Beamon couldn't put his finger on. Something telling him that the bland aura emanating from the man had been carefully and purposefully crafted.

He finally looked up when Beamon was only a few feet away. "Nicolai. I was just rereading some information Joseph put together on you."

His upper-crust British accent seemed to be too careful for English to be his native language.

"Anything interesting?" Beamon said.

"Fascinating, really. You've had quite a career."

He stood and came around the desk. His gait was graceful and relaxed but didn't betray anything about the man. They shook hands and Volkov pointed to one of two chairs in front of his desk. Beamon sat.

"Can I get you something to drink?"

"Sure. Maybe a sparkling water?"

Volkov walked over to a small refrigerator against the wall and pulled out two. He poured them into heavy crystal glasses and handed one to Beamon before taking a seat in the chair next to him.

Beamon forced himself further into his Nicolai persona, using it to keep himself calm, to keep the rage and hate building inside him from surfacing.

This had to be the man—the son of a bitch who had casually given the order to extinguish Chet Michaels's life. Beamon was suddenly very aware of the .357 still holstered against the small of his back. He looked around, confirming at least the illusion that they were alone. If he pulled his gun, would he have time to get a shot off? Probably. Of course, he'd almost certainly be dead seconds later, but not before he got to watch this bastard's brain leak all over the tasteful stone floor.

No question, it was an option worth considering.

"I know we've never met," Volkov said, "but we had a common associate in South Africa. Carl Munchen."

Beamon didn't react to the name, though it seemed to be a fairly bad sign that Munchen was connected with the man sitting in front of him. The FBI had credited Nicolai with his assassination.

"I'm really in your debt," Volkov continued. "I can't tell you how convenient Carl's death was to me."

"I've never been to South Africa," Beamon said honestly.

Volkov smiled and took a sip from his glass. "Of course. My mistake."

"I don't mean to be rude, but who are you and why am I here?"

"I'm sorry, I assumed Joseph had told you. I'm Christian Volkov."

Beamon kept his expression passive, giving away no indication of recognition, but also not admitting to being unfamiliar with the name.

The truth was, he'd never heard of Volkov. The FBI was aware that men like him existed, though—floating like ghosts from country to country with a handful of semilegitimate passports and involving themselves in drugs, arms dealing, gambling, counterfeit goods, slavery, and many other "businesses."

The money and political power men like this controlled was staggering. But because of the carefully international nature of their crimes, they were virtually untouchable. America's own law enforcement agencies could barely stand each other. The idea of international coordination sophisticated enough to catch and prosecute someone like this was more or less a joke.

"And who are you?" Volkov asked. "Nicolai is just a name on an Interpol file."

"Call me Mark."

"I'm glad we could get together to talk, Mark."

Beamon wondered if Volkov had gotten a dossier on Chet before he'd had him killed. If he knew that Chet had been only thirty-three. If he knew Chet's wife's name. If he knew that both of Chet's parents were still alive to attend their son's funeral.

Volkov crossed his legs, revealing work boots where Beamon would have expected a pair of two-thousand-dollar loafers. "I have to admit, Mark . . . I'm not sure I understand you."

"How so?"

"I've been asking myself why someone like you would get involved with Carlo Gasta. Why you would involve yourself in something so unpredictable and banal as the theft of a shipment of heroin?"

"Gasta owed me money. He killed a young FBI agent I had been cultivating."

Volkov frowned. "Chet Michaels. Yes. Unfortunate."

Beamon had to struggle not to pull his gun out and blow the back of Volkov's smug head off. "If Gasta managed to succeed in getting ahold of the heroin, he'd have the money to pay me. He's fairly stupid, though, and it seemed unlikely that he'd be able to do it on his own. I didn't involve myself directly—just a bit of consulting."

"How much?"

"Consulting?"

"Money."

"Three million, U.S. But it was more the principle than the cash."

Volkov put his empty glass down on a small table next to him, and Beamon couldn't help thinking about the fingerprints it contained. He already figured his chances of leaving there alive at less than fifty percent, though. With some of the guy's china in his pants, his chances would probably decline to around zero.

"And the entire operation was wonderfully successful," Volkov said. "Thanks, in part, to a number of attractive women taking their clothes off on critical thoroughfares. I assume that was your doing."

Beamon shrugged. "Apparently there was a leak somewhere. The police knew where the transaction was going to take place. If Gasta had been captured, I wouldn't get paid."

Volkov nodded thoughtfully but didn't speak. The silence wasn't overtly threatening, but after about a minute Beamon started wondering if he'd said something he shouldn't have.

"I have to say in all modesty that I don't make a habit out of being outsmarted," Volkov said, finally breaking the silence.

Beamon considered the seemingly out-of-place comment for a moment. "It was you," he said finally. "You leaked the location to the LAPD."

"And it was my expectation that Carlo Gasta would be arrested with a gun in his hand, surrounded by a Afghan drug dealers and heroin. But because I underestimated him—and by that, I mean that he would be able to convince you to get involved—I've lost both him and the drugs." He paused for a moment. "Though I understand that the Afghans' bodies are now in the hands of the American authorities."

Beamon took a sip of his Perrier. "And you'd like me to tell you where Gasta is."

"Yes."

"I honestly don't know."

"And if you did?"

"I wouldn't tell you. First, if Gasta gets arrested, I don't get paid. Second, while he owes me two of the three million for the trouble he's caused me, the other million is payment for my involvement. Double-crossing an employer—even an idiot like Carlo Gasta—would be bad for my reputation."

Volkov leaned back in his chair, raising the front legs off the ground, but didn't say anything.

"May I ask why you're so interested in someone like Gasta? Why would you care about him one way or another?"

"He's become unstable, unreliable. Wait . . . a burr under my saddle. Is that right?"

Beamon nodded.

"On the street he's become a liability. In the court system he could become an asset, if you understand me."

Unfortunately, Beamon understood perfectly. "Criminal Darwinism."

"Excuse me?"

"Criminal Darwinism," Beamon repeated. "If you think about it, the police are the natural predators of criminals. And, like all predators, they generally take only the weak and stupid. In the end, all they succeed in doing is culling the herd, making the whole stronger. And smart criminal organizations will take it one step further—purposely giving up people who are causing problems to further their own purposes and to appease law enforcement officials and politicians."

"Criminal Darwinism," Volkov repeated. "May I use that? I've never heard it expressed so eloquently."

"Be my guest," Beamon said, taking another sip of his water. He wanted a cigarette something awful, but guessed that this guy was one of those assholes who didn't allow smoking in his house. Yet another reason to want him dead. "I have to wonder, Christian: Why is it you're being so open with me?"

"You seem trustworthy."

"Should I translate that as I'm never going to leave here alive?"

"I'm many things, but I am not a . . . a . . . sore loser."

It suddenly occurred to Beamon that it really wouldn't matter if "Nicolai" talked. The FBI, the cops, the politicians—they all wanted Gasta so bad they could taste it. The fact that his arrest was convenient for an international crime lord was neither here nor there. Like Laura said: What were they going to do—tell the press that Carlo Gasta was just some small-time crook and that the man in power was out of America's reach?

"Having said that," Volkov continued, "it is my intention to see Gasta in jail. Can I count on you to not interfere?"

"You have me at a disadvantage."

"It isn't my intention to threaten you."

"Well, then, I have to say that I want my money and your plan doesn't work for me. I mean, I wish you well, but in this case our interests seem to conflict."

"I understand." Volkov stood and walked to his desk, pushing the intercom button on his phone. "Joseph, could you come in here for a moment, please?"

Beamon adjusted himself in his chair and moved his hand subtly closer to his gun. He was probably going down, but not before he did everything in his power to make sure Christian Volkov preceded him.

Joseph appeared a moment later, looking about as threatening as kitten. "What can I do for you, Christian?"

"We have Nicolai's bank account number, don't we?"

Joseph looked at Beamon and recited the one Laura had given him when they'd put his cover together.

"Is that correct?" Volkov asked.

Beamon hadn't actually memorized it but felt depressingly confident in the competence of Volkov's organization. He nodded.

"Joseph, please wire three million dollars into that account as soon as the banks open."

Joseph nodded and disappeared again through the door.

Beamon wasn't sure exactly what had just happened, but when Volkov stretched his hand out, he stood and took it.

"It's my understanding that your obligations to Carlo Gasta are finished and that now the money isn't an issue. Have we reached an understanding?"

"I guess we have."

Volkov put a hand on Beamon's back and walked him to the door. "Joseph will take you back to my plane. We'll have you on the ground in L.A. in a few hours."

Beamon passed through the door but then stopped and turned around. "Oh, Christian. Those raviolis with the green sauce . . . Give your chef my compliments."

Volkov's smile seemed strangely genuine. "François has been perfecting that recipe for years. He'll be very happy to hear you enjoyed it."

Beamon followed Joseph back outside and climbed into the Expedition again. He intended to do everything in his power to see Christian Volkov dead. But he'd spare the chef if at all possible.

Beamon glanced at his watch. They'd been in the air for almost two hours and he still hadn't been thrown out the window. He looked around him again, though for no particular reason. The plane was pretty much empty. It was just him, the less-than-dangerous-looking female pilot, and a handful of really good puff pastries.

He popped another in his mouth and thought about what had just happened. It was almost certain that he had just sipped Perrier with the man he was looking for—the man ultimately responsible for Chet's death. And on the surface that seemed like a step in the right direction. But was it really? What did he really have that he hadn't had yesterday? A description of a medium-sized man of unknown nationality, with medium-length brown hair, almost certainly living somewhere on the planet earth.

The worst part, though, was that their business together appeared to have been concluded. It seemed highly unlikely that the paths of Nicolai and Christian Volkov would ever cross again. The question was, what could he do about that?

He could hijack the plane, fill it with an FBI SWAT team, and force the pilot to take him back. But Volkov would see that coming a mile away. Besides, what was the likelihood he was anywhere the FBI could operate, anyway?

Assuming that Volkov actually wired him the three million—and Beamon had a strange feeling he would—the FBI could try to trace the money back. Another waste of time. If there was one thing organized-crime lords could do, it was make money materialize out of the ether.

He could track down Gasta and sweat him for information on Volkov. But what were the chances Gasta had ever even seen this guy? Based on Chet's description of the man he and Gasta had met, it was one of Volkov's people and not the man himself.

His last, and equally bad, idea was to save Gasta from the cops again and see if he could make Volkov angry. An action that would almost certainly get him summarily executed.

"Fuck!"

A moment later the pilot appeared from the cockpit. "Did you need something, sir?"

Beamon twisted his face into a polite smile. "I sneezed."

"God bless you."

37

MARK Beamon couldn't even seem to muster the energy to yawn. The memory of the last time he'd slept was starting to get fuzzy, as was his ability to think coherently. He'd gone so far as to stretch out on the bed in the back of Volkov's jet, but that nagging feeling that Wolfgang was going to jump out of a utility hatch and slit his throat had kept his eyes from closing. All in all, it had been a long flight.

He slumped over in the backseat of the car and leaned against the window. It took a few moments for him to realize that he had no idea where they were. He wasn't all that familiar with L.A., but he'd swear he'd never seen this part of town before. A jolt of adrenaline partially pulled him from his stupor and he reached behind him, once again wrapping his hand around the butt of his gun.

"Are you sure you know where you're going?" he said to the back of the driver's head.

"Yes, sir. In fact, we're here."

The Mercedes turned and glided to a stop in the courtyard of an elegant-looking hotel.

"This isn't where I'm staying," Beamon said.

"I believe it is, sir. Room 305."

Beamon didn't move for a moment but then decided to just go with the flow. He jumped out of the car and entered the hotel, striding purposefully toward the man manning front desk. The lobby was otherwise empty. Business and vacation travel had more or less ground to a halt since the launcher photograph had appeared.

"Hi. I'm in, uh, Room 305."

"Of course, sir. Welcome." The man handed him a card key. "I've been instructed to tell you that all of your expenses are being taken care of by your employer. Please let us know if there is anything we can do for you."

A thin smile spread across Beamon's face as he turned and started for the elevator. Volkov obviously wasn't finished with him. And that meant he had another shot.

The room turned out to be enormous—a two-bedroom suite with a large balcony overlooking a garden. Fresh flowers were everywhere, and a bottle of champagne was accompanied by a personal note from the hotel manager that included his home number should any problems arise that couldn't be solved by his staff. Even more interesting was a box about six inches square topped with an elegant bow. A bomb? No, too melodramatic: Volkov had his chance and passed it up. Beamon opened it and found another cell phone to add to his growing collection. A sticky note on top of it read: *You might find this profitable.*

What few possessions he'd had at his other hotel were arranged neatly in one of the bedrooms, along with an elaborate assortment of sweets on a heavy silver platter. Beamon sat down on the bed and grabbed a fork, turning his personal cell phone on and retrieving his messages as he attacked a piece of fresh cheesecake. An impressive five from the Director's secretary, each with increasing urgency. The last one was from Laura. He checked the phone Gasta had the number to next. Nothing.

Sighing quietly, he dialed Laura.

"Hello?"

"Did you miss me?"

"Mark! Where have you been?"

"I honestly have no idea."

"We've got to meet."

It suddenly occurred to him that he didn't know where his rental car was. Still confident in Volkov's efficiency, he took a quick look around and found the keys next to a note giving the car's location in the hotel's parking lot.

"Just us again, right?"

"Yeah, just us."

"What are you still doing here?" Beamon said, sliding into the booth across from Laura. Her hair had pulled itself partially from the band tying it back, and individual blond strands were floating around in the breeze created by an overhead fan. Dark circles had painted themselves beneath her eyes, and a tall glass of milk sat in front of her on the table. Despite his own situation, he couldn't help feeling a pang of concern. Her pieces usually fit together so tightly.

"Looking for you."

"Why? I delivered Afghans. I don't think I can help you any more."

"Maybe I was just worried about you. After we talked you just disappeared again. I thought something might have happened to you."

A man appeared and slid a beer onto the table. "On me—for having the guts to leave your house."

Beamon guessed he was the empty diner's owner by the bitterness in his voice.

"Thanks."

"So? Did something happen to you?" Laura said when the man retreated out of earshot.

Beamon shook his head. "What's going on, Laura? You look like you're on your last leg."

She pushed her glass of milk around on the table with her index finger. "You were right."

"About what?"

"Have you been watching the news?"

"No."

"It's all turning against me, Mark. I haven't found the launcher and I haven't found the people responsible for it being here. The pressure's getting worse, and it goes all the way up. The President and Charles Russell are pushing to create yet another oversight committee—this one just to look over my shoulder. So I'm going to end up with a bunch of thirty-year-old Ivy Leaguers second-guessing everything I do and trying to make themselves look good at my expense."

"Don't take this so personally, Laura. Politicians have always had a love-hate relationship with the Bureau. Every time they want to take a bribe or chase a skirt, they have to wonder if we're taping it. Now they get their revenge. It's not you."

She just kept playing with her glass of milk. "You know, I kind of always wanted to be you. I wanted to be the person everyone called when things got really tough. The kind of person who'd do what had to be done. . . ."

"How do you like it?"

"It's more than I bargained for. Knowing that a rocket could come out of nowhere at any minute and hit anything. And that if it does, it's my fault."

He wanted to tell her that it wouldn't be her fault—that it would be the fault of the assholes who actually fired the rocket. But people had been telling him similar things for years, and it never helped. The buck had to stop somewhere.

"How did you handle it, Mark?"

He opened the can of beer and took a swig. "I drink, remember?"

When she looked up at him, he swore that her eyes looked a little wet.

"There's more," he said. "What is it?"

She wiped at her eyes, confirming his suspicion. "The press . . . they're starting to turn on me, too . . . starting to say that I don't have what it takes to be in charge. . . ."

She pulled out a roll of Tums and offered him one. He shook his head.

"Are you getting *anywhere*, Laura?"

She shook her head. "Everything I've done has been a waste of time. We're pretty sure that the rocket and launcher were manufactured somewhere in the former Soviet Union. Guess where that piece of detective work got me."

"Knowing the Russians as I do, I'd say nowhere."

"Exactly right. We're following up on your drug angle, trying to make deals with some of the big traffickers to see if they know anything about how a rocket launcher might have been smuggled into the States and who might be involved. Guess where that's getting me."

"Knowing drug traffickers as I do, I'd say nowhere."

"Right again. We're still tracking sales and rentals of trucks big enough to haul this thing—unfortunately, they don't have to be all that big—and have local cops looking for them on the roads. Know where that's getting me?"

"Just a guess here. Nowhere?"

"Worse! I've got people chucking the Bill of Rights right out the window! Yesterday some cops about a hundred miles from here had a kid in a U-Haul facedown on the road with a gun in the back of his head. He was a surfer and had a good tan. They thought he might be Arab."

"Lovely."

"And finally, I've got a bunch of politicians wanting me to point my finger so they can start lobbing cruise missiles—but there's nowhere to target anymore. They're putting a lot of pressure on me to say Sudan or whatever so that they can look like they're hitting back. You know where *that's* going to get me?"

"Feeling responsible for the deaths of thousands of dirt-poor Sudanese women and children who had nothing to do with any of this?"

"Goddamn right!" she nearly shouted.

Beamon reached across the table and grabbed her hand. "Laura, you're going to have to calm down or you're going to die. I'm serious."

"How can I calm down? I am a complete failure! The only decent leads I have came from you. And it's not even your case." She popped another Tums and began chewing violently.

"It could be worse."

"How?"

"You could be me."

She looked up at him. "The Director said that the only reason he'd accept for you not returning his calls was that you were dead."

"Still wanting Gasta, is he?"

Laura just raised her eyebrows.

He wondered how much he should tell her. It was possible that the information he had could help, but it also had the potential to blow up in their faces.

"An interesting thing happened to me, Laura. I was walking around after we talked last night, and some German guy comes up to me—to Nicolai—and tells me his boss wants to meet me. Next thing I know, I'm on a very nice jet for about twelve hours. When I get off I'm God-knows-where and I meet this guy named Christian Volkov. . . ."

Laura pulled out a piece of paper and a pen. "You know how to spell that?"

"He didn't say. Do your best and run it though the computers. You should call Jonathan Drake at the CIA, too, and see if he can turn up anything."

She nodded. "What did he want?"

Beamon leaned back in the booth but didn't answer.

"Mark, what did he want?"

"He just seemed to want to talk about some of the things I'd done, to size me up. I couldn't figure it out, but when I got back, he'd moved me to a nice hotel and put me up in a suite. I think he's courting me as a potential employee. It was an interview."

Keeping secrets from her was harder than he thought it would be.

"So you think he's the one who Chet met with? The one behind Gasta?"

"Him or one of his people. Probably . . . maybe."

She looked at him searchingly for a moment. "Are you holding out on me, Mark?"

"Yes."

"You don't think you can trust me?"

"I'm absolutely certain I can trust you—you've already started lying to the Director to try to protect me. I don't want you to go down with me, Laura."

"I want the information, Mark. Then you and I can decide what to do with it. But I want everything."

"Honestly, Laura, I doubt this guy has much to do with your problem."

"But are you sure?"

"No."

"Could he be involved in terrorism?"

"Directly? I doubt it. Volkov's a businessman. Besides, this is a guy who seems to really cherish his anonymity. Terrorism is high profile and a money-losing proposition any way you look at it."

"So you think he has no connection to this?"

"I didn't say that. If he's behind Gasta, then he's involved with Afghan heroin on some level. If we're right and Mustafa Yasin is tying to get control of the heroin trade in the Golden Crescent, maybe Volkov is backing him. Or maybe he's backing the other side. I honestly don't know."

"But either way, he might have information on where the launcher came from and where it is now."

"It's possible. He strikes me as a guy with a lot of information."

"What else?"

"You're sure you want to hear all this."

"I'm sure."

"He's the one who called in the tip to the cops. The real reason he wanted to talk to me was because I interfered by helping Gasta get away. He paid me three mil not to get in the way next time."

"Dollars? Three million dollars?"

"I'm guessing it's already in my account. I think he wants Gasta in custody so he can roll over on some people Volkov has no use for any-more."

"It's like that depressing theory of criminal Darwinism you have."

"I thought you never listened to my theories."

"I'm not sure I understand, Mark. If it's true that he wanted Gasta arrested, why tell him to execute the Afghans? The cops would move in before it happened or would start a shooting match that Gasta would probably get killed in. A dead Carlo Gasta couldn't roll over on inconvenient people. It seems that this Volkov was leaving a lot to chance."

And that was something that bothered Beamon too. Volkov didn't seem the type.

They sat in silence for a few minutes, considering the problem. Finally, Laura spoke.

"The Director wants Gasta. He's responsible for the death of an FBI agent and the deaths of those Afghans. Not to mention the drugs. What are you going to do?"

"I'm not going to do anything. I don't even know where he is."

"You think Volkov will find him and phone in another tip to the cops? That he wasn't just screwing with you?"

"That's what I think."

"If you're confident, we can probably use that."

"Use it?"

"Are you confident?"

"I think so. Yeah."

Laura pulled her phone from her pocket and dialed.

"Director Caroll? Mark Beamon just called me."

The shouting on the other side of the phone was audible from across the table.

"He in pretty deep, sir, and hasn't been able to get to a phone. He doesn't know where Gasta is right now, but he's doing everything he can to locate him. He thinks it will take another day, maybe two. Yes, sir. He's going to contact us but he says it won't come directly from him—it's too dangerous. It will be another anonymous tip. Yes, sir. I don't know—that's what he told me. I only talked to him only briefly. Thank you, sir."

She shut off the phone and looked up at him. "See where that gets us."

"You're being stupid, Laura. I'm beyond saving—we both know it. It's time for you to start distancing yourself from me, okay? This situation is only going to get worse."

She started playing with her glass again, seeming to not hear him.

"What is it now?" he said.

She didn't answer.

He grabbed the glass. "Laura?"

"Remember when we talked a few days ago? When I told you that finding the guy behind Gasta wasn't going to be a priority for the Bureau?"

"Yeah."

"Well, that was true, you know."

"I know."

"I . . ."

"Spit it out, Laura."

"I didn't need to say that. I . . . I did it on purpose. I wanted—I needed—you to pull one of your crazy stunts. I was desperate."

Beamon was caught off guard by the statement and wasn't immediately sure what to say. In the end he just laughed. "I always knew you were an evil bitch."

"Mark, I'm serious."

"Me too."

"If you lose your job . . ." her voice trailed off.

"No great catastrophe. It's not that good a job."

She finally found the resolve to look him in the eye. "Do you want to see where your crazy stunt got us?"

"What do you mean? I thought you said you were getting nowhere."

"I did. I said *I* was getting nowhere. So far, though, your record's not bad."

38

"DIAL the phone, Mark."

"No."

"Dial it."

"Look, I don't want to, okay? What am I going to say?"

Laura accelerated the car slightly and flipped down her visor, blocking the glare off the empty desert highway in front of them.

"It doesn't matter what you say. You just need to say something. She's worried about you or she wouldn't be leaving messages at my house."

"Tell me where you're taking me."

Laura pulled her phone from her pocket and dialed a number into it. "Carrie? Hey, it's Laura. Sorry I didn't get back to you sooner. Yeah. . . . You can't even imagine."

Beamon grimaced, knowing what was coming.

"Hey, guess who's sitting right here next to me? None other. . . . Want to talk to him? Hang on."

Beamon made a halfhearted attempt to look pissed off but was just too tired. He took the phone and pressed it to his ear. "Carrie? Hi. How are you?"

"I'm okay, Mark. Where have you been? The people at your office just say you're out. It's all been very secret agent. . . ."

He had to admit, as out of control as his life had gotten over the last week, it was great to hear her voice. Even better live than on the machine.

"It's probably not as interesting as it sounds," he lied. "I got conned into doing an undercover job for a friend."

"Aren't you a little old for that kind of thing?"

"Thanks, Carrie. Always nice to talk to you."

"That's not what I mean. I mean that you're the SAC–Phoenix. Is it common for people in your position to do undercover work?"

"Like I said, just a quick favor for a friend."

"Anybody I know?"

In fact, it was. Chet Michaels had been a first-office agent in Flagstaff, where Carrie lived and Beamon used to work. In fact, Chet had been at Beamon's apartment when Carrie had asked him to the wedding that was technically their first date.

"No. No one you know."

"Well, I bet you're really good at playing the desperate criminal type."

"I've already made over three million dollars."

She laughed. "If it was anybody else, I'd think that was a joke."

"Tax-free. I'm thinking about switching careers."

"So you're doing okay? You're not going to get yourself shot at."

"Nah. I'm good. A little tired. Maybe I *am* getting too old for this."

"I'd like to get together and talk, Mark. How much longer is this job going to last?"

Beamon stared out the window, squinting against the sun. It was a good question. The rest of his life? "Turns out it could be a little longer than I thought."

"Really? What about the inspection? Is that done? How did it go?"

The inspection. He'd almost forgotten about that.

"No, it's not quite finished," he said, not knowing if it was true or not. "I think it's going to turn out better than I thought." Definitely a lie. "What do you want to talk about?"

"Maybe it would be better to wait until we can get together."

He glanced over at Laura, who was pretending not to be listening. "Are you finally dumping me?"

"Mark! No. It's nothing like that. Kind of the opposite, actually."

"Well, you've got me now, and I can't guarantee when we're going to get to talk again. Maybe you should just say what you want to say."

There was a brief silence over the phone. "Okay. I will. It's about what we talked about at dinner . . . about your job."

"Yeah?"

"I told you that I thought you could do really well at it if you tried."

"Mmm-hmm."

"I've been thinking about that. Maybe it's all about doing what you love. Someone once said to me that life is not a rehearsal. Counting on getting your reward after you die is kind of a leap. So maybe what it's really about is making yourself happy."

"What happened to striving for mental health, balance, and self-improvement?"

"As much as I hate to admit it, I'm starting to feel the irresistible pull of your philosophy. . . ."

"My philosophy?"

"Psychotic, self-destructive, hedonistic wacko-ism."

"So you're giving up obsessive soul-searching, self-doubt, and Amish-like discipline?"

"Touché. What I'm saying is that if a little denial and a couple of beers helps get you through the day, it's not such a bad thing. And if you hate that job, why not just take a demotion or whatever you have to do to get back to the one you loved? When you're lying on your deathbed, you won't be thinking, Damn, I wish I'd have gotten a higher SES rating. . . . Mark? Are you still there?"

Was it possible that she had finally convinced herself to take him back full-time, just when it was too late? The gods continued their mean streak where he was concerned.

"Yeah, I'm still here. I'm just surprised."

"Me too."

Another long silence.

"Emory's been asking about you."

Laura had pulled off the main road and was heading toward an old prefab house sitting in what looked like the middle of nowhere.

"You tell her I'll see her—see you both—soon. Look, Carrie, I've got to go. But don't worry, okay? Laura's watching out for me."

"That makes me feel a little better," she said, sounding genuinely relieved. "Hurry up and finish what you're doing. I'd like to talk some more."

"Me too."

He hung up and handed the phone back to Laura as she eased the car around the dilapidated house to a more discreet parking space in the back.

"Thanks a lot, Laura. Now I'm really depressed."

She set the brake and jumped out, leaning back through the open door. "I think I have something that's going to cheer you up."

The house was simplistic in design, nothing more than a slightly crooked box surrounded by a yard devoid of anything but sand, and open expanses in every direction. It was as if the building had fallen from the sky and landed there by chance.

"Is this where the FBI's putting you up, Laura? I've got a four-thousand-dollar-a-night suite. Maybe I could put in a good word for you with Christian."

She ignored him and pushed the front door open. After his eyes adjusted, he saw that the interior was about what he'd expected: furniture with the stuffing hanging out, a dirty shag carpet, water-stained walls. The windows had been covered with thick black cloth, creating a depressing gloom.

"Where are we?" Beamon said.

"This is it, Mark. We traced the van those Afghans were driving. It wasn't easy, but it led us here."

Beamon looked around him again. "Is the FBI watching the house? You just told the Director you couldn't find me."

"A friend of mine is in charge of surveillance. He agreed to take a coffee break for an hour."

Beamon shook his head. "Stupid, Laura. But since we're here, did you find anything? Is there a connection to your terrorists?"

She shrugged enigmatically.

"Did you check phone records?"

"Yeah, but we didn't find anything interesting. There was somebody here holding down the fort, though."

Beamon spun around to face her. "There was somebody here? You've got somebody alive?"

She nodded, a real smile spreading across her face for the first time that day. "He's not talking yet, but we've got him."

"Have you been able to figure out who he is?"

"We haven't been able to identify any of them yet. We're running their prints and photos through every law enforcement agency we can think of. Somebody will claim them. Eventually."

"But you don't have anything concrete to link them to the terrorists. I mean, they're probably just drug dealers, right? Just because you come from Afghanistan doesn't mean you're a terrorist."

"I've got one more thing to show you."

He followed her into the kitchen and then down a rickety staircase to the dirt floor of the basement. The light wasn't very good—provided by a single bare bulb—but he could see that there wasn't much down there: A plywood table with a long, wooden box on it was about all. Laura strode over and pulled the top off the crate.

"Jesus . . ." was all Beamon could get out. It was just like in the picture: about ten feet long and pitch black, with small fins at the base and a conical nose cone. What hadn't been visible in the photo, though, was the elegant Arabic script etched on it in gold.

"What does it say?"

"'Death to the great Satan,' jihad this, jihad that. Typical Muslim terrorist stuff."

He ran his hand along its cold surface, feeling the individual letters. "Jesus," he said again.

"What do you think?" Laura said. "Not bad, huh?"

"Your long shot seems to have come in. My hat's off to you."

"Remember what I said about your sins being forgiven if we turned up something," she said. "I think this qualifies as something."

"Where did it come from?" Beamon said, strangely mesmerized by the deep black of its surface.

"Like I said, probably the former Soviet Union. Built mostly out of spare parts from old multiple launch ammunition, with a few parts specifically, if crudely, manufactured for it. Our people says it's not particularly sophisticated, but it'll get the job done."

Beamon nodded.

"Apparently—and you're not going to believe this—there's at least one organized-crime outfit throwing these things together and selling them. The beautiful paint job wasn't done by the terrorists: They're sold this way. It's all about marketing. This unit's called . . . I think it translates into something like Fire of God. They package them to appeal to their buyers. If they sold one to the IRA it would probably have a picture of the pope on it."

"We live in a very strange world," Beamon said. "Does this mean you've tracked it back to the group that sold it?"

"It's not that simple. These outfits are like smoke, Mark. More than likely a bunch of former KGB agents feathering a retirement nest. You wouldn't believe the maze. You can't tell where crime ends and politics starts over there."

"So you don't know how many more of these are out there?"

She shook her head.

"Then you're assuming that the launcher is on the road," Beamon began, "that this is just one of a number of cells holding a rocket."

"Right. Somewhere we've got a truck with the launcher in it and he's waiting for word to go to a cell with a rocket. Maybe this is the only one, but I doubt we're that lucky."

"Well, you can be sure he won't come here. The thing with Gasta's been all over the TV. Whoever's running this operation knows that this cell is blown."

"Hopefully, the rocket and the launcher aren't together yet. We've been leaking information to the press to keep the panic fairly high. It's killing the economy, but I'm guessing that's al-Qaeda's plan. They won't crawl out of their holes until things start going back to normal." Laura looked down at the rocket. "If we're right and Yasin is trying to set himself up in the heroin business, we've got real problems. He's going to have a whole lot of money and connections to the Russian crime machine. There's no telling how many of these toys he'll be able to buy."

Beamon nodded. "I wouldn't even worry about that. What I'd worry about is that his relationship with the Mexican smugglers is going to mean he can get anything he wants into this country anytime he wants."

The sound of a cell phone ringing startled them both and set them to patting their pockets.

"Mine," Laura said, putting it to her ear. She hung up after a moment and began towing Beamon toward the stairs. "Your friend works fast, Mark."

39

LAURA steered the car through the small industrial park, finally gliding to a stop in front of a utility truck parked sideways across the narrow road. A man in coveralls immediately climbed out of it and began walking in their direction. Laura rolled down the window.

"Ma'am," he said touching his hard hat politely, "we've got a busted gas main in here and we've had to close down the entire area. It shouldn't take long. Hopefully we'll be done with the repairs in a few hours."

Laura flipped open her FBI credentials and held them up so that the man could see them. He crouched down and leaned into the window a bit. "Our guys are almost in position and we've got the area locked down. We'll be breaching in probably five minutes." He pointed to the warehouse behind him. "Go around there and I'll have someone meet you."

"Thank you," Laura said, rolling up the window and pulling away. In the side mirror Beamon watched the "workman" talking into a walkie-talkie.

"I admit it's not ideal, but it could be worse," Laura said, picking up the conversation they'd been having before they were stopped.

Beamon laughed. "Your optimism is actually starting to cheer me up. Keep it coming. Seriously."

The situation she was talking about was the anonymous tip that had been received regarding Carlo Gasta's location. While the enigmatic Christian Volkov had been right on time, he'd called the cops and not the FBI. Based on what Laura had told the Director, he would assume that the tip had originated with Beamon and see it as Beamon giving him the finger.

"We can just play it off as a mistake," Laura said. "Tell him that—"

"Give it up, Laura," Beamon said as she parked the car and they got out. "The cops are about to catch Gasta and he's going tell them all about Nicolai."

"Are you sure? Gasta's afraid of you, right? And he's an insecure ass. Are you sure he wouldn't just forget about Nicolai and take credit for the heist himself? He's screwed either way."

"Laura . . ."

"And even if he does implicate you, he's not going to do it right away—he's going to wheel and deal. We still have some time."

"Not as much as you think."

A shadowy figure standing in the door of the warehouse in front of them motioned them over. "Agent Vilechi?" he said when they got within whispering distance.

She nodded. "And this is my associate." She didn't give a name.

"Could you follow me please?"

The LAPD had taken over the second floor of a vacant warehouse, which was now filled with ten or so men moving urgently back and forth, talking quietly into phones and radios, gazing into video monitors, making notes on clipboards. The windows at the far end of the expansive space had been covered in a similar way to the ones in the old house he and Laura had just left. Beamon was about to peek out of one when a rather unhappy-looking man started hurrying across the floor toward them.

"Agent Vilechi. I'm Lieutenant Troy Marsten. I'm in charge of this operation."

"Call me Laura," she said smoothly. "We appreciate you letting us watch. We won't get in your way."

He glanced up at Beamon but that was the extent of his acknowledgment.

"We've got real-time video of all sides of the target building and we just got fiber optics in through the skylights." He pointed to a line of monitors on the floor, and Beamon crouched down to examine the different views of the warehouse across the street.

The exterior wasn't all that interesting, but there seemed to be a fair amount of activity inside. The building was one huge room with ceilings that were high enough to make the entire space visible to the overhead cameras. He could make out five men inside, but the angle and quality of the image made them impossible to recognize. The van parked in the middle of the concrete floor wasn't quite so hard to identify, though. He remembered that vividly.

A voice came over Marsten's walkie-talkie and he held it up to his ear. "They're ready to go. Is everyone up here ready?"

There was an affirmative murmur from the group as they crowded around the monitors. Marsten put the walkie-talkie to his mouth. "Go! I repeat: Go!"

Black-clad men carrying battering rams suddenly materialized on-screen and made quick work of the warehouse's doors. A moment later they were inside and Beamon redirected his attention to the interior video. The five out-of-focus figures inside froze for a moment and then began to scatter, but it was too late. A cascade of glass fell past the camera as the skylight was smashed and a sniper shoved his gun through.

It didn't take long for the chaos to turn to order. Within two minutes the five men were lying on their stomachs, handcuffed, and the members of the SWAT team were sweeping the building. A few more minutes passed before Marsten's walkie-talkie came to life.

"We're clear in here, Troy. We've got five Caucasian males and one of 'em is Carlo Gasta. . . ."

A loud cheer went up in the room.

"We've also got a whole lot of something I'd bet is heroin."

Another cheer, augmented with a little backslapping.

"All right," Marsten said. "Good job. Is it safe to let the vultures in?"

"Go ahead. We've got it under control."

"You heard him," Marsten said to the men surrounding him. "Let 'em out."

One of his men pulled the blankets off the windows and waved. Beamon and Laura watched as three television vans careened down the narrow road and skidded to a halt.

"Where were you keeping them?" Beamon asked as the cameramen set up their equipment and reporters messed with their hair.

"We had them penned up on the south perimeter."

The activity level notched up again as the door to the warehouse opened and a stream of well-guarded wise guys came pouring out. Gasta was last, straining against his handcuffs and the men holding him. The gold chains around his neck flashed in the sunlight when he tried to kick a reporter who got a microphone too close to him. It seemed that he'd temporarily forgotten his love affair with the media.

Beamon could see that he was shouting, but couldn't hear what. It didn't matter. All in all, it was the easiest three million dollars he'd ever earn.

40

MARK Beamon had been impressing himself for the last ten minutes by managing to lie completely still in the middle of the large hotel bed without the aid of alcohol. Despite a bottle of champagne within easy reach, he was nearly completely sober. But it was starting to give him a headache.

The large television at the foot of the bed was replaying Carlo Gasta's captured for the fiftieth time. Leaked information on the van and heroin had led the media to begin speculating on a connection between Gasta and the excitement two nights before, allowing for some more gratuitous stripper footage. Beamon could almost feel the advertising rates going up. He figured he should be getting a piece of that action, but then remembered he'd already been more than fairly compensated.

The full-screen image of Gasta's enraged face faded and was replaced by a lively interview with a big-haired blonde in a rather small halter top, then, less interestingly, to the head of the LAPD. Finally it settled on the ever-present Charles Russell.

"I think we're sending a message that we aren't going to put up with this garbage." He was standing about halfway up a set of marble steps, framed dramatically by the Capitol. His suit, hair, and shirt were impeccable but his tie was slightly loose, hinting at the hard work he was doing for the American people.

"We have zero tolerance for organized crime and drugs, and you're starting to see the results of the initiatives of this administration. We are one hundred percent behind our law enforcement people and are doing everything possible to support them. It's that kind of partnership between Washington and the local agencies that produces results. . . ."

Beamon grimaced and looked longingly at the bottle of champagne. He'd met Charles Russell no less than three times and could say with some certainty that he didn't know the meaning of the word *partnership*. He was the kind of politician who asked a question and then instantly glazed over if you gave him an answer he didn't want to hear. Russell's answer to everything was more jails, more cops, fewer rights, more things illegal. Punish, punish, punish.

"The capture of Carlo Gasta—one of the most powerful organized-crime figures in America, and perhaps the world—will be a major blow. . . ."

Beamon tuned him out and lit a cigarette. Honestly, he was probably being a little hard on Russell. Most politicians did everything for appearances, creating ineffective initiatives with no real goal other than more votes on Election Day. The ineffective policies Russell created were actually based on things he believed in. And while Beamon strongly disagreed with the theory that you could incarcerate and execute your problems away, he had to admit that Russell came off as fairly sincere in person. Crazy, megalomaniacal, and misguided—but sincere.

". . . terrorism investigation, sir?"

Beamon caught the tail end of the reporter's question and returned his attention to the television.

"We have a coordinated effort between every law enforcement organization in America focused on finding these people, and I understand that the FBI is following substantial leads."

"Sir, there's speculation that—"

"I don't want to hear any more speculation," Russell responded angrily. "Unless you've got facts or sources who'll use their names, I've got no time for this. . . ."

"Good for you," Beamon said, hitting the MUTE button and lying back on the bed. Russell hadn't mentioned Laura or the plan to set up an oversight committee to pick apart her investigation. In the end Beamon guessed that Russell's oversight idea was just saber rattling. If he got himself too personally involved, he'd set himself up to take the blame if a rocket attack ever came. No, he'd find some patriotic-sounding reason that adding yet another layer of oversight wouldn't work and then create a committee to Monday-morning-quarterback the investigation when it was over.

Beamon turned on his personal cell phone and checked for messages. Nothing. The Director's office seemed to have stopped calling. He guessed that P.C. was going ballistic at the Gasta tip going to the cops, but with one rocket to Beamon's credit, he would have to proceed carefully. And, as Laura had pointed out, that gave Beamon some time. But how much?

The truth was, there was no way to know. And what made that so maddening was the fact that there was nothing to do but wait for Laura to turn up something he could work with, for Volkov to contact him again. He concentrated on the launcher, trying to come up with an angle that Laura hadn't already thoroughly attacked, but his brain was pretty much broken down at this point.

The most productive thing he could do was get some sleep. With a little luck he'd doze off with a cigarette in his hand and burn the hotel down with him in it.

Beamon closed his eyes and forced himself to relax. He thought about Chet, picturing his bright-red hair and those stupid-looking freckles across his nose. He remembered first meeting him in Flagstaff—an impossibly young and ridiculously overeager first-office agent. But he'd had what it took to do something in the Bureau. He'd been smart, honorable, hardworking . . .

Beamon squeezed his eyes shut a little tighter and pushed the memory away. He'd have plenty of time to think about Chet. More time than he'd want. Not now, though. He only had a few days at best before the Director discovered the truth about his involvement in the death of those Afghans. The question he had to answer was: What was he going to do with that time?

First, get some sleep. He knew from experience that it would be a waste of time to try to think even moderately deep thoughts when he was this tired. He stubbed out his cigarette and flicked off the light, promising himself that he'd figure it all out in morning.

Beamon awoke suddenly, confused and groggy. The television was still silently covering the Gasta story and the room was still nearly dark.

"Hello?"

The only answer was a ringing cell phone overpowering the ringing in his ears. All three phones were on the nightstand, and he had to fumble through them to figure out which it was.

"Yeah," he said noncommittally. They all looked pretty much alike and he wasn't sure who he was supposed to be when he answered anymore.

"Mark. I'm sorry, did I wake you?"

Beamon shook his head violently and looked at the clock. He'd been asleep for almost ten hours. The heavy hotel curtains were keeping the daylight out.

"Still nursing a case of jet lag."

"Have you tried melatonin?" Volkov said. "There's some on the plane. I should have told you."

"That's okay. I'm fine actually. Just needed to catch up a little."

"Are you watching television?"

"Yeah. It's playing *The Carlo Gasta Show*. You move fast."

"We don't have a problem do we?"

"I told him I'd help him with the Afghans. I did and I've been paid. No problems."

"That's a very enlightened attitude. Turn to CNN for a moment."

Beamon grabbed the remote and began flipping through channels until he found it. He'd expected a bunch of alarmist crap about terrorism or another angle on Gasta's arrest, but found a story on the recent coup in Laos instead. He turned the sound back on and listened to the description of General Yung's desperate takeover from the Communist government.

It was a strange juxtaposition: politically sympathetic narrative over brutal images of jungle fighting, explosions, and lines of small, thin men with their arms tied behind them being run up muddy roads.

"Pol Pot reincarnated," Beamon said finally.

"Yes, they're all the same. One general replaces another, one president replaces another. A burst of violence that briefly attracts the attention of the world and then the less media-friendly strangulation of the country's population."

"What's this have to do with me?"

"I had a very profitable relationship with General Yung's predecessor. Wait a moment . . . wait . . . there! You can see him in the right-hand corner of the screen."

The camera had panned quickly over a smoking treeline, and for a brief moment a group of bamboo pikes topped with human heads was framed in the picture.

"Looks like you've had a little setback," Beamon said, lighting a cigarette and listening to the narrator discuss the former government's involvement in heroin trafficking. Funny how that subject kept coming up.

"That kind of thing really upsets me," Volkov said.

"Beheadings?"

"No—sensationalist, irresponsible reporting."

"I don't follow you."

"All this talk about government corruption—as though all governments aren't corrupt. And then they have the gall to deride the former president as a Communist and in the same breath involve him in narcotics."

"I guess I see your point," Beamon said. "Drug trafficking does seem to be pretty firmly in the free enterprise camp."

"The truth is, he was a brutal dictator who nationalized companies not for philosophical reasons but so he could bleed them into his Swiss bank account—the actions of a capitalist with real conviction, as far as I'm concerned. But in some ways he was anti-American, and that leaves only two categories in which to put him: Communist or Muslim. And he since he was Buddhist . . ."

Beamon had never met an international crime lord before but had to admit that Volkov wasn't what he'd pictured. The man was kind of . . . chatty.

"In any event, Mark, I need to negotiate a relationship with General Yung, and I thought you might be interested in being my representative."

"Excuse me?"

"Laos has products that I'm interested in, and a friendly government is always helpful. I'd like you to go to Laos and talk to the general on my behalf."

Beamon looked up at the screen again and watched people fleeing a burning village while being shot at from the trees.

"You know, Christian, I have to tell you . . . it looks kind of unpleasant there."

"Media hype," Volkov replied dismissively. "I'm not asking you to fight the war. Just to open a dialog."

"I don't know. I might not be a great choice. I've never gotten a handle on the Asians. Their motivations have always seemed kind of murky to me."

"Really? If I had my way, I'd deal with them exclusively. Oh, not the politicians, of course. Never the politicians. But their businessmen. For thousands of years the Chinese government has hated merchants—put them in the same category as criminals. If you were a Chinese entrepreneur, you never knew when the government would suddenly decide to send someone to execute you, or imprison you, or banish you—though often it had a great deal to do with how much money various government officials owed you. And when the businessmen and traders ran from that persecution, they spread across the Pacific Rim, creating some of history's greatest centers of commerce. To them all business is illegal—selling cars is no more or less dangerous or immoral than selling drugs. Keeping a—I think you Americans would say 'low profile'—is a matter of life or death."

"The Jews of the East," Beamon said, quoting a book he'd read while getting what, until now, had been a completely useless history degree at Yale.

"Precisely. Industrious people consistently persecuted. The problem with what most people call 'organized crime' in the West is the low class of people involved. America is by far the best example of this. It's the land of opportunity. Anyone with intelligence and drive can make a wonderful life for himself in a career more palatable to polite society. People who choose the underworld in the U.S. tend to be the ones who couldn't compete above."

"Like Carlo Gasta."

"Exactly. In Thailand, or Laos for that matter, a man like Carlo Gasta would have never risen to a position of responsibility."

"You're quite a salesman, Christian. An exotic locale, umbrella drinks, a chance to bone up on my Southeast Asian history. It sounds like I should be paying you."

Volkov laughed. "So you're interested?"

Actually, he could think of very few things he wanted to do less than put himself in the middle of a brutal civil war on the other side of the world. But he suspected that if he turned Volkov down here, he'd never hear from the man again. And if that happened, his chances of putting a bullet hole in him someday would decline to about zero.

"Money?"

"We're talking about a diplomatic call here, Mark. All jokes aside, I'm guessing you'll be well fed and drink some wine. I don't think this is a particularly high-dollar job."

"Christian, please. There's a shooting war going on over there and no one seems to know exactly how it's going to turn out. I'd hate to see my head on a piece of bamboo."

"We'll come to a number when you get back, based on how difficult the job turned out to be. Suitable?"

Beamon's impression was that he had to worry much more about Volkov killing him than quibbling over payment. "Fine."

"Wonderful. I'll send some preliminary intelligence to your e-mail address and have the rest for you on the plane." There was a short pause. "I'm glad you've agreed to go."

"Do you mind telling me what it is exactly you're after?"

"I want to know if you think the general will be able to create stability in his country and if he's hostile to me and my organization."

"And if you don't like the answers I come up with?"

"Then we'll discuss what you would charge to help me solve that problem."

Beamon nodded into the phone. This week he'd already helped an infamous Mob boss kill a bunch of heroin traffickers and now he was plotting the assassination of a foreign head of state. Maybe next week he could find time to start World War Three.

41

"Is Gasta talking?"

The car was moving lazily along the maze of rural roads outside L.A. Beamon glanced back again but saw only darkness. Still not sure how Christian Volkov had managed to find him the first time, he had let his paranoia run free in ensuring they weren't being followed. If Volkov ever put him together with Laura, it seemed likely that his lifespan would be significantly shortened.

"He talks a lot but he doesn't say anything," Laura replied. "We're pressuring him with the disappearance of Chet, but he isn't going to admit anything about that. He doesn't know about you and we can't tell him without blowing your cover. At this point the LAPD has him dead to rights on the drug charge and they're working to firm up the case against him for the execution of the Afghans. In the end, though, it will be interesting to see how that plays with a jury: LOCAL MOB ANTIHERO KILLS AFGHAN TERRORISTS."

"Is he trying to deal?"

"He's playing it cool and his people aren't saying anything at all—they're trusting Gasta to make a deal for them all. The New York families are nervous enough about what Gasta knows to have coughed up some serious money for his legal team, and they can obviously smell something. When it comes out that these Afghans had a rocket, the price of what Gasta knows about them is going to go through the roof."

"Don't buy it. He told me everything he knows already and it wasn't much."

"I'm not sure I have anything to buy it with. The LAPD isn't going to be anxious to deal away their collar, and we can't go after him for Chet's death because of your position. At this point I just want to keep him isolated enough that he can't shoot his mouth off and somehow screw up my investigation."

"How do you plan to do that?"

"I've convinced everybody involved that it makes sense to move him out of L.A. to the middle of Nowhere, West Virginia. We're saying it's for his protection, but really it's just to put some distance between him, the press, and his lawyer. I had to make a lot of promises to even get that, though."

"What did you find out about Volkov's bank that wired me the three mil?"

"A maze of offshore accounts that leads nowhere."

"Big surprise. Great."

"There was one interesting thing, though." She reached behind her into the backseat, feeling around until she found a large roll of paper. "Take a look at this."

Beamon pulled the rubber band off it and flipped the dash light on. It turned out to be an unmanageable four feet long, covered with what looked like an impossibly complex flow chart.

"I had a team of our accountants put this together. What you're looking at is a graphical representation of the organizations involved in sending money to and receiving money from Carlo Gasta. At the top there you'll find three shell companies that had direct contact with Gasta in one way or another."

"Who owns those companies?"

"That's what the rest of that stuff is. They're all offshore corporations chartered in countries that allow corporations as opposed to individuals to be owners. Basically little islands that create laws to cater to money laundering."

"Christ," Beamon said, running down the hundred or so companies and the lines and arrows connecting them. Laura was a whiz at this kind of crap but it didn't mean much to him. He'd never succeeded in getting his mind to wrap around this level of detail.

"Quite a mess, huh? From the top of the page to the bottom, it spans thirty years."

"So the companies that gave birth to all this were incorporated in the seventies?"

"Yup."

"But it all must lead to someone; there has to be a starting point."

"There *were* a couple of names on the original companies. I can guarantee you that they're either fictitious or long dead."

"As usual, I find myself in complete disagreement with you," Beamon said.

"That they're dead or fake names?"

"No, that this is interesting. I mean, where does this get us?"

"A little patience, Mark. I'm not to the good part yet. Flip the paper over."

With some difficulty Beamon did as she said and found a similar though much shorter flowchart.

"What you're looking at now is what you asked about—how you got paid your three million from Volkov. This little maze only goes back about fifteen years."

"How do these shell corporations and banks connect to the ones related to Gasta?"

"That's what's interesting: They don't. There are no overlapping organizations or owners at all."

Beamon considered that for a moment. It proved nothing, but it did bring up some disturbing possibilities.

"What are you thinking, Mark?"

"I don't know what to think."

"How old do you figure Volkov is?"

"That doesn't mean anything, Laura."

"It's worth talking about, though. How old?"

"Early forties."

"So the network that paid Gasta was started when Volkov was what? Thirteenish?"

"He could have built on a structure that he inherited from someone else. And he could have a hundred totally separate networks that he uses for different things. In fact, I'd expect it."

She nodded. "But it's an interesting concept. We've been wondering why Volkov would suddenly turn on Gasta—his own man. But what if he didn't? What if Gasta isn't 'his guy'? What if there's somebody else involved here?"

"You tell me," Beamon said, holding up the paper in his hand. "Is there anything concrete here? Anything we can really use?"

"Probably not," she admitted. "There's no starting or ending point. We're running all of these dummy corporations against other organized-crime investigations we've done, trying to get some point of reference—a real company or a person that's connected to them but we haven't been able to get either."

"Okay, let's change the subject, then. What about the house you found the rocket in?"

"Nothing there, either. The guy that owns it never met the renters face-to-face. No prints that didn't belong to the guy we found there or the men Gasta killed. No calls have come in and no one has come anywhere near the house. Not that we really expected them to, since the Afghans Gasta killed are all over TV. I wish we could have kept it quiet—maybe the guy with the launcher would have just rolled up one day."

A cell phone started ringing and Beamon cursed under his breath as he pulled three from his pocket. He finally figured out which one it was and picked up.

"Yeah."

"It's me."

The voice belonged to a friend of his at the National Security Agency whom he'd called the night before.

"I've got what you want," the man said quietly.

Beamon had told him to keep the conversation fairly cloak-and-dagger and to expect payment for the service he was providing. He doubted that Volkov was listening, but if he was, having a contact at the NSA wouldn't hurt Nicolai's reputation any.

"I've e-mailed you our analysis of General Yung and the situation in Laos, along with some stuff from the CIA. The data is sketchy and it's too early to come up with any hard conclusions about the stability of the region. But you have everything we have now."

"Do you know how much support he's getting from the U.S.?"

"We're being pretty noncommittal at this point, but word is we see him as an improvement over the old regime and we'd like to see him hold on."

"Were you able to get anything personal? Anything like what we talked about?"

"I think so. He's a car nut."

"Really?"

"Yeah. Subscribes to no less than five auto-buff magazines and must have gone through a hell of a lot of trouble to get them when he was living in the jungle with his opposition movement. People close to him say that if he isn't talking about politics, he's talking about cars."

"Fine. I'll take a look at the data you sent tomorrow. Expect payment through the normal channel."

There was a click on the phone when his friend hung up.

"Who was that?" Laura said.

"Friend of mine from NSA."

"What are you doing with them?"

"They're giving me what they have on Laos."

"Laos? What, the coup there? Why do you care about that?"

"Volkov called me last night and asked me to go over there and see if I can help him build a relationship with General Yung."

"General Yung? Why didn't you tell me this?"

"I just did."

"You're not thinking about going, though, right? The guy's a psychopath. Have you been watching what's going on over there on TV?"

Beamon shrugged. "I didn't say it was a good job. But it's the one he gave me. I don't see that I have much of a choice."

"Of course you have a choice!"

He ignored her and dialed a number into his phone. Surprisingly, Christian Volkov picked up personally.

"Christian. It's Mark."

"Is everything all right? You haven't changed your mind, have you?"

"No, but I need something. I have information that General Yung is a fanatic about cars. I need something good to take along with me—like a Ferrari or something. Oh, and a cargo plane to fly it there."

There was a brief silence over the phone that was impossible to read. Time to see if organized crime was as efficient as some people contended.

"You know, Mark, I don't think there are very many paved roads there. And now, with all the bombing . . . Hang on. . . . Joseph! What was that elaborate four-wheel drive we rode in last time we were in Saudi Arabia? . . . Really? . . . Mark, Joseph says Lamborghini made a sport utility vehicle. I think that might be more appropriate."

"Sounds good to me."

"Joseph! I need one of those on a cargo plane tomorrow. It's going to go to Laos with Mark. . . . What? . . . Good question, hold on. Mark? Would he have a color preference?"

"Uh, I have no idea."

"Probably black," Volkov said. "Military dictators love black. Is there anything else?"

"Yeah. I don't know anything about cars. Could you send me information on why this truck's so great—why it's better than others?"

"Of course. Good-bye, Mark. I'll see you soon."

"And that," Beamon said after hanging up, "is why we'll never stop organized crime."

"Why?" Laura said.

"How long do you think it would take me to get the FBI to put a Lamborghini on a cargo plane and fly it to Laos?"

"Twenty years?"

"Volkov's going to do it in twenty hours and he gave me a choice of color."

"Please explain to me what you're doing here, Mark. You're not really going, right? You're just making him think you are."

"No, I'm really going."

"Think about this for a second," Laura said. "You're an FBI agent and you're going to negotiate on behalf of a major organized-crime figure with a foreign leader who the State Department is probably already talking to. I mean, I've told everyone at Headquarters who'll listen that you're responsible for finding the rocket, but that's only going to go so far. The Director's never going to authorize you to do this. Even if he wanted to, it would take six months for *him* to get permission."

Beamon lit a cigarette. "I'm going to do what it takes to get Christian Volkov. And in the process I'm going to help you find your launcher. So, what are you worried about? Has it occurred to you that Laos is one of the major heroin producers in the world?"

The silence in the car extended for more than ten minutes.

"You're going too far," Laura said finally. "You're leaving yourself no way out."

"There's already no way out for me."

Another long silence.

"Mark. I'm asking you not to go."

He turned toward her but couldn't read anything from her expression. She'd go along with him if he asked her to—he knew that. But by keeping her mouth shut on this, she'd end up getting crucified alongside him.

"Tell you what, Laura. You tell the Director my plan. See if he goes for it."

She turned toward him for a moment, an expression of relief and gratitude playing across face. "Thank you, Mark."

42

THE driver snaked the BMW through the small private airport, finally coming to a halt in a secluded back corner. Beamon leaned forward over the seats to get a better look at the blinding white of the jet parked on the tarmac in front of them. It was smaller and sleeker than the one he'd flown in to meet Volkov a few days earlier. How many of these things did the man have?

"The pilot's already on board, sir. Is there anything else I can do for you?"

Beamon hadn't brought much in the way of luggage: a laptop with a pair of underwear, a white dress shirt, and a toothbrush stuffed in the side pocket of the case. It was his sincere hope that his time on the ground in Laos would be measurable in hours and not days. Minutes would be even better.

"That should do it, Charles," Beamon said, throwing the door open and stepping out into the scorching sun. The moment he did, a tinny version of "The Star-Spangled Banner" began to play in one of the pockets of his blazer.

He had gone to an electronics store earlier that day and a rather enthusiastic young woman had helped him organize his growing collection of phones. The one the FBI had the number to got a faceplate that looked like a flag and the patriotic ring. Gasta's got green snakeskin and "Taps." Volkov's rated a slightly more attractive blue snakeskin and an ominous fugue. Finally, he'd added an expensive satellite phone to his arsenal. In the unlikely event that he could figure out the instruction manual, it was supposed to work anywhere in the world.

He stopped halfway to the plane and turned his back to it as he flipped the red, white, and blue phone open. The BMW he'd arrived in was already disappearing around a hangar.

"Hello."

"How are things going?" Laura said.

"I'm not bad, I suppose."

"Were you able to get out of that trip to Laos like you thought?"

Beamon was confused for a moment. He'd never said he thought he could get out of it, or even that he'd try. It suddenly occurred to him that she was signaling him. Someone else was on the line.

"Didn't work out," he said. "I'm pretty much roped in at this point." For good measure he threw in "Sorry, I know you're against it."

"Mark, I talked to the Director and he won't okay this trip. We just don't have the authority."

"Well, I'll tell you, Laura, I'm not really in a position to turn back now."

"Mark, I don't think you understand. The Director's giving you a direct order. You're not to go to Laos."

Beamon sighed quietly. He'd known that this would be P.C.'s reaction. The only reason he'd had Laura ask was to get her off the hook. "Look, I gotta go, Laura. . . ."

"Mark—"

"Don't hang up this phone, Beamon!"

He recognized the voice. The man himself.

"I'm glad we could finally catch up, sir," Beamon lied. He turned in a slow circle to make sure no one was within earshot. The plane was the only thing within two hundred yards, and despite the open door, it looked deserted.

"You will *not* go to Laos," Caroll said, dispensing with any pleasantries. "You're an employee of the United States government and are not going to negotiate with a foreign dignitary on behalf of organized crime. We're supporting this new regime and it would be a disaster if

General Yung discovered that we sent an undercover FBI agent to talk to him."

Beamon really didn't have time for this. There was undoubtedly a world-class lunch getting cold in the jet.

"Like I said, I'm really not in a position to turn back, sir."

"Well, then, put yourself in a position to turn back, goddamnit. We're risking an international incident!"

"An international incident? With Laos?" Beamon said, feeling strangely bored by the conversation despite the fact that he knew he was about to finally, irretrievably, end his career. It felt like shooting a lame horse. "What are they going to do, sir? Spit at us from across the ocean? Besides, if you don't tell Yung, he'll never find out. And if he does, he'll get really angry and make an official statement which will be played once on the eleven o'clock news, right after a story about a yam that looks like Teddy Roosevelt."

The silence over the phone suggested that the Director was uncharacteristically speechless. Unfortunately, it didn't last.

"I want you to listen to me very carefully," Caroll said, enunciating with exaggerated clarity. "You are officially removed from this case. I expect you in my office tomorrow morning."

Beamon looked down at the phone and, before he knew what he was doing, hung it up. It felt kind of . . . liberating. No need to worry about how he was going to weasel out of this thing anymore. Every bridge was now burning brightly behind him.

"Hey, how you doing, Tegla?" Beamon said as he entered the plane. The now familiar dark face of his pilot peaked out from the cockpit. "Mark. It's nice to see you again."

"Same here." He took a seat in a plush leather chair. It didn't look like this plane had a bed, but the chair was about as comfortable as they got.

"If you're ready, we'll get underway," Tegla said ducking out of the cockpit and closing the door in the side of the plane.

"Sounds good."

"François made you some more of those shrimp raviolis you like so much. I'll heat them up as soon as we're in the air."

Beamon smiled. Man, how he loved those things. Ten or twenty would almost certainly be enough to make him forget his problems.

"Oh, and Mark? You'll find some documents under your chair: Christian thought you'd like to review them en route."

Beamon retrieved them and leafed through the well-organized folder, which contained, among other things, a brief history of Laos, recent newspaper articles, an up-to-date analysis of what he was getting himself into, and everything you ever wanted to know about Lamborghini four-wheel drives. All in all, it looked at least as thorough as the data he'd received from the NSA.

What it didn't include, though, was a clear outline of exactly what it was he—Nicolai—was supposed to accomplish there. Of course, it didn't take a great deal of imagination to figure out. Laos had only one thing that would interest a man like Volkov. Heroin.

Volkov was wondering if his relationship with the prior regime was going to come back to haunt him. Would Volkov's support for Yung's sworn enemy be held against him? Even if Yung was the forgive-and-forget type, it seemed likely that his first order of business would be to wipe the slate clean—to renegotiate his predecessor's arrangements.

It seemed to Beamon that Volkov needed to know two things: First, had the region become so unstable that Yung couldn't reliably deliver product even if he wanted to? And second, was he considering hitching his wagon to someone else? Neither of these questions would be easy to answer in what would hopefully be an extremely short visit. But then, Volkov would certainly know that. So why this trip?

The landing gear hitting the ground jolted Beamon awake and caused the Laotian history book he'd been reading to slide to the floor. After God knew how many shrimp raviolis and an amazing almond-encrusted salmon, keeping his eyes open had become absolutely impossible.

"Are we there?"

"No, Mark. We're switching planes."

He looked out the window and into complete darkness. How she'd managed to hit the runway, he had no idea.

Tegla gathered up the pieces of the file that Beamon had strewn around during the flight, and he watched her take the armload of documents to the shredder in the back of the plane.

"Christian hates paper," she explained as she finished destroying the information, then hurried back across the plane and opened the door in its side. Beamon grabbed his laptop and followed her outside into a rain so hot, it felt like a shower. He looked away from the plane as she closed the door, letting his eyes adjust to the darkness. By the time she came alongside him, he could make out the large, curved shapes of the hangars in front of them.

"This way," Tegla said, flipping an umbrella open and sharing it with him as they started toward a dead-looking cargo plane.

"This part of the trip won't be quite as comfortable, but it won't be as long, either," she said as they entered the plane.

It was basically hollow and completely empty except for a large sport utility vehicle tied down with what looked like a heavy net. Beamon examined the gleaming truck in the dim light while Tegla busied herself in the cockpit. He leaned close to the windshield, careful not to put a spot on it with his nose, and studied the leather and polished wood interior. Volkov didn't disappoint.

The sound of the props started as a low rumble and turned deafening very quickly. Tegla reappeared for a moment and pointed to a jump seat, which Beamon strapped himself into.

He finally noticed a nervous feeling in the pit of his stomach when the plane began to taxi. The only thing certain about his trip to Laos was that he was completely on his own. The FBI sure as hell wasn't behind him, and the fact that Volkov needed to send him on this little errand suggested that his power base in Laos was pretty much nonexistent. Or maybe even worse than nonexistent: Maybe Yung was openly hostile. Was Volkov sending him into the lion's den, just to see what would happen? If Yung mailed Beamon back in numerous small boxes, Volkov would be able to safely assume that his relationship with Laos had soured.

This time a jolt of adrenaline accompanied the impact of the landing gear and Beamon found himself wide-awake as Tegla wrestled the plane across a less than smooth runway. The light that was bleeding around the curtain leading to the cockpit didn't look completely artificial, so Beamon assumed it was daytime, though he had no way to confirm that. He felt his back pressed into his seat as the plane decelerated, and he gripped the armrests tightly until it finally came to a full stop.

"Are you ready, Mark?" Tegla said, hurrying past him and starting to free the Lamborghini. Beamon helped her carefully drag the cargo net to the floor and then tossed his laptop in the backseat and climbed behind the wheel. The cargo doors at the back of the plane were already almost half open when he backed past Tegla.

"What's your plan?" he said, rolling down the window.

"To wait here for you to return."

Beamon frowned slightly. He hated the thought of her staying there alone, but he seriously doubted she'd be any safer with him. "You gonna be okay?"

"Fine," she said confidently. "I've got work to do here."

"Thanks for the ride," Beamon said, depressing the accelerator and coaxing the truck down the ramp onto what in Laos passed as a runway.

He was immediately surrounded by no less than ten young Asian men who paid him no attention as they circled and pointed at the vehicle, talking excitedly. Interestingly, not a single one of them actually dared touch it.

"Any of you boys speak English?" he said through the open window.

They all looked at one another and then back at him. An argument that seemed sure to last awhile ensued, so Beamon took the time to get a feel for his surroundings. There wasn't much to see: jungle, a few distant columns of smoke rising above the trees, two military jeeps that had seen better days. Brief bursts of gunfire were audible but sounded pretty far away. There was a burning chemical smell in the air that he'd never encountered before. Of course, he generally avoided wars.

"'I love the smell of napalm in the morning,'" he muttered, quoting one of his favorite movies. "'It smells like . . . victory.'"

The argument seemed to have lost most of its intensity and all but two participants.

"Any time now, guys."

They looked up at him, shouted a few more obscenities—he didn't need to speak the language to translate—and finally came to an agreement. After having the dirt carefully brushed from their clothing by their compatriots, the two men climbed into the Lamborghini—one in the passenger seat and one in the back.

The kid in the passenger seat pointed to one of the jeeps and said something. Beamon threw the truck into gear and followed the dilapidated military vehicle as it started through the jungle on a narrow, muddy road.

Based on the chatter between his new friends, he guessed that they were impressed with the smooth, quiet ride. When he flipped on the stereo and Frank Sinatra's voice filled the vehicle, they squealed in delight.

The photographs and descriptions he'd seen didn't really do the small city of Luang Prabang justice. The architecture was an elegant mix of Asian and French and blended beautifully with the landscape. The man in the passenger seat pointed right and Beamon eased the truck onto an empty cobblestone street dominated by an impressive white building that he knew to be the Royal Palace Museum. Beyond a few burn marks in its white façade and some damage to the roof, the century-old building looked as if it were going to make it through yet another coup.

The jeep he was following came to a stop just as three men appeared from the museum and started across its courtyard. Beamon jumped out of the truck and jogged up to meet them. The man in the middle, wearing a neat military uniform, was easily recognizable as General Yung. Beamon decided to take the fact that the leader of the country had bothered to acknowledge his arrival personally as a good sign and not just a sign that the general was anxious to get the torture under way immediately.

"Sir," Beamon said, unsure whether to bow or extend a hand. "I'm so pleased that you've taken time from your schedule to meet with me."

Yung was a hard-looking man. It wasn't his features, though—they had the delicate aesthetic that everyone in this part of the world enjoyed. It was something else. A thousand atrocities lurking just beneath that buttery-smooth skin.

Yung extended a hand, solving at least one of Beamon's problems.

"I, too, was pleased when Mr. Volkov told me you were coming. It is a pleasure to make your acquaintance."

His English was heavily accented but easily understandable, as the information he'd been provided had promised.

Yung was clearly struggling to keep his attention on Beamon as they exchanged a few diplomatic platitudes. After about thirty seconds he couldn't stand it anymore and his eyes flicked briefly to the Lamborghini parked only a few yards away. Beamon smiled and handed him the keys.

"Christian wants to apologize for not coming personally. Unfortunately, it's very difficult for him to travel right now. He hopes that you'll accept this a token of his respect."

Yung stared down at the keys in his hand and then at the truck. He actually licked his lips.

"It's a wonderful vehicle," Beamon said. "You know, only three hundred were made. Christian understands that you're a busy man, but everyone needs occasional moments of leisure."

Yung's gave the keys to one of the men standing next to him, who promptly descended the steps and drove the truck away.

"Mr. Volkov is most kind," Yung said with practiced coolness. "Khan will show you to your room so that you may rest. We will talk later."

Beamon smiled politely. So far, things could be going a lot worse. He'd bet the whole three million he'd made over the last week that within five minutes, General Yung would be speeding through the capital in his new Lamborghini, shooting out the window at the peasants.

43

THE room Beamon had been given was at the back of the palace and was dominated by a massive carved bed with lamps at each of its corners. The bathroom was modern, in a British sort of way, and the mattress was comfortable enough. Large windows, thrown open to provide a view of the Mekong River, let a damp breeze flow through, and with it the strangely unmistakable odor of war.

Despite the fact that he was desperately tired, he couldn't sleep and ended up just sitting there with his back against the ornate headboard, replaying the events of the last few weeks. His old job and the inspection report that by now was sitting on his desk seemed more like a television show he'd once watched than his life. Chet, the Afghans, Volkov, and now General Yung were his whole world now. Except maybe for Carrie. Where did she fit into all this?

He didn't know how long he sat like that. Time seemed a more fluid concept in this part of the world. He guessed four hours, based solely on the fact that it was how long he predicted it would take Yung to run the gas-guzzling Lamborghini out of fuel.

The man who finally entered the room motioned for him to come but obviously didn't speak any English. Beamon flipped his legs off the bed and followed.

Yung came out from behind his desk when Beamon entered and they shook hands again. The general's mood seemed as sunny as could be expected from a murderous sociopath. He waved around the sparsely furnished room. "You'll have to excuse the condition of my office—we have been quite busy. I don't have time for the excesses of my predecessor.

Beamon saw the afternoon degenerating before his eyes.

"I am going to give the country back to the people. I intend to create a progressive government that will focus on education, health care, and economic growth. A government committed to human rights. A new Utopia."

Beamon couldn't help wondering if all those people whose heads were decorating the tops of bamboo pikes knew what happened to the old Utopia.

"I admire your vision," Beamon said, mostly because he couldn't think of anything more clever.

Yung seemed happy enough with the response and retrieved a half-full bottle from behind his desk.

Beamon wasn't sure what to make of it. If he had to guess, he would say the greenish brown liquid was the bodily fluids of a very old, very sick man. As for the chunks floating around in it, he didn't even want to speculate.

"Would you have a drink with me, Mark?"

Was he serious? He was going to drink that?

"Excuse me?" Beamon said, trying to stall. He'd once said that he'd never met an alcohol delivery system he didn't like. That statement was starting to look a little rash.

"Would you like a drink?" Yung repeated, rephrasing slightly and trying to speak more clearly.

There was no good answer. In the end, though, it seemed more prudent to take a risk on the booze than to insult the man.

"I'd love one."

Yung poured them both a shot and handed one to Beamon, who smiled and raised the glass. Yung proved that he was indeed serious by swallowing the liquid in one mighty gulp, and Beamon followed suit.

The intense burn helped cover up the fact that it tasted just like it looked. Beamon clenched his teeth together and smiled, trying to keep the shot from coming right back up on the general's floor. Fortunately, the bottle disappeared back behind the desk and the Yung sat, indicating that Beamon should do the same. He swallowed a couple more times, concentrating on defusing his gag reflex as he took a chair.

"I was very disappointed that your predecessor saw fit to leave so quickly. And without telling anyone . . ." Yung said. "Have you been able to locate him?"

That brought the shot about halfway back up Beamon's throat. He kept what he hoped was a serene smile on his face as he swallowed again and tried to recalculate his position in light of Yung's statement. Volkov had forgotten to mention that he'd tried this before. Had he told his first man to turn around and come back, deciding that it was too dangerous and that they'd find a more expendable negotiator? Or had Yung killed the guy and dumped his body where no one would ever find it? Either way, Beamon's first foray into diplomacy was taking a turn for the worse.

"We were disappointed too," Beamon finally managed to get out. "That's why I'm here. We're very committed to building a strong relationship with you."

Noncommittal yet meaningless. Bill Clinton couldn't have done better under the circumstances.

"A strong relationship like the one you had with my predecessor?"

According to the information Beamon had, Yung's coup had been something of a surprise to both Christian Volkov and the American intelligence community. The CIA had maintained limited contact with Yung over the years but hadn't given the man enough credit. Volkov seemed to have had a similar opinion, underestimating the general's strength even more profoundly. He'd maintained no relationship at all with Yung, dealing exclusively with Laos's late president.

Beamon cleared his throat. His mouth tasted like old kitty litter. "Wasn't it Sun Tzu who said 'Be so subtle that you are invisible, be so mysterious that you are intangible, then you will control your rival's fate'? You followed these principles too well, General. Christian was not aware of your strength. He was taken by surprise." If he got much better at kissing psychoass, somebody was going to make him an ambassador.

"Our business relationship with your predecessor was satisfactory," Beamon continued. "Though obviously his Communist leanings concerned us. An environment where capitalism and freedom are encouraged should be beneficial to us both. And to the Lao people."

"You provided him money and weapons to use against me," Yung said, obviously not willing to let this go easily. Beamon felt himself start to sweat more than the heat and humidity could account for.

"As you know, General, business relationships go two ways. He provided us with what we wanted and we provided him with what he wanted. There was no political agenda whatsoever. Christian would never presume to interfere in the politics of your country. It is not his place."

Yung nodded thoughtfully, though Beamon had no idea whether he was buying any of this crap.

"But you are wondering if I am in control," Yung said finally. "If perhaps you should back someone else?"

"There is no one else," Beamon said truthfully. "But we watch the news. We hear the reports of rebel—Communist—strongholds in the north and we're concerned. It's in both our best interests to see Laos stabilized. . . . Stabilized under your authority."

By the time Beamon was led out of Yung's office, he was feeling fairly ill. The sweat was running freely down his face, and his stomach was quivering pathetically. He managed to make it to his room, but when he got there it was all he could do to step through the door, slam it shut, and sag against it.

"Shit," he mumbled, putting his hand to his head and mopping away the heavy film of perspiration. When he looked up again, he saw a shadow move across the dark room. Well beyond being able to think or move quickly, he just stood there helplessly as the shadow approached.

His imagined assassin turned out to be a little girl. She looked to be twelve or thirteen, with long, shiny black hair and big, dark eyes. Something like a kimono was draped over her thin body and it glimmered in the dim light coming through the open window.

"You look bad."

At least that's what he thought she said. His stomach suddenly decided it was done cowering and rolled over violently, forcing him into a weak sprint for the bathroom where he threw up with impressive force and then flopped down on the floor.

"You look very bad."

The nausea and fever that had started only a few hours ago seemed to be doubling every minute or so.

"I'll be all right in a minute," he managed to get out.

The girl ran a washcloth under the water and put it on his forehead. "Yes?"

"Thank you."

After about five minutes of lying on the floor with the girl hovering over him, he decided he could stand and try for the bed. She grabbed his arm with surprising strength and supported a considerable amount of his weight as he staggered along. Without her help he doubted he would have made it.

The bed was more comfortable than the floor, but he immediately began to wonder if the relocation had been a good idea. The bathroom was now a very long twenty feet away.

Another wet cloth was pressed against his forehead and he closed his eyes, breathing deeply. He didn't have time for this.

"You better now?" The girl said, quickly running through her inventory of English words.

"Yes, thank you."

As long as he concentrated on ignoring the nausea and didn't provoke it by moving, he'd be okay.

The cloth was pulled from his forehead, and a few moments later he felt something much softer and heavier pressing against his body. When he opened his eyes, he found the now naked girl lying on top of him, rubbing herself gracefully against him.

He pushed her off and scooted away, in the process falling off the bed. The motion was too much for him and he had to make another dash for the bathroom.

When he was finished purging what little was left in his stomach, he propped himself against the doorframe. The willowy little girl, still naked, was standing only a few feet away looking worried.

"You no like me?"

Beamon couldn't help letting out a weak laugh. He stumbled forward and pulled a blanket and pillow off the bed, handing them to her. Trying to explain his reluctance to have sex with a girl who should have been shooting spit wads at her classmates in the sixth grade would probably be a little too much for her limited vocabulary. "I like you very much, but I'm real sick. Do you understand?"

Another worried nod.

"You sleep on the floor, okay?" he said.

The knock on the door was insistent enough not to be a first attempt. Beamon lifted his head off the pillow and squinted against the daylight streaming through the window. The girl, who had apparently completely lost her kimono, was standing at the base of the bed, staring at him with those big dark eyes, now full of panic. When the banging on the door started again, she swung around and faced it, her back pressed against the bed's footboard.

Beamon was still groggy, but his head had cleared enough to understand the problem. If Yung thought the girl hadn't done her job entertaining his guest, there would be a punishment involved.

He pushed himself into a sitting position and grabbed her under her arms, pulling her up onto the bed and throwing half the covers over her. She immediately snuggled up to him.

"Come in," Beamon tried to shout, but it came out at more of a conversational volume.

An unusually stocky Asian man stomped through the door a moment later. "Ten o'clock," he said. "I come back ten o'clock."

"What time is it now?"

He didn't seem to understand. Beamon pointed at his wrist.

"Nine o'clock," he said forcefully and then disappeared into the hall.

The girl rubbed up against his leg and he shoved her out of the bed and onto the floor.

With more than a little help from his grateful young assistant, Beamon had showered, shaved, and dressed by ten. He had a headache that felt like a concussion and could barely walk in a straight line, but he didn't look that bad. It was hard not to wonder if James Bond ever had to contend with explosive diarrhea during his travels.

"Mark!" General Yung called as Beamon stepped unsteadily from the car. "Did you have a pleasant evening?"

"I did," he lied, then added, "The girl was lovely." Amazing how much time he spent keeping the women in his life out of trouble.

Yung smiled. "I know that you are concerned with my ability to control rebel activity. . . ."

The sound of a helicopter suddenly became audible and Beamon looked up at the sky, wondering if it was coming to shoot at them. Yung didn't seem worried.

"I thought I would show you."

"Show me what?" Beamon had to raise his voice over the sound of the approaching chopper.

"Show you that I am in control."

The helicopter finally came overhead and made a less than graceful landing about fifty yards away. Beamon just stared at it. He was barely keeping his stomach and bowels in check on solid land.

"I'll tell you, General. After our conversation last night, I'm convinced. I have no doubts whatsoever that you are going to succeed in stabilizing your country. In fact—"

"No, no, Mark. You should see for yourself. Mr. Volkov would expect it, I think, and I want you to be able to report back to him with absolute confidence."

Great.

The helicopter ride, more than an hour of back-and-forth over the jungle and open fields south of Luang Prabang, proved little more than that Beamon's illness was far from over. While it was true that the countryside directly below looked peaceful enough, thick smoke and the unmistakable glow of a fire were easily visible to the north. Yung was purposefully oblivious to this, though, and seemed to have no intention of taking him in that direction.

". . . educate the villagers, teach them what it means to be free and economically secure . . ."

The general had been talking nonstop through the archaic headphones squeezing Beamon's ears. For the most part he'd tuned his host out, instead concentrating on not vomiting in his lap.

The sound of the engine deepened slightly and they began losing altitude. Beamon leaned over and saw the emerald-green rows of what he assumed was rice as they descended. The helicopter landed hard, despite the soft earth, and Yung pointed to a small village a few hundred yards away. Beamon didn't catch what he said but gratefully followed him out of the whirring death trap and onto semisolid ground.

"This is a rebel village," Yung shouted, putting a hand against Beamon's back and propelling him toward the small grouping of huts. "Loyal to the Communists. I sent men here last night to secure it."

Beamon could see that the show had been carefully staged. The occupants of the entire village—probably twenty people—were lined up in front of their huts, guarded by no less than five men in grubby fatigues. They were obviously terrified, and Yung's appearance with an unidentified white man didn't seem to be helping any. Beamon moved his eyes along their frightened faces, trying not to focus too long on the women and the children clinging to them.

"How do you know that this is a rebel village, General?"

"Intelligence," he said vaguely.

Beamon didn't know what to do. This was all being orchestrated for him—for Volkov. He'd be willing to bet anything that Yung had no idea of these people's political leanings—assuming they had any beyond getting the rice crop in so they didn't starve.

Yung nodded to one of his soldiers.

"Wait!" Beamon shouted, but it was too late. His weakened voice was completely lost in a burst of machine-gun fire. In less than twenty seconds the villagers had gone from living, breathing people to shredded pieces of dead flesh. Beamon staggered back a few steps before his eye picked up movement where there shouldn't have been any. A child—a young boy of about four—jumped up and began to run, screaming. Yung made a bored hand gesture and one of his men chased the child down. Apparently wanting to seem frugal with his boss's ammunition, he used his machete instead of his gun to finish the job.

"As you can see, Mark, I *am* in control. And I will only get stronger."

Beamon's peripheral vision was starting to go blank and he tried to bring it back by biting down on the inside of his cheek and concentrating on the pain. *You will not pass out,* he told himself, just before everything went black.

44

HE'D had the dream before.

It always started out as impenetrable smoke slowly twisting itself into human form. For a moment it clung to the soldiers like clouds on mountains, and then it was gone. There were five of them—all with impeccable uniforms, Asian features, and skin burned almost black by the sun. They were all laughing.

Beamon walked forward, as he always did, toward one of the soldiers, who seemed to be trying to comfort a crying infant. There was something wrong, but what it was got trapped between conscious thought and the pull of his dream.

He made it to within ten feet of the armed men when the one holding the child tossed it toward his companions. They all moved toward the baby as it arced through the air, but only the quickest was rewarded. He caught it on the tip of his bayonet.

Beamon came awake but he didn't open his eyes. The first few times he'd suffered through that nightmare, he'd bolted upright, covered in sweat. Now he just drifted out of it with a brief but powerful sense of despair.

He knew where it came from but had no idea why. It was a World War Two class he'd taken in college that had included vivid descriptions of certain Japanese military practices that had been lost in their new status as Friend of America. Why that image out of so many?

The pounding in his head quickly began to disperse the memory of the dream, and he tried to focus on where he was and what had happened to him.

The village.

"Mark?"

Beamon heard the voice but didn't react.

"Mark?"

He finally opened his eyes and looked into a worried Asian face that he didn't recognize.

"How are you feeling?" the man said in heavily accented English.

It took some effort for Beamon to lift his head from the pillow, but when he did he saw that he was back in his room at the palace. General Yung himself was standing at the foot of the bed, looking anxious.

"I think I'm okay," Beamon croaked.

"Your temperature is coming down," the man said. "You're going to be fine."

The general seemed genuinely relieved. "Mark, why didn't you tell me you were ill?"

Beamon struggled into a sitting position, noticing for the first time the IV running into his still bruised arm. It seemed unproductive to point out that he had been feeling fine until Yung had poisoned him with his Laotian moonshine. "I've been fighting the flu for a few days now, General. I thought I was getting over it."

"Doctor Ki will take good care of you," Yung said. "If you need anything at all, please have someone contact me immediately."

"Thank you."

"You rest now," the doctor said, and they left him alone.

Beamon closed his eyes again. He couldn't think of anything else to do.

Thousands of miles from his White House connections, the infamous Mark Beamon didn't look like much. Just another soft, weak, middle-aged bureaucrat. But he was a lucky son of a bitch—there was no denying it. And having lucky enemies could be dangerous.

Jonathan Drake spun a chair around backward and sat, leaning his thick forearms on the back. It was after midnight in Laos, and the only light in the room was the sick glow of Luang Prabang coming through the open window.

In the semidarkness the FBI agent could have been dead—lying motionless under damp blankets far too heavy for the climate. Helpless.

Drake had heard whisperings of Beamon's unauthorized visit to Laos through his and Alan Holsten's contacts at the Bureau. In light of the continued deterioration of his position, it had seemed prudent to make a quiet appearance.

Although it was hard to tell from Alan Holsten's growing panic, the situation seemed to have temporarily stabilized. While it was true that Carlo Gasta was in custody, it was also apparent that he wasn't talking. And even if he did, Drake was just "John" to Gasta—a man who supplied him with cash and intelligence but who had no other identity. The FBI had al-Qaeda's L.A. cell and a rocket, but their investigation was once again stalled. Mustafa Yasin was obsessive about keeping his individual terrorist cells separate, and the Russians were stonewalling.

In the end, though, the situation was certain to begin to deteriorate again, and Drake wasn't confident that he could stop the slide. What he did know, though, was that Christian Volkov was behind all of it. As long as Volkov was allowed to anonymously manipulate this situation, there would be no end to it.

Beamon stirred and Drake watched him, trying to detect signs of consciousness.

Honestly, he wanted to just kill the FBI agent now. There would never be a better opportunity. But where would that leave him? Holsten was still quietly working to distance himself from this operation, and Drake knew that if he didn't regain control soon, he would find himself dangerously alone. No, Beamon was his best chance of finding Volkov quickly. The FBI agent wouldn't be difficult to control—he had been all but abandoned by his organization and was in dire need of a friend.

"You look like shit," Drake said aloud.

Beamon's body tensed visibly beneath the blanket, and he turned his head in Drake's direction. "Who . . . who's there?"

Drake leaned forward and allowed his face to be illuminated by the glow coming through the window. It took a few seconds for Beamon to recognize him.

"Drake?"

"You're a long way from home, aren't you, Mark?"

"I should have known you assholes were behind General Yung."

"Oh, we weren't behind the coup—that just happened. But now that it has, we might as well try to use it to our advantage." Drake shrugged, disinterestedly. "I'm not really involved in any of this. It's not my area."

That was almost true. In fact, he had gone to great pains to keep his relationship with General Yung from the CIA operatives who worked this part of the world.

"Uh-huh," Beamon said, feeling around on the nightstand next to him. A moment later, a flame flared and the scent of tobacco began to obscure the stench of sickness in the room. "Just looking out for me, Jonathan? I'm touched. I didn't know you guys cared. . . ."

"What are you doing here?" Drake said, ignoring the sarcasm. "I hear that you're representing Christian Volkov."

Beamon didn't say anything, instead just lay there, working on his cigarette.

"The Bureau is being pretty tight-lipped about you, Mark. But I've got friends over there. It seems that you were undercover on an investigation into Carlo Gasta's organization. A friend of yours got killed. I'm sorry to hear about that."

A well-formed smoke ring floated toward Drake but disbursed before reaching him.

"That's where the story gets all confused," he continued. "As near as I can tell, you have no authority here at all."

"You're right there," Beamon said.

"That you have no authority?"

"That it's all confused."

Drake laughed with calculated ease and motioned around him in the dark. "No kidnappers or bank robbers here, Mark. Welcome to my world."

"What are *you* doing here?" Beamon said.

Drake didn't answer immediately, creating the illusion that he was trying to decide how much he should say.

"I think the same thing you are. But I'm not doing as good a job."

"Would you care to be more specific?"

"I'm after Volkov. I have been for years."

"Really?"

Drake nodded. "Volkov represents a whole new kind of organized crime, Mark. People like him are wielding economic and political power that in some ways is greater than the largest international corporations— but they pay no taxes and answer to no authority. The U.S. can't afford to keep ignoring them."

"Sounds serious," Beamon said. Drake couldn't tell if the comment was meant to be sarcastic.

"I think you'd agree that we'd live in a better world if people like Christian Volkov didn't exist. But I've never been able to get close to him. You have. What I want to know is how you got from Carlo Gasta to Christian Volkov in the span of a week."

Another smoke ring. This time Drake had to dodge it.

"He was involved with Gasta," Beamon said finally. "I guess it has to do with heroin. Gasta was buying and I gotta figure that Volkov is selling— or, more precisely, brokering. My getting involved was an accident, really. Volkov was impressed with my résumé."

Even in his weakened condition, Beamon was guarded. It was obvious to Drake that the FBI agent wasn't going to volunteer information easily.

"Why are you here, Mark?"

"I'm starting to wonder that myself."

"Well, let me tell you my theory," Drake said when it became obvious that Beamon was finished talking for the moment. "You want Volkov because you think he ordered Gasta to kill your friend. And I think you're right. But I'll tell you what else I think—I think that you're all alone on this and that you have a snowball's chance in hell of getting

Volkov working by yourself. Shit, even if the FBI *was* behind you, you wouldn't get him. He never sets foot in the U.S. and if he did, he'd probably be having dinner at the White House."

"Do you have a point?" Beamon said.

"Ever consider working for the CIA?"

Beamon didn't answer.

"Look, Mark, let's call a truce here, okay? I'll tell you what I know and you tell me what you know. Then we can talk about what we can do to help each other."

"And if I don't want to?"

"Then I'll just walk out of here and let you go back to working all alone on an undercover operation that doesn't exist. Maybe one of these days you'll meet Volkov and then you can just flash your creds and tell him he's under arrest."

Beamon lit another cigarette from the embers of his first one. He was obviously unsure what to do. But it was just a matter of time. He really had no choice.

"What happened to the first guy Volkov sent here to negotiate with Yung—the one who disappeared? Did you have this same conversation with him?"

Mark Beamon once again proved not to be as stupid as he looked.

"I didn't know Volkov had sent anyone else," Drake lied. Actually, he'd left Pascal and his pilot to rot in the jungle. "I don't have ears in Volkov's organization. I only know about you through the FBI."

Beamon nodded at the perfectly credible story, but it took another few minutes for him to arrive at a decision.

"Chet Michaels was inside Gasta's organization," he said. "There was a lot of money coming in from offshore accounts—I'm guessing that Volkov was the source. He's laying the groundwork for a new drug cartel in Afghanistan."

"A new cartel in Afghanistan?" Drake said. Just how much had Beamon figured out?

"Al-Qaeda's skirmishes correspond to the poppy-growing and heroin-refining areas in that region. Put that together with Volkov, Gasta, and the dead Afghans in L.A., and the implication is obvious: Volkov is helping Mustafa Yasin take over the Middle Eastern heroin trade. But then, you already knew that."

There was nothing to gain at this point with a denial that Beamon wouldn't believe. "Yeah, I knew that."

"Somehow, Chet's cover was blown," Beamon continued. "At that point I believe Volkov ordered Gasta to kill him. He probably also ordered Gasta to kill that group of Afghans. Why? I'm not sure. Maybe to try to stop any further terrorist acts. He strikes me as a man who doesn't like that kind of publicity."

Beamon leaned his head back onto his pillow, obviously finished. Drake knew that it was his turn now, but took a few seconds to run through what Beamon had told him. He was damn close. His only significant lapse was assuming that Volkov was the only player in this and that he had ordered Michaels's death. And of course he was unaware that the support for al-Qaeda was actually a now-abandoned effort on the CIA's part to crush them.

Drake started slowly, careful to offer only information that Beamon probably already had or that wouldn't be particularly useful. It was a balancing act. He had to build trust without giving him anything substantial.

"Volkov is not directly involved in terrorism—he's only interested in money and power. If increased terrorism is a by-product of him getting what he wants, though, then I don't think he really cares."

"Why now? The opium trade has been around for a thousand years."

"But it changed significantly when the Taliban gained control of most of Afghanistan. The supply of cheap high-quality heroin coming out of Afghanistan went through the roof, and that cut into the Asians' market share." Drake motioned around him. "Obviously, Volkov is heavily involved with the Asians."

"So he's looking to hitch his wagon to the Afghans."

"Exactly—he sees them as the future. But the production and refining system was really fragmented and unsophisticated, particularly after all our bombing runs. In the end it is easier for Volkov to support a consolidation under Yasin than to try to deal with literally hundreds of small players. He's been supplying al-Qaeda with arms and intelligence through his Russian connections for over a year."

"And if all goes well, Yasin ends up with a billion-dollar income, connections to Russian organized crime, and near-foolproof smuggling lines into the U.S."

"That's about the size of it. The FBI is doing everything it can to find the launcher, but they're missing the big picture. It's just the tip of the iceberg if Yasin is able to consolidate his position in the Golden Crescent."

"Do you know who Volkov is? I mean, who he is *really*?" Beamon said.

"We're honestly not sure. We think he was born Mihai Florescu in Romania sometime around 1958. His parents were killed in one of the government's purges and he ended up in an orphanage. He has no formal education to speak of—he's completely self-taught. Ironically, we hear that he always wanted to be a college professor—literature, I think it was. Kind of funny. Anyway, he ended up on the street, like a lot of kids did during Ceauşescu's regime, and got into dealing in black-market goods. He had a knack for it but still ended up in jail when he was about fourteen. Apparently, somebody there saw potential in him, because when he got out, he went to work for a criminal organization of some sort. And he moved up. It starts getting fuzzy after that. As he got older and wiser he got harder to track. He became at least ten different people and a hundred different offshore corporations."

"Why didn't you say anything about this when we met with you in Langley?"

"Volkov has powerful friends, Mark. I wasn't going to take any chances. The more people that know about this, the better the chance Volkov will find out that I'm after him. And if that happens, I'm a dead man."

"Why tell me, then?"

Drake grinned. "As I see it, you don't have any friends at the FBI willing to listen to you." He let the smile fade. "Look, Mark. I'm putting my life in your hands by talking to you about this. Some of my own people don't know this much."

"Likewise," Beamon said.

"So we're outcasts. The question is: Should we be outcasts together?"

There was a long pause before Beamon spoke. "I guess maybe we should."

"Great. Do you have any ideas?"

"No good ones. When—if—I leave here, I'm guessing I'll be going to see him."

"Face-to-face?" Drake said, genuinely surprised. "You're going to meet him face-to-face?"

"I reckon. Maybe you can use some of that fancy equipment you guys spend so much money on to track my plane."

"Maybe. We'll give it a shot. But in case we lose you for some reason, look for clues as to where you are and pay attention to what his plans are—particularly if they relate to where he's going and where we might have an opportunity to intercept him."

"Yeah," Beamon said quietly.

Drake had to struggle not to smile. The great Mark Beamon was going to lead him straight to Volkov, and the CIA would be able to get rid of them both in one fell swoop. Then all he'd have to do was figure out how to get to Gasta and the immediate danger would be over.

Beamon started coughing and for a moment looked as though he was going to throw up.

"You okay, Mark?"

"Yeah," he said after he'd caught his breath. "Fine."

"So do we have a deal?"

45

ONE thing about being high-class criminal talent—you ended up spending way too much time in helicopters.

Beamon glanced down at the top of the rolling carpet of alpine grass and stunted trees, and then at the expanse of blue water still miles away. It was a beautiful view—the day was nearly perfect: sunny, warm, and mercifully calm. Despite the conditions and the skill of the pilot, though, his stomach was on the verge of rebellion.

He'd stayed on for another half a day in Laos to give himself time to have one more polite but ultimately inconclusive discussion with General Yung. After that he'd been whisked back to his plane with effusive well-wishing aimed both at himself and Christian Volkov.

Five hours of sleep en route and the horse pills provided by Yung's doctor had brought him back from what felt like the brink of death to about ten feet from the brink of death. Another few days and he hoped to be back to his normal state of poor health.

Beamon leaned forward, careful not to upset the delicate balance that was keeping the dry heaves at bay, and searched the deep blue sky. Did the CIA have a plane up there, just out of sight? Was Jonathan Drake watching him via satellite? And most important, how did he feel about his new position as CIA stooge?

Honestly, he didn't much like Drake and had always felt a little like the mongoose to the CIA's snake. Probably not a fair evaluation of the Agency, but he just couldn't help himself—their motivations and results had always been hopelessly murky, and now, with the implosion of the Soviet Union and their proven ineffectiveness in the Middle East, their place in the world was even more confused. In this particular case, though, motivations were more or less irrelevant. He and Drake seemed to want the same thing: Christian Volkov's head on a platter.

Besides, it was hard to be morally indignant when he was more or less officially employed by organized crime. And as much as he hated to admit it, it felt good to have somebody behind him. Even if it was the Agency.

The helicopter began to lose altitude as the land below them disappeared into what looked like an inland sea. The pilot adjusted their trajectory a bit, aiming at a small white speck miles away. As they got closer the speck turned into a boat and then the boat into a yacht and then the yacht into what could only be described as a ship. Beamon looked down at it as they circled and examined the long, graceful lines of the gleaming hull. Based on the scale provided by the people on deck, his best guess at length was two hundred and fifty feet.

They touched down on the bow and Beamon jumped out, running beneath the downdraft toward a man dressed in the white shorts and shirt of a crewman.

"If you could follow me, sir."

Beamon trailed the man along the walkway, glancing up again at the sky and hoping again that someone was watching.

"Mark!"

Christian Volkov broke off from the men he was talking to and strode toward him, drink in hand. He gave Beamon's shoulder a friendly squeeze. "How are you? Are you feeling better?"

He'd obviously heard about his negotiator's less-than-dignified performance in Laos. "A lot better, thank you, Christian."

"There are some people I'd like you to meet. Do you feel up to it?"

"Sure."

Volkov put a hand on his back and led him across the broad stern, where no less than ten people were standing around, talking and drinking. The pattern was fairly simple: The men were all middle-aged Asians and the women, with one exception, were all tall, mid-twenties, blond and barely dressed. Obviously, Volkov knew how to throw a party.

"This is Mark—the man I was telling you about."

Beamon shook hands with two as yet unidentified men, one of whom said something in what sounded like Chinese. When Volkov laughed politely, Beamon was suddenly overcome by a sense of how sick, slow, and stupid he felt. The son of a bitch spoke Chinese.

"He says that you look like you've been drinking General Yung's, uh, would the expression be 'home brew'?"

"Yes, it would," Beamon said. "And he's exactly right. Refusing to have a drink with the general struck me as rude."

They all laughed again, and the man on the right spoke to Volkov in more than respectable English. "Your associate is very wise, Christian. Best not to insult the general."

"Excuse me, gentlemen." The voice was youthful and feminine, with an upper-crust British accent.

Beamon turned and found its source to be the one exception to the herd of blondes roaming the deck, grazing hors d'oeuvres. Like the others, she was tall, twenty-something, and gorgeous, but her hair was a deep, shiny brown and her eyes were almost black. Her skin was also fairly dark— probably half from the sun and half from her parents. Whatever had created the color, it looked exactly right against her pale pink bikini. Perhaps Volkov didn't share his Asian friends' penchant for the California ideal.

"Mark, I don't think you've met Elizabeth."

"I don't think I have. Hello, Elizabeth."

She smiled beautifully. "Can I get you a drink, Mark?"

"Just a water, please."

"Fizzy or regular?"

"With Alka-Seltzer, if possible. So, fizzy, I guess."

Another dazzling smile and she was off to the bar.

"Why don't I have my doctor fly in, Mark. He can have a look at you."

Beamon shook his head. "I got some pills in Laos. I'll be fine."

To Volkov's credit he looked genuinely concerned.

"How did you find the general, Mark?" one of the men he'd just met piped in.

Beamon had no idea who these two Asians were. If he had to bet, he'd say one was from Thailand and the other from Myanmar—the other two corners of the Golden Triangle. Since their Lao counterpart's head was currently topping a pike outside of Luang Prabang, they undoubtedly wanted to know if General Yung would complete their little triad again. Unfortunately, Beamon had no idea what they knew or how much to say. He glanced over at Volkov but couldn't read anything from his expression. A test.

"He has a wonderful sense of hospitality," Beamon said. "But next time I think I'll stick to bourbon."

"Is he in control?"

"I didn't have time to investigate that fully. Obviously, I saw what he wanted me to see. He gives every appearance of consolidating his power, though there is resistance. How organized it is, I can't say for certain."

Being a criminal was turning out to be a lot like being a politician. Talk a lot but don't say anything.

Another woman glided up to them, ignoring Beamon and sliding an arm around one of the Asian's waists. It was kind of an odd sight: her glistening, six-foot body pressed against the five-foot-six, pudgy, middle-aged man. Not surprisingly, he didn't seem to be overly upset by the interruption.

"All you do is talk about business," she said with a pout that briefly blotted out the sun. "The food is getting cold."

The man smiled. "You're right. We've been unforgivably rude. Perhaps we can talk later, Mark?"

"I look forward to it," Beamon said as the two men allowed themselves to be led to greener pastures.

"Are you sure you're all right, Mark?" Volkov asked again. "My doctor can be here in a few hours."

"I just need some rest and I'll be good as new."

Volkov looked past him. "Elizabeth, could you take Mark to his cabin, please?"

She handed Beamon a tall glass and he took a sip of the cold, fizzy liquid. For the thousandth time in his life, he said a quick, silent prayer for the souls of the brilliant men who had invented Alka-Seltzer.

"Sure. It's this way, Mark."

"Maybe we can get together tomorrow morning," Volkov said as Beamon was led away.

"Sure, Christian. Whatever works for you."

"Here you are, Mark."

The room was enormous and richly decorated in cheerful colors and polished brass. It kind of reminded him of the hotel suite Volkov had put him up in except for the three large portals looking out on the water.

"Thanks, Elizabeth," he said, tossing his laptop on the bed and eyeing the white marble shower through the bathroom door.

"Is there anything I can do to make you feel better? Believe it or not, I actually took a massage class at university."

Somehow he did believe it. That was the other thing about being a criminal—women seemed to love them. It must be have been the sense of danger, the rebel ideal. Helicopters, cash, and beautiful young women. At least at this level it looked like crime did pay.

For a moment he actually considered her offer. His introduction to Laotian moonshine had left his body feeling like the good general had run him over with that new Lamborghini. What he didn't need, though, was Jonathan Drake pulling up in a battleship, only to find some bikini-clad twenty-something sitting in the small of his back. The story would undoubtedly somehow make its way back to Carrie.

"You know, I think I'm just going to take a shower and crawl in bed."

"You're sure there's nothing I can do?"

"Hit me over the head with a monkey wrench."

She looked down at her nearly naked body. "Now, where would I keep a monkey wrench?"

"Then, I guess that's it."

"My number is on the phone directory next to the bed," she said, turning and walking back out into the hall, or whatever you called them on boats. "Ring me if you need anything."

Beamon decided to skip the shower and just flopped on the bed fully clothed. The events of the past weeks had become an unfathomable tangle at this point. And worse, doubts were beginning to creep into his mind, amplifying his headache.

He closed his eyes, considered setting the alarm, but decided against it. With a little luck he'd wake to the sound of machine-gun fire and the sight of Christian Volkov with some CIA guy's gun in his mouth. Then he wouldn't have to think about any of this anymore. It was just getting too complicated.

46

A BURST of sharp, loud noises brought Mark Beamon back to consciousness and he rolled over in the luxurious bed. Gunfire? He smiled and moved his arm to shade his eyes from the powerful sunlight beaming through the portals behind him. Had the CIA finally decided to get off their asses and make an appearance?

The sound came again and Beamon's smile faded.

"Come in," he yelled, propping some pillows behind him.

He didn't recognize the man Elizabeth ushered through the door, but based on the black leather bag in his hand, he could guess.

"Mark, this is Samuel Magnussen—Christian's doctor."

"Nice to meet you," Beamon said, shaking the man's hand from his position on the bed.

"And you," he said, with one of those Scandinavian lilts that sounded more like a mild speech impediment than an accent. "How are you feeling this morning?"

"A lot better," Beamon said honestly. "I told Christian not to bother you."

"It's no bother," he said, digging though his bag.

The exam was quick and standard: eyes, ears, nose, throat, blood pressure, temperature. Based on the doctor's expression, it looked as if he were going to live.

"I honestly don't recognize these pills," he said, examining the unlabeled bottle given to Beamon by Yung's doctor. "But you're feeling better and I wouldn't presume to second-guess a Lao physician about what is almost undoubtedly an illness relating to something you ate or drank there. . . ."

"Drank," Beamon said.

"Just so. I suggest following his recommendations. You'll be fine."

He left, but Elizabeth remained. Like Volkov, she had an expression of concerned that seemed genuine, but hers was so much more attractive. "Mark, if you feel up to it, Christian would like to speak with you."

"Tell him I'm going to take a shower and get dressed. Say a half an hour?"

"Fine."

"Mark!" Volkov stood and ducked under the umbrella shading him from what looked like the noon sun. Beamon would have reset his watch, but that would have meant he'd need to know roughly where on the planet he was. Somehow he guessed that information wouldn't be forthcoming.

"How are you feeling? Samuel tells me you're going to make it."

"It was touch and go there for a while, but I think I'm on the mend."

Volkov pointed to a chair across from him and Beamon took it, shooting one last glance at the sky before going under the umbrella. Still no CIA. Had they lost him? Were they organizing an attack? Was he somewhere beyond the Agency's long reach?

"So, how did you really find the general, Mark?"

Beamon looked around him. They were alone on the stern of the boat. Volkov's Asian guests had either gone or were still sleeping off their evening with the blondes.

"He's a nutcase."

Volkov smiled. "And that surprised you? They're all insane, Mark. Those in power are those willing to do what it takes to gain power. While the context varies, depending on the region, the rule itself is inviolable."

"Well, I'll tell you, Christian, he sees himself as some kind of revolutionary messiah. Kind of a combination of Papa Doc, Gandhi, and Keynes, depending on the particular moment."

Volkov nodded, prompting him to go on. Beamon just sat there, silent. "That's all?"

"I think I've answered all the questions you wanted answered. I've earned my paycheck."

Volkov laughed. "I was hoping for something more than a ten-second description of General Yung's delusions."

"No you weren't."

"I wasn't?"

Beamon popped a cigarette into his mouth and began patting his pockets for a lighter. To his surprise, Volkov pulled out his own and flicked the flame to life. Beamon leaned into it and nodded his thanks.

"So tell me, Mark. What was my motivation for sending you there, if not to get a detailed description of the atmosphere?"

"What happened to the last guy you sent, Christian?"

"The last guy?"

Beamon dragged in a lungful of smoke and let it roll from his mouth as he spoke. "He disappeared. Either you pulled him back because you thought he was in danger or he's buried in the jungle somewhere. Either way you needed to send someone else to talk to Yung. Not because you wanted to know about stability or competition—things a two-day trip couldn't determine—but because you wanted to know if your emissary would survive the trip. Maybe you even have some people on the ground there. If I'd been killed, you might have been able to figure out who did it and why."

Volkov turned away and looked out over the water. "I think you're being a little cynical, Mark. It's true that your safe return suggests certain things, but I thought it very unlikely that anyone would move against you there. And I *am* interested in your impressions."

"My impressions . . ." Beamon repeated. "You sent me out there as bait, Christian. My impressions are going to be expensive."

"How expensive?"

Beamon thought about that for a moment. When he'd been a first-office agent, he'd stuck his neck out for less than twenty grand a year. So that translated into . . .

"Two million."

"Fine. Joseph will wire it this afternoon."

"And this afternoon I'll give you my report."

"I have to wait?"

"I don't think Yung's going to lose his grip on Laos or make any deals with your competitors today. He's afraid of you, Christian."

Volkov's expression became thoughtful.

"Isn't that what you want?" Beamon said. "A wise man once said it's better to be feared than loved."

"Machiavelli's statement was overly simplistic, Mark. Fear's a difficult balancing act. If someone's too afraid, they become panicked and dangerous. Not afraid enough, and they get bold. Generally it's a combination of fear and love that works."

Beamon nodded and took another drag on his cigarette.

"Who was in your room that night in Laos, Mark?"

Beamon had considered the possibility that Volkov would know something about Drake's visit. But his question and the fact that Beamon was still alive suggested that he didn't know Drake's identity or what was said. Beamon tried to stay relaxed and talked in smooth, even tones.

"An old associate."

"What did he want?"

"He wanted to know what I was doing there."

"And what did you tell him?"

"I told him the truth—that I had a client who had a business relationship with the prior regime and was interested in a relationship with the new regime."

"Is this man my competition for General Yung's business?"

"The heroin business?" Beamon said. The word had yet to be uttered and he watched Volkov's reaction carefully. There was none. "No. He's more a broker in information than tangibles."

Volkov nodded silently and Beamon braced himself for cross-examination.

"Thank you, Mark."

"That's it?" Beamon said, surprised.

"Not entirely. If you're interested, I might have something for you in the U.S. A much more difficult job, but the pay would be better."

"Another setup?" Beamon said, not yet ready to be dismissed. Where the hell were Drake and his storm troopers?

"I didn't set you up in Laos, Mark. The job had risks, but you knew that going in. Besides, every time we meet, I see more of your value. I'm starting to wonder if I can afford to let anything happen to you."

47

MARK Beamon turned his rental car into a narrow alley without slowing, barely keeping the back end from slamming into a fire hydrant as the tires lost traction. After he'd managed to wrestle the vehicle back under control, he looked in the rearview mirror at the quiet L.A. street behind him. Nothing—just like after his last five extremely illegal maneuvers.

The town seemed dead. Not surprising, he supposed. The media had just broken the story about the rocket found outside of town, and a man with an Arabic accent had immediately called in to no less than five of the major local radio stations, assuring the good people of L.A. that it was only one of many. Any day now Allah would rain fire down on this most immoral of cities.

Volkov had provided the jet with the bed in the back for Beamon's return flight, and he was mending rapidly. In fact, he figured the hint of headache and nausea remaining was more the result of the mysterious pills prescribed by General Yung's doctor than the bug that had gotten hold of him.

He pulled the red, white, and blue phone from his pocket and speed dialed Laura's number.

"Hello?"

"Laura. Where are you?"

"Still in L.A."

"Why?"

"Waiting for you to get back."

"I figured I was persona non grata now. Don't you have anything better to do?"

"You are, and no, thanks, for pointing it out. My side of the investigation is mostly in the hands of the street agents and the science guys. Coordination and oversight on that end isn't taking much effort. I'm still working our best lead—the Afghans and the rocket we found here."

"The Director's still miffed?"

"You have no idea."

"What's he doing?"

"About you? Nothing that I know of. The doors are closed to me now, Mark. They figure I've taken your side but they can't prove it."

"Okay, what do you *think* he's doing?"

"Not much would be my guess. Gasta's still not talking, so my story that you didn't have anything to do with the drug heist is holding. He can't say much about your trip to Laos without making himself look like he's not in control. And since the press has ahold of the L.A. rocket story, I leaked that you're the one who found it. He's got to tread carefully." She paused briefly. "Did you ever play that game when you were a kid where you pull little sticks out of a tube until everything inside comes crashing down? I feel like that's what we're doing."

"A little after my time, but I take your point," Beamon said, wondering why it hadn't all come crashing down already. The FBI was getting lazy. "You and I are still okay, though. Right, Laura?"

"Yeah," she said. "We're okay."

"I'll be at the Starlite Cottage Motel on Sepulveda in about a half an hour, registered under the name Bolten. Meet me there." He hung up and dialed another number from memory.

"Yeah, go ahead."

"Drake! Where the fuck were you?"

"The problem wasn't where I was, Mark, it was where you were. We don't make a habit out of flying into Russian airspace without an invitation."

"Goddamnit," Beamon muttered. "What about those spy satellite things you guys are always bragging about?"

"They don't work that way—you know that. Did you get anything on where he might be headed? If we can get a little more notice, we might have time to make a deal with the local government and get in. . . ."

"Or maybe he'll go to one we're not so afraid of," Beamon said.

"Yeah. I mean, if we find out he's in Cuba, we might just be able to go in there and grab him. But Russia . . ."

"Shit!" Beamon shouted in the empty car.

"So, did you meet with him, Mark? Face-to-face?"

"Yeah."

"What happened?"

"Nothing." Beamon floored the car, running a very yellow light as he watched the rearview mirror. "I met a couple of Asian guys but didn't catch any names. Heroin dealers from Thailand and Burma if I had to guess. And I told him about Laos."

"That's it?"

"Well, he knew someone talked to me in my room."

There was a stunned silence over the phone for a moment.

"What did he say, Mark? Tell me exactly!"

"Relax, Jonathan. He didn't know who you were or what we said. If he did, I'd be at the bottom of a Russian lake right now."

"What did you tell him?" Drake was trying to hide it, but he sounded scared.

"I pretty much told him the truth—that you were a former associate who traded on information."

"And what was his reaction?"

"Honestly, he didn't seem to care."

"You're sure, Mark. You're sure that's all you said."

"If he finds anything out, Jonathan, I'm dead before you are. So if I suddenly disappear, start looking for a good plastic surgeon. If not, don't worry about it."

That seemed to calm him down a bit. "So you're telling me you didn't get *anything* that we might be able to use?"

"You mean other than the goddamn mile-wide trail I gave you? Not really. He did say he might have another job for me. That's it. It's his move."

Just as it always was. He was getting pretty tired of being dumber and slower than this asshole.

"Let me know the minute he gets in touch with you, Mark. Seriously— the *minute*."

"I will. See if you can get your act together next time. Volkov is starting to make us look like a couple of amateurs. It's getting embarrassing."

The hotel room was pretty basic—nowhere near the opulence of the one Volkov had provided him and that he would return to later that night. He was fairly certain that no one was watching or listening, though. For now, anyway.

He pressed a handful of ice against his forehead and sat down at a small desk, centering a pad of hotel stationery in front of himself. First he wrote down the names of the actors in the drama he'd gotten himself involved in: Chet Michaels, the Afghan heroin dealers, Carlo Gasta, Christian Volkov, Mustafa Yasin, General Yung, and now Jonathan Drake. Staring down at the list, he tried to get his mind to put some sense to what was going on.

Too many goddamn players. This kind of thing just wasn't his forte.

The ice was starting to melt down his face, so he stuffed it in a pillowcase and pressed it against the back of his neck, trying to concentrate. Despite the complexity of this thing, he couldn't shake the feeling that he was missing something. Something obvious.

The knock broke his train of thought just as the effort was beginning to amplify his headache. He crossed the room and pulled the door open, starting back toward the bed without bothering to look who was there.

"Mark, are you all right? What happened in Laos?"

He flopped down on the mattress and pressed the ice-filled pillowcase against his forehead again. "I didn't find your launcher, if that's what you mean."

"What *did* you find, then?" she said.

That was something he didn't really want to think too hard about. "I basically did exactly what Volkov wanted me to. In fact, I did such a great job, I made another two million."

"You're becoming very successful."

"Was there ever any doubt?"

"I guess not."

"I'm hoping you're doing better," Beamon said.

"Not much. We've identified the men Gasta killed. No surprises and not much help. All four are thought to be tied to al-Qaeda, one we suspect was involved in the attack on the USS *Cole*."

Beamon sighed quietly. "Any known associates we can look for?"

"Not really. The information we have on these men is sketchy at best. Honestly, we're probably worse off than we were before. The tightening of the connection to al-Qaeda is getting the military's trigger finger itchy."

"Are they going to move on it?"

"Not yet. With the exception of Charles Russell, who's taken a pretty uncompromising scorched-earth stance, I think Congress and the President are going to wait and watch. They won't admit it, but having a rocket launcher buzzing around has made them all a little more thoughtful—well, that and the fact that they're not sure who to shoot at."

Beamon leaned back against the headboard. "So after all this, what we've learned is where the launcher *won't* be."

Laura nodded. "The threats are just smoke. With all this plastered across the TV, we can safely say that Yasin will target somewhere else. He's gotten what he wanted in L.A.—fear."

"We can always just hope that's the only missile they have and that now they're out of ammo," Beamon said.

"Seems overly optimistic."

"Yeah. What else you got?"

"My fingers crossed that you've turned up something that can help me? At this point I'll take anything—no matter how far-fetched. The fact that I'm here should tell you how desperate I am. If the Director finds out, I'll be as dead as—" She cut herself off.

"As dead as me?"

"I'm sorry, Mark. I—"

He waved his hand, silencing her. "I'm not that easily offended. I wish I *could* help you, Laura, I really do. But I have to admit that I'm stuck. I can almost make things fit together, but not quite."

"How so?"

Beamon took a deep breath. "Christian Volkov. Based on my trip to Laos for him, we can assume he's involved with the Asian heroin machine. The Afghans are horning in on the market, though, and he wants a piece of that action. So he backs Yasin and helps him take over the Golden Crescent."

Laura nodded, but didn't say anything.

"And then there's Carlo Gasta," Beamon continued. "We assume he's one of Volkov's U.S. connections—a cog in the new Afghan distribution system Volkov is setting up. It all couldn't be more simple. Two of the classic and most easily understood motivators are at play here: money and religion."

He had purposely left out Jonathan Drake's visit to him in Laos. It seemed safer to keep that to himself for now.

"Okay," Laura said, "based on those assumptions, what's happening? Let me give it a try. Everything was going great—al-Qaeda is having success in the Golden Crescent and is starting to sell heroin in the U.S. to people like Gasta. But that's not ultimately what Yasin wants—he wants to destroy the U.S. So he uses some of his new contacts in Russian organized crime to get this boutique rocket launcher and he uses his new friends in Mexico to smuggle it here. Next thing you know, they're sending snapshots to the press. How would a man like your Christian Volkov react? We've got to figure he'd get spooked and decide he needs to distance himself from this whole thing. He tells Gasta to get rid of the Afghan drug dealers. . . . But why? Did he think that it would put an end to any further terrorist acts? Maybe these Afghans could identify his role in this thing? And in the meantime he finds out about Chet, who he met face-to-face. He gives the order to get rid of him too."

"That's the worst theory I've ever heard. And I can say that with real certainty because it's pretty much the same one I came up with."

Laura looked down at the floor. "Yeah, it's pretty lame."

"Three problems jump out at me," Beamon said. "First, Chet didn't meet Volkov. When you meet this guy, it's on his turf and you have no idea where in the world you are. I doubt he ever sets foot in the U.S. Best case, Chet met one of Volkov's people. Second—and it hurts me to say this—Christian Volkov isn't afraid of the FBI. As far as we're concerned he doesn't exist, right? And even if the FBI figures it out, I doubt we'd be able to get him. Third, let's not forget that he's the one who called the cops in on Gasta. How the hell does that fit into all this?"

"So if he's not afraid of us and Chet didn't meet him, why'd he have Chet killed?"

Beamon slid the pillowcase down over his eyes and stared into the cold darkness. "I'm not sure he did."

"What? I thought the only reason you were here is because you wanted to get this guy."

"Those bank records you went through can't even put him together with Gasta," Beamon said. "You told me yourself that there was no connection between the accounts I was paid through and the accounts that Gasta was paid through."

"There could be ten different explanations for that."

"Yeah, but . . . I don't know, Laura. You should meet this guy. He's . . ."

"A sadistic criminal mastermind?"

"That's just it. He's really not. Is he ruthless? Yeah, sure. But he's not ten feet tall with horns and a pointed tail. Honestly, he seems like a pretty reasonable guy. Is he a criminal? I don't know. . . . It kind of depends on your perspective and which side of which border he's standing on at the time."

"What the hell are you talking about, Mark? He's a heroin dealer and God knows what else. He makes his living pedaling death and misery to the world."

"That's true. But certainly not on the scale of a Philip Morris or Anheuser-Busch."

"Going native, are you?"

"Look, I just watched an entire village of farmers get gunned down in cold blood and a little kid get hacked apart by a guy with a machete. Christian Volkov didn't have anything to do with that. You know who did? The new president of Laos—a man America is supporting."

He sighed quietly and sunk deeper into the mattress. "Don't listen to me, Laura. I'm just frustrated out of my mind. The answer's right in front of us—I know it is. We just can't see it."

He fell silent, turning the myriad pieces of this investigation over and over in his mind, trying to create a coherent theory. Nothing. He knew from experience that he'd been concentrating on the problem for too long. He wouldn't solve it tonight.

48

THE big-screen television was barely visible in the glare coming through the hotel suite's windows. It wasn't the image that was important, though, it was the commentary that was so damaging. Small hand-to-mouth businesses shutting their doors permanently, people panicking about the huge drop in the values of their retirement accounts, big corporations laying the groundwork for government handouts. Could America take a year of this? What about two?

Instead of giving the FBI credit for turning up the terrorist cell in L.A., the media had decided to use it to give credibility to their baseless reports of suspected Muslim fanatics with batteries of rockets in every city in America. Any tip, however unsupported, became certain death lurking just around the corner for hundreds of Americans. And it was quickly becoming Laura's fault.

Next, the politicians would jump on the bandwagon and FBI management would start to back away from her. Someone would have to pay for the American people's fear and suffering. Someone always had to pay.

Beamon continued to pace back and forth in front of the television, as he had been since he'd woken from his deathlike five-hour nap. Physically and mentally, he felt as if he were back to about ninety percent, and with most of his neurons firing again, a coherent theory had finally formed. He'd been trying to punch holes in it for more than thirty minutes now, and so far he couldn't find any fatal weaknesses beyond the fact that it seemed a little far-fetched. For the first time in all this, he had something that fit all the facts.

The knock at the door startled him and he stopped pacing abruptly. He hadn't given anyone the location of the hotel suite that Volkov had provided—not even Laura. Unless it was a lost room-service guy, it stood to reason that one of Volkov's people was on the other side of that door. Why? Clearly the man preferred to give orders long distance. Why would he send someone personally with no warning?

Beamon stood motionless in the middle of the floor, staring at the door. He knew that his tenuous cover would eventually fall apart—the only reason it had lasted this long was probably because Volkov had to deal with the same inefficiency as everyone else when it came to getting information out of the U.S. bureaucracy. At some point, though, his informants would take the doughnuts out of their mouths and get back to him on the identity of the enigmatic Nicolai.

He grabbed his .357 off the nightstand and walked quietly across the room. Holding it casually behind his back, he took a deep breath and pulled the door open.

"Mark! My God, you look like a new man. Can I come in?"

Beamon stepped aside to let Elizabeth through and then cautiously poked his head out the door and looked both ways. The hall was empty.

"Nice room," Elizabeth commented as he closed the door and locked it. "Christian usually puts me in the Holiday Inn."

Except for the British accent, she was almost unrecognizable as the bikini-clad girl on Volkov's boat. She was wearing a tan silk blouse and an elegant but form-fitting black skirt. Her dark hair flowed across her shoulders and framed a face that suddenly seemed to exude an unlikely combination of youth and worldliness. Had all that been there before? Probably. It seemed almost certain that, in her former nearly naked state, he hadn't really given a great deal of thought to her face.

"You have a balcony out here?" she said, striding across the room and gazing out at the light of the setting sun playing across the city.

"What are you doing in the States?" Beamon asked, sliding his gun into the waistband of his slacks.

"Christian wanted me to come and pick you up. Are you free this evening?"

Good question. Had Volkov's people managed to follow him earlier? Did they know about his meeting with Laura? Had they been able to figure out who she was?

"For what?"

She turned and smiled. "I don't know. He just told me to come and get you. So? Are you free?"

He didn't have any choice, he knew. If he was going to keep this ball in play, he'd just have to assume that his cover was solid until someone finally put him out of his misery.

"I guess I am."

"Great! I've got a car downstairs."

Elizabeth pushed a garage door opener on the visor and turned the car off the winding road toward a nondescript iron gate surrounded by densely packed trees. They eased through as it opened and then accelerated up a steep and winding driveway that went on for about a quarter of a mile. The house suddenly became visible when the grade leveled out— a graceful building constructed of red stucco, intermittently lit by tiny spotlights set into a well-tended yard.

Elizabeth let the car roll to a slightly bumpy stop in the cobblestone courtyard and Beamon jumped out.

"You coming?" he said.

"I've got a few errands to run actually. I'll see you a little later."

He watched her turn and disappear down the driveway again, suddenly realizing how quiet it was.

"Mark!"

Beamon instantly recognized the young man jogging across the uneven ground.

"Joseph. It's good to see you."

They shook hands and Joseph motioned toward the front door. "Come on in."

The interior was pretty much what he expected—high ceilings and an open floor plan, tastefully decorated in an understated southwestern theme.

"Just through those doors," Joseph said. "Christian's by the pool."

"Christian's here?" Beamon said, unable to disguise his surprise.

"Yeah. Out by the pool."

Beamon pushed through the door at the back of the house and found himself on a large terrace overflowing with brightly colored flowers and dominated by a kidney-shaped pool.

"Mark! How are you feeling?" Christian Volkov said, circumnavigating some deck furniture and shaking his hand warmly.

"Much better, thank you."

"Samuel wanted me to follow up. Not having any problems?"

"No problems at all," Beamon said, a little distracted. They seemed to be alone on the terrace, and it suddenly occurred to him that he was armed and, assuming he hadn't been officially fired yet, within his jurisdiction. It was conceivable that he could actually arrest Volkov. The only problem was that for some reason the idea seemed absurd.

"Did Joseph offer you a drink?"

"No."

Volkov shook his head, smiling. "He has a very sharp mind, but I need to work on his social graces."

"He seems like a good kid."

"Oh, he is—the crown jewel of my college recruiting program."

Beamon laughed but then realized that Volkov wasn't joking. "You're serious."

"Of course. One of my associates found him working two jobs, putting himself through the equivalent of a community college in Australia. He was doing brilliantly and at the same time helping to support his parents and siblings. One of my companies gave him a scholarship to get an M.B.A. in America and then a job when he graduated. Now, seven years later, he's one of my executive assistants."

"Part Aborigine, isn't he?" Beamon said.

Volkov nodded. "There's still very real bigotry in Australia against the native people. And where there's bigotry, there are very talented, very frustrated people looking for an opportunity."

"No Americans?"

Volkov shook his head and took a sip of the drink in his hand. "Of course, I employ a great number of Americans in my U.S. corporations, but none are close to me. Could you excuse me for a moment, Mark? Please make yourself a drink."

Volkov went inside the house and Beamon wandered to an outdoor bar next to an elaborate stainless-steel grill. He poured himself a club soda while trying to picture Volkov barbecuing with friends. What would the conversation be? *So I think if we assassinate the foreign minister of Swaziland, we can gain control of the drug flow through there and insert a puppet regime. Do you want Swiss or cheddar on your burger?*

"Bad news," Volkov said as he came back through the door. "François has refused to make the shrimp raviolis you like so much. I tried to insist but he threw a spoon at me. Apparently they don't complement what he's preparing. The good news is that whatever it is he's making, it smells wonderful."

"I'm not worried," Beamon said. "I have nothing but confidence in François."

"Well founded, I think. What are you drinking, Mark?"

"Club soda. I'm not much of a drinker."

That elicited a broad smile from Volkov. "I'll tell you what, Mark. Let's make a pact. We're going to have a nice evening: a night of conversation instead of giving orders and worrying about who's sneaking up behind us. I'll promise not to have you killed for what you say tonight, and you promise likewise." They shook hands, consummating the agreement, and then Volkov reached behind the bar and pulled out a bottle of wine. "I've been wanting to uncork this for a while," he said. "It's a '49 Yago Condal . . . from Spain."

Beamon looked skeptically at the bottle. "You might want to wait for better company, Christian. I don't really know one wine from another."

"Honestly, I don't either," he said, gazing down at the thin, angular bottle. "I like the history of it, though. Think about what Spain had been through in the years before this wine was produced. They had managed to stay out of World War Two, but their own civil war had left them ostracized by most of the world and in the hands of a military dictator. . . ."

Beamon couldn't believe he was finally getting to use his history degree. If only his father were alive to see it. "But they'd only have to stick it out a little longer. The world needed Spain's help with the Koreans. And Franco would turn out to have a fairly good record as military dictators go."

Volkov smiled as he uncorked the bottle and poured it gently into a carafe. "That's very true."

About halfway through the apparently arduous decanting process, a tinny rendition of "The Star-Spangled Banner" started playing in Beamon's pocket.

"Would you excuse me for a moment, Christian?"

"Of course."

Beamon walked along the edge of the pool and put the phone to his ear. "Yeah."

"We've got problems, Mark." Laura's voice. "The L.A. office followed up on those strippers who helped Gasta get away. When they described the guy that hired them, guess who it sounded like?"

"Jesus, it's about time they figured that out. I was starting to get embarrassed for you guys."

"Jesus Christ, Mark. You went and hired them yourself?"

"I needed reliable gals. No way to know if they're worth rubbernecking unless you look 'em in the, uh, eye."

"Mark! For God's sake! We've got four dead bodies and now they know you were directly involved. This goes way beyond the Laos thing."

"Wait till they find out I used an FBI credit card."

"You didn't."

"Mine was over the limit."

"The Director's going to have a heart attack. I don't even know what to tell you here."

Even though he'd known this was coming, Beamon had expected to feel fairly emotional when the actual hammer dropped. Now that the moment was here, though, he didn't feel anything.

"So, where do I stand, Laura?"

"I don't know. Caroll wants you in his office first thing tomorrow morning—and this time you'd damn well better show up. Maybe you can cut a deal—convince him that he doesn't want the press to get ahold of this. . . ." Her voice faded for a moment. "Shit, Mark. I don't know . . . I'm so sorry. This is my fault. I got you into this."

"Don't be stupid. I got myself into this."

"Can I tell him that you'll be on a plane tonight? That you'll be there tomorrow?"

"What about all those other things you've got me working on," Beamon said, looking behind him. Volkov was paying him no attention at all—he seemed absorbed by his wine bottle.

"We're going to have to go on without you. It may be already too late for you to save yourself here, Mark. I don't know. But I guarantee that if you miss this meeting it's all over."

He didn't respond.

"Mark?"

Laura's investigation was dead in the water but his continued to move forward. Whether Volkov was actually behind Chet Michaels's death was starting to become a question mark, but either way he was the key to all this. If he wasn't responsible for Chet's death, he knew who was. And he was almost certainly in bed with Mustafa Yasin.

"No. A face-to-face meeting is out of the question."

"What?"

"You heard me."

"Mark, we tried to work around management on this thing and we had a pretty good run. But now it's time to try to save yourself."

"It's too late for that—we both know it. Look, I'm a little busy right now. I'll call you later."

"Mark, wait—"

Beamon turned off the phone and stuffed it in his pocket as he walked back to the bar. Volkov handed him a glass of wine.

"I'm surprised to see you in L.A., Christian."

"I have a computer technology company based here. Internet gambling."

"Internet gambling?"

He nodded. "It's an enormous growth industry with really exciting potential for innovation. The younger generation that's been weaned on computers will be coming of age soon and won't have patience for conventional games like blackjack. Everything is going to have to be an elaborate multimedia experience. Imagine, every personal computer more interesting than Las Vegas."

"I'm not much of a computer person myself," Beamon said, taking a sip of the wine. It was pretty good. "Tell me, Christian . . . I'm curious. How did you get into this?"

"Computer gambling?"

"Organized crime."

"That label—it's so . . ."

"Melodramatic?"

"Yes. Though I suppose it's correct. On some level I am a criminal. I just don't think of myself as one."

"But isn't it true that you're involved in the heroin trade?"

"And currently heroin is illegal in the U.S. and Europe, though much more destructive products are not. Gambling, on the other hand, may or may not be legal, depending on where you happen to be at the time. You can give a dying cancer patient morphine to relieve his suffering, but not marijuana. The numbers racket used to be very profitable for the American Mob. Now the government's taken it over, called it a lottery, and enforced its monopoly."

"I suppose, like everything, it's a matter of perspective," Beamon prompted.

"You would be surprised to know how much money I give conservative politicians and right-wing Christian groups. The only competitors I really fear are the governments. It's best for me if all things pleasurable remain illegal."

"You didn't answer my question. How did you get involved in all this?"

"I'm sorry." He took a thoughtful sip of his wine. "I was unlucky enough to have not been born American. Where I grew up, 'crime' was the only way to survive. Despite the communist ideals of the country where I was born, the gap between the haves and have-nots was too wide to see across. Of course, business prospered there, but only for those connected to the government and under its protection. If any private citizen managed to make a life for themselves, the police called them traitors, murdered them, and then gave their burgeoning enterprise to one of the ruling elite. In any event, I fell in with a group who were close to a powerful official and were therefore allowed to operate. I had an aptitude for the work and did well. When the Soviet Union collapsed, I was able to move in on the less efficient operations that were no longer protected by the government and military. Since then I've continued to grow." He motioned toward a table with two chairs pushed up to it and they both sat.

"It's funny, really. This isn't where I pictured myself. But there was always another deal to be done. As you know, you either grow or you die in this business."

"So now you make a living providing the people what they want," Beamon said. "Drugs, women, black-market goods, whatever. Victimless crimes."

"Crimes in which one is a willing victim would be more accurate."

The opening was there. Beamon tried to decide whether this was a safe moment to test his new theory. Probably not, but he doubted a better time would present itself.

"What about supplying weapons to al-Qaeda so that they can take over the heroin trade in the Golden Crescent? Are all their victims willing?"

Volkov's eyes flashed briefly but otherwise his expression remained passive. Beamon knew that there was no going back now: He had let on that he knew more than he had been told.

"The American government can supply anyone they want with arms," Volkov said. For the first time there was a hint of anger in his voice. "They themselves have armed the Afghans, the Iranians, and the Iraqis, to mention only a few. They have overthrown democratically elected governments and replaced them with despots to further their interests and the interests of American corporations. Of course, this is all legal because they can arbitrarily define legality and intimidate the rest of the world with their military and economic power."

"I didn't mean to offend you, Christian."

"You haven't."

Beamon reached into his pocket and pulled out a cigarette. The act of lighting it calmed him down a bit. "I certainly didn't mean to imply that you were looking to get in bed with Yasin."

Volkov didn't respond immediately, and Beamon couldn't help being a little impressed with himself. He was playing chess against a more skilled opponent and had made him hesitate. For the first time Volkov was having to think before he spoke.

"But didn't you just suggest that I was involved in that very thing?"

Beamon shrugged and feigned disinterest in continuing the conversation.

"You obviously have something to say, Mark. Say it."

"Remember our pact," Beamon said.

"I remember."

Beamon took another sip of his wine and set his cigarette in a thoughtfully provided ashtray. "It was something you said to me a few days ago. You said that you'd deal with the Asians exclusively if you could. Why? Because they're intelligent and reliable. They have the same philosophy as you. The difference between the illegal and legal is arbitrary at best. Yasin, it seems to me, is on the other side of the spectrum. He's motivated by religion, by politics, by his own delusions. Overall, an unstable and unpredictable man. Not your kind of guy."

Beamon paused to take a drag off his cigarette. So far so good. He wasn't dead yet.

"Go on," Volkov said.

"Okay, I will. Yasin is in the process of taking over as much of the heroin machine in Afghanistan, Pakistan, and Iran as he can—not just production but refining and distribution. And he's doing that with weapons and intelligence provided by you. But he's in for a bit of a surprise, isn't he?"

"Is he?"

"I think so. His little war has caused a fairly serious disruption in the flow of heroin out of that region, and everyone down the line is starting to get nervous. They're starting to worry that Yasin and his people are nuts and are going to be impossible to deal with."

Beamon paused again, this time to take a sip of wine. Volkov didn't seem ready to speak, so he figured he might as well continue.

"I'm guessing that sometime soon, all the support you're giving al-Qaeda is going to come to an abrupt halt and you and your Asian friends will use the nervousness of the Mexican, American, and European distributors to move right on in. You'll have nearly complete control of the world heroin trade before Yasin knows what hit him. That's why you needed me to go talk to General Yung. Before long you're going to need as much product as the Asians can provide."

Beamon leaned back in his chair and folded his hands over his stomach. His cards were pretty much on the table now. Volkov still wasn't reacting, though. He was just sitting there, staring off into the darkness. It was almost a minute before he spoke.

"It's a fine line, Mark. . . . You want clever people working for you. But there's such a thing as too clever."

"Remember our pact," Beamon said again.

"I remember. And you do the same."

49

JONATHAN Drake crossed the driveway quickly, still wondering why he was there. Was being asked to meet at Alan Holsten's suburban home a vote of confidence, or was it because the DDO didn't want to be seen with him at Langley?

The latter was the most likely answer. The game Drake had been playing was almost over, and it looked like he was going to lose. Holsten was simply trying to decrease his chances of getting caught in the ensuing storm.

Drake jumped up onto the front porch but didn't have to knock. The door opened almost immediately and Holsten, wearing a golf shirt and a pair of tan slacks, motioned him in. The entry was dark, as was the rest of the house. It was almost eleven and it looked as though Holsten's wife and two daughters were already asleep.

Drake silently followed his host through the house and into a windowless office, thinking through the events of the past few weeks one last time.

He knew now that the loss of Gasta to the L.A. police had been the beginning of the end. With al-Qaeda's L.A. cell now in the hands of the FBI, and Mark Beamon inexplicably finding a way to get close to Christian Volkov, it was only a matter of time before someone glimpsed the truth. Admittedly the puzzle was complicated, but nearly all the pieces were available now.

At this point the only thing that could solve his immediate problems would be the deaths of both Christian Volkov and Mark Beamon—something that in the short term seemed unlikely.

"Where do you stand, Jonathan?" Holsten said, closing the door to the claustrophobic home office behind them. "Do you have any movement?"

Holsten's liberal use of the word *you* made it even clearer that he was continuing to back away from this operation and planned to leave his subordinate holding the bag to whatever degree possible. Drake knew that if he told the truth tonight, he would leave Holsten considering options that would end with him dead. He had to get out before it came to that.

"Beamon's fully on board," Drake said. "He wants Volkov and is willing to do whatever it takes to get him—he's already thrown away his career and probably his life."

"He wants Volkov because he thinks Volkov ordered the death of his friend," Holsten said. "What's he going to do when he finds out that it was actually you?"

The anger that had been so evident in their recent meetings was gone, replaced by a cold monotone that made Drake even more certain that it was time to cut and run. Holsten had a beautiful home, a prominent social standing, an important job, a family. He would do whatever was necessary to protect that.

"There's nothing that would lead him to me, Alan. How could he possibly find out about my involvement?"

"Volkov might tell him. And Gasta can identify you."

Drake shook his head. "Why would he believe Volkov, the man who he thinks killed his friend? No, our biggest problem with Beamon is that the FBI's starting to actively look for him."

"They won't find him if he doesn't want to be found," Holsten said.

"Which is good for us—he's the key to all this. He tells me that he can position Volkov so we can get him. And based on his reputation, I'm willing to bet that he can do what he says."

Drake watched his boss's face carefully, trying to see if he believed the string of lies he was being told. One week—that was all the time he needed to sell Beamon's identity to Volkov and use the money to disappear.

"And you'll take them both out," Holsten said.

Drake nodded. "Volkov's organization is completely reliant on him—particularly now that Pascal, his former number two, is dead. With Volkov gone, there will be a feeding frenzy as his enemies rip apart his organization and divide it up for themselves. By the time the FBI's investigation leads them that far—if it ever does—Christian Volkov will be nothing more than a hazy maze of legends and hearsay."

"And Gasta?"

"Neither he or any of his people have said a word."

"They will."

"Eventually. Right now he's dealing with the New York families through the lawyer they provided him. They're telling him that they'll kill him if he says anything. And the FBI is telling him that they can protect him out of one side of their mouth and threatening him with the death penalty out of the other."

"It's just a matter of time," Holsten said. "He'll have to deal."

"Alan, he has no idea who I am—only a physical description and a maze of dummy corporations and overseas banks that have no connection to organized crime. The FBI wanted Gasta and now they've got him. They want to believe al-Qaeda is behind the launcher and now they have evidence of that. They're not going to dig deeper. Why would they?"

Drake fell silent and let his boss consider what he'd just heard. A bead of sweat threatened to trickle out of his hairline and down his nose, but a slight adjustment of his head kept it in check.

"What are you hearing about Laura Vilechi's investigation?" Holsten said finally.

"I'm hearing the same thing you are—that it's going nowhere."

"An attack is coming, though, Jonathan—have you been watching the news? People are starting to come out of hiding and go to work, go shopping, put their kids back in day care. When the fear fades too much, Yasin's people are going to use that launcher. And when they do, the FBI's investigation is going to get a huge shot in the arm. People are paying attention, Jonathan. They remember anyone who looks Arab. They're watching for contrails. It isn't going to be a surprise."

"By then Volkov and Beamon will be gone, Alan. I guarantee it."

50

THE combination of overeating and Laotian antibiotics was starting to make Beamon feel sick again. Despite that, he broke off a small piece of lighter-than-air piecrust and popped it in his mouth. When he swallowed, his stomach rumbled audibly.

"That was undoubtedly one of the finest meals I've ever eaten, Christian."

"I'll pass that on to François. He'll be pleased you enjoyed it."

After Beamon's recitation of his apparently correct theory regarding Volkov's plan to double-cross Mustafa Yasin, the conversation had become somewhat subdued. Quiet small talk about the area, art, history, food. Volkov seemed a bit distant, as though he were trying to make a decision—probably whether or not this would be Beamon's last meal. Could he afford to have an independent operator running around with the blueprint for a takeover of the world heroin trade and the knowledge that he was facilitating al-Qaeda's war on America?

Beamon nodded his thanks as Elizabeth cleared his plate and then looked out over the shimmering pool into the darkness. A beautiful setting. But for what? It seemed unlikely that Volkov had asked him here just for the considerable pleasure of his company.

Finally the answer came. Volkov reached into his pocket and pulled out a scrap of paper, sliding it facedown across the table toward Beamon.

"I want you to talk to Carlo Gasta for me. To give him a message."

Beamon's eyebrows rose a bit. "From what I hear, he's under heavy guard by the FBI. They seem to think the New York families would like to see him dead. His lawyer is the only person with access."

"If it was easy, I'd get someone cheaper to do it."

Beamon laughed. "I appreciate your confidence in me, Christian, but what do you want me to do? *No one* is getting in to see him."

"How much?"

Beamon pulled out a cigarette and lit it. He had to admit to liking the crime business just a little bit. It was a world where anything was possible. The only question worth asking was the one Volkov just posed. The interesting thing was that it was remotely possible that he actually could get to Gasta. But if he did, it was because of his connection to the FBI. When did you go from being undercover to being on the take? The line was surprisingly fuzzy.

"My fee would be ten million, plus expenses, which could be substantial. And there would be no guarantees. If I can't pull it off, I'd still want five million to cover my out-of-pocket."

Volkov shrugged. "Fine."

"But before I agree to anything, I want to know why. No more going in blind like I did in Laos. How does Carlo Gasta fit into all this?"

"Criminal Darwinism, remember?"

"But Gasta's just a moron—we both know that. I mean, he's probably got some dirt on a few wise guys, but no one who could bother you much."

"You tell me why, then," Volkov said. "You must have a theory."

"Honestly, you have me stumped. It seems like bad timing. You have enough on your plate right now."

"Why don't you work on it."

Beamon took a thoughtful pull on his cigarette. "I will. I figure if Chet Michaels, a wet-behind-the-ears kid from the FBI, could get close enough to scare you, I sure as hell can."

Volkov didn't say anything for a moment, instead just staring across the table in a way that made Beamon strangely uncomfortable.

"Let me help you a bit, Mark. I had nothing to do with the death of

Chet Michaels. In fact, I've never had any contact with Carlo Gasta at all. He's probably vaguely aware of my existence, as most people in his position would be, but we've never spoken or had business dealings together."

Beamon took another drag on his cigarette, hoping it kept his surprise from showing. He hadn't been prepared for the quiet forcefulness of Volkov's statement. The man was undoubtedly a hell of a liar, but was he that good? Why would he bother to lie, anyway? Chet was dead and Nicolai, while a powerful fabrication, was no real threat to him.

Beamon finally realized that he hadn't reacted for far too long. Chet Michaels had been nothing more than a valuable business asset to Nicolai.

"I've been paid for the inconvenience Chet's death caused me. Who was responsible is just an interesting intellectual exercise at this point."

Volkov patted the corners of his mouth with his napkin and stood. "I'm afraid I have to go. But I'd like you to stay and be my guest here. I think you'll find it more comfortable than the hotel."

"Thanks, but . . ."

"Really, Mark. I insist."

Obviously, Volkov wanted to keep an even closer eye on him than the hotel would allow. Beamon wanted to refuse, but he suspected Volkov wouldn't take no for an answer.

"Thank you, then. I accept."

"And I'll leave Elizabeth with you. I think you'll find—"

Beamon held up his hand. "I appreciate the offer of the house, Christian, but I really don't need . . . companionship."

Volkov looked a bit perplexed for a moment, then smiled. "Oh, of course—the boat. I'm afraid you have the wrong impression of Elizabeth. While she is very beautiful, she wasn't with the women entertaining our Asian friends. She's another one of my executive assistants. Joseph is wonderful with mathematics and business. Elizabeth's talents are languages and people. I say talent, but I really mean genius—and that isn't a word I use often. She speaks nine languages fluently and is conversant in a number of others. She even reads and writes Mandarin, which is something I struggle with."

Beamon didn't bother to hide his surprise. "How'd she fall into your net, Christian? I'd think a nice English girl with her talents would be immune to your charms."

"Oh, she's not English. She's Albanian. I first heard about her when she was only fourteen. Her father was a small-time criminal and was using her as a translator. In fact, he was renting her out as a translator to other criminals and politicians who needed things done discreetly."

"And you hired her away?"

"Not exactly. Her father sold her to me for the outrageous sum of twenty thousand U.S. dollars."

Beamon wasn't quite sure how to respond to that. "Sounds like a bargain."

"Perhaps the best I ever made."

51

THE expansive flagstone patio, now illuminated only by the shimmering lights from the pool, was completely silent. Volkov had gone almost an hour ago, followed closely by the inestimable François and a literal wheelbarrow load of cooking accessories "that felt good in his hand." Elizabeth was somewhere in the house, Beamon guessed, but right now it looked totally dark behind him.

He pulled the red, white, and blue phone from his pocket, turned it back on, and retrieved his messages. There were only two: Both were from Jonathan Drake, wanting to know if Volkov had reappeared yet. He didn't think he'd answer those right away.

A light came on behind him and he craned his neck to see Elizabeth step out onto the patio, wearing only a nightshirt. She sat in the chair across from him, a lovely but disappointingly nonthreatening example of the new world of organized crime. Maybe she had a poisoned needle hidden in her hair or something. Probably not.

"I've set up the master bedroom for you, Mark—it's the one on the ground floor. You should get some sleep."

He tapped the bottle of bourbon he'd found in the patio bar. "I'm just going to finish my drink, thanks."

"Is there anything else I can do for you tonight?"

"I think I'm good."

"You're sure?"

"I'm sure."

She started to rise but sat back down when he spoke again.

"How did you come to work for Christian, Elizabeth?" He couldn't help being a little curious about her side of the story.

"He bought me from my father when I was fourteen," she said simply.

"So he owns you?"

"You can't own another person, Mark. Where I come from, you might call it an adoption. I can leave anytime I want—in fact, Christian has offered to help me find a . . . I guess you'd say 'normal' job. It's just never been the right time."

"It would be hard to be ripped from your family at such a young age, though," Beamon probed. He'd never met a slave before.

Her expression seemed to darken for a moment, but it might have just been the light.

"My father wasn't a kind man."

"So now Christian is like a father to you?"

She actually laughed at that. "Christian has been wonderful to me and I owe him a lot—probably my life. But do I think of him as a father?" She shook her head. "You probably haven't noticed this because, well, of who you are, but Christian can be a little intimidating. In his defense, he tries not to be, but . . . well, it doesn't really work."

"So, how would you describe your relationship, then?"

She thought about the question for longer than it probably deserved. "He's like a cross between an uncle and a really brilliant professor that you love, but who's on kind of a different level."

Beamon nodded and took a sip of his drink. "Good night, Elizabeth."

He sat there for another hour, staring off into the darkness and working through the rest of his cigarettes before he dialed his phone.

"Hel . . . hello?"

"I didn't think you ever slept."

"I thought I'd give it a try to see what it was like," Laura said, in a slightly muffled voice. "Are you okay?"

"I need to talk to Carlo Gasta."

"What?"

"In person. Oh, and alone."

"Are you joking?"

"Nope."

There was some rustling and he imagined her sitting up and turning on a light.

"Well, you can't, Mark. They're moving him to West Virginia tomorrow for safekeeping. Saying that security is tight would be an understatement. No one is seeing him except his lawyer and people directly involved in the investigation. Did you get the message I left you?"

"No."

"As of tonight, the FBI is officially looking for you. The director's set up a five-man team."

"Who's on it?"

"He only picked people who truly hate you."

"I guess there were people lining up for the job."

"Just the opposite, actually. People were scattering like someone had thrown a grenade. The consensus seems to be that it was a no-win situation—that if you didn't want to be found you weren't going to be found. None of this is public yet, but it won't stay quiet forever. Then the press is going to get involved. . . ."

Beamon lit his dead-last cigarette. Even *his* bulletproof lungs were starting to feel heavy. "I'm getting closer, Laura. We're on the right track."

"Have you come up with a theory that works?"

"I think so."

"Damn!"

"What?"

"I worked on it all night. I thought this was it—this was the time I was going to beat you."

"Being inside, I think maybe I had an unfair advantage."

"Tell me."

"You don't have time."

"I don't?"

"You're going to be too busy figuring out how to get me in to see Gasta, remember?"

"Mark, I'm telling you, forget it. There *is* no way."

"You said they're moving him tomorrow. Who's doing it?"

"Scott Reynolds is coordinating."

"Then call him."

"You know him. You call him."

"But he'll listen to you—he thinks I'm nuts, remember?"

She didn't respond immediately, but he knew she was still there because he could hear her breathing.

"Okay. Look, I'll call him and tell him what you want. But that's it. Then you're on your own, Mark."

Beamon hung up the phone and looked down at the scrap of paper Volkov had given him. It was full of names—most he recognized, a few he didn't. Primarily mid-level mobsters with the occasional second-tier executive. The message he was supposed to deliver to Gasta was that he could give up any or all of the men on this list to cut a deal for himself, but that everyone else was strictly off-limits.

The question Beamon couldn't answer was why. It would be a hell of a coup for law enforcement, but what did it do for Volkov? These people were gnats to him. What would rolling on these guys do for him that was worth the ten million that Beamon was going to charge him to do it?

He kicked his feet up on the table and let the blue light flowing from the pool hypnotize him. What was he missing?

He wasn't sure how long he'd been sitting there when the ringing of his phone broke him from his trance. He assumed it was Laura and picked up. "Yeah."

"Beamon, you son of a bitch, do you know where I am?"

He recognized Scott Reynolds's voice immediately. The question seemed rhetorical, though, so he didn't bother answering.

"It's four in the morning and I'm on a fucking pay phone behind a closed restaurant—standing here like a goddamn criminal. Unlike you, I *like* my career."

Reynolds had been a hell of a street agent before his very successful move into management. There was no question that he was a stand-up guy, but he had a lot to lose.

"I take it you talked to Laura."

"How sure are you on this, Mark? I want goddamn guarantees. If I risk screwing myself here, are you going to find this fucking launcher?"

"I don't know, Scott. But I think I've got a shot."

"Odds?"

"Two chances out of five. That may be a little optimistic."

"Son of a bitch! Couldn't you just have lied?"

"Not this time, Scott. You need to go into this with your eyes open. I'd understand if you say no."

"Shit! You know I've never liked you, Mark. Never." There was a short pause. "We're flying him to West Virginia tomorrow. The plane is going to have problems and we're going to have to land at a private strip—something remote. I'll let you know where. You won't have much time and it's up to you to figure out a way to get there."

"Fine."

Beamon hung up the phone and walked into the house, finding Elizabeth's room after a short search of the upstairs. She was curled up under a pink sheet, looking even less than dangerous than she had earlier.

"Elizabeth," he said quietly. "Elizabeth?"

Her eyes opened slowly. "Mark?"

"Sorry to wake you, but I need you to do something for me."

She reached clumsily for the nightstand and felt around for a pair of glasses, which she perched on her nose. "Sure, Mark. What is it?"

"I need a jet tomorrow. First thing."

"No problem. I'll have one flown in."

Beamon was still sitting on the deck when the sun started to rise. Layers of color began to appear above distant hills as the morning beat back the shadows that surrounded him.

He wiped the dew off his phone and started to dial again. It was a hard call to make but he had no choice. As much as he wanted to believe that he was just paranoid and hopelessly cynical, it would nag at him until it finally drove him nuts.

"Hello?" Laura sounded awake this time.

"Morning."

"How did it go? What did Scott say?"

"Do you really want to know?"

"I guess not."

"I need you to do something for me."

"What?"

"How many times do you think the FBI's investigated crimes that the CIA may have been involved in?"

"You mean in total? I don't know. A lot."

"And how many of those investigations did we drop before they knew we were looking?"

"If I had to guess, I'd say more than half."

"And how many of that half involved offshore companies and banks that they were using to finance operations that they wanted to keep quiet?"

"What are you getting at, Mark?"

"I want you to pull those files—all the investigations into the CIA that we shut down for one reason or another and that involved overseas shell corporations."

"Why?"

"I want you to compare the shell companies to the ones that were funding Carlo Gasta."

The sun was blinding now and Beamon had to shade his eyes with this hand. "Laura? You still there?"

"I'm still here but I'm not sure what you're telling me. Are you saying the CIA is involved in this? If you are, we need to—"

"Will you do it?"

"Are you going to tell me why?"

"It's probably nothing. I'm just trying to cover the bases."

"That's a bunch of bull, Mark."

"Will you do it?" He repeated.

She took a deep breath and let it out into the phone. "I'll try. They don't just keep those files lying around the coffee room, though, you know? And I'm guessing it would be better if no one knew I was pulling them."

"Much better. Call me if you find anything." He hung up the phone and turned his chair so his back was to the sun.

He hadn't been overly suspicious of Jonathan Drake trying to keep al-Qaeda's skirmishes in Afghanistan quiet. Spooks were like that; pointless secrecy was coded into their genes. He hadn't even been terribly worried when Drake had shown up in Laos. His story about tracking international organized criminals seemed credible—particularly with the Agency searching for its post–Cold War place in the world. The possibility that CIA would be involved in helping al-Qaeda had never crossed Beamon's mind. But getting in bed with Christian Volkov to set them up? That sounded like *just* the kind of thing those creepy sons of bitches would be involved in.

52

"I GOTTA take a piss," Carlo Gasta said to the man sitting across from him.

"Hold it."

"Fuck you! Take these cuffs off! I've got the right to go to the fucking bathroom!"

Scott Reynolds looked up from his magazine for a moment and then out the window of the jet. Then he just went back to his article. Gasta glared at him, but it didn't take long to realize that he was being completely ignored.

"Screw you," he said, yanking one of his shackled hands painfully over to the seat belt clasp in his lap. With some effort he managed to release it and jumped up from the seat. Without a word and without looking up, Reynolds stuck a foot out and used it to shove Gasta back into his seat.

"Son of a bitch!" Gasta spat out as he fell backward, further straining his already full bladder.

He wanted to kill these bastards more than he'd ever wanted anything in his life. If he could just get free of the shackles securing his hands to the chain around his waist, he'd rip Special Agent in Charge Scott Reynolds's throat out. What did he have to lose? He was fucked and he knew it.

So far he and his men were keeping their mouths shut while he negotiated with the families about what he would and wouldn't say. Or, more accurately, while the families pointed out all the different ways they could get to him no matter what the Feds did to protect him.

Eventually, though, he'd have to deal. When the FBI found out that he'd done their man Chet Michaels, he'd have to talk a blue streak just to stay alive. He'd just have to take his chances with the boys in New York.

The mysterious John, who had started all this shit, had slunk away like a scared dog. At least that's what it looked like. In truth John probably wouldn't be able to contact him even if he wanted to. Gasta was broke and his son-of-a-bitch lawyer was being paid by the families. No way he was going to get any messages that didn't go through New York first. And unless he wanted to get stuck with some moron of a public defender, that situation wasn't going to change anytime soon.

A sudden urgent buzzing coming from the cockpit broke Gasta away from his violent revenge fantasies, and he leaned out into the aisle to try to see what was going on. Reynolds and the other two Feds flying with them did the same.

"What's going on up there?" Reynolds shouted.

"We've got a warning light!"

"What the hell does that mean?" Reynolds said, getting out of his seat and walking to the front of the plane. Gasta leaned out farther, trying to see into the cockpit.

"We've got an engine overheating," Gasta heard the pilot say. He sounded scared.

"What the fuck's going on up there?" Gasta shouted, feeling his own fear starting to build. He glanced out the window and saw and empty red landscape some thirty thousand feet below. "Hey! We're not going to crash, are we?"

"Shut the fuck up!" Reynolds yelled back.

Gasta struggled to get his seat belt back on as the pilot radioed that they had a mechanical problem and were going to try to set down at an airstrip twenty miles away.

"I can't reach my belt! Somebody buckle it for me!"

No one responded.

"Hey! Buckle my fucking belt!"

He looked up hopefully when Reynolds turned toward him, but the FBI agent just took a seat near the cockpit.

"Hey—"

The plane dropped suddenly, making the words catch in his throat. Gasta closed his eyes tightly and held the arm of his seat in sweaty hands, saying a silent prayer as the jet began to buck violently and the pilot's shouts became more urgent.

"We're going in too fast! Fuck! Pull up! Pull up!"

Gasta felt the tears begin to flow down his cheeks and he almost lost control of his aching bladder. "Oh my God, oh my God," he kept repeating. "I'm going to die."

There was a gentle bump and he felt the plane decelerate smoothly before coming to a graceful stop. When he opened his tear-filled eyes he saw the pilot standing in the cockpit door.

"Shit, I'm sorry, guys. That alarm just meant my microwave popcorn was ready."

Everyone in the plane burst out laughing.

Still confused about what just happened, Gasta didn't resist when Reynolds grabbed him by the shirt and pulled him to his feet.

"If you pissed on our seats, I'm going to beat the shit out of you."

"I . . . I didn't," was all Gasta could manage to get out.

"Why don't we go take a walk while they eat their popcorn," Reynolds said, pushing Gasta toward the now open door in the side of the plane. When he got to the stairs, Gasta saw another small jet parked on the otherwise deserted airstrip.

"What's that?" he said, coming to an abrupt halt.

Reynolds gave him a shove from behind and he nearly fell to the ground. "Don't worry, Carlo. You're safe. I'd never let anything happen to a nice guy like you."

The old office in the back of the hangar didn't have much in it other than two chairs and a thick layer of dust. There was no power, so light was provided by a couple of broken windows and a sizable hole in the roof. An appropriately ominous meeting place, Beamon thought. He'd have to compliment Scott on his choice if he ever got the chance.

He'd heard the FBI's jet land about two minutes earlier and he could actually feel the adrenaline starting to trickle into his bloodstream. It was starting to look a lot like he was working for Christian Volkov. Even to him.

Another extremely long minute went by before Carlo Gasta appeared in the doorway, looking scared as hell. Reynolds gave him a shove forward, then disappeared back outside. Beamon clicked the timer on his watch. He had ten minutes.

"I told you hitting the Afghans would be risky."

"Fuck," Gasta said in disbelief. "You set me up. I can't believe it—you're a goddamn Fed!"

Beamon shook his head slowly. "I swear to God, you're one of the stupidest sons of bitches I ever met. If I was a Fed, would I have planned that heist for you? Would I have helped you get away from the cops? Jesus Christ, the only thing I left for you to figure out on your own was where to stash the stuff—and you couldn't even handle that."

Gasta was obviously confused, as he was meant to be. He just stood there and stared, trying to get his tiny mind around what was happening.

"Sit," Beamon ordered, pointing to the chair in front of him. Gasta did as he was told.

"Where's my money, Carlo?"

The fear visible in Gasta's eyes intensified.

"You do remember the three million you owe me."

"I . . . the cops . . . They got the drugs."

"Excuses. It's always excuses with you Italian guys."

"Are you . . . are you going to kill me?"

"I don't know. I guess it depends. Honestly, I was just going let it go—too much time and effort for not very much money. But the guy I'm working for has suddenly taken an interest in you. Why? I have no idea."

"I thought you worked on your own."

"I do. Call him a client. His name is Christian Volkov."

Gasta's eyes widened and he tugged uncomfortably at the shackles keeping his hands bound to his waist. "There's no such person. You're trying to scare me. Christian Volkov is just a bullshit story. He doesn't really exist."

"Well, that bullshit story just went through a whole lot of trouble and expense to get you and me together. You should be flattered, really. Do you have any idea how much it costs to get an FBI special agent in charge to fake engine trouble on a Bureau jet? More money than you've ever seen in your life."

"What does he want with me?" Gasta said, starting to sound a little panicked. "I don't know anything about him. I've never done anything to him."

"Now, that's not entirely true. Because of you, his negotiations with the Afghans have stalled. You've cost him a lot of money."

"But I didn't mean to. I didn't know. . . ."

Beamon pulled the piece of paper Volkov had given him from his pocket and held it in front of Gasta's face.

"Do you recognized the names on this paper?"

He nodded nervously.

"These are the people that you can give up. Do any deal you can— but only with these names."

Gasta scanned the paper carefully. Beamon had actually considered modifying it—adding a few names. Then, when Gasta gave up people who hadn't been approved, Volkov would have him killed. Chet Michaels would be partially avenged and Beamon would sleep a little better. But that was too much like murder.

"My lawyer won't do it," Gasta whined. "He works for some of the guys on that list."

"We've lined up a new lawyer for you. One of the top men in the country. As a favor to Christian, he's agreed to take you on pro bono."

"They'll kill me."

"They'll certainly try. I'd suggest getting some kind of protective custody worked into your deal."

"But if I do that, then you wouldn't be able to get to me, either," Gasta said, a thin smile spreading across his face. Beamon shook his head in disbelief. The little pissant had gone from nearly soiling himself to wanting to negotiate in five short seconds.

"You're in protective custody now," Beamon said, pulling his .357 from its holster. He pressed it against Gasta's forehead and pulled the hammer back. "Do you feel safe?"

53

MARK Beamon picked at the food in front of him as the small jet he was on sped smoothly to . . . where? He hadn't even bothered to ask. His best guess was that he was being taken back to Christian Volkov's luxurious hideout du jour so that he could report on his meeting with Gasta. What would he say? The truth, probably. It was hard not to feel at least a little uncomfortable with the fact that lately the only person he ever told the truth to was Christian Volkov.

"Tegla, can I use my phone?"

The pilot's dark face peeked out of the cockpit. "Of course, Mark."

He turned it back on and dialed to pick up his messages. Laura. Laura again. And Laura again. He cleared the messages and punched in her number.

"Hello?"

"It's me."

"Jesus, I've been trying to get in touch with you forever. Where are you? Can we get together and talk?"

"I don't know where I am exactly—I'm on a plane. If it can wait, I should be back in L.A. in a day or two."

"It definitely can't wait."

She sounded strange. Fear?

"I don't know what to tell you first, Mark."

"How about the good news. I could use a little cheering up."

"Uh, okay. The Director said that if you're not found within the week, the whole thing's going public. You'll be an officially wanted man."

Beamon took a deep breath and let it out. "That's the good news?"

"Everything's relative."

"Didn't Einstein say that?"

"What's going on with this CIA thing, Mark?"

"What do you mean?"

"We had to go back a lot of years. During the S&L crisis the FBI did an investigation of a Minnesota bank that was going under. It was connected to a bunch of offshore corporations, and when it started to look like it might be a front for funneling money to the Noriega regime, the investigation was just shut down and sealed with no explanation."

"If it was sealed, how'd you get ahold of it?"

"I have friends in this organization too," she said. "You know Tim Lang, right? He was the lead investigator. I talked to him and he said, confidentially, that he was ninety percent sure the CIA was behind that bank."

Beamon moved to the seat farthest from the cockpit, pressing the phone closer to his mouth and speaking quietly. "So, are you telling me that there's a connection to one of the companies financing Gasta?"

"That's exactly what I'm saying, Mark. One of the offshore corporations connected to that bank has an ownership interest in a company that has an ownership interest a company that's involved in a partnership that has a partner who—"

"What the hell are you talking about? Are they connected or not?"

"They're connected. It's complicated, but they're connected."

Beamon felt his jaw tense and he gritted his teeth with near audible intensity. This was supposed to have been an exercise in paranoia—an impossible angle that he needed to cover just to make himself feel better. He hadn't expected Laura to find anything.

"What about Volkov?" Beamon said through a slightly constricted throat. "Are there any CIA connections to the institutions that he used to pay me?"

"None that we could find. What's going on, Mark? Why is the CIA involved with Carlo Gasta? What's their connection to the Afghans?"

"Shit!" Beamon spat out. The fucking CIA.

"Mark, are you going to tell me what's going on?"

Beamon slammed a fist into the plastic window of the jet, making it flex perilously.

"Mark?"

"Do you really want to know?"

"Probably not, but at this point I think I have to."

Beamon glanced toward the front of the plane. Tegla was wearing a set of headphones and had apparently missed his tantrum. "The CIA is involved with Volkov and they're supporting al-Qaeda's bid to take over the heroin business in the Middle East."

"Why would the CIA be involved in something like that?"

"Think about it, Laura. They support Yasin while he picks fights and makes enemies of every drug refiner and trafficker in the region. The supply flowing through Mexico into the U.S. starts to get disrupted because of the fighting. People start getting nervous about dealing with Muslim fanatics. . . ."

"Are you saying this is all a setup?"

"Of course it is. Remember my trip to Laos and the Asians I met on Volkov's boat? When the disruptions from the Middle East are at their worst and Yasin's organization is spread as thin as possible, Volkov and the CIA are going to pull their support and replace al-Qaeda with the Asians. Yasin's going to find himself cut off from the weapons and intelligence and money he's come to rely on, and everyone in the Middle Eastern drug trade who's still alive is going to want him and his men dead. And you know who will be there to help all that along?"

"The CIA."

"But it didn't quite work out," Beamon continued, his anger still building. "Al-Qaeda managed to get one of the toys they'd been supplied into the U.S."

"So the CIA got scared," Laura said. "And they pulled out, trying to cut ties to anything that could connect them to this . . . Jesus. Chet."

"And finally we get an explanation of why Volkov fingered Gasta: He wanted to keep the CIA occupied, and putting Gasta in the hands of the

FBI would definitely throw a wrench in their plan to get themselves out of this. And something I never told you—I ran into Jonathan Drake in Laos. He wanted me to help him find Volkov. And I fell for it." Beamon shook his head. "Jesus, if it hadn't been for Volkov making sure he was out of their reach, he and I would both be dead right now."

"Mark . . . do you remember the description of the man Chet and Gasta met with?"

Beamon remembered it exactly. Drake.

"Mark, are you still there?"

"I'm here."

"We've got to call the White House. You've got to talk to Tom Sherman about this. We're really exposed here."

"We'll talk when I get back . . ." Beamon said. "Figure out what we're going to do."

"Back from where?"

"Hell if I know."

54

"**Just** curve around to your left and you'll find him," Elizabeth said. Beamon nodded his thanks and started forward along a path constructed of what looked like loose volcanic gravel. He didn't know much about trees, but the ones lining the path looked like something that would grow in the American South: large and bushy, with long tendrils hanging nearly to the ground and a sweet smell. The sky was a uniform blue without so much as a streak of haze to break it. . . .

He shook his head and forced himself to stop investigating for a moment. He had no idea where he was, and a botanical survey of the area sure as hell wasn't going to help—he didn't know a magnolia from an aspen.

As Elizabeth had promised, Volkov was just around the bend, sitting on a bench surrounded by a well-tended flower garden. He didn't look up from what he was reading when Beamon approached.

"Good book?" Beamon said, stopping a few feet away.

"Absolutely fascinating," Volkov responded, still staring down at the page. "It's a sort of nonrevisionist history of the United States. I've never completely understood the American psyche by reading other texts— they were always too cluttered with noble intangibles like fleeing religious persecution and the quest for freedom. Do you know what prompted the Boston Tea Party?"

"London giving the East India Company a monopoly on tea imports?"

"Yes, but it wasn't the oppression of the masses that was the issue. It was Sam Adams's blind hatred of the British and the fact that one of the wealthiest men in the Colonies, John Hancock, saw these kinds of legal monopolies cutting into his profit margin. When I look at how America has evolved, that makes much more sense to me than a saintly painting of George Washington crossing the Delaware in search of freedom and equality."

"Washington had a favorite general," Beamon said. "A big guy; they called him Ox Knox. When Washington got into the boat to cross the Delaware, Knox was already in it. Do you know what Washington said to him?"

"Most the books I've read would have him saying something like 'Forward to free God's people.'"

Beamon shook his head. "He said, 'Shift that fat ass, Harry, but do it slowly or you'll swamp the damn boat.'"

"Exactly! Right there—more insight into the American mind than a hundred 'I regret I have only one life to give for my country.'" Volkov slammed the book down on the bench next to him. "Have a seat, Mark. How did things go in Utah? Isn't that where you took the jet? Utah?"

Beamon sat down on a surprisingly comfortable boulder and studied Volkov for a moment. How deeply was he involved with the CIA? At one time probably pretty deeply, but now the CIA undoubtedly wanted him dead. They would be running hard and fast from this thing with the Afghans, but it was a fair bet that Volkov didn't have that option. The kind of people he dealt with would expect him to live up to his agreements.

"Expensive," Beamon responded finally. "Utah was expensive. I had to call in a lifetime's worth of markers to get this done."

"You did it? You spoke to Gasta?"

Beamon nodded.

"And?"

"I think I got my—your—point across. But even with the names on that paper, I don't know what kind of a deal they're going to give him. The Feds will try to get him with the death of Chet Michaels."

"Yes, I suppose they will. Do you think he can be trusted to stay within the parameters I've set for him?"

"He's afraid of you. I made sure of that."

"That isn't an answer."

"It's the only one I have."

"I appreciate how difficult a job this was, Mark. The ten million you requested will be deposited in your account this afternoon. If you have any other expenses that need to be covered, let Joseph know."

Beamon nodded.

"Are you all right, Mark?"

"What do you mean?"

"You seem—I don't know. Tense. Upset."

Beamon cursed himself silently. He was too angry right now; it was compromising his ability to think straight. The sudden redirecting of his quest for revenge from Volkov to his own government had thrown him. He was having a hard time centering himself again. "I guess I'm just a little tired. Maybe we could talk later."

"Of course. Get Elizabeth to put you up in the guesthouse."

"And if I'd rather go back to L.A.?" Beamon said, a little too indignantly.

Volkov's brow knitted. "What's wrong with you today, Mark? If you want to go back to L.A., I'll have someone fly you there. Are you sure you're all right?"

55

"RISE and shine, Mark."

Elizabeth strode across the large room and threw open the curtains, sending a beam of heat and light across the bed. Beamon had decided against going back to L.A. the day before, finally admitting to himself that he felt safer here with Volkov—out of the Agency's and the FBI's reach.

He just needed a little time to figure out his next move—or, more accurately, how he was going to get that son of a bitch Jonathan Drake. Before this was over he'd see that bastard dead or behind bars for the rest of his life. Preferably dead.

"Christian would like to see you in about an hour, Mark. Can you make it?"

"Yeah, I can make it."

"You don't look that great. Did you sleep at all?"

"Some."

"You know what you need?"

He propped himself up on his elbows. "What?"

"A good breakfast." She motioned toward the door and a man in a white uniform entered, pushing a cart topped with covered silver trays.

"François!" Beamon said, recognizing the man instantly. "My savior. How are you this morning?"

"I am well, Mark. Very well," he said through a thick accent. "I think you will be quite pleased with what I have prepared for you this morning. It is . . . an American medley, I think you would say."

"I put some clothes for you in the closet, Mark—I think they'll be your size. Christian will be in his office at eleven."

"Thanks, François," Beamon said as the man parked the cart near a set of windows overlooking Volkov's endless property and then disappeared out into the hallway. The fact that he was starting to like the staff as much as he begrudgingly liked Volkov was yet another source of worry to him.

"Do you need anything else?" Elizabeth said.

"You wouldn't happen to have a cigarette."

"Of course not."

"Then, that's it."

She started to leave but paused at the door. "François made sausage, eggs, and hash browns. He's never seen a hash brown in his life, but he tried very hard. You should tell him how good they were, no matter what."

"No problem. And hey, Elizabeth . . . thanks—for everything. Really."

She looked a little self-conscious. "Sure, Mark. My pleasure."

Beamon showed up at Volkov's office door five minutes early, freshly showered and clothed in a luxurious pair of slacks, a linen shirt, and a pair of shoes that probably cost what he made in a month at the FBI.

The slacks would have been a perfect fit had he not just sucked up François's breakfast like a Shop-Vac. The sausage had obviously been handmade and delicately spiced with something characteristically uniden-tifiable and wonderful. And the hash browns . . . what could he say except that he respected a man who wasn't afraid to use lard. Being able to eat without feeling nauseous was a nice change of pace. More proof that Carrie was right and he really was nuts. Being doomed seemed to agree with him.

He stood in front of the closed door for a moment, trying to think back only a few weeks to his life before all this. More and more they seemed like someone else's memories. Thoughts of Carrie caused him to sag a little. She'd been so gung-ho for him to quit the Bureau and take a job in the private sector. He wondered what she'd think if she could see how successful he'd become.

Beamon took a deep breath and pushed through the door, walking across the stone floor with confidence he didn't feel. Volkov was sitting behind an expensive-looking but unremarkable desk, talking to someone sitting in one of two chairs lined up in front of it. Beamon could only see the back of the man's head as he approached.

"Mark! Right on time," Volkov said. "Are you feeling better this morning?"

"Much, thanks."

"Then I'd like to introduce you to someone."

Jonathan Drake stood and turned toward him. "It's a pleasure to meet you, Mark."

Beamon almost stopped short but managed to keep himself moving. He plastered a polite smile across his face and offered his hand.

"Have a seat, Mark," Volkov prompted. If he sensed that anything was wrong, he gave no indication.

Beamon released Drake's hand and sat. What else could he do but wait to see where this was going?

"That breakfast was wonderful, Mark. François made me the same thing you had. Hash browns . . . a truly sublime creation."

"His were particularly good," Beamon mumbled, focusing on Drake in his peripheral vision.

"Mark, here, has taken on some of Pascal's duties," Volkov said. "I don't know if you're aware that he disappeared in Laos."

"I wasn't," Drake responded smoothly. "I'm sorry to hear that."

"Jonathan has a proposition for me, Mark. I thought you might help me assess it."

Out of the corner of his eye Beamon saw Drake look over at him.

"This might be something we should talk about alone, Christian."

Volkov didn't react to the suggestion and Drake was forced to take the hint that his request for a private audience had been denied.

"We've both worked very hard on this . . . operation," Drake started. "And we've both made commitments. I think it's safe to say that you and I agree it's too late to pull out."

Volkov nodded and Drake cleared his throat.

"It's come to my attention that my boss, Alan Holsten, the deputy director of operations, has no intention of going through with this. He's concerned solely about his personal exposure and he wants out."

"I see," Volkov said calmly.

Beamon kept his eyes focused on the floor in front of him, trying to stifle his rage enough to think coherently about what was happening. He could come up with about twenty scenarios, but they all seemed to end the same way—with him dead.

"As you can imagine," Drake continued, "Holsten also wants to destroy anything that can connect him to the Afghans. Unfortunately, that includes us. I'm guessing that this doesn't come as a surprise to you."

Volkov's expression turned thoughtful for a moment. "A disappointment, Jonathan, not a surprise. But as you say, I've made commitments. My course is set. Now, what is it you want?"

"What do I want? I want passports and money—ten million dollars. I want to disappear from the CIA's radar and live out the rest of my life comfortably."

Volkov frowned and looked at Beamon. "Everybody wants ten million of my dollars all of a sudden."

When Beamon didn't respond to the inside joke, Volkov refocused his attention on Drake. "I'm sure that I would sleep better knowing that you are 'living out the rest of your life comfortably,' but I don't think it's worth that much to me. I assume you have something more valuable to offer than my peace of mind."

"I do. Information."

"Ten million dollars' worth? That would have to be a very tantalizing piece of information."

"It is. I think you'll consider it a bargain at that price." He turned toward Beamon and smiled arrogantly. "We haven't heard from you, Mark. What do you think?"

They locked eyes for a few seconds, but Beamon knew that Drake had him. This was where he was going to fail—four feet from the man who had ordered Chet's death.

"It's not that much money in the scheme of things," Beamon heard himself say. "Why not?"

"I agree," Volkov said. "So, what do you have for us Jonathan?"

Drake turned back toward Volkov and crossed his legs casually. "I discovered yesterday that Nicolai is a fabrication of the FBI." He motioned toward Beamon. "Your replacement for Pascal is actually an undercover federal agent."

Volkov considered that for a moment. "You don't disappoint, Jonathan. That is an interesting piece of information. Is this just an accusation or do you have proof?"

Drake leaned over and picked up the file that had been lying on the floor next to him. He tossed it onto Volkov's desk. "It's all in there."

Beamon was staring at the floor again, his mind an uncharacteristic blank. This was it. He was going to die and Drake was going to stroll out of there with ten million dollars.

Volkov made no move to reach for the file on his desk. "Is this true, Mark?"

He didn't respond.

"I'm capable of opening a file."

Beamon looked up at him. "Yeah. I guess it is."

Volkov pursed his lips for a moment and then reached into one of his desk drawers. When his hand reappeared, there was a gun in it. Despite the fact that Volkov was undoubtedly one of the most powerful criminals in the world, Beamon couldn't help thinking how unnatural he looked holding the weapon. The idea that Volkov would do his own killing had never really crossed his mind.

"Wait," Beamon said, holding a hand out and looking over at Drake, who was just sitting there, smiling serenely.

"For what?" Volkov said.

"I delivered your message to Gasta like you asked, and you still owe me money for that."

"Yes. . . ."

"There's one thing I want to do before I die. Give me three minutes instead of the money and we'll call it even."

Volkov placed the gun on the desk, but his hand didn't move more than a few inches from it. "I'm intrigued. You have your three minutes."

"Thank you," Beamon said, and then lunged from his chair—not at Volkov but at Drake. His fist caught the much larger CIA man completely by surprise, connecting solidly enough to tip him over backward in his chair.

Beamon wasn't sure if the soft crunch he'd felt was Drake's nose or the bones in his own hand, but it didn't really matter. Drake was lying on the floor, flinging blood back and forth as he shook his head in an effort to regain his bearings. But it was too late. Beamon swung an expensive Italian leather shoe into the man's ribs with all the anger and frustration he'd been choking on since Chet's death. This time the cracking of bone was accompanied by an incredibly satisfying squeal as the wind went out of Drake's lungs. Just like a pig.

"You stupid piece of shit," Beamon screamed, slamming his foot down again, this time on Drake's unprotected chest. "I traced the bank you used to pay Gasta back to a CIA operation from the eighties. That kind of sloppy shit really pisses me off."

Drake made a grab for Beamon's ankle but wasn't quite fast enough, and ended up exposing his arm to another vicious kick instead. The adrenaline running through Beamon had obviously increased his strength, because he heard the bones in Drake's muscular arm snap.

"Did you know Chet Michaels was married?" he shouted, continuing to kick the man. "He and his wife had just bought a house."

"Stop," Drake said weakly, trying to sit up. Beamon grabbed him by the hair and slammed the back of his head into the stone floor.

"He was getting a lot of pressure from his parents to have children, but he was going to wait a couple of years . . ." Beamon said, breathing hard. He was lining up to deliver another kick to Drake's ribs when he felt a hand on his shoulder. He spun around and found Christian Volkov, gun in hand, standing behind him. He'd honestly almost forgotten Volkov was there.

"Enough, Mark. That's enough."

Beamon turned back toward Drake, who was still conscious, and waited to get shot in the back. Instead, Volkov walked around him and crouched down beside the CIA man. For a moment Beamon thought he was going to try to help him to his feet, but he made no move to.

"The Central Intelligence Agency . . ." Volkov said, his back inexplicably presented to Beamon. "A completely unpredictable lot. Impossible to do business with. Just another of the world's insane government organizations—no better than in Laos."

The blind rage that had gripped Beamon was starting to fade, replaced by confusion. And that confusion turned to shock when Volkov aimed his pistol at Drake. The CIA agent managed one last act: to raise his arms in terror before the deafening crack of the gun sounded. The bullet went through one of his hands before entering his forehead and blowing most of the back of his head off.

Volkov rose from his crouched position, spattered with blood, and picked up the chair Drake had been sitting in. "I'm sorry, Mr. Beamon. I should have let you do that." He tossed the gun onto his desk and sat down.

It took a few moments for Beamon to realize that Volkov wasn't going to kill him. In fact, from his position, Beamon figured that he could reach the gun on the desk before Volkov could. Despite that realization, though, he didn't move. "What did you call me?"

"Mr. Beamon. You are Mark Beamon, aren't you? The special agent in charge of the FBI's Phoenix office?"

Beamon fell into the chair next to Volkov. "How long have you known?"

"Since right before our first meeting."

Beamon gazed down at the thick stream of blood running from Drake's broken head. A moment later two men he'd never seen before walked in and unceremoniously dragged the body out.

He and Volkov sat in silence for a long time. Beamon could feel his hand starting to swell and stared blankly down at it.

"So here we are." Volkov said finally, breaking the silence.

Beamon looked up at him, still unsure what had just happened. "Where is that?"

"A decision point, I suppose. Do we go forward or go backward?"

"I . . . I'm not sure I follow you."

"The CIA approached me with this plan some time ago: to support al-Qaeda in a takeover of the heroin business in the Middle East. They correctly assumed that Mustafa Yasin would use the tools we provided to mount a violent and campaign against the current drug lords, causing a disruption that would allow the Asians to move in and replace Iran, Pakistan, and Afghanistan as America's supplier of choice. And at that point the CIA planned to offer support to Yasin's victims in all this, creating an internal war that would at worst keep him occupied for years to come and at best kill him and most of his men."

"Why you?"

"I have strong relationships with the Asians and the Russians. As you can imagine, though, I resisted becoming involved. There were significant risks, not the smallest of which was the possibility that Yasin would use his new contacts and weapons against the U.S. But I really had no choice. If I didn't cooperate, one of my competitors certainly would have. And if the plan succeeded, they would have generated an opportunity for my Asian associates that I hadn't, and created a strong relationship with America's intelligence community. So, despite the risks, I had to get involved." Volkov paused for a moment. "But then, I assume you knew most of this already."

Beamon nodded.

"You live up to your reputation, Mark."

"You said we're at a decision point," Beamon said, now looking at the trail of blood Drake's head had left on the floor. It was kind of hypnotic. "What is it we have to decide?"

"You already know the answer to that. We only have one path ahead of us. Do we take it or not?"

"What if we don't?"

"Then the status quo that the CIA has created is maintained. Yasin consolidates his position in the heroin trade, putting an end to the disruptions his war is causing. He becomes one of the wealthiest men in the world and gains inroads to a very sophisticated smuggling network—which he uses to wage war against your country."

"That doesn't sound particularly attractive. I assume you've come up with an alternative?"

"We simply finish what has been started."

Beamon almost laughed, but managed to keep it in check. "Are you asking me—an FBI agent—to help you flood America with Asian heroin?"

"My sources suggest that it would be more accurate to call you a *former* FBI agent. And your streets are already flooded with Middle Eastern heroin, so I see no great harm in it."

"I don't think so, Christian."

Volkov leaned forward, resting his elbows on his knees. "If I were to write a dictionary, do you know how I would define the word *government*? I'd define it as 'a crime organization ruthless and powerful enough to do away with all those who can meaningfully oppose it.'"

"I understand your point, Christian, but I've got a line in my head that I try not to cross. It's not always logical, but it's there. Can you understand that?"

"Would it make you feel better if I hired a group of mercenaries to slaughter thousands of people in some small South American country, then put on a uniform and called myself *El Presidente*? You could be an ambassador."

"I don't see myself as an ambassador."

"And I don't see myself as a hypocrite."

Beamon considered his position—something that didn't take very long. Options were fairly scarce.

"I want the launcher."

"Are we negotiating?"

"I guess we are."

"And if I get you the launcher, I want your contact in the White House."

Beamon shook his head. "No. I wouldn't get Tom involved in this even if I could. I owe him my life."

Volkov didn't seem particularly upset by the refusal.

"Then I want you, Mark. Not to stand by and avert your eyes, but as an active participant. My assistant—my executive vice president, you could say—was killed recently. Probably by Jonathan. I need someone to stand in his shoes."

"What about Elizabeth and Joseph?"

"They're both brilliant, but they're children."

Beamon leaned back in his chair and focused on Volkov. "You know that killing Drake isn't the end of this. You still have Alan Holsten to deal with. He'll do whatever's necessary to protect himself."

"Yes, of course you're right. What I hope to have gained by Jonathan's death is some temporary confusion, and possibly plausible deniability for Holsten. Perhaps he can paint Jonathan as a rogue agent?"

"Perhaps."

"Do you know him?"

"Holsten? In passing. He's an ass. But he's not an idiot."

Volkov nodded. "So where do we stand, Mark?"

Beamon sighed quietly. "Can I use your phone?"

"Of course."

Beamon walked around the desk and dialed Laura.

"Hello?"

"It's me."

"Are you all right? Where are you?"

"I'm with Volkov."

"Mark, we've got to get together and talk face-to-face. I'm serious here. This thing with the CIA . . ."

"Don't worry about it. I'm taking care of it."

"What do you mean, you're 'taking care of it'?"

"I'm taking care of it. Let's leave it at that."

There was a short pause over the line. "Gasta's starting to talk, Mark, working out a deal. It looks like we might get some interesting stuff out of him. He's got a new lawyer too—a serious piece of high-class talent. Can I assume that this is all your doing?"

"I need you to do me a favor," Beamon said, ignoring her question. "Call my secretary. Tell her to get my credentials out of my desk—she knows where they are. Mail them to the Director with a letter of resignation. Tell her to sign it for me—she's good at that. I'll send him one with my signature on it when I get a chance."

"Are you sure that's what you want?"

"No, but I don't think I have much of a choice at this point."

"He's still going to come after you, Mark. Your involvement with Gasta, the Afghans . . ."

"I know."

"I don't understand what you're doing here, Mark."

"What I'm doing is helping you find your launcher, Laura. I'll call you."

He hung up the phone and sat down behind Volkov's desk. "I guess I'm officially in your employ. Do you have medical?"

Volkov laughed. "In fact, we have a very good plan through one of my American companies. I'll have Elizabeth do the paperwork."

Beamon pulled out a cigarette and lit it. Of course. He should have known.

56

"HOW many goddamn people did we have watching him? How many?"

Alan Holsten slammed the door to his office and spun around to face his executive assistant—normally a very competent and unflappable thirty-five-year-old man. Right now he looked like a scared kid.

"Four, sir. We don't—"

"Four men? You had four men on Jonathan Drake, plus electronic surveillance and real-time access to his bank records, and you lost him?"

"Sir, we don't know how he did it. But it was obviously intentional and well planned—"

"Of course it was intentional and well planned, you stupid son of a bitch! That's why I had you watching him! Fuck!"

"Sir, we think this is only a temporary loss of contact. We're doing everything we can to find him, and we expect to reacquire him soon."

"And why do you expect that?"

"Because he didn't take anything, sir—just the clothes on his back and the money in his wallet. We've frozen all his accounts and are watching for him to try to access them."

Holsten dropped into his chair and closed his eyes, trying to ease the headache that was in the process of turning blinding.

"Sir—"

"Shut up!" Holsten shouted. "Just stand there and be quiet!"

His assistant had no idea what was going on—only that Holsten had wanted Jonathan Drake watched. But now Drake was gone and the implication was obvious. He had painted a fairly attractive picture of their situation last time they'd met. But now Holsten knew that it had all been a lie designed to keep him docile long enough for Jonathan to set up his escape.

Now he was the only one left who had been directly involved in the Afghanistan operation. If it came to the surface, he would be the one singled out for responsibility. Everything he had, everything he'd worked for, would disappear in a matter of hours.

Holsten rubbed his temples and tried to concentrate. Mark Beamon was the key to this. Drake would sell Beamon's true identity to Volkov and use the money to disappear forever. There might still be time.

"Mark Beamon," Holsten said. "What do we have on him?"

"The FBI's stepped up their search for him but with no success. From what we can tell, the task force they've created isn't working very hard. The consensus seems to be that if he doesn't want to be found, he won't be."

"Can *we* find him?"

His assistant shrugged. "I honestly doubt it. The FBI is set up for this kind of thing and he's one of theirs. I'm not sure why we would be more successful—"

"Bullshit!" Holsten leaned forward over his desk and jabbed a finger toward his assistant. "We *are* going to find that son of a bitch! What isn't the FBI doing? What are they missing?"

His assistant smoothed an imaginary wrinkle from his expensive suit and cleared his throat nervously. "He has a confidante, sir. Laura Vilechi— the lead investigator on the rocket launcher investigation. The FBI's already talked to her and she swears she has no idea where he is."

"But we think she's holding out."

"It seems likely. Beamon's generated a number of leads on the launcher case, and based on his reputation, there's no reason to believe he's stopped working it. . . ."

Holsten nodded. "Then I think we need to talk to her. Very quietly. Do you understand?"

"Yes, sir."

Holsten leaned back in his chair and chewed the end of a pencil compulsively. Another angle the FBI wasn't considering was Christian Volkov, who they weren't aware existed. Volkov almost certainly knew where both Drake and Beamon were, but it was unlikely that he would expose himself. At least, not intentionally.

"Contact the Mexican attorney general too. I want to talk to him."

"I'm sorry, sir. . . . Did you say the attorney general of Mexico?"

Holsten nodded.

It was certain that Volkov would move forward with the CIA's plan to oust the Afghans from the heroin trade—he'd made too many commitments to walk away now.

The key to the changeover from Middle Eastern to Asian heroin was in the Mexican distribution lines. The attorney general of Mexico was up to his eyeballs in the narcotics trade—little happened without his knowledge and approval. It might be possible to catch up with Volkov there.

"Tell him I have a proposal for him that he'll find interesting. No one else is to know that we're talking, though."

"I understand, sir. I'll contact him right away."

57

THE gravel path was longer than he'd thought. After a half a mile or so, it had turned to dirt, winding itself through shaded stands of trees and floral-scented clearings, meandering ever forward.

They'd been walking for over an hour now, with Volkov doing most of the talking, telling the fascinating and probably rather selective story of his life, and running down the basic structure of his organization. With that background in place, he finally made his way to more current issues.

"The situation is a simple one, Mark. You already know it. Middle Eastern heroin floods into Mexico through a number of channels and is transported across the border into the U.S. Al-Qaeda has at this point managed to gain control of enough of the supply to begin dealing directly with the Mexicans. Until recently they had been bringing in relatively small shipments through other avenues and selling directly to people like Carlo Gasta."

"Just to pay the bills," Beamon said.

"Exactly. They needed the cash, but didn't yet have the critical mass to create the necessary relationships."

"Shouldn't you have moved a little earlier? I mean, if they're already at the point where they're building relationships with Mexico . . ."

"No, it was important for the Mexicans to meet Mustafa Yasin's people. It's been a complete disaster, of course. Inexperience, language barriers, Muslim fanaticism, unstable supply . . . And to make matters worse, word of al-Qaeda's methods has spread across the Middle East.

Now, if their target sees them coming, they destroy everything and all Yasin ends up with a burned-out shell."

"Making the disruption you're counting on even worse. I suppose the rocket launcher and all the publicity hasn't hurt, either."

Volkov nodded gravely. "It certainly added to the Mexicans' fears. But—and I want to be clear on this, Mark—I regret what's happened to your country. The effect on Drake and the CIA has more than offset any benefits with the Mexicans—not to mention the hundreds of millions I've lost because of the destabilization of the American economy." He stopped for a moment and looked directly into Beamon's face. "I know that as a man who's dedicated his life to the FBI—to an ideal—you must think of me as rather . . . amoral. Perhaps even evil?"

"I don't know what I think of you, Christian. I really don't."

He seemed to accept that and started walking again.

"So you need the Mexicans," Beamon said. "You need them to agree to dump the Afghans and start doing business with your Southeast Asian friends. I honestly don't see how you're going to pull that off, Christian. There are too many people involved, too many opportunities for the Afghans to circle their wagons. I mean, you'd have to do this impossibly fast—the changeover would have to happen almost instantaneously. How do you even know that Yasin hasn't already noticed you laying the groundwork for this thing?"

"Simple—because I haven't done anything yet. No one knows the status of this but you and me. Holsten might suspect, of course, but he can only guess at this point."

Beamon looked at him out of the corner of his eye. "When is it you think all this is going to happen?"

"Next week."

Beamon laughed—partially at the absurdity of Volkov's statement and partially at the fact that he was strolling along a dirt path, planning a multibillion-dollar drug deal. "Next week, huh? Just when are you going to get around to letting the people involved know?"

"As you said, Mark, leaks are unacceptable. Everything has to be done at the very last moment possible. It's vital that everything happen quickly and smoothly. The narcotics business, you might be surprised to know, is primarily based on trust."

"I'm not sure I see how, in a matter of hours, you're going to convince all those people that they should dump their current suppliers and move their business to you."

"You let me worry about that."

"Okay, I will," Beamon said. Volkov had done exactly what he said he was going to do so far. No reason to start doubting him now. "What about the CIA? You still have the same problem you always did. Even with Jonathan dead, Alan Holsten isn't going to want to risk being left twisting in the wind if the FBI comes up with any of this. He must know that I'm involved and that I've gotten close to you. Jonathan probably would have had to tell him that much."

"Certainly, he is . . . what would you say? A wild card?"

"That seems optimistic. I'm guessing he wants you dead more than anything he's ever wanted in his life."

"Oh, I think he probably wants you dead more."

"Good point. Either way, he's going to be pulling out all the stops right about now. He knows at least part of your plan, so this is his chance. After you succeed—or fail—you'll just disappear again. If he's going to find you, he's got to do it now."

"If he's going to find *us*, Mark. Us."

Beamon frowned. He wondered if it would actually be possible for him to piss off any more U.S. government agencies. As far as he knew, he was still in the good graces of the Park Service. . . .

"Perhaps he won't be as aggressive as you think," Volkov said. "It seems a foregone conclusion that it's in America's best interest that I complete this deal."

"But it's not in *his* best interest. The FBI already sees the connection between the drugs, Gasta, and al-Qaeda. And a complete changeover in America's heroin supply structure isn't going to be lost on the DEA. Holsten won't take a chance that someone from the FBI might eventually arrive at your door to find you still alive. And as far as Jonathan's disappearance causing confusion that you can use, don't count on it. Count on Holsten assuming that Jonathan ran and sold me out or is in the process of selling me out for retirement money."

"I suspect you're right, Mark. But my course is already set."

They walked in silence for a few minutes, Beamon smoking furiously and Volkov calmly enjoying the near-perfect day.

"Can we change the subject a bit?" Beamon said finally.

"The launcher."

"That's the only reason I'm here, Christian."

"Yes, I know. . . . According to my intelligence, four rockets were smuggled into America. The FBI has one."

"Jesus," Beamon muttered.

"As you probably already guessed, the remaining rockets are held by three separate cells, with no contact with or knowledge of the others. The launcher is in a truck with a driver who's familiar with the unit's operation. He has no idea where the cells are located until he is contacted by Mustafa Yasin himself. What you might not know is that each cell also has a shipment of heroin that came in with the rockets. The sale of the heroin was being set up through Jonathan before he was aware of their terrorist ambitions. Now, though, after Gasta's attack on the L.A. cell, Yasin has pulled his people back. He's suspicious. But he's also desperate for cash."

"Do you have the locations of the cells?"

Volkov laughed quietly. "You give me too much credit, Mark. I managed to keep my relationship with Yasin from completely falling apart by seeing that Gasta was arrested. But he still thinks Gasta might have been under my control. It was a serious blow to the trust between us."

"We need to figure out a way to find those rockets, Christian."

"I understand, Mark, and I'll do everything I can to help you. But I have to say that I'm not hopeful."

58

I**T** was nearly midnight but Laura Vilechi still couldn't sleep. She had been sitting on the bed in the small L.A. hotel room for two hours now, flipping the channels on the television to see if the press had found another colorful way to say that her investigation was a joke.

In truth, it was hard to blame them—facts were facts. Despite all the theories, manpower, and scientific minutiae, she'd gotten almost nowhere. Her only stroke of brilliance had been dragging Mark into it and then manipulating him into throwing his life away to help her.

She looked over at her cell phone on the nightstand, trying to will it to ring. She had no idea where Mark was now—or even if he was alive. How long would it take for a man like Christian Volkov to figure out that he had an FBI agent—hell, a well-known FBI agent—working for him? And what would happen when he did?

She pushed herself into a more upright position on the bed and looked across the room into a large mirror hanging on the wall. The flowing blond hair and bright-red pajamas didn't exactly create an imposing image. Maybe the press was right. Maybe she wasn't up to the task of running an investigation of this size and complexity. Hundreds, perhaps thousands, of lives at stake, and it was looking as though the FBI had entrusted them to just another semicompetent bureaucrat. As long as Mark was pointing her in the right direction, she might manage to do a thorough but uninspired job.

She concentrated on the mirror harder, examining the deepening lines around her eyes that, she'd told herself, were badges of wisdom. Now they just looked like stress, age, and lack of sleep.

Finally sliding off the bed, she walked into the bathroom and began stuffing her things into a leather bag sitting on the edge of the tub. Gasta was in West Virginia, and the physical evidence from the terrorist cell here—including the rocket and the bodies—had been carefully packaged and flown to the FBI's lab. L.A. was dead as far as this investigation went. It was time for her to get off her ass, get back to D.C., and work harder. Enough self-pity. And more than enough waiting for Mark to do her job for her.

The knock on the door startled her and she leaned out of the bathroom, feeling her mood darken even further. Another damned reporter. It was the third time they'd tracked her down, despite her efforts to steer clear of them. Maybe *they* should be looking for the launcher.

"Who is it?" she said, padding barefoot toward the door.

She was only a few feet away when she heard the lock click. A moment later the door was thrown open and two men in dark suits rushed in. She turned and ran for the nightstand and her gun but wasn't fast enough. One of the men grabbed her from behind and clamped a hand over her mouth while the other quietly shut the door.

Laura surprised herself by half remembering her Quantico self-defense training and executed a sloppy countermove that was obviously anticipated. Her instructor would have been completely disgusted. She tried again, this time going for the man's groin, but whoever he was, he was strong as hell and good at this kind of thing. There was no way to get free.

She was lifted off her feet and swung around to face the other man, who was now standing calmly in the middle of the room.

"Ms. Vilechi," he said quietly. "I'm sorry about the melodrama." He pulled an identification card from his pocket and held it up in front of her. "We're from the CIA. We just need to talk to you."

She felt her feet hit the ground and the arms holding her withdraw. When she glanced behind her, though, she saw that the man had only retreated a few inches and was ready to grab her again if necessary.

"Have you been watching too many movies or something?" she said, trying to use anger to hide her fear. "What the hell do you think you're doing? If you'd have shown up ten minutes later, I'd have been wearing my gun and I might have shot one of you."

"Calm down, Ms. Vilechi. Like I said, we're sorry about the entrance—we just needed to talk to you."

"Then talk and get the hell out of here," she said, forcing herself to follow the man's advice to calm down. If Mark's suspicions about he CIA were right, she might actually be in danger here. How desperate were they at this point?

"Maybe we could find a more suitable place," the man said. "We'd appreciate it if you could come with us for a little while."

It obviously wasn't a request, but Laura knew she had to treat it as one. If she looked scared, they'd think she knew something. And the truth was, she really didn't. She made a show of glancing at her watch.

"I've got two hours before I have to get on a plane back to D.C. You can have one of those hours if you drop me at the airport afterward. Let me call my office and tell them I'm not going to need a car."

"That won't be necessary, ma'am. This won't take long."

She started chewing her lip before she realized she was doing it. Despite his politeness, he obviously wasn't going to take no for an answer.

"I don't suppose you mind if I put some clothes on."

The man motioned to his partner, who examined the bathroom. "It's fine."

"Please do. Leave the door open just a crack, though, please."

They watched silently as she gathered her things from the closet. Her gun was next to her phone on the nightstand, but there was no way to get either.

She went into the bathroom and pushed the door almost closed, concentrating on steadying her breathing. She was now officially scared. The CIA didn't screw around with high-ranking FBI agents and then just let them go back to work the next day to tell the tale. Was Mark right? Had they killed Chet? Were they going to do the same thing to her?

She pulled on her slacks and buttoned up her blouse, trying to think. She could scream, but the hotel was pretty soundproof and they'd be through the door in about two seconds. Maybe on the way out? No, they would have planned for that somehow.

"Are you ready, Ms. Vilechi?"

She took a few deep breaths and stepped out of the bathroom. One of the men led the way to the door and the other stayed behind her as they exited into the hall.

They'd made it about ten feet down the corridor when two men appeared from a small enclave that housed the floor's ice machine. Less than three seconds later they had both CIA agents lying on their stomachs, each with a nearly invisible strand of wire looped tightly around their necks.

Laura retreated a few feet but then stopped, not sure what to do. Distinguishing friends from enemies wasn't as simple as it had once been. The men holding the garrotes were both thin, with short, dark hair and nice but nondescript suits. She was fairly certain that she'd never seen either of them before in her life.

"Mark Beamon sends his compliments, ma'am," one of the men said through a thick accent that sounded German. He looked up at her and smiled politely. "Would you mind very much opening the door to your room?"

She knew she should be running for the stairs but instead found herself pulling her key card from her pocket and holding the door open while they pulled the two suddenly very cooperative CIA agents inside.

"Mark asks that you perhaps make yourself difficult to find for a few days," the German man said, still with that relaxed smile. He didn't seem particularly concerned by the fact that he was on the verge of strangling an agent of the U.S. government.

"What . . . what about them?"

"We'll take care of them."

"You're not going to kill them, are you?" she said. "You can't kill them."

"Mark was very specific that they not be harmed."

She looked down at the blood starting to flow from the shallow cuts opening around the neck of the man who had grabbed her earlier. The German followed her gaze.

"Not to be harmed in any permanent way," he corrected.

59

"I HEAR you met Wolfgang," Beamon said into the satellite phone Joseph had finally managed to teach him to use.

"Mark! What the hell's going on?"

"Alan Holsten is pretty interested in finding me. It stood to reason that he'd try to go through you."

"Alan Holsten? You mean Deputy Director of Operations Alan Holsten?"

Beamon walked across the wide terrace and examined an enormous pot full of blooming flowers. "You know him?"

"The DDO," she said quietly. "That's great, Mark. That's just great."

"Can you make yourself scarce while I get all this straightened out?"

"No, I can't make myself scarce—I'm in the middle of one of the biggest investigations in the history of the FBI. I may not be doing a very good job, but I can't just disappear."

"You're doing a great job, Laura. You don't know it but you're getting closer and closer. Can you get some protection, then? If not, you're welcome to keep Wolfgang."

"I don't need European mercenaries watching my back," she said, the anger and frustration audible in her voice. "I'll get some people from the FBI."

"Find people you've got some history with, Laura. Holsten's got a lot of influence, and you're his best bet to get to me."

"How far would he go to accomplish that?"

Beamon didn't answer. The truth was he didn't know.

"Mark, we need to talk to somebody at the Bureau about all this. It's getting too big for us to handle alone. . . ."

"Give me and Christian a couple of days, Laura. I don't need a leak here, okay?"

"You and Christian. . . . Getting to be good friends are you?"

"I'm not sure what we're getting to be."

"It was supposed to be a joke, Mark. The correct response is that you're setting him up and about to get him."

Beamon laughed. "I'm not going to get *him*, Laura. Even if I wanted to, I doubt I could. Christian's a reasonable guy with what's starting to look like a pretty clear agenda."

"Can I ask you a question?"

"Go ahead."

"What side are you on, Mark? Do you know anymore?"

"America's side," he said, then laughed again. "Damn, that sounded patriotic. Somebody get me a flag."

"What about Jonathan, Mark? Should I be worried about him too?"

"Jonathan's dead."

There was a short silence over the line. "Did you . . . did you kill him?"

"No, Laura, I didn't kill him. But he's still dead, and that takes care of about half our problem. This thing with al-Qaeda is too lunatic-fringe for a lot of people to be involved. I'm guessing that Drake and Holsten dreamed this one up on their own. So now we've just got to steer clear of Holsten for a little while."

"Just Holsten. Great."

"What's going on with the launcher?"

"Nothing," she said miserably. "It could be anywhere. I'm working with DEA, local narcotics people, and Immigration, but I'm not hopeful. At this point, pathetic as it sounds, we're waiting for a launch and hoping to get something from that."

Beamon turned away from the flowers and wandered back to the house. "I'm working on it, Laura. I expect to have something for you soon. I don't know what, but something."

"I hope you're right."

He pushed through a set of glass doors and found Christian Volkov sitting with his feet on his desk, speaking an unidentifiable language into a telephone headset. He waved toward a chair.

"Look, I've gotta go, Laura. I'm checking my messages, so if you need me, leave one."

"Mark?"

"Yeah."

"I know what you've given up to help me. I just wanted to say . . . well, thanks."

He hung up the phone just as Volkov tossed his headset onto his desk.

"I'm sorry, Mark. I've tried, but I think it's hopeless."

"What's hopeless?"

"Finding your rocket launcher. The Afghans are still blaming me for the deaths of their people in L.A., and the fact that I had Carlo Gasta arrested hasn't really helped. At a minimum they wanted him dead."

"You're telling me that you can't get a single thing out of them that could help me?" Beamon asked, not bothering to hide his skepticism. Volkov hadn't failed at anything since they'd met.

"I can't just come out and ask where they're keeping their launcher and the rockets, Mark. They're already suspicious and wouldn't tell me even if they weren't. Besides, the Arabs just aren't phone negotiators. They're technophobes by nature—they only trust face-to-face meetings."

"Meaning?" Beamon said.

"Meaning that I can set up a meeting if you want me to. You can go and physically sit down with Mustafa Yasin. Personally, I'd recommend against it. I think it's unlikely that you'd get anything useful—much more likely that they'll just kill you as payment for their men who died in L.A. An eye for and eye and all that. . . . It wouldn't be a pleasant death, Mark."

"You paint such a rosy picture."

"An accurate picture, I think."

Beamon pulled a lighter from the fancy ashtray that had appeared next to the chair he favored and lit a cigarette. "But you want me to go, don't you, Christian? I mean, it works for you. I convince Yasin to trust you again or they kill me and get their eye for an eye. Either way, your relationship with al-Qaeda is improved. And the more they trust you, the easier it's going to be for you to screw them."

"For God's sake," Volkov said, letting his feet fall from his desk loudly. "I just told you not to go. In the long run, your death would cost me more than it would gain me. Listen to me very carefully, Mark. You didn't cause any of this—it was the CIA's doing. Leave it to the American authorities to straighten out. It's their job."

Of course, Volkov was right. He wasn't an FBI agent anymore. In fact, it was hard to imagine how he could get much further from his former life at the bureau.

"I can't just let this go, Christian."

"No, of course you can't. And I won't insult your intelligence—if you get killed doing something that I believe is pointless and extremely dangerous, I'm going to do everything I can to use your death to my advantage. I won't be happy about it, though."

"I feel so much better, knowing that you'll feel a brief moment of remorse before you use my mutilated corpse to help you hook America's children on Asian heroin."

"I do what I can," Volkov said, leaning to his right and looking around Beamon. "Elizabeth. Come in."

Beamon twisted around in his chair and watched her approach. She was dressed head to toe in a flowing black gown that revealed nothing of her. Even her eyes were partially obscured by black mesh.

"That's a new look," Beamon said suspiciously.

"You're going to need a translator, and I speak Arabic."

Beamon frowned. He hated being predictable. "That's doesn't seem like such a good idea. I think I'll just go this one alone."

"I'm afraid that's impossible," Volkov said. "Many of Yasin's people don't speak English, and he refuses to. You have to have a translator."

"Look, I think—" Beamon began.

Elizabeth cut him off. "We're just about ready to go, Mark. I've gathered some information for you—you can read over it on the plane."

"But—"

She pulled off her headdress and looked at her watch. "Forty-five minutes?" Then she spun on her heels and hurried out of the office.

"It's not my first choice to send a woman—Elizabeth particularly—into this," Volkov said. "I'd appreciate it if you'd make sure she returns."

Beamon turned back to him. "I don't want her, Christian. I'll make do."

Volkov shook his head. "Everything in life costs, Mark. The price for a chance at saving America from itself may be your life *and* Elizabeth's. I think it's too expensive. But it's up to you."

Beamon stared out the window, trying to convince himself that he had a choice. But he didn't. How many people would die if that launcher was used? Besides, Volkov was right—this was going to be a fairly delicate piece of negotiating, and he wasn't going to get far using just his charades skills.

"I'll bring her back."

"If it was anyone but you, I wouldn't let her go at all." Volkov reached for a glass of water on the desk and took a quick sip. "You have three days, Mark. On Saturday I'm going to cut the Middle East off from the Mexican distribution lines. When that happens, my relationship with the Afghans is going to sour very quickly, and Yasin's people in America will be completely out of my reach—and out of yours, too, I think."

"Three days. Okay."

"Be very careful, Mark. I won't be available to help you—even if I could. I'm leaving for Mexico tonight to meet with the attorney general."

"Of Mexico? Salvador Castaneda?"

Volkov nodded.

"Why?"

"Why do you think?"

Beamon shrugged. "We know that Castaneda is a facilitator of nar-cotics trafficking—taking bribes and such. And we know that President Garcia looks the other way. That's why Mexico's been decertified. Our relationship with them is probably at a hundred-year low."

"Actually, Castaneda is much more powerful than your DEA imag-ines. He doesn't take bribes so much as he oversees his country's nar-cotics machine. He's the critical link in coordinating traffickers with the military and police. Actually, he's quite an administrator. If he weren't such a sadistic, backstabbing cretin, I'd be looking to make him part of my organization when he leaves office."

"So that's it," Beamon said. "That's how you're planning on pulling this off. He has all the contacts and can coordinate the whole thing for you."

Volkov nodded. "He'll prefer dealing with the Asians, I think. More money, less risk."

"That's a lot to hang on an 'I think.'"

Volkov smiled. "Not to worry. I'll make him an offer he can't refuse."

60

ANOTHER goddamn helicopter.

This one was a Russian military rig with two rotors, an enormous cargo hold, and an absolute minimum of creature comforts. Beamon had already plowed through the box lunch François had prepared and now all there was to do was gaze out over the mountainous, sunburned landscape below. He felt a long way from home.

Another half hour passed before he spotted what looked like a small encampment in the distance. He leaned forward, as though that would help him penetrate the dusty haze that seemed to blanket this part of the world.

"Is that it?" he shouted into the microphone suspended in front of his mouth.

The pilot nodded.

"Not too close. Land a good half mile away."

The young man behind the controls flipped a few switches and the wildly vibrating helicopter smoothed out a bit as it started to descend. Individual structures were starting to become visible, and Beamon gave the encampment they were hurtling toward another quick look before sliding out of his seat and ducking back into the cargo hold.

"We're there," Elizabeth said with quiet resignation that made her hard to understand over the noise. She was strapped into an uncomfortable-looking jump seat, wearing all her Muslim garb with the exception of the elaborate headpiece.

"Yeah, we're there," Beamon shouted. "I'm sorry I got you into this, Elizabeth. My plan was to come in here alone."

She reached up and grabbed his shirt, pulling him close enough that she could speak in a more or less normal tone. "You asked me once why I didn't just get a real job. Why didn't you?"

Beamon shrugged. "I guess 'cause I'd miss the rush."

"Same with me. But I suppose you have to live with the fact that sometimes the rush is a little more than you bargained for."

A broad, nervous smile spread across her face, and Beamon couldn't help returning the grin. Had there been women like this when he'd been in his twenties? Not that he could remember.

"Get ready," he said, starting toward the back of the airship. He fell to his knees when the skids hit the ground but managed to haul himself back to his feet with the aid of a large crate, which he then slid behind.

The sound of the engine was quickly dying as he dialed a number into his satellite phone.

"Hello?" came an Irish voice.

"Daniel? It's Mark. How are things?"

"Fine. Everything's quiet."

The engines went silent but the helicopter continued to rock gently, buffeted by the wind attacking the fuselage.

"Is she there?"

"Yeah, it's pretty early here."

Beamon had sent Daniel and another of Volkov's men to watch Carrie's house, with orders to do whatever was necessary to keep her safe. He thought it was unlikely that the CIA would go after her, but who knew what Holsten would do if he started feeling truly desperate?

"Okay. Thanks, Daniel." He hung up and then took a deep breath before dialing Carrie's number.

"Hello?" She sounded groggy, but years as a doctor had made her accustomed to being awakened at all hours.

"Carrie!"

"Mark? Where are you? I can barely hear you. Are you back in Phoenix?"

"Not exactly. I'm still kind of tied up on this investigation."

"That's interesting. I'm hearing that you quit the FBI. Is that true?"

"Who told you that? Laura?"

"No. Laura keeps telling me everything is fine. But I think she's lying. She sounds . . . I don't know. Horrible."

"Then, who?"

"Two FBI agents I didn't know showed up at my door yesterday. They wanted to know if I could help them find you."

"What did you tell them?"

"Everything I know, which is nothing. They said I should call them right away if I heard from you."

"You do that, Carrie. Call them right after we hang up and answer all their questions as truthfully as you can. More than likely they're listening to this conversation anyway."

"Are you kidding? You think my phone is tapped?"

"Probably," he said honestly. If not by the Bureau, certainly by the CIA.

"What's going on, Mark? Did you really quit? And why do they want to find you so badly?"

"The answers are yes and it's a long story."

"Maybe they want you back?" she said with uncharacteristic optimism.

Beamon couldn't help smiling despite his position wedged behind a crate full of weapons on a Russian helicopter in the Afghan desert. "Yeah, they want me all right."

"What are you going to do?"

"I actually picked up a really lucrative consulting contract," he said. Not a lie. "Sorry I didn't call sooner, but I wanted to straighten things out first. There hasn't been a lot of time."

"That doesn't explain my phones being tapped. Is your client the Mob or something?" The joke sounded a little strained. It would have been a lot more strained if she knew she wasn't thinking big enough.

"Mark?"

Beamon spun around and saw Elizabeth peeking around the crate he was hiding behind.

"They're coming," she said. He nodded and she disappeared again.

"Look, I have to go. I just wanted to say . . ." *Good-bye* came to mind. "I just wanted to say hello."

He turned the phone off before she could say anything more and followed Elizabeth to a large set of sliding doors that had been thrown open to the desert.

The wind was cold and filled with enough sand to actually sting his skin as he jumped to the ground. He helped Elizabeth out of the helicopter and looked through the black mesh into her eyes.

"Show time," he said as they started forward to meet the approaching group of well-armed men. While nasty-looking machine guns seemed to be in good supply, none were yet pointed at his head. A good sign.

"The man in front, the kind of tall one," Elizabeth said, "is Mohammed Wakil. He's one of Yasin's top people. Did you read the stuff I gave you on him?"

Beamon nodded.

"He speaks enough English to pick up a word here and there, so be careful what you say to me. . . ."

"You sound scared, Elizabeth."

"I am. Aren't you?"

"Yeah. It's fine to be scared, but it's not so good to sound scared, okay?"

Wakil stopped in front of them, but the young boys accompanying him just passed by and headed straight for the helicopter. It was stuffed with gifts, though nothing quite so benevolent as the Lamborghini he'd taken to Laos. Mostly Russian rifles, heavy machine guns, and land mines. All the wonderful little gadgets that people turned to when there were a few dollars to be made, or their god spelled his name differently from their neighbor's god, or they thought Marx and Engels's book was better than Adam Smith's . . .

Wakil spoke in Arabic and Elizabeth whispered the translation in Beamon's ear.

"He wants to know if you're Mark."

"Tell him I am."

Wakil turned and motioned for them to follow. Beamon glanced back at the helicopter one last time and saw Wakil's men throwing boxes recklessly through the cargo doors, shouting gleefully.

"He wants us to go with him, I think," Elizabeth said.

Probably not a bad idea. He didn't know much about military weaponry but guessed some of it didn't react well to being thrown from helicopters. The last thing he needed was to be blown to bits by the Islamic version of the Hitler Youth.

The encampment he'd seen in the distance was just that—an encampment. It consisted of five large tents, a few worn-out military vehicles, and a few camels. Honest-to-God camels. He leaned into Elizabeth's ear. "Just like in the movies."

Her only response was a short nod that was almost imperceptible beneath the folds of black cloth.

Wakil pushed open a flap and indicated that they were to enter. Beamon went through first, with Elizabeth a little too close behind. Inside, the ground was covered with colorful rugs and pillows, and the sound of the wind was replaced by the sound of flapping fabric.

Beamon stood motionless near the entrance, looking down at the man sitting cross-legged on the floor. You had to say one thing about Christian Volkov: The son of a bitch was well connected. Three weeks ago, Beamon would have laughed at anyone who suggested that he would one day be standing five feet from Mustafa Yasin.

He couldn't help being a little mesmerized by the man. Yasin was even more impressive in person than in his pictures. He exuded a charismatic intensity like no one else Beamon had ever met. When he spoke he did so quietly, but the sound easily overpowered the drone of the wind on the tent.

"He invites you to sit," Elizabeth said.

Beamon sank onto a dusty pillow and Elizabeth knelt next to him. He heard the flap open and two women—at least, he assumed there were women under there somewhere—entered, carrying trays of food. They were laid in front of Beamon and he took the hint, beginning to eat reluctantly. It looked and tasted a hell of a lot better than General Yung's home brew, but he guessed it was just as deadly. As a precaution, he'd gulped a few antibiotics and a bottle of Pepto on the way there. Yasin didn't eat.

"Christian regrets not being able to come here himself," Beamon said, mimicking his successful performance in Laos. "You understand that it is very difficult for him to travel now."

Yasin didn't react, just stared out along his impressive nose.

"I'm here," Beamon continued respectfully, "in hopes that we can again find the trust that we lost through our mistake of employing Carlo Gasta in America."

Elizabeth's translation still got no reaction, so Beamon just shut up. He needed something to tell him he was on the right ass-kissing track here. For all he knew, he was just digging himself in deeper.

Yasin sat with statuelike stillness. Signs of life were minimal until he finally spoke.

"Our brothers are dead or being held hostage by America's FBI because of your man, Gasta," Elizabeth whispered, her lips brushing Beamon's ear. "And he stole from us. How can you possibly atone for that? How can you expect to regain our trust?"

Of course Gasta was completely unconnected to Volkov, but now probably wasn't the time to go into the CIA's involvement.

"We believe," Yasin continued, "that Christian Volkov either ordered this action or that he cannot control his people."

"Christian did not order it," Beamon said. "Why would he? He's taken great risks and incurred great expense to build a relationship with you. In the past he has come here personally in friendship."

The conversation was frustratingly slow with Elizabeth translating both sides.

"Then why is Gasta not dead? He is in the custody of the American authorities, where he is in a position to expose us all."

"It was the best option under the circumstances," Beamon answered. "Carlo Gasta was greedy and looking to go out on his own. He had backing to do so from our enemies. Christian had him arrested and has made it clear that his only chance at survival is by informing on those people."

In truth Beamon still hadn't figured out why Volkov had gone to such great lengths to get Gasta to roll over on a bunch of more or less irrelevant wise guys, but this imaginary explanation worked well in the current context.

"Even if the men who turned Gasta against us aren't indicted immediately," Beamon continued, "they've been rendered harmless. It would have been impossible to kill them all, but Christian has created a situation where the American authorities will do our job for us. And the compensation for the heroin you lost is on the helicopter we came in. Right now your men are unloading double the heroin's value in weapons, and we're making arrangements to purchase the remaining heroin that your people have brought into America."

Yasin was obviously suspicious. "You still wish to buy our product?"

"Of course. It was our agreement."

Al-Qaeda was being squeezed financially by its ambitions in the region and the loss of its financial cornerstone, Osama bin Laden. They were desperate for cash, and Beamon's payment in weapons instead of currency didn't go very far to solve that problem.

"When?"

"As soon as we can set up meetings between your people and ours."

Yasin frowned regally. "And I should trust you?"

"I told you the circumstances of your men's deaths as openly as I can. Of course, if you aren't comfortable dealing with our people, I understand. It may take time, but we are committed to rebuilding our relationship. Perhaps we should just postpone the transactions indefinitely. Until you're confident again."

It was a risky suggestion, but Beamon was fairly certain that Yasin didn't have the U.S. contacts to unload that much product without the help of Volkov or the now permanently indisposed Jonathan Drake. The question was: How badly did he need the money?

Yasin stood suddenly. "Excuse me for a moment."

He disappeared through the tent flap, giving Beamon a glimpse of the armed men—boys—outside.

"How am I doing?" he whispered to Elizabeth.

"I think they're going to kill us."

"Really? I thought he was starting to like me. I can be very charming, you know."

"Yeah, I know."

"We're not dead yet," he whispered as Yasin reappeared and sat in front of them again.

Beamon felt Elizabeth's grip on his arm tighten as the Arab spoke, but he wasn't sure how to interpret the pressure.

"He says he'll agree to one transaction," she whispered excitedly.

Beamon nodded slowly, stalling for a few moments. He needed all three—he had to locate all the rockets, not just one. And he needed to do it before Christian blew this whole thing up.

"We would be happy to do all three," he said as smoothly as possible. "We have the money set aside."

"One," Yasin responded in forcefully. "Then we will discuss the others."

It wasn't difficult to see that the man wasn't going to change his mind. One was all they were going to get. That meant he had to pick the cell that was going to use their rocket first in order to have a chance at getting ahold of the launcher.

"When?"

"Tonight." Yasin clearly wasn't an idiot. He wasn't going to give Beamon enough to time to set up an ambush.

"Where?"

"El Paso, Texas."

Beamon needed more information than that. He needed to know where the others were. He needed some clue as to where the launcher was going to be.

"Texas," he said, shaking his head slowly. "Texas could be a problem. As you know, the Mexicans are very concerned about the disruption in their heroin supply. If they were to find out you're going around them directly to the American market, it could destroy everything we've worked to build. Would it be possible to choose a place where the Mexicans have fewer ears?"

Yasin stroked his long beard thoughtfully. "New York."

Beamon laughed quietly. "You pick difficult locations, my friend. Right now Carlo Gasta is informing on some of the most powerful organized-crime figures in America, most of whom are based there. New York is a powder keg." He glanced over at Elizabeth, but she seemed to be having no problem getting across the concept of a powder keg.

Yasin's face darkened and he focused his piercing stare on Beamon, who stared back but tried to remain passive. Finally the Arab stood again and walked out of the tent without a word. When he was gone, Elizabeth whispered in Beamon's ear. "You're trying to find out where all of them are?"

He nodded. "And he's trying to decide out if I'm just pumping him for information so I can set him up again. But he can't figure how I could possibly use the general locations of well-hidden terrorist cells to my advantage."

"I'm a little curious about that too."

Yasin was gone a solid five minutes this time. When he returned, he sat again and said simply, "Las Vegas."

Beamon took a deep breath and let it out slowly, giving himself a few seconds to think. That was it—those were the three locations. If he were a terrorist, which one would he go for next? Where would he send the launcher?

"We have no people in Las Vegas right now," Beamon said, hoping that Yasin would assume that with no infrastructure there, Volkov's organization would have a hard time setting up an ambush. "Maybe New York would be better. The Mob is in an uproar, but at least we have a reliable organization in place. I mean, if you want to do it tonight. . . ."

Yasin's dark eyes narrowed. "No. Las Vegas. If you don't have people there, send them. Tonight."

"I can't convince you—"

"No."

Beamon affected a worried expression and stood. "I'm going to have to leave immediately to try to get this set up. As a show of good faith, I'll have the money wired to your account in Iraq immediately and you'll be able to confirm the transfer before you send your people."

Yasin blessed him with a short nod.

"Okay," Beamon said, pulling a notepad from his pocket and jotting down Laura's cell phone number, then handing it to Yasin. "I'll have my people on their way to Vegas in a few hours. Have your people call this number and tell the woman who answers where and when they want to meet."

The helicopter's cargo hold was just a dirty, empty cavern when they returned, but it was still one hell of a welcome sight. They couldn't take off immediately because Yasin's men had been so intoxicated with their new toys, they had uncrated them only a few feet away. Beamon watched them through a small window as they moved the mess of materiel to a safer distance.

A sudden high-pitched, warbling scream made him jump and he spun around to see Elizabeth peeling off her *burka* to reveal a pair of khaki shorts and a white blouse.

"Jesus Christ," Beamon said, clutching his chest. "A little respect for the condition of my arteries, please."

"Sorry, Mark. Women in this part of the world do that when they're happy. It seemed appropriate. I never thought we'd leave here."

"Ye of little faith," Beamon said, dialing Laura's number into his satellite phone.

"Hello?"

"It's Mark. Listen, a nice man named Mustafa Yasin is going to call you at this number—so find yourself someone who can translate fast. He's going to want you to send people to buy some heroin from a group of his men in Las Vegas. I'm going to take care of paying for it, so you don't need to worry about that. Just pick it up, thank everybody nicely, and have someone very quietly follow the bastards. Then all you're going to do is settle in and watch them. Don't—I repeat, *don't*—do anything else. Just surround the shit out of them and hide. Do you understand?"

"Mark, what—"

"Do you understand?"

"Yes."

"Are you going to be able to get anyone to help you with this? I can get you some people if you need them. . . ."

"No, I'll take care of it."

He clicked the phone off and once again hoped that Vegas had been the right guess.

Elizabeth sat down on the dirty floor a few feet away from him and hugged her knees to her chest. "You're trying to find the launcher—the one they're using to threaten the Americans with. . . ."

Beamon nodded, suddenly realizing that he didn't know what Elizabeth had been told about him. He assumed that she still thought he was Nicolai.

"I have to ask you, Mark: Why Las Vegas? Why not El Paso or New York?"

"Why do you think?"

"Because he mentioned it last, right?"

"I hadn't really thought of that. Good point, though."

"Why, then?"

"You've got to remember that if Yasin's people use that launcher, they expose themselves and risk getting caught. He has to make it count. I see El Paso as a transition point. I'm guessing that his people smuggled the rocket over the border there and are waiting for instructions on where to go. Think about it. What's in El Paso? I mean, what's there that would make a real statement? If you blow something up, you'd probably get more Mexicans than you would Americans."

"Why not New York, then? That would be a statement."

"These rockets have a range of only about twelve miles and no real guidance system. If you wanted to hit something major, you'd have to have a pretty straight shot and be only be only a few miles from it. Besides, they've already hit New York. They want to make the point that no one is safe no matter where they are."

"So, by process of elimination, Las Vegas."

"More than just elimination. Huge buildings with profiles that are the proverbial broad side of a barn, surrounded by empty desert. And the best part is that the casinos are full all the time, making them a fantastic nighttime target."

"No visible contrail at night."

"Precisely. With the cover of dark, their chance of getting away is a hell of a lot better."

The helicopter started to vibrate as the engines began to warm up.

"Pretty smart, Mark. I hope you're right."

61

THE ring of fire in the sky seemed like a different sun than the one he knew. Christian Volkov always looked forward to summer—the long, warm afternoons reading outside, the landscape coming to life. The Mexican sun, though, wasn't so benevolent. It shone mercilessly, burning and finally killing everything beneath it.

The plane that had dropped him on this desolate airstrip had taken to the air as soon as he'd disembarked, moving out of reach in case the situation deteriorated. Volkov looked out over the red dirt and broken rocks that made up the landscape around him and searched for any sign of human habitation. Except for the makeshift runway, there was nothing. No roads, no structures, no sign of the bleached garbage that clung to the rest of Mexico.

It wasn't long before a plume of dust appeared on the horizon and began to lengthen steadily. He knew he should feel frightened or at least nervous. He rarely entered the world of the people he did business with, preferring to maintain the cocoon of misdirection and confusion he'd constructed around himself by having them come to him. In this instance, though, he'd had no choice. Mexico was the key to his future now, and there was little chance that the attorney general could be persuaded to leave his borders or be swayed by one of Volkov's messengers.

The source of the dust was visible now: No fewer than four Mexican army jeeps speeding recklessly toward him across the desert. When they were only a few hundred meters from him, the column split, sending two of the jeeps flying past him on either side. All four vehicles skidded to a stop simultaneously, engulfing him in a choking cloud of red dust that forced him to hold his breath and close his eyes. His welcome thus far was less than hospitable. It could only be a bad sign.

By the time the air cleared, the jeeps in front of him were empty and being used as cover by no fewer than eight men, each with a firearm aimed at him. Volkov turned in a slow circle, confirming that the soldiers behind had taken an equally aggressive posture.

As he came around to his original position he saw another vehicle following the same path the jeeps had but at a much slower speed. It looked like some kind of American sport utility, though he couldn't be certain of the make. Like his new friend Mark Beamon, he knew very little about cars.

The vehicle rolled to a graceful stop behind the dirty, fatigue-clad men guarding him, and Volkov watched a man in khaki slacks and a white golf shirt step out.

"Alan Holsten, I presume," Volkov said as the man closed the gap between them on foot. He had a smallish frame and a soft, well-tended look to him that hadn't been completely apparent in the photos Volkov had seen. In person he looked very much the product of his wealthy and pampered upbringing.

"Mr. Volkov," he said. "Or should I say Mihai Florescu?"

It had been a long time since Volkov had heard his real name spoken. He wondered if there was any spark of that boy left in him.

"I suppose you're surprised that Castaneda would turn on you like this."

Volkov looked around him again. The guns had been raised in deference to the CIA man's presence but were still at the ready. "*Surprised* may be too strong a word. But I am disappointed that he'd make such an obvious mistake."

Holsten let out a loud, condescending laugh. "That's your weakness, Christian: arrogance. Do you know what you are?"

"I know exactly what I am, Alan."

Holsten wagged a finger at him. "There it is again—that fatal arrogance. Tell me, then. Are you a businessman? A victim of an unjust homeland? A revolutionary? Let me clue you in, Christian—you're just a drug dealer. Maybe a little wealthier and a little smarter than some hood on the street, but no different."

Volkov didn't argue. He didn't seem to be in very good position to debate, and nothing Holsten had said was really untrue.

"Jonathan created quite a file on you, Christian. And I gave Castaneda a copy of it. Do you know what your other weakness is?"

Volkov shook his head.

"You're what we Americans call a control freak. You don't delegate. I told Castaneda that Pascal was dead and that there's no one left in your organization with any kind of real power or ability. If you were to disappear, what would happen? You'd have a bunch of kids in their early thirties running around, trying to figure out what to do while your enemies divide up your empire."

"With the help of America's CIA, of course," Volkov said.

"I'm sure there would be something we could do to facilitate the disintegration of everything you've built."

Holsten gave a nearly imperceptible nod, and Volkov's hands were wrenched behind him and handcuffed. Instead of the cold he'd expected, the metal was painfully hot.

"Jonathan tells me you measure everything in risk and return, Christian. If that's the case, you should appreciate the attorney general's position. Because there will be no one left in your organization to be afraid of, there isn't much risk attached to killing you. And in return he gets the undying gratitude of the Central Intelligence Agency. Not a bad deal, huh?"

Volkov remained silent.

"Nothing to say, Christian? I'd heard you always had something to say."

It seemed certain that he and Holsten would have a chance to speak soon—and under much more unfavorable circumstances. The CIA would undoubtedly want to know everything.

Volkov allowed himself to be led to one of the open jeeps and didn't resist when a length of chain was run through his handcuffs and secured to a metal loop in the backseat. This had always been a possibility, he knew, but he'd miscalculated it as a small one. It seemed that he had overestimated Castaneda. The attorney general had made a grave error in choosing Holsten over him. The CIA could never be trusted.

The jeep jerked forward and Volkov pressed his nose and mouth into the fabric of his shirt against the dust. He could feel a strange sensation of excitement that wasn't entirely unpleasant. His normally unshakable control over the events of his life was completely gone now. What would the next day bring?

62

"Mark!"

Beamon had barely stepped from the plane when he spotted Joseph running across the tarmac toward him. Surprisingly, he found himself back in the same place he'd left from—wherever that was. Was Volkov finally running low on stylishly appointed holes-in-the-wall?

Beamon lit a cigarette, having refrained from smoking during the private jet portion of his flight there. That was one thing Russian cargo helicopters had going for them: NO SMOKING signs were scarce.

"Evening," Beamon said, letting a gust of wind extinguish his match. The black sky was completely starless, and the air was filled with a fine mist.

"I'm so glad you made it back," Joseph said, his breath coming a little hard.

"Really?"

Joseph nodded sincerely. "We've lost contact with Christian. I've put three calls in to Salvador Castaneda but he won't speak to me."

Beamon took a long drag on his cigarette, not sure how he felt about Volkov's disappearance. "I'm sorry to hear that."

"Christian said that if he disappeared, you were in charge."

Beamon looked over at Elizabeth, who had just jogged up alongside him. "Excuse me?"

She put a hand on his shoulder. "Christian said that you were to be put in complete control of everything should we lose contact with him."

"What do you mean, 'complete control of everything'?"

She shrugged. "His businesses, his holdings. Everything."

Beamon tossed the cigarette down onto the tarmac and ground it out with his shoe, still not quite sure what he was hearing. "You don't mean *complete* control—he just wants me to do something for him, right? What is it now?"

Elizabeth and Joseph looked at each other, obviously not sure what to make of his confusion.

"I don't know how else to explain it to you," she said. "Christian didn't leave any instructions for you. . . . He just said you'd take over."

Beamon let out a short laugh but stifled it when he saw how serious Elizabeth and Joseph were. What was the joke? With Volkov there was always a catch. Some hidden agenda.

"Okay. Great. I'm in charge, right? Fine. Joseph, transfer a hundred million dollars into my account."

"The 413 account? The same one we've been using?"

That wasn't the response Beamon had expected. "Uh, yeah."

"Do you have a preference as to what accounts we pull from? There might be some tax—"

Beamon held up his hand, silencing the young man, and started walking toward the car parked at the edge of the runway. The little bastard was going to do it—he was going to transfer a hundred million dollars into his account. Volkov really had put him in charge of the organization. Why?

He stopped suddenly when it occurred to him that he'd managed to transform himself from the SAC–Phoenix to one of the world's wealthiest and most powerful organized criminals in less than a month. Carrie was right. He did have what it took to make it in the private sector.

He started walking again, shaking his head.

"Mark—" Elizabeth started.

He put a finger to his lips. "Shhhh."

Another few seconds of thought and his situation seemed much clearer. Christian Volkov had once again covered all the angles. What options did Beamon realistically have? He could try to get his job with the FBI back and dismantle Volkov's organization from the inside. But what would be the point? Even in the unlikely event he stayed out of jail and the Director could be convinced to take him back, he knew that every time he shut something down, one of Volkov's competitors would immediately act to fill the void. He'd end up with fifty different nutcases running fifty different illegal enterprises and al-Qaeda solidified as one of the richest drug-trafficking organizations in the world. There would be terrorists using Rolls-Royces as car bombs all over the globe.

Joseph and Elizabeth slid into the front of the car and Beamon stretched out in back. He watched through the window as the rain started in earnest, turning the dirt road to Christian's—now his—house to mud.

To the dismay of his companions, Beamon started laughing.

Christian Volkov. You just had to love the guy. He'd managed to turn his organization over to the only person in the world who he knew aspired *not* to be the most powerful criminal in the world. The only person who would actually want him back.

"What?" Joseph said. Both he and Elizabeth twisted around in the seat to look at him.

"Watch the road," Beamon said. "What are we hearing from . . ." He had a hard time saying it. ". . . Our people?"

Elizabeth smiled and let out long breath as she faced forward in her seat again.

"The military appears to have taken him into custody just after he was dropped off in Mexico. There was an American with them who seemed to be in charge."

"Do we have a physical description?"

"About five feet nine inches. Fairly thin and a bit pale. Dark hair cut short. Tan slacks and a white shirt."

It had to be that preppy asshole Alan Holsten. The bad news was that Holsten had proven smart enough to get ahold of Christian Volkov. The good news was that if he'd made a personal appearance, it meant he was hanging out there all by himself. Beamon would bet money that the CIA's director didn't know anything about this dumb-ass operation.

"Do we know where they took him?"

"No. I've been on the phone twice to Charles Russell's office, hoping to get him to intercede on our behalf, but I have no idea what name Christian was using to deal with him. Without that we have no access. It's sort of like a code word."

Beamon leaned forward and poked his head over the seats. "Charles Russell, the politician?"

"Yes."

"Goddamn," he said, flopping back in the leather seat. There it was. The piece of the puzzle that he hadn't been able to fit. How Volkov intended to pull this off. What had he said when they were having dinner in L.A? "You wouldn't believe how much money I give law-and-order politicians . . ."

"The Mexicans seem to know that Pascal is dead . . ." Joseph continued.

"Christian's old number two?"

"Yeah. He'd been with Christian for years. He knew everything and would have been able to hold the organization together. Now Castaneda thinks there's no one capable of standing in for Christian. They think that if they kill him, there won't be a reprisal."

The car slid to a stop in front of the house and Beamon jumped out, heading directly toward Volkov's—his—office with Joseph and Elizabeth right behind. He dropped into the chair behind the desk and looked down at the phone, trying to decide what he was going to do.

"Mark?" Elizabeth said, pulling him from his daze. "Should Joseph get Attorney General Castaneda on the line for you?"

Beamon looked up at her. He'd come this far. "What the hell. Why not?"

Joseph dialed the phone for him and gave him the headset. Interestingly, it fit perfectly.

"This will go through to his executive assistant. She speaks English."

Beamon listened to it ring for a few seconds before a woman answered.

"*Buenas tardes . . .*"

"Hi. You speak English, don't you?"

"I do."

"Great. This is Mark Beamon calling on behalf of Christian Volkov."

"I'm afraid the attorney general is unavailable."

"May I leave a message?"

"Of course."

"I am the former special agent in charge of the FBI's Phoenix office. In Mr. Volkov's absence I'm overseeing his business interests. If Mr. Castaneda needs confirmation of this, I suggest he use any contacts he has at the FBI."

If his contacts were good enough—and Beamon guessed they were—Castaneda would find someone at the FBI who would tell him that Special Agent Mark Beamon had resigned and disappeared and was now being actively sought in connection with the deaths of four Afghan heroin dealers.

"Do you have all that?"

"Yes, sir. I have it."

"And one more thing," Beamon said, deciding to take the power of Volkov's office for a quick spin. "I expect to be on the phone with Christian within the hour. If I'm not, I'll have to"—he paused meaningfully—"make other arrangements to contact him. Thank you."

He hung up and started dialing again, looking up into the anxious faces of Joseph and Elizabeth as the phone on the other end of the line rang. He couldn't tell if his identity had been revelation to them or if they'd already known. It didn't really matter.

"Hello?"

Beamon pulled a drawer open and put his feet on it. "Laura. How are things going? Have you heard from the Afghans yet?"

"Are you kidding? The FBI is now the proud owner of enough heroin to get half the country high."

"Already? You've outdone yourself."

"It didn't have anything to do with me—those guys were on fire to do the deal. When they called they gave me two hours. I barely made it."

"Were you able to track them?"

"Yeah. They're holed up in a house outside of Vegas. We've very quietly surrounded it but won't move until you give the go-ahead."

"What about the launcher?"

"I don't know. We can't get close enough to get a good look without tipping them off. We're gathering what information we can without making contact."

"Have you found anything interesting?"

"Nothing so far. Look, Mark, everyone here is pretty nervous about just sitting here. If they don't have the launcher, we might be able to get something out of them that *will* help us find it. Every minute we don't do anything . . ." She drew short of speculating how many innocent lives were in the balance.

"But you're staying put, right? No one's cracking."

"We're solid. We don't move until we get the okay from you."

"You're a good man," Beamon said.

"What? I lost you there for a second. Where are you? It's kind of hard to hear."

He suddenly realized he had no idea where he was. He'd gotten so used to being perpetually lost, he hadn't thought to ask.

"I'll call you soon, Laura. Hold tight, okay?"

63

"I have to say that I don't understand you, Christian. I'd heard how smart you were, how brilliant. But now here you are, playing a stupid game." Alan Holsten spread his arms wide, as if presenting the room they were in for the first time.

It was fairly stereotypical, almost a cliché in Volkov's mind. The closeness of it, the blue paint peeling from the walls, the bare wooden floor. The heat. No doubt every army interrogation room in Mexico looked almost identical.

He adjusted himself into a more comfortable position in the old wooden chair as Holsten began to circle. Volkov wasn't bound, but neither was he armed. Holsten, on the other hand, had a loaded pistol on his khaki hip, and there were a number of armed men just outside the door.

"I know all about you," Holsten said. Oddly, he had the same aura as many of the third-world maniacs Volkov had dealt with: soft but with a simmering desperation and an infinite capacity for cowardice and cruelty.

"I know about the Romanian orphanage, the time you spent in prison, the people you've killed. . . . You're apparently a very disciplined man and I admire that. But I have no constraints here. We both know that you'll eventually tell me what I want to know."

That was undoubtedly true, but "eventually" could be a long time. A lot could happen in "eventually."

Probably nothing would, though. It seemed likely that Mustafa Yasin had killed both Mark and Elizabeth. And Joseph was loyal, but in the end would find himself powerless.

Volkov couldn't help letting his mind wander to Elizabeth and the day he'd taken her from her father. He shouldn't have let her go to Afghanistan. He should have found another way.

"Answer my question," Holsten said.

"I think I already have. Twice."

"I want the goddamn truth: *Where is Jonathan Drake?*"

Volkov took a deep breath and let it out, burning a good five seconds. It wasn't much, but every little bit would help.

"As I told you, I gave him the ten million dollars he asked for and he's disappeared."

"And you don't know where."

"Why would I care, Alan? He provided me with all the information he had and certainly would never again be in a position at the CIA that would be useful to me. If I had to guess, I would say Brazil. It seems a popular country with Americans who need to get lost."

"And al-Qaeda?"

"On that front you've won. Without my involvement, Yasin will eventually solidify his ties with the Mexicans, making him one of the wealthiest drug lords in the world. And he'll use that position to kill thousands of Americans." For the first time Volkov looked directly into Holsten's eyes. "Congratulations. When I'm dead, your part in all this will be completely obscured. You'll be able to use al-Qaeda's newfound strength to increase the CIA's budget and inflate your own importance."

Holsten raised his moisturized, manicured hand and struck Volkov across the face. The blow was laughably weak, though the satisfied smile spreading across Holsten's face suggested that he'd enjoyed the small taste of the violence to come.

"You're right, Christian. It's an unfortunate situation, but there is no reason for me not to use it to my advantage. And to do that, I need quick and decisive victories in the war against al-Qaeda. I need to know exactly what areas they control, their strength, access to weapons, where Yasin and his council can be found. And I need information on your organization—your contacts, financial resources, business transactions in process . . ." His smile broadened. "I'll get all those things—I guarantee it. We have plenty of time."

Volkov opened his mouth to speak but fell silent when the metal door at the back of the room opened and a fat Mexican soldier entered carrying a cell phone. Holsten held his hand out but the man just walked past him and offered the phone to Volkov.

"What the hell's going on?" Holsten shouted.

The soldier, who almost certainly spoke no English, ignored him.

"What the fuck is going on?" Holsten screamed, pulling his gun and aiming it at Volkov. The Mexican stepped between them and moved forward until the barrel of the pistol was pressed to his chest.

Holsten froze. What else could he do? Shoot? Undoubtedly he realized that the Mexican's well-armed friends sitting in the hallway would take exception to that.

Volkov crossed his legs casually and pressed the phone to his ear. "Hello?"

"I hear things aren't going so well down there." Volkov smiled at Mark Beamon's lazy American accent.

"It didn't work out exactly as planned. So often this is the case. I take it your trip went more smoothly."

"It could have been worse, but we'll see what comes of it. . . . Charles Russell, huh."

Volkov smiled again. "Of course. Who else?"

"I should have known. You delivered Carlo Gasta to the cops and now he's rolling over on half of New York. As the terrorism and law enforcement oversight czar, Russell's getting a hell of a lot of good publicity from all that."

Volkov looked up to see that Holsten had holstered his gun. The Mexican was standing in the doorway now, making sure that everything stayed under control.

"And I'm not finished yet. With a little luck, I might be able to put him in the White House."

"Oh, I'd be disappointed if you didn't."

There was a brief silence over the phone that Volkov couldn't read.

"What are you going to do, Mark?"

"You haven't left me with a lot of choices, have you? I got you a meeting with Castaneda. Holsten will be there, too, though—I couldn't get you a one-on-one. I hope what you have to sell is as good as I think it is. Your chair hurts my back."

The line suddenly went dead. Beamon had hung up.

64

"WHO the hell do you think you're dealing with? We had an agreement!" Alan Holsten shouted, pacing back and forth across the thick carpet, jabbing his finger in the air. Their surroundings had improved significantly: Peeling paint had given way to cherry paneling and the unbearable heat had been extinguished by the central air conditioning of the attorney general's office.

"Can I offer anyone tea?" Salvador Castaneda said, carefully rearranging three cups on a silver service in an obvious effort to mask his nervousness.

Castaneda had sided with Holsten and now was being put in the awkward position of having to reconsider that alliance. He would be reluctant to reverse himself at this late date, though, and would be strongly biased toward continuing his support for America's Central Intelligence Agency. Despite his boorish behavior, Alan Holsten had the edge.

"I'd love some," Volkov said calmly.

"Milk?"

"Please."

Holsten came to a stop in the middle of the office and watched the bizarre ceremony with his mouth half hanging open.

"What the hell—"

Castaneda waved his hand and, surprisingly, Holsten shut up. He was obviously not too conceited to recognize that he was at the very edge of his sphere of influence and that the Mexican was in control.

Volkov accepted his tea with a calm, graceful smile.

"I intend to speak frankly because I believe that the time for subterfuge is past," Castaneda said, leaning against his desk. He was a handsome man in a calculated sort of way, with a thin mustache and well-tended hair that always made Volkov think of old American movies.

"It goes without saying that all of the decisions I've made have been based purely on business and that I hold no personal animosity toward anyone in this room."

Volkov took a sip of his tea. "Could I have a sugar, please?"

"Of course." Castaneda used a pair of small silver tongs to drop a cube into Volkov's cup.

"Jesus Christ," Holsten muttered, continuing to throw away his advantage. It was critical for Volkov to play up the difference between them—the unthinking volatility of the CIA versus his organization's calm, predictable, efficiency.

"We had a deal," the attorney general continued, talking to Holsten but looking at Volkov, "based on your assurances that there was no one capable of keeping Mr. Volkov's organization together."

"There is no one," Holsten said emphatically.

"I have to disagree. A few hours ago I received a call from a former FBI agent named Mark Beamon, who insists that he is very much in control. And I've confirmed through the FBI that he is currently being sought for questioning in relation to the Afghans recently killed in Los Angeles."

Holsten opened his mouth to speak, but Castaneda ignored him. "I'm familiar with Mr. Beamon, as I think most people involved in my kind of business are. He was a dangerous opponent when he was with the FBI. Now, though"—he shook his head—"unbounded by the confines of that organization, I believe him to be fully capable of filling Mr. Volkov's shoes."

Volkov saw Holsten's face go blank for a moment. He'd assumed that Beamon was dead and was having to very quickly switch gears.

"Beamon is an undercover FBI agent," he stuttered. "His job . . . his job is to *destroy* Volkov's organization. . . ."

"According to my information, he has resigned his position and is a wanted man. The charges against him are grave and seem to be easily proven. No, I think Mr. Beamon knows that he can never return to the U.S."

"This is insane," Holsten said, starting to pace again. "He's an FBI agent, for Christ's sake!"

Americans could be so blind, Volkov thought as he stirred his tea. To Holsten the idea that a government employee with Mark Beamon's reputation would go to work for organized crime was ludicrous. But Salvador Castaneda certainly would not share that sentiment. He was one of the most powerful politicians in Mexico and was a pivotal player in the illegal narcotics trade. In Mexico, as in many countries, the line between organized crime, politics, the military, and the police was blurry at best. Based on the world he had been born to, Castaneda would have no reason to believe that Beamon would do anything but run Volkov's organization to the best of his ability and reap the significant financial rewards for doing so.

"Mr. Holsten," Castaneda started again, "you have offered me two things: first, protection from Mr. Volkov's organization—something it would appear that you can't deliver, since you don't even know who's running it. And second, you've offered me the friendship of the CIA. But now there is some question as to whether that is yours to give. When I spoke with Mr. Beamon, he suggested that you have no backing for this operation, either at the CIA or within the political framework. In his mind, my best-case scenario is that you stay in your position for the next eight years until you are forced to retire. He makes a compelling argument that your career will not survive the next twelve months, though."

"Mark Beamon has no idea what he is talking about!" Holsten managed not to shout, but the anger in his voice was obviously just at the edge of his control. "Like you said, he isn't even an FBI agent anymore.

And even when he was, he was nothing more than the special agent in charge of an office thousands of miles from Washington. He has no idea about the inner workings of the CIA."

"Then I suggest we get your boss, the Director, on the phone. We should discuss this situation fully and decide exactly what kind of support I can expect going forward should I decide to give you Mr. Volkov."

When Holsten just stood silently the middle of the office, Castaneda nodded knowingly and turned to Volkov. "What is it you ask of me?"

Volkov set his empty cup down on the table next to him and cleared his throat. "You're aware of al-Qaeda's ongoing takeover of the heroin refining and trafficking capabilities of the Middle East. And I know you're aware of the supply problems and increased scrutiny Yasin's involvement has caused and will continue to cause.

"Of course."

"My proposal is simple and mutually beneficial. We replace your current Middle Eastern suppliers with my associates in Asia."

Castaneda stared at him for a moment, blinking. "Simple? You think this is simple? And when exactly would you propose we do this?"

Volkov smiled easily. "I'm free Friday."

The attorney general laughed out loud. "Is this a joke?"

Volkov shook his head and pointed to the phone. "Have your assistant call Charles Russell's office. Use the name Paul Holt."

Out of the corner of his eye, Volkov could see Holsten's head swiveling back and forth as he tried to understand what was happening. He tensed visibly when Castaneda shrugged and pressed down the intercom, asking his assistant to do as Volkov instructed. A few moments later her voice came over the speaker on Castaneda's phone, telling him in Spanish that he was being connected.

"What . . . what did she say," Holsten asked. Castaneda ignored him and handed Volkov the phone.

"Hello? Mr. Russell?"

"Yes."

"I'm here with Salvador. Would you have a moment to speak with him?"

"Put him on."

Volkov handed the phone back to Castaneda, who sat down behind his desk and pressed it to his ear. He spoke very little, mostly just nodding as he listened to Russell's proposal. After about five minutes he gently replaced the handset and stared across the desk at Volkov. "Mr. Russell seems to have a great deal of confidence in you. He makes a compelling argument that I should give serious consideration to whatever you propose. I'm listening."

Volkov picked up his cup and refilled it from the pot on the desk. "On Friday we will coordinate an effort through your military and police to arrest Afghan and other Middle Eastern narcotics distributors in your country, confiscate their inventory, and destroy or take control of what infrastructure they have in place. The effort will be heavily publicized, with American reporters along on the raids. It will come out that this was a highly confidential operation, coordinated by you, President García, and Charles Russell. Of course, all press releases from the Mexican government will go through Russell's people for approval and distribution."

"Of course."

"Then, I'll coordinate the shift in supply to my Asian associates and give you my word that all of this"—he waved his hand in a lazy arc, indicating Castaneda's involvement in his kidnapping—"is behind us."

"And if I refuse?"

"Then you'll continue to be tied to an increasingly unstable heroin supply under the intensifying spotlight brought about by al-Qaeda's terrorist activities. And then, of course, there's Mark Beamon. I'll be dead, but you'll still have him to deal with. I honestly don't know how he'll react."

"This is absurd," Holsten said as Castaneda sank further into his soft leather chair. "We can help you stabilize your Middle Eastern supply lines and we're asking almost nothing in return. Why would you bend over backward for Charles Russell—an elected official—at the risk of making an enemy of the CIA?"

Castaneda finally met Holsten's gaze. "I'm beginning to think that you don't speak for the CIA, Alan. And what Russell has offered me is quite valuable."

"What?"

"In return for my cooperation, he has guaranteed the certification of Mexico's antinarcotics effort for as long as I am in office. Are you prepared to offer more?"

65

CHRISTIAN Volkov twisted his head slowly back and forth, trying to relax the knot in the back of his neck. Thanks to the eminently reliable Mark Beamon, he had arrived back at his home in nearly untouched condition. The one exception was a light bruise on one cheek, thanks to Alan Holsten, and the inexplicable ache in his neck that accompanied it. Well, not entirely inexplicable. He just wasn't as young as he once was.

The expansive room was dimly lit, making the myriad monitors and television screens more easily visible. There were no fewer than ten people lined up along the wall, most sitting in front of computer terminals with headsets similar to the one he was wearing. Volkov walked toward the open door leading to a broad terrace but didn't step through. He just turned and stood with his back to the doorway, letting the breeze chill his sweat-dampened skin and listening to the chorus of Spanish voices filling the room.

As expected, Castaneda had enthusiastically accepted Charles Russell's offer of guaranteed certification for Mexico and the opportunity to replace the volatile and highly public Afghans with the efficient and shadowy Asians. Now all Volkov had to do was perform the nearly impossible task of coordinating the end of Mustafa Yasin's brief narcotics career.

Surprisingly, the only disastrous glitch so far had been Volkov's inability to convince Castaneda to keep Alan Holsten incommunicado during the transition. It seemed that holding the CIA's deputy director of operations against his will was too much to ask. Not surprising, but it added an additional facet to an already insurmountably complex situation.

"We've got a plane with a mechanical problem stuck in Panama," Volkov heard Elizabeth say. She sounded a little panicked. "Can we cover it?"

Joseph spoke quietly to one of the people sitting along the wall as he gazed at the computer screen in front of him. "I'm not sure. . . . We might be able to bring in a cargo plane we have on the ground in Nicaragua. Are we in contact with them?"

Volkov wiped the perspiration from his upper lip and listened intently to his assistants' conversation. He had been entrusted with literally hundreds of millions of dollars' worth of product and virtual control of the Mexico's military and law enforcement, based on his insistence that he would succeed in this. If he didn't, he'd spend the rest of his short life running from the people he'd failed.

Elizabeth tapped a button on the phone attached to her hip and started speaking quietly into her headset, pacing back and forth across the room.

"Elizabeth?" Volkov prompted.

She held up a hand and continued to talk, finally clamping a hand over her headset's microphone. "We're okay. They can be in the air in a few minutes. We're looking at no more than an hour's delay."

"Let the people on the ground know and tell them the price of the shipment will be cut by one third for the inconvenience," Volkov said.

She nodded and went back to speaking quietly into her headset.

With the latest of what seemed like a hundred problems averted, Volkov tried to calm himself and focus on the big picture for a moment.

His entire future was to be determined by two critical hours, one of which was already gone. Timing was everything now. The literally hundreds of drug traffickers, Mexican police, and soldiers had to be coordinated with absolute precision. Once the Afghans had been led to the slaughter, Volkov immediately had to appease an extremely nervous Mexican narcotics machine with hundreds of tons of Asian heroin. And all of this had to be accomplished so effectively that resistance to the new order of things would seem completely pointless.

"Joseph! Have you located that ship yet?" Volkov said.

The young man spun around to face him and shook his head. "I've been on to everyone, Christian. The Mexicans have flown all over the area and it's just not there. It could have sunk, but the weather's calm and clear."

The ship in question was part of an Afghan heroin shipment that was scheduled to come ashore in half an hour to rendezvous with a group of Mexican smugglers. Of course, that plan had changed a bit. During the exchange of something like three tons of heroin, the Mexican police would descend, confiscate the product, and arrest everyone involved—all under the watchful eye of a CBS camera crew. And then, after all the pictures had been taken and interviews given, the media would be escorted away and the Mexican traffickers would be freed along with the heroin and their money. The Afghans, on the other hand, would not fare so well. They would disappear forever.

"If the Afghans don't arrive, we are going to have to take responsibility for filling the order."

"We're down to one backup plane in the area, Christian. If we use it now . . ."

"Do it," Volkov said. "If we have any more problems, we'll have to solve them as they arise. Reroute the American television crew to Belao and notify the police there to be mindful that they're being watched."

"Okay, Christian."

"And find that damned boat!"

Joseph gave him a frightened nod and leaned over the shoulder of a man staring into a computer screen.

The crux of the entire operation was knowing the precise moment that the Afghans discovered that their people were being captured and killed all over Mexico. When that time came, Yasin would order them to pull back and be ready to defend themselves. The element of surprise would be gone.

"Do you think they're on to us?" Elizabeth said. "Do you want us to go to phase two?"

He honestly didn't know.

"Christian?"

"No. Not yet. We're going to stay with our original plan."

The phone on Volkov's hip began to ring and he jabbed a button, activating his headset. "Go ahead."

"We have completed number fourteen," a deep voice said in Spanish.

Volkov jogged over to an empty computer terminal and scrolled down, skimming the various operational summaries until he got to fourteen. It was a raid on an airstrip in central Mexico that the Afghans used as transition point.

"What did you find?"

"Four men and approximately one ton of product."

"Hold on. . . . Joseph! Fourteen's completed—they've got one ton of product."

"One moment, Christian."

He tapped a few commands into a laptop and concentrated on the screen. "Okay, Christian. Just tell them to leave the stuff there. We can use it as a backup in case we run into any more problems."

Volkov reactivated his headset. "Clear the area and leave the product in place."

"Understood. What about the four men?"

Volkov frowned. There was really only one possible answer. "Make sure they're never found."

The line went dead and he pulled the mike away from his mouth. "Joseph! What about that ship?"

"Still nothing, Christian."

Volkov took a deep breath and let it out. "Where's Mark? Is he on the ground in Mexico yet? Are we in contact with him?"

"Who knew the Mexicans even had helicopters that could get off the ground?" Mark Beamon shouted, taking a drag on his cigarette. The young blond man sitting across from him had an intense mix of fear, determination, and nausea on his face that prompted Beamon to move his feet out of the kid's likely vomiting range.

The large airship was being buffeted around like a badminton birdie and there were no windows, leaving their location and ultimate destination a complete mystery. In addition to the two of them, there were fifteen Mexican soldiers crammed into the cargo hold, increasing the ambient temperature to over a hundred. Beamon's cigarette deadened his sense of smell a bit, but the stench of sweat and bad breath—some of it his own—was still nearly unbearable.

The thing that kept him from beating the blond kid to the punch and throwing up on his own shoes was the fact that his curiosity was powerful enough to keep him distracted. What the hell was he doing here?

Castaneda had obviously gotten a good story from the FBI, because he'd dusted Christian off and sent him on his way pretty quickly after their conversation. Beamon saw it as a testament to his criminal talent that he could pluck Volkov from certain death with a mere phone call. His résumé was starting to look pretty good if he just left off all the FBI crap.

The problem was that Volkov, after arriving home safely and without so much as a thank-you, had banished Beamon to a run-down military base in a region of Mexico that even scorpions avoided. He'd spent a few hours on the ground there and then had been herded onto this helicopter with a bunch of people he couldn't communicate with to fly to God knows where.

The obvious implication was that he had served his purpose and Volkov wanted to be rid of him. Hopefully the obvious answer wasn't the correct one in this case. Try as he might, though, he couldn't come up with another explanation.

Beamon lit another cigarette from the embers of his first one and looked up at the blond American kid in front of him again. Nausea had now overtaken determination as the easiest thing to read in his face. The pale green hue was hard to miss.

"What's in there?" Beamon shouted, nodding toward a hard suitcase on the young man's lap.

"Camera," he managed to get out.

"A camera for what?"

Talking seemed to make him feel better and his voice gained strength. "I work for Fox. I'm here to get the story."

"What story?"

He shrugged. "Whatever story there is, I guess. Do you know where we're going?"

"Nope."

Beamon felt his phone start to vibrate and he plugged it into an elaborate set of headphones that canceled out the noise from the helicopter.

"Hello? Hello?" He said into the mike hanging in front of his mouth.

"Mark?"

It was a little hard to hear but not too bad. Laura's voice was clearly recognizable.

"How are things going out there?" he said. "Are you okay?"

"We're still in position around the Afghans' house. It was quiet until about two minutes ago. Suddenly we're seeing a hell of a lot of activity."

"Shit," Beamon muttered and looked at his watch. An hour and fifteen minutes into Volkov's operation.

They'd been working on the assumption that when Yasin figured out he'd been screwed, the first people he'd warn would be his holy warriors in America. This was the signal that it was time for a blitz.

"Laura! Laura—are you still there?"

"I'm here, Mark. I can barely hear you."

"Go ahead and move in. But be careful—they're probably expecting you."

"Are you sure we should go now, Mark? Look, there's still no sign of the launcher. Maybe—"

"Trust me, Laura. It's not going to get any better—it's only going to get worse."

"Okay, Mark. We're on it."

Beamon clicked off the line and stared down at the phone for a moment. What now? Did he warn Volkov, the man who was probably sending him to his death? As much as he didn't want to, he had little choice. In the end, his and Volkov's interests were more or less the same: They wanted al-Qaeda crushed.

He dialed the phone and listened to it ring. When he leaned his head back, he saw that the young man in front of him had his camera out of its case and was aiming it right at him.

"What the hell do you think you're doing?"

The line picked up and Christian Volkov's voice came over the headphones. "Mark? Mark? Are you there?"

"Hang on." Beamon grabbed the lens of the camera and pushed it away. "I'm not the story you're looking for. You got that?"

The young man took his words for the threat they were and laid the camera in his lap.

"Yeah, I'm here," Beamon said into the mike. "Yasin's got us. If I were you, I'd light a fire under this thing."

"I understand. Hold on. . . . Elizabeth! Call everyone in, right now. We aren't going to be able to coordinate things from here anymore. Tell them it's possible that the Afghans will be ready for them. . . ."

When Beamon looked up, the camera was back in his face. He couldn't summon the will to push it out of the way again, though. He might as well let it capture what he'd become—a key player in providing on-time delivery of quality heroin at reasonable prices. When someone finally put a bullet in him, he'd probably end up as the assistant manager of Hell's Wal-Mart.

"Mark—are you still there?"

"Yeah."

"How is everything going? Are you all right?"

"I'm great, Christian," he responded suspiciously. "I'm just great."

66

LAURA Vilechi ran crouched as low as possible, finally throwing herself to the ground next to a prone man in desert camo. He didn't move from his position examining a double-wide trailer about a hundred yards away through the scope of his rifle.

"Anything new?"

He shook his head almost imperceptibly. "Based on what I can see through the gaps in the curtains, they're still pretty excited. No one's come outside, though."

Laura straightened the sunglasses on her face and peered over the mound they had taken cover behind. The sun-bleached home was the only building in sight, erected in a broad depression with a dry riverbed running through it. They were only about forty miles from the Las Vegas strip, but it might as well have been a hundred miles. With the exception of the trailer and the barely discernible dirt road leading to it, there was nothing but empty, rolling desert and mountains for as far as the eye could see.

She pulled a pair of binoculars from a pocket in her fatigues and scanned the terrain but didn't see anything she hadn't seen a hundred times before. The building was more than two decades old and, according to the plans the manufacturer had faxed her, encompassed exactly eleven hundred and twenty square feet. There was no phone service, no garage, no outside storage sheds. Power was provided by a propane tank and a generator. The only foliage in sight was a few bushy trees growing in front of a low ridge that rose about fifteen feet high near the riverbed.

"Mark says we go in now," she said, rolling onto her back and staring up at the unbroken blue of the sky.

That actually got the man next to her to divert his attention from the house for a moment. "What about the launcher? There's nowhere down there big enough to hide it. If we blow this thing now . . ."

He didn't finish his sentence. He didn't have to. They'd been there for two days, praying that a truck big enough to carry the launcher would roll up. But now it didn't look like that was going to happen. If they went in now, they guaranteed that the launcher would never show up—that it would be diverted to another, unknown site. It was a no-win situation.

"He says the activity we've seen is because they know they've been compromised." She sighed quietly. As much as she wanted to, second-guessing Mark in this kind of situation was almost never productive. He wouldn't have told her to move if he wasn't sure.

"Shit," she muttered, and then pulled out a walkie-talkie and spoke into it. "We're going in. Is everyone in position?"

She got an affirmative from her entire team, as she knew she would. They were all good people—handpicked by her from the substantial man-power she'd been given. Headquarters was completely unaware of this operation—she was doing it completely on her own authority. If it blew up in her face, her men could honestly say they were just following orders.

"Okay. Everything nice and easy, according to Plan C as in Charlie. Set your watch in five, four, three, two, one, now. Five minutes to get into breach position."

She hung the walkie-talkie on her belt and pointlessly patted the bulletproof vest she was wearing. Her heart rate was already way up, and the sweat on her face had turned cold despite the relentless Nevada sun. She rolled on her side and faced the man lying next to her. "What about you, Jim? Are you ready?"

He nodded and they both started crawling forward through the sharp rocks and dust. Her torso was protected but she could feel the blood starting to run down her elbows and knees as they were attacked by the desert floor. Oddly, though, there was no pain. It was being drowned in adrenaline.

They made it to their designated position, an unimpressive dirt rise about thirty feet from the house, with time to spare. This was, by far, the closest she or any of her team had been. The indistinct forms that had been appearing and disappearing behind the curtains now took shape, turning unmistakably human for the first time.

The people inside the house were moving urgently now—none were framed by the window for more than a second. Her instincts told her that Mark was right. They were packing up and getting ready to move out. How, she wasn't sure—there was no vehicle in sight. And that was the one glimmer of hope she still had.

Laura looked up at her partner, who was watching the house from near the top of the rise, and put the walkie-talkie's earpiece back in her ear.

"Is everyone in final position?"

She got four affirmatives out of four. They had the house more or less surrounded, with ten people grouped in pairs behind what little natural cover the area provided. There had been three separate plans: A through C, in order of optimism. A had assumed that the truck would show up and that everyone would come out of the house. With four good snipers on her team, that had been as close to a no-brainer as they were going to come. B had been to kick in the doors and go in fast and hard— the assumption being that they had surprise on their side. The worst-case scenario, which of course was the one they were faced with, was the less certain Plan C.

Laura depressed the button on the side of her walkie-talkie. "Are we scrambling cell phone transmissions?"

She got an affirmative from the team handling the microwave device behind the house.

"All right. Do it."

A moment later a deep, heavily amplified voice broke the silence.

"This is the FBI. We have your position surrounded. Come out of the house with your hands up!" The instructions were then repeated in Arabic.

The response was easily predicted: the sound of breaking glass, quickly drowned out by the deafening roar of automatic rifle fire.

Laura and her partner ducked as a spray of bullets kicked up enough dirt that they both found themselves spitting it from their mouths. The sound of gunfire gained in frequency and volume as the FBI agents surrounding the trailer joined in.

Another well-timed burst of adrenaline helped Laura crawl around the edge of the small hill and begin returning fire. The bullet impacts near her had stopped and there seemed to be no flashes coming from the house, suggesting that the men inside had dropped to the floor to try to survive the barrage.

"What was that?" she heard her partner yell.

"What?"

"Listen!"

She did, and heard the mechanical whine of an engine just below the disorienting roar of their guns.

"Where the hell is that coming from?" she shouted, rolling a little farther out into the open. She still couldn't see anything, but the sound was definitely getting closer.

"Where—"

A voice coming over her earpiece cut her off.

"It was in a goddamn cave! Laura are you reading me? We've got a Frito-Lay truck coming across the riverbed toward your position! There was a cave in the ridge behind the house! The entrance was covered with trees!"

She crawled desperately back behind the rise and over her partner, who had stopped firing but was still searching for a target. Except for the ringing in her ears and the roar of the approaching engine, everything had gone silent.

"There it is!" Laura said when the truck appeared from behind the house. It looked like it was going at its absolute top speed over the broken terrain, jumping up over the ruts and obstacles in the road and then slamming down hard enough to bottom the shocks. It swayed dangerously as it came around the corner, sending a spray of dust that hung in the still air.

"Eric!" Laura yelled into the walkie-talkie. "It's coming up on your position! Can you get the tires?"

The ridiculous fact was that because of the difficulty in recruiting for this illegal operation, they had no backup at all. And because of the open terrain, their cars were over three miles away. If the truck made it past them, there was actually a possibility that it could disappear again.

"Eric, did you read me?"

The truck hit a sharp-edged horizontal rut and she saw one of the front tires blow. When the rear tires hit, they both blew. Obviously they hadn't been designed for fully loaded off-road use. A single gunshot took out the last tire.

The scene was almost comical now. The truck's engine was gunning desperately and it was jumping wildly over the uneven ground, but Laura guessed it was only making about ten miles an hour. The road smoothed out after another few hundred yards, though, and she guessed the driver would be able to coax it up to fifteen or so. He probably wouldn't make it far, but she couldn't take that chance.

"I'm going for the truck," she yelled into her walkie-talkie. "Cover me."

Her partner grabbed her by the back of her flak jacket before she could break into the open. "Laura, they're waiting for that. They stopped shooting to conserve their ammo to keep us away from the truck!"

She just looked at him and shrugged. "That thing won't get far on four flats, but it might get close enough to Vegas to get a wild shot off before we can stop it. If I miss, get on the phone to the Vegas cops."

The gunfire started again in earnest the second she cleared her cover, masking the sound of the struggling truck. She heard the distinct hiss of rounds as they sped by her head, but forced herself to ignore it and just run. Sprinting past the lumbering vehicle, she finally stopped directly in its path.

The position made the truck an easy target and temporarily provided cover from the men shooting at her from inside the house. The drawback was that in about three seconds she was either going to be run over or she was going to have to dive out of the way and put herself back in the line of fire.

Her rifle was on full automatic and she squeezed off a volley at the truck's radiator, making sure that no matter what happened, it wouldn't ever make it to the highway. Then she emptied her clip into the windshield.

It didn't stop—or even slow down—forcing her to drop to the ground and roll out of the way. She lay motionless with her face pressed into the dirt and her hands over the back of her head, waiting for the inevitable barrage that would kill her. When, after a few seconds, it didn't materialize, she raised her head enough to see that the muzzle flashes coming from the house had gone dark. Flipping over on her back, she saw that the truck was still moving and had managed to make it to the smoother dirt of the road that would eventually take it to the highway. Despite the better surface, though, it was going slower and slower.

One more quick glance toward the house and she got to her feet and started sprinting up behind the truck. Still no gunfire. Hopefully that meant the men in the house were out of ammo, too injured to fire, or dead. Of course, it could just mean that they were lining up their shots really carefully this time.

She had her Glock in her hand when she finally caught up to the driver's side door. The engine had caught fire and the cab was quickly filling with smoke, despite the damage she'd done to the windshield. All she could see of the driver was an outline in the haze. He looked uninjured, gripping the wheel tightly and continuing to gun what was left of the burning engine. At this point the truck's top speed was no more than four miles per hour.

"Stop the truck and get out!" she yelled, aiming her pistol at what looked like his head.

He ignored her.

"Stop the goddamn truck!"

The engine finally died, and she could see him jerking on the steering wheel in frustration. He was less than a shadow now, a vague shape in the smoke.

The flames were licking the windshield and at least some had made their way into the cab—something she assumed would convince him to do as she'd told him. But it didn't.

The fire inside grew and he just sat there. Finally, Laura ran up and grabbed the door handle, burning her hand as she pulled on it. Locked. She raised her gun to try to break the window but felt a pair of powerful arms grab her from behind and begin dragging her back.

"Time to go!" came the familiar voice of her partner. He was right. There was no way to know if there was a missile or other kind of explosive in the back of that truck. Or, for that matter, if the gas tank would explode. She turned and ran with him, finally jumping into a ditch a couple of hundred yards away.

She immediately rose to her knees and looked back at the burning vehicle. Flames were jumping thirty feet in the air and the driver's door was still firmly shut. "My God," she said quietly, shaking her head as though she could dislodge the image of the man calmly burning inside.

She fell back into the ditch and pressed her back against the dirt wall. "Is everyone okay?"

"Not a scratch on anybody. I had them all pull back to a safe position in case that thing goes off. We didn't have time to check out the house, but we've got guys covering the exits. I'm guessing there's no one in there alive, though."

Laura slumped forward, trying to will her heart to slow down.

"You're one lucky woman," her partner said. "Those guys wanted you something awful when you went for the truck. They all came out in the open and started shooting—pretty much an act of suicide. It's a fucking miracle that we took them all out before you caught a bullet."

67

BEAMON wouldn't have guessed that it was possible, but his luck seemed to have actually taken another turn for the worse. At the behest of a major international crime lord, he was being force-marched through a hot, wet Mexican jungle by a column of angry-looking soldiers who seemed to speak no English. And to top it off, the whole thing was being captured on camera by the enthusiastic kid behind him.

Looking on the bright side of things was starting to be a little difficult. The only truly positive things in his life right now were the shotgun in his hand and the .357 holstered in the small of his back. Beyond that, the only thing he could think of was that they were going generally downhill.

The column stopped abruptly and Beamon used the brief rest to look around him. He and his new companions weren't really on what anyone in their right mind would call a trail, but his sense was that they were moving in a generally straight line. The five well-armed men behind him and seven in front didn't exactly inspire confidence. About half were grossly overweight and no fewer than four were wearing gaudy gold jewelry that negated the effectiveness of their camo and marked them as "consultants" to the local drug trade.

"Would you turn that fucking thing off," Beamon whispered harshly.

The cameraman took a prudent step back but kept rolling. "Are you kidding, man? This is great stuff! Superdramatic."

Beamon leaned his shotgun against a tree and toweled the sweat off his forehead with his sleeve. "What's your name?"

"Tim," he said, panning the jungle and the men around them.

"Look, Tim, why don't you get your ass out of here? Get one of these guys to take you back to the helicopter. I don't know where we're going but I'm guessing it's not somewhere you're going to want to be."

Tim looked around the camera's eyepiece. "Then, how come you're still here?"

"Because I figure somebody's going to shoot me either way."

The column started again and Beamon grabbed his shotgun before being swept forward.

"Nah," he heard the kid say. "I think I'll just stick with you guys." His tone suggested that he thought Beamon was trying to trick him into giving up an easy Pulitzer.

The man directly in front of them looked back and put a finger to his lips. The rest of the soldiers were taking their guns off their shoulders and checking them as they continued forward. Beamon pushed the safety off his shotgun and stepped behind a tree, grabbing the young cameraman by the collar and pulling him off the trail. Surprisingly, the rest of the column moved by without protest.

"What are you doing?" Tim said.

"When you're not sure who to trust, it's best not to have anyone behind you." The last Mexican passed by and Beamon stepped back out, following at a distance of about ten feet.

The jungle seemed to get denser as they continued, the songs of invisible birds growing in volume and coming from every direction. What he wouldn't give to be standing on Carrie's back deck, eating one of her horrible low-fat appetizers and looking forward to a fibrous, organic, salt- and sugar-free entrée.

A colorful bird finally came out of hiding and Beamon heard his new video biographer stop to get a shot of it. A moment later the entire jungle erupted in the sound of automatic gunfire. A thick tree branch was cut in half only about a foot away, and Beamon felt a sudden, searing pain in his shoulder.

He dove toward the frozen cameraman and managed to take his legs out from under him. Tim landed hard, trying to protect his camera, and Beamon dragged him behind the trunk of a tree.

"You all right?" Beamon said.

At first he thought the kid was terror-struck from the bullets singing through the air, but it turned out that the little bastard was just calculating a better camera angle. He shoved Beamon out of the way and eased his lens around the tree—apparently to make sure he got an artistically composed photo of the person who was about to kill them.

Beamon just shrugged and stayed close to the tree. His shoulder was killing him and he ripped the sleeve off his shirt to take a look. It wasn't pretty, but the large area and relative shallowness of the wound suggested that he hadn't been shot. More likely, it was just wood splinters from a bullet impacting one of the surrounding trees.

He was starting to seriously consider trying to get a look at who was shooting, but then it occurred to him that the less-than-cautious cameraman was already taking care of that.

"See anything?" Beamon shouted over the noise.

"Just our guys!" Tim said, panning the camera. "They're moving toward the edge of a clearing. I can't see into it, though. I think whoever's shooting at us is probably there. Should we move up?"

Beamon pulled a slightly bent cigarette from of his pocket and lit it. A bullet smacked into the edge of the tree he was behind and he ducked involuntarily. This time the wood shrapnel missed him.

"Come on, let's go up!" Tim said excitedly. "I've got everything I can from here."

"I don't know if you've been paying attention, son, but there are people shooting at us up there."

"You're just going to hide back here and let your guys do the fighting for you?"

"They're not my guys," Beamon said, not elaborating on the fact that he figured at least one, maybe all, had been slipped a few bucks to make sure he caught one in the back.

"We can't just sit here forever," Tim observed.

Unfortunately, that was probably true. So what were their options? Make a run for it, get lost, and die of Montezuma's revenge somewhere in this godforsaken jungle? Or . . .

He suddenly remembered that this was what he'd been telling himself he'd wanted for years—to go out in a blaze of glory. Film at eleven. He'd quit the FBI, he was guilty of planning the murder of four Afghan drug dealers, he'd gotten Chet killed. Was there any real point to hiding behind this tree like a coward? Even if he managed to get out of here alive, Christian Volkov and Alan Holsten would almost surely come after him to make sure he never talked about what he knew. Well, fuck them. Fuck all of them.

He took a final drag and flicked the cigarette into the jungle. "You want some good footage? Let's go get you some."

Despite the fact that whoever was shooting didn't seem to be specifically shooting at him, there were a hell of a lot of bullets flying overhead as he slithered out from behind the tree. He stayed on his belly, inching his way toward the nearest of the soldiers they'd hiked in with.

It turned out that he was dead—hung up on a branch with bullet holes everywhere but mostly concentrated within the loop of a heavy gold chain he'd been wearing. A twenty-four-karat bull's-eye.

Beamon pulled the body down and used it for a shield as Tim crawled up beside him and gleefully propped his camera on the dead man's bleeding chest.

A quick look around suggested that the force they had come in with was nearly gone. There were broken bodies everywhere and the few men still alive were hiding, not shooting. Beamon wasn't in a position that allowed him to look into the clearing, but the sound coming from it was enough to be sure that he wasn't up against an M16 or AK-47. He was willing to bet that whatever was being used to pin them down came off the top of a tank or something. A bullet impacting a tree behind him confirmed that suspicion when it created a deep crater eight inches in diameter.

When he looked over at Tim, the camera was pointed directly at him again.

"What are you going to do now, Mark?"

Beamon laughed. For some reason the question sounded like a TV commercial he'd once seen. If he remembered right, the appropriate answer was something about a trip to Disneyland.

The constant stream of bullets ripping through the forest seemed to have redirected themselves about twenty feet to his right, so Beamon rolled over and crawled to large tree at the edge of the clearing. Peering around it, he saw that they were at the edge of a narrow landing strip. It was about forty feet away and covered with an enormous camouflage net that would make it impossible to spot from the air. A medium-sized metal building splashed with earth-tone paint was another fifty yards beyond. The gunfire, though, was coming from two fixed machine guns surrounded by sandbags. Both were manned but the rate of fire was slowing a bit. They seemed to be aware that they had made their point.

Beamon pulled back and scanned the jungle behind him. As near as he could tell, there were only three men left alive and uninjured from the group he'd come in with. Volkov had done a hell of a job setting this up—no one was going to walk away.

He looked over at Tim and saw that he was still filming, no doubt pretending that there was some kind of bullshit war-correspondent heroism in all this. Beamon knew better.

He leaned out around the tree and aimed his shotgun at the closest of the machine-gun nests. The person manning the gun wasn't even visible behind the huge metal plate at the back of the barrel, so Beamon just fired at the narrow slit used for sighting.

A direct and utterly pointless hit. He threw himself to the ground as the guns revved up again and focused on his position. The destruction around him was filling the air with enough dust and vaporized wood to make it hard to breathe. If they couldn't shoot him, they were going to suffocate him.

Beamon covered his ears and remained motionless, waiting for some body part he'd become fond over the years to get blown off. It seemed like an hour, though it was probably only a few seconds, when the bullet impacts suddenly stopped. The guns were still firing, but no longer at him. A moment later a deafening mechanical whine combined with a deep, rhythmic thudding became clearly audible over the machine guns.

He inched forward and peeked out from behind the tree, holding a hand up to protect his eyes from the sudden wind that had kicked up. It took him a moment to compute that it wasn't wind at all but the downdraft from a helicopter hovering over the clearing. He squinted and looked up at it, seeing that it wasn't anything like the one he'd flown in on. This one was black, angular, and bristling with dangerous-looking weapons.

The Gatling gun hanging beneath its fuselage had already completed its work on the first machine-gun nest, and Beamon watched the line of small explosions in the dirt as the helicopter redirected its firepower to the other nest. The sandbags blew apart and the gun itself was shredded in a matter of seconds.

The airship turned gracefully and brought its gun to bear on the small building across the airstrip, causing it to completely collapse in less than a minute. Then the helicopter just turned and disappeared into the bright blue sky.

"Enough with the camera already!" Beamon said, turning on the young man who had been following him around for the last hour. "I swear to God I'm going to shoot you!" Tim didn't look particularly intimidated by Beamon's tirade. It probably seemed kind of mild after the day they'd had. When Beamon began reaching for his gun, though, he took a step back.

"I guess I've got some background stuff I could do."

"I thought you might," Beamon said as he watched the cameraman stroll off toward a neat line of bodies baking in the setting sun.

Only five of the Mexicans he'd come in with had survived—three without a scratch and two with relatively minor injuries. The men who had manned the machine-gun nests hadn't faired quite so well and had been left where they'd died. Removing their bodies would have involved a shovel and a sponge.

A survey of the collapsed building revealed that it had been stacked with individual bags of what he assumed was heroin. Most had been penetrated by bullets, and no one seemed anxious to get too close without a respirator. If anyone had been inside when the Gatling gun had turned on the building, they were dead. Nothing could have survived.

What all this had to do with him remained an unanswered question. The surviving Mexicans seemed to have no interest in shooting him and had been genuinely impressed by his futile shot at the machine gunners. They also suspected that he was the one who had called in the chopper. Of course, that had to have been Volkov. But why?

The satellite phone that he'd turned back on about half an hour earlier started to ring and he picked it up.

"Hello."

"Mark! It's Laura."

"What happened?" he asked, sitting down on the edge of an old stone well.

"You aren't going to believe it."

"Tell."

"We got it."

"What did you say?"

"I said we got it."

His breath leaked from his mouth and he felt some of the tension in his body ease.

"You're sure. You got the launcher?"

"And another rocket! There isn't much left of the launcher itself—the truck caught on fire. But this is definitely it. The FBI is now the proud owner of one slightly melted Russian rocket launcher!"

Beamon started to lean back but caught himself when he remembered he was sitting above a well. "Congratulations, Laura. You did it. Any of our guys get hurt?"

"Nothing worth mentioning."

"What's the Director saying?"

"What *can* he say? I've got the launcher."

68

"**JESUS!** What are you using? A spoon?"

Christian Volkov watched silently as the doctor continued digging around in Beamon's shoulder.

"You had a great number of wood splinters, Mark. That was the deepest—and the last." He irrigated the wound and taped a large bandage over it before gathering up his torture devices and walking silently from the room.

Beamon motioned toward the elaborate bank of unmanned computer terminals against the wall. "So, were you able to get the space shuttle down safely?"

Volkov smiled. "If I understand your question, the answer is yes. Everything went as smoothly as could be expected. No significant resistance."

Beamon had actually considered just pretending that none of this had happened, but the see-no-evil, hear-no-evil defense seemed a little strained at this point.

"And the Afghans?"

"In Mexico? Almost all dead. A few escaped, but I expect them to be found within the next twenty-four hours."

Beamon eased his shirt back on and began buttoning it.

"Is something wrong, Mark? It's not just the shoulder. . . . You look unhappy."

"I guess I'm just trying to figure out where 'flooded America with Asian heroin and exterminated every Afghan south of El Paso' is going to fit on my résumé."

Volkov shrugged. "Yasin is cut off from his income stream, and the support he enjoyed from me and the Central Intelligence Agency is gone. In addition to that, you found your rocket launcher. It seems to me that you have very little to complain about. Everything went beautifully, no?"

"For you, maybe. And for Laura. She found the launcher and you're on your way to being the wealthiest man in the world—if you're not already. As for me, I'm still wanted by the FBI for helping Carlo Gasta kill those men in L.A.—among other things."

"You're turning into a real glass-is-half-empty person, Mark. It doesn't suit you."

Beamon stood and stuck his hand out. "It's been interesting knowing you, Christian."

Volkov didn't move from behind his desk. "Are you going somewhere?"

"By my reckoning, we're even. I was kind of hoping you'd just let me walk out of here. Was I being naïve?"

"I'm not sure I agree that all our accounts have been settled."

"No?"

"As I see it, I still owe you for taking my message to Carlo Gasta. Ten million, wasn't it? Plus expenses?"

"If you just have one of your planes take me home, we'll call it good."

"Home? Do you mean back to your apartment in Phoenix? My understanding is that the FBI has two men waiting for you there. As you say, your activities over the past month haven't been . . . um, within the normal parameters set out by your government. You've been in a similar position in the past, haven't you? You don't seem to learn from your mistakes."

"There's a difference this time."

"What's that?"

"I'm actually guilty. Sort of fundamental, don't you think? I'm going to have to go back and face the music sometime."

"Face the music for what? For finding a rocket launcher that would have killed hundreds if not thousands of people before it was located? For stopping Mustafa Yasin from gaining enormous wealth and power? Perhaps Alan Holsten and Charles Russell will be kind enough to leave their beautiful homes and families to visit you in prison."

Beamon frowned. Admittedly, his return to the U.S. wasn't something he was looking forward to.

"As I see it, you have two options," Volkov said. "I can pay you the money I owe you and provide you with a new identity that will allow you to live out a luxurious retirement abroad . . ."

Beamon tried to picture that—skipping from one place where he didn't speak the language to another place where he didn't speak the language, wandering through the rest of his life with nothing to do. He'd die of boredom.

"You said I had two options. That's only one."

"Stay and work for me."

Beamon laughed.

"Why do you think that's funny? It's a serious offer."

"I'm an FBI agent, Christian."

"No you're not. You're an unemployed man wanted in his own country."

"I don't see myself as some kind of international crime lord."

Volkov smiled mischievously. "A bit too late to avoid that designation, isn't it? You've just helped orchestrate the largest drug deal in history. The best you can do is take the first option and be a *retired* international crime lord. Try to think outside the box for a moment, Mark. In the greater context, what do I do that's so horrible?"

"Well, you peddle drugs that destroy people's lives and cause incredible misery and suffering."

"Nonsense. People don't subject themselves to misery and suffering voluntarily. I'm surprised that you would be so unsympathetic."

"Unsympathetic?"

"How would you react if some teetotaler made the observation that bourbon had caused you nothing but misery and then presumed to take it away from you?"

It was a good point.

"You supply weapons that are used to butcher innocent people."

Volkov opened his mouth to speak but Beamon held up his hand and silenced him. "I know what you're going to say: that my own government has done the same thing in Guatemala, Cuba, Libya, Afghanistan, and God knows how many other countries for reasons no better than yours. The difference is, I don't work for that branch of the government."

"I was going to say no such thing, Mark."

Volkov reached into one of his drawers and pulled out a pistol. For a moment Beamon thought he'd argued too well, but Volkov just put it down on his desk and dug what looked like a set of car keys from his pocket, which he placed on the desk next to the gun.

"Once again, Mark, I'd argue that people pursue things that give them pleasure. I've put two things in front of me. One I will give to you. Do you want the gun so you can use it to kill someone of a different race or creed or political philosophy than yours? Or would you prefer the car—a Ford Excursion, I believe. Low miles. Leather . . ."

Beamon could see where this was going but responded anyway. "I guess I'd have to take the car."

"Of course you would—you're an American and Americans are obsessed with the acquisition of wealth. The pleasure you might get from killing, say, a black man would pale in comparison to the pleasure you'd get from owning a nicer vehicle than your neighbor." Volkov pushed the keys and gun a little farther across the desk toward Beamon. "Now, imagine you're Northern Irish. Or Congolese. Or Croatian. Which do you choose, Mark?"

Beamon frowned but didn't speak. The really absurd thing about Volkov's argument was that it was about ninety-eight percent true.

"So it's agreed," Volkov said, leaning back in his chair. "You'll stay and work with me. Not because you want to, but because you have no other choice."

"I appreciate the offer, but I don't think so."

Volkov shook his head sadly but his eyes seemed to smile. "Poor Mark Beamon. So confused, yet so predictable." He leaned to his right a bit, looking past Beamon through the open door of his office. "Elizabeth! Do you have those tapes ready?"

She appeared a moment later, hurrying across the room in a yellow skirt and black blouse that were probably very stylish but made her look a little like a bee. Beamon watched her put a video into one of the televisions bolted to the wall.

"How's the shoulder?" she asked, walking over and gently tracing her finger around the bandage beneath his shirt. "Does it hurt a lot?"

"I'll survive."

She blinked her big brown eyes and then disappeared out the door.

"Another reason to come work for me. Elizabeth seems quite taken with you. . . ."

"A girl that age would kill me."

"Somehow I knew you'd say that." Volkov jabbed at the remote on his desk and the television on the wall came to life.

The camera work was jerky, adding an interesting sense of claustrophobia and desperation to the footage of him and a column of Mexican soldiers marching through the jungle. It turned even more dramatic when the bullets started flying and he pressed his back against a tree, his inadequate-looking shotgun at the ready. Some strategic editing had removed the part where he'd sat around smoking and considering making a break for it.

The camera panned over his mutilated comrades and then cut to a distant view of one of the machine-gun nests before following him as he leaned out from his cover and fired his shotgun. The tiny screen made the act look impossibly heroic when it was actually stupid, futile, and perhaps suicidal. A little more artful editing made it appear that he and his Mexican comrades had managed to single-handedly defeat the machine gunners.

"No helicopter," Beamon commented.

A slightly pained expression crossed Volkov's face. "You know, it was a Russian model and might have clouded the issue."

"What issue?"

"What issue? Why, your incredible heroism in the service of your country, of course. The thing with the shotgun . . . that may be the most moronic act I've ever witnessed. If I'd for a moment thought you'd do something like that, I would never have sent you. It did made for some riveting footage, though."

"Seemed like a good idea at the time," Beamon mumbled.

Volkov laughed and leaned over in his desk again. "Elizabeth! Where's the voiceover on this thing with Mark in Mexico? The audio is just a bunch of shooting and yelling now."

"That's a preliminary edit we got from Fox, Christian. They haven't finished the narrative yet, but I understand it's going to make Mark look like a saint."

Beamon watched his image as the camera followed him to the destroyed building full of heroin and then tightened on his face as he gazed thoughtfully down at his fallen comrades. The whole thing was wrapped up by a big narcotic bonfire that he knew for a fact had never happened.

"Christian, how did you—"

"Shhhh. It gets better."

The screen went blank for a moment. When it came back on, the image had changed to one of Charles Russell standing behind a lectern.

"Blah, blah, blah," Volkov said, fast-forwarding a bit before hitting the PLAY button again.

". . . *agencies involved, from local law enforcement to ATF, DEA, and the Central Intelligence Agency, as well as substantial resources abroad.*" Volkov paused the tape for a moment and glanced at Mark. "I'm guessing that would be me." He pushed PLAY again.

"*Having said that, special recognition has to go to the FBI, which took the lead in this and really pulled out the stops to find that launcher before anyone could be harmed. First, I want to single out Laura Vilechi, who coordinated what seems to me to be an impossibly complicated investigation. But most of all, I'd like to commend Mark Beamon, who many of you are familiar with.*" He shook his head in a strangely engaging gesture of disbelief. "*Mark really put himself in harm's way on this thing. And he delivered—*"

Volkov hit the FAST FORWARD button again. "The rest is about his involvement in all the drug arrests in Mexico. You know the speech—'a new era in cooperation with the Mexican authorities, a major blow to heroin trafficking and organized crime . . .'"

Beamon wasn't sure he understood what was going on. He just sat there with his mouth shut.

The jerky motions on the screen slowed to normal speed again when Laura appeared, speaking to a room packed with reporters. *"I have to say that I really can't take credit for any of this. Mark Beamon came up with the initial concept of the terrorist cells being linked to narcotics trafficking and he turned up the location of the launcher—almost getting killed in the process. . . ."*

Volkov cut the tape off and the screen went blank. "She goes on like that for quite a while, downplaying her involvement. That's a loyal friend you have there, Mark. Don't take her for granted." He leaned out around the desk again. "Elizabeth! Are those last two we saw—the ones with Russell and Vilechi—airing yet?"

"They're in heavy rotation, Christian. Those weren't copies sent to us—I taped them right off American TV."

Beamon scooted his chair around so that he could look directly at Volkov. "I don't mean to be dense, but I'm not sure what's going on here."

"I believe your career was just saved—though I have to tell you that I'm personally insulted that you'd go back the FBI when you could work for me. In any event, I understand that your director is preparing a press conference that will continue to shine a very favorable light on you."

"Why?"

"I don't think he has any choice at this point. The FBI needed a win and he isn't going to risk tainting it."

"You know what I mean, Christian. Why did you do this?"

Volkov shrugged. "You've helped me a great deal since we first met—and you saved my life. It was the least I could do. Though, honestly, I don't think any of this is in your best interest."

Beamon couldn't help being skeptical. "That's it?"

Volkov played with the remote on his desk. "Of course, if I can't have you working for me directly, having someone highly placed in the FBI might be useful."

Beamon laughed. "It's true that I crossed the line on this thing, Christian—maybe a few times—but I'm not going on the take, for Christ's sake. It's just not my style. I'm a windmill tilter by nature."

"'On the take,'" Volkov said with disgust. "Don't be absurd, Mark. I'm merely suggesting that we could be of help to one another from time to time."

"No offense, Christian—I've got nothing against you. In fact, I'm embarrassed to say I kind of like you. But it would make me very happy if we could just avoid each other for the rest of our lives." He twisted around in his chair to face the open door to the office. "Elizabeth! Can I grab a plane back to Phoenix?"

"Sure, Mark. I've got to bring one in. Give me about an hour."

Beamon stood and offered his hand for a second time, and for a second time Volkov didn't move.

"So you're going to allow the director of the FBI to just tear up your letter of resignation and give you back your old job as the SAC–Phoenix. You're going to return to an organization that has taken every opportunity to pillory you—and probably will again. Back to a government that supplied al-Qaeda with weapons and ordered the death of a young man you were close to. And for all this they'll pay you a pathetic government salary and promise you a barely livable pension."

"You make it sound so attractive."

"It's actually bourbon, right?" Volkov said, standing and walking through the open doors behind him to a bar on the terrace.

Beamon nodded and followed him into the cool evening air, though he wasn't sure why.

"Okay, I understand that you don't want to work for me," Volkov said, handing him a full glass and pouring a vodka for himself. "Have you ever considered starting a consulting company? You'd be free to take other contracts, of course, but I think I could probably offer you enough business that you could make a living. In fact, you could probably make a very comfortable living."

"You're a real piece of work, Christian. I just helped you do the biggest drug deal in history and still you've almost got me convinced that you're just a misunderstood businessman. Thank you, but no."

"Then, what? What are you going to do now? Back to Phoenix and the FBI? It seems like a waste."

Beamon took a sip of his bourbon. After being virtually certain that his future would be spent in a prison cell, his old job and life should have seemed pretty attractive. Why didn't they?

"Perhaps a guaranteed minimum contract for your new consulting company would help. You make what . . . a little over a hundred thousand dollars a year?"

Beamon nodded.

"What if I guaranteed you, oh, I don't know . . . a hundred thousand a day."

Beamon felt his eyebrows rise involuntarily and he did a few quick mental calculations. "That's thirty-six point five million a year."

"Twenty-six million," Volkov corrected. "Five-day work week."

Beamon smirked. "I just helped you make a hundred billion, and now you're quibbling over a few dollars."

"Are we negotiating?"

"No, we're not. I'm—"

"Here's an interesting example of the kind of thing I could use help with," Volkov interrupted, pulling a small piece of paper from his pocket and handing it to Beamon. "This came across my desk yesterday. The men at that e-mail address have nuclear material to sell and are looking for a buyer."

Beamon glanced down at the paper, then tossed it on the bar. He wasn't going to play this game. "That shit's never weapons grade. It always ends up being the dirt out of a Chernobyl flowerpot or something."

Volkov shrugged. "Based on the information I have, I believe that this *is* weapons grade. And I believe they have a significant amount available."

Beamon wasn't immediately sure how to respond. "Are you going to broker it?" he said finally.

Volkov shrugged. "Everyone loves a war, Mark—there's good money in it. But this . . . it's an investment in chaos. Frankly, there's nothing I hate more than a terrorist. Despite that, you wouldn't believe the number of them that I come across. They always need something. Weapons, passports, information, training . . ."

"This is blackmail."

"Of course it's blackmail. I'm a criminal, remember? So, what do you think? Would your new consulting company be interested in finding a buyer for this product?"

Beamon looked down at the piece of paper on the bar but didn't move.

"There's no reason for you to make a decision this very minute, Mark. François has been planning tonight's dinner for days. Perhaps you'd like to join me?"

Beamon stayed focused on the paper. "Is he making those shrimp things?"

"I understand that he is."

69

ALAN Holsten slammed his cell phone repeatedly into the dashboard of his car as he sped through the silent suburban neighborhood. Over the last five days all his power and connections had proven to be completely useless.

With Carlo Gasta's help, Charles Russell was in the process of decimating the New York crime families, and through Volkov and Salvador Castaneda he had created the illusion of crushing the Mexican heroin trade. Russell's alliance with Christian Volkov and been very productive, helping the politician turn both himself and Mark Beamon into heroes of the war on organized crime and terrorism when they were actually in bed with both.

He slammed his phone into the dash again at the thought of the press Beamon was getting. As a disgraced FBI agent wanted for murder, Beamon had been a serious threat. As a well-connected national hero, he was the most dangerous man alive. Volkov could be counted on not to pick a fight with the CIA—he'd won and there was no profit in continuing a feud. Beamon, though, was clearly a man who held a grudge.

Holsten threw the phone into the passenger seat and cursed loudly in the empty car. He had people working around the clock trying to locate Beamon before he could slip back across the U.S. border, but with no success so far. At home the FBI agent would be nearly untouchable, but if the CIA could get to him in Mexico or the former Soviet Union, his sudden disappearance would get lost in an impenetrable maze of jurisdiction and corruption.

He glanced at his watch. Just after midnight. Despite the hour, he picked up his phone, confirmed that it was still working, and dialed a number at Langley.

"Yes, sir."

"What have you got?"

"We're still working on it, sir. Beamon hasn't contacted anyone at the FBI—they seem to have no more idea where he is than we do. Laura Vilechi's reappeared but she's heavily protected now. We're also watching Carrie Johnstone and monitoring international flights, but I think it's unlikely that he'd be flying commercially. . . ."

Holsten shut off the phone without another word and slammed it one last time into the dash before hitting his garage remote and skidding into his driveway.

He jumped out of the car and stalked through the dark house, stopping abruptly when he spotted a dim light bleeding from beneath the door to his home office. Had he left it on? He always kept the door locked, but his wife had a key in case of an emergency. Had she been in there?

Holsten started toward it but slowed again when the unmistakable scent of tobacco smoke hit him. No one ever smoked in his house—Kate didn't allow it. He finally stopped five feet from the door, not entirely sure what to do.

"Kate?" he said quietly. "Are you in there?"

"I'm afraid she isn't."

Holsten spun toward the unfamiliar voice and, when he did, found an automatic pistol hovering an inch from his face. He froze, staring at the gun with an intensity that made it impossible for him to see the man holding it. His knees suddenly felt weak and for a moment he thought he was going to fall.

"Please," the man said, flicking the barrel toward the door to the office. His voice was youthful and the accent almost certainly German.

Holsten tried to get a look at his face but could see little in the darkness: short hair, eyes cast in shadow, a nondescript nose.

"Please," the man repeated.

Holsten could feel the sweat beginning to run down his sides but managed to calm himself enough to speak. "What do you want?"

The man's answer was simply to pull the hammer back on the pistol.

"Okay! Okay, I'm doing it," Holsten said, turning slowly and opening the door to his office. "Just stay cool. I'm the deputy director of operations at the CIA. Think very hard about what that will mean if you hurt me."

Holsten felt the barrel press into the back of his head, prompting him through the door.

"I hear you've been looking for me, Alan."

The contents of his desk had been emptied onto its top and Mark Beamon was sifting through the piles of documents. Holsten wasn't sure what to say. He just stood there, listening to the door being closed behind him.

"Cat got your tongue?" Beamon said, looking up from an open file.

"What are you going to do to me?"

The FBI agent scowled. "Your wife and daughters are fine—they're upstairs sleeping. Nice of you to ask, you fucking lowlife."

Holsten was trying to focus, to run though his options. There weren't many. Beamon had made it back to the U.S. and he had heavy support— Russell in the Cabinet, Tom Sherman at the White House, Peter Caroll at the FBI, and, perhaps most significantly, Christian Volkov.

"Sit."

Holsten did as he was told.

"I think," Beamon said, speaking slowly, "that we both pretty much know what's happened over the last month and who's done what to whom. For instance, I know that you and Jonathan Drake are responsible for arming Afghan terrorists, and I know that you approved the assassination of Chet Michaels."

Holsten opened his mouth to protest, but Beamon silenced him with a wave of his hand.

"I don't want to hear it, Alan. I didn't come here to talk about the past. I want to talk about where we go from here."

"Where's Jonathan?" Holsten said.

"You'll be happy to know he's dead. I don't think he'll protest too much when you try to shift the blame for all this onto what's left of his shoulders."

Holsten wasn't sure what he was hearing. Was Mark Beamon saying that he was just going to leave this thing alone?

"What do you want?"

"I want to come to an understanding. The FBI—particularly a woman named Laura Vilechi—isn't finished with this thing. She'll be tracking back that launcher and determining exactly who was involved, and she'll be trying to figure out who's ultimately responsible for Chet's death. She already knows a lot and I'm guessing that's she's eventually going to come around to you. Also, I think she's still pissed off about you sending those goons to her hotel."

Holsten began to feel a little nauseous at the realization that the FBI was already hard on his trail. What was he going to do? Was it still viable to go after Vilechi?

"Why are you telling me all this?"

"Because you'd have found out anyway. And you'd have come up with some dumb-ass scheme to get rid of Laura and obscure your involvement in all this. I can already see it in your beady little eyes: You're wondering how you can get to her—get both of us—aren't you?"

"What do you want?" Holsten asked, suddenly wondering if he was being recorded. "You've got nothing on me and I deny everything you've accused me of. Be careful how you go forward on this—you're not the only person in this room with powerful friends."

"Look, Alan, I don't plan on being involved in this investigation going forward—I've done my part. But I can't allow you to harm Laura or anyone working for her. Any other method you want to use to try to weasel out of this thing is fine with me, but Laura and her team are off-limits. Do we understand each other?"

A thin smile spread across Alan Holsten's face. "Since you seem to think I'm some kind of criminal, I have to ask a hypothetical question. What would I get in return for this favor?"

"You wouldn't believe the things I've done over the last month, Alan. How many deaths I've been involved in. At this point, one more wouldn't make much of a difference to me. So the answer is that you get to live." Beamon pointed to the man standing next to the closed door. "If anything happens to Laura, you'll spend the rest of your short life looking over your shoulder and wondering when Wolfgang here is going to put a bullet in you from seven hundred yards away."

EPILOGUE

BEAMON stopped in the middle of the well-manicured lawn and pressed the phone to his ear a little harder. The sun was about to drop behind the horizon and a hot wind was starting to kick up.

"I'm sorry, sir, but this isn't really negotiable."

"Don't push me, Beamon," Peter Caroll said. "You think you've put yourself in the catbird seat, that you're above the law. Let me assure you that you're not."

Above the law. He'd never really given that cliché much thought. Now, though, he found himself in a strange position. Despite his bluster, the Director would not be anxious to see Beamon brought to justice for the things he'd done because it would badly taint one of the FBI's few true victories in recent memory and dispel the illusion that Caroll was continuing to "turn the organization around."

"Actually, sir, right now, I think I pretty much *am* above the law. If you'd like to test your political juice against mine, be my guest."

"Look, this isn't productive," Laura cut in. "Let's get back to the issue at hand. Can we do that?"

When the Director's voice came over the phone again, the raw fury in it made him sound a little like someone was strangling him. If only it were true . . .

"Beamon, you are protecting people who are selling material that could be turned into a bomb that could kill millions! How do you think that would play in the papers?"

Beamon started across the grass again, shaking his head miserably. The FBI's insistence on arresting people selling nuclear material was infuriating. Billions of tax dollars were pissed away every year on shameless pork, and the government couldn't set aside a few million to make America the world's best-paying and most reliable purchaser of this crap.

"I don't care how it plays in the papers," Beamon said. "You bust these guys, and the twenty-five other guys behind them are going to get a little bit smarter about how to avoid us next time. It's very simple, sir. All we have to do is go in there, pay them their money, and tell them that we have an insatiable appetite for radioactivity and unlimited funds to pay for it. Inside a year, every asshole with so much as an old glow-in-the-dark watch will call us first."

"You're suggesting that we encourage the trade in illicit nuclear—"

"That's exactly what I'm suggesting! There's tens of thousands of pounds of it lying around half-guarded storage facilities all over Russia, and I think we ought to just whip out our checkbooks and buy it all."

"Director Caroll, Mark is making sense—"

"Be quiet, Laura!"

Beamon frowned deeply. The fact that this pissant bureaucrat could talk to someone like Laura Vilechi that way proved that all was not right with the world.

"I'd like to know how you came upon this information and exactly what your motivation here is, Beamon. I'm guessing that Christian Volkov is involved. But what I can't guess is what your percentage in the deal would be."

Beamon rolled his eyes. Years of working his ass off for the FBI, making people like this prick look good, and he still couldn't get a moment's respect. But then, he didn't really work for the FBI anymore and he wasn't sure he ever wanted to again.

"Laura, has anyone talked to Chet's wife yet?" Beamon said, deciding to pretend the Director didn't exist as he jogged up a short set of stairs and rapped on the door of a freshly painted suburban home.

"Uh, Scott's going tonight."

The porch light went on and Beamon took a hesitant step backward for some reason. "My offer is still open to go in his place."

"Beamon—" Caroll said, trying to cut off their conversation. Laura, obviously feeling a little bulletproof herself, talked over him.

"Scott says it's his job and he's going to do it."

"I'll drive to Vegas tomorrow. I want to tell her . . . tell what happened. She'll want to hear it from me."

The door in front of him suddenly opened and a little blond girl with a tooth obviously missing in front ran out and grabbed his hand. "Mark!"

"I missed your birthday, didn't I, Emory? Seven's a big one."

"Come on, come on, come on!" she said, desperately tugging on his hand. "You're on TV again."

He let himself be pulled through the door and led through the foyer. "Look, Laura, I gotta go. Why don't y'all give me a call when you make a decision on that nuke thing."

ABOUT THE AUTHOR

Kyle Mills lives in Jackson Hole, Wyoming, where he spends time skiing, rock climbing, and writing books. He is the bestselling author of *Rising Phoenix, Storming Heaven, Free Fall,* and *Burn Factor.*